TATTOO MEMORIES

BY
L. ANN

TATTOOED MEMORIES

Copyright © 2020 by L. Ann.

All rights reserved.

No part of this book may be used or reproduced in any manner whatsoever without written permission except in the case of brief quotations embodied in critical articles or reviews.

This book is a work of fiction. Names, characters, businesses, organisations, places, events and incidents either are the product of the author's imagination or are used fictitiously. Any resemblance to actual persons, living or dead, events, or locales is entirely coincidental.

Cover design by A.T. Cover Designs

Interior Formatting by Crow Fiction Designs

Edited by Margot Mostert

First Edition: July 2020

ASIN: 9798665055701

L.Ann Online -

www.lannauthor.com

https://clubdamnation.com

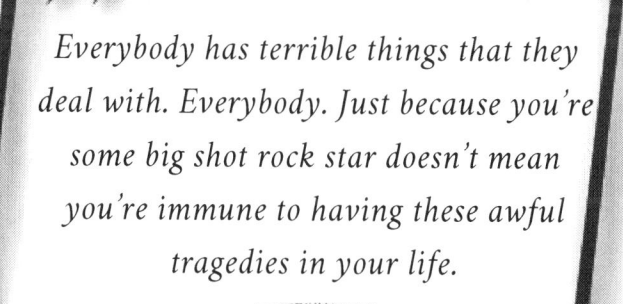

Everybody has terrible things that they deal with. Everybody. Just because you're some big shot rock star doesn't mean you're immune to having these awful tragedies in your life.

ALEX LIFESON ~ RUSH

Dedication

Angela, Brenda, Fiona, Jennifer, K. Elise, Tami, Tommie. You have no idea how important you were during the writing of this book. Without you, it probably still wouldn't be written!

To Kalli - the person behind the song lyrics for Forgotten Legacy. Thank you for letting me use your words!

Margot - I know I'm a pain in the ass, but you put up with me anyway. Thank you for taking all my idiosyncrasies in your stride (I expected way more eye-rolls!).

Last but definitely not least - Aubrey of A.T. Cover Designs. What can I say? This cover is everything!

PLAYLIST

Into The Void - Nine Inch Nails
Jerk - Neurotic Outsiders
Miss Jackson - Panic! At The Disco
Sex And Candy - Marcy Playground
She Hates Me - Puddle of Mudd
Somebody That I Used To Know - Mayday Parade
Seven Nation Army - The White Stripes
Memories - Maroon Five
Migraine - Twenty One Pilots
12 Rounds - Bohness
BangBangBang (Acoustic) - Deal Casino
I Miss You - Blink 182
One Little Lie - Simple Creatures
Better Now (Acoustic) - Etham
Demons - Jacob Lee
Scars - Boy Epic
IDGAF (cover) - Panic! At The Disco
Everything About You - Ugly Kid Joe
Ain't No Rest For The Wicked - Cage The Elephant
Tumblin' Down - Venus In Furs
Bath Salts - Highly Suspect
Middle Finger - MISSIO
Porn Star Dancing - My Darkest Days
Tainted Love - Marilyn Manson
Choke - I Don't Know How But They Found Me
Talk Dirty To Me - Poison
Church - Fall Out Boy
Primal Scream - Motley Crue
I Can't Go On Without You - Kaleo

Loverboy - You And Me At Six
Back Of My Mind - Two Feet
Heroin - Badflower
Sleeping In - All Time Low
Is This Love? (cover) - Blacktop Mojo
Chicago - Highly Suspect
Why Worry? - Set It Off
Play With Fire - Sam Tinnesz
Say Something (cover) - Boy Epic
Cancer - My Chemical Romance
Stay - Thirty Seconds To Mars
Iris - Goo Goo Dolls
Right Left Wrong - Three Days Grace
Devil Devil - MILCK
Not Gonna Break Me - Jamie N Commons
Hate Me - Blue October
Dirty Little Secret - The All American Rejects
Control - Puddle of Mudd
Strawberry Lipstick - Yungblud
Satellite Kid - Dogs D'Amour
Level of Concern - Twenty One Pilots
Born For This - The Score
Rock Bottom - Grandson
Bad Day - Daniel Powter
Ain't No Sunshine - Shawn James
Way Down We Go - Kaleo
Mother Mary - Badflower
I'm Sorry - Hothouse Flowers
Lost The Game - Two Feet
I See You - MISSIO
Red Ballon - Deal Casino

TATTOOED MEMORIES

PROLOGUE

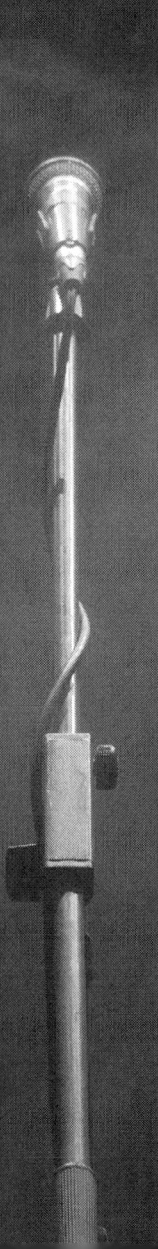

INTO THE VOID - NINE INCH NAILS

Future

SOMEWHERE IN LA.

Her head throbbed. That was one of the first things she noticed when she woke up. The second thing was the warmth. How long had it been since she'd last felt anything other than cold? It was the warmth of being indoors, of central heating. She shifted position and that was when she noticed the third thing—the thing that snapped her eyes open.

She was in a seated position, and her hands were raised to shoulder height, chained to the sleek chrome radiator against the wall.

"What the hell?" she whispered, and even keeping her voice low made her head hurt. She gave an experimental tug, hoping that somehow her wrists would slip through the metal hoops of the cuffs, but no such luck.

"Oh good, you're awake." The male voice came from behind her, *close* behind, and her body jerked in surprise. Twisting her head around as far as she could, she tried to see him, but he was just out of sight and all she could catch sight of was a dark brown sleeve.

"I thought I might have given you too strong a dose this time. I didn't want to kill you, but it wouldn't have mattered really," the voice continued, and his conversational tone scared her more than it would have if he had sounded aggressive.

"Who are you? What do you want with me?" she demanded, but she wasn't really sure if she wanted to hear the answers. No one in their right mind knocked someone out and chained them to a radiator, so whatever he wanted, it was nothing good.

"This is *his* house," her unseen captor ignored her question. "Do you know that? Has he brought you here?"

"Him? Who?"

"How often do you think he sneaked away to be with his other little whores when he wasn't with you? You don't truly think he's been faithful, do you? That's not in his nature."

She shook her head—a mistake, she conceded—as dizziness made her vision blur. "I don't know what you mean." She pulled on her arms, trying to free them again. "Why have you brought me here? Who are you?"

"You're not fooling me with your innocent act. The only reason you're with him is for what he can give you. Why else would you have forgiven everything he did?" Her captor strode around and crouched in front of her. "Look at me."

She swallowed. She'd been around long enough to know that seeing the face of the person who'd kidnapped her was a clear statement that she wasn't going to survive whatever he'd taken her for. She didn't want to look at him, but couldn't help it. Her eyes widened in sudden recognition and fear.

Sandy blond hair, blue eyes, a face that was neither ugly nor handsome—*normal* looking, she realised. Someone you wouldn't look twice at in the street. Nondescript, that was a good word to use. She almost laughed at the way she was describing him in her head. Like it mattered what he looked like!

"If you let me go, I won't tell anyone you brought me here," she tried to bargain, fighting to keep her voice from shaking.

"I can't do that. He needs to understand that he can't go through life doing whatever he damn well pleases with no consequences." She watched as he reached behind him and lifted a gun.

"Please … please don't kill me," she whispered, shrinking back against the radiator.

"*Kill* you?" he paused in the middle of sliding the bullets into the barrel. "I don't *need* to kill you. You will die though … testimony to the excesses of his life and the bad decisions he constantly makes."

"I … I don't understand."

"You will … or maybe you won't," he told her and raised the gun.

"No, no!" She cried out and tried to reach toward him, forgetting her wrists were cuffed.

He smiled. "This is the only way to show him everything is

his fault. A life for a life," he said and pulled the trigger.

She screamed.

※

The venue was dark, filled with hot, excited bodies. There was a low steady thrum vibrating through the floor, through the veins of the people in the crowd, building anticipation. It heightened their emotions, played with their senses, synced with their heartbeats until the stadium was a gasping mass of bodies hovering on the edges of orgasm.

A light joined the thrum, flashing on then off too quickly for their eyes to adjust, giving brief glimpses of the empty stage, and then one long low guitar note sounded.

The crowd drew a collective breath, held it …

The thud of a drum, the low heavy beat of a bass guitar …

And then …

> *My heart is dying, slowly withering away,*
> *I am without my soul day after day.*
> *Forced to continue my purposeless existence,*
> *Separated by an endless distance.*

The voice whispered out, low and raspy, yet still heard clearly above the music. Husky, compelling, forcing the crowd to take heed, to listen to the pain its owner suffered.

> *Detached from myself and the rest of the world,*
> *Apart from my reason, I am naught and ephemeral.*
> *Gone is my love and my mind has followed,*
> *My sanity and happiness swiftly swallowed.*

The lead guitar cried out and the singer's voice soared, sharing their agony.

Ripped apart by a force of nature unseen,
My future in exile is a path unforeseen.
Torn from your heaven and cast in this pit of hell,
Tortured within the cage, the Gods lonely realm.

As the music dropped lower, and then fell silent, the lights flickered once … twice … then stayed dark and the thrumming beat began again, building, rising.

Filled with a dark, empty cold rage,
Eternally growing is a hunger no other can sate.
An ache for destruction leaves me numb,
For keeping me away from my only one.

A spotlight shone onto the stage, highlighting the single figure, standing dead centre and leaning toward the microphone.

The crowd roared.

My once grey eyes now filled with ice,
Much like an angel in a beautiful disguise.
Loneliness eats at the heart of men,
A plague you can't cure nor entirely prevent.

He lifted his arms and a large screen lit up behind him, displaying pitch-black wings. From the view of the crowd, it looked like they emerged from the singer's back. With arms outstretched, he threw back his head and his voice rang out.

I suffer immensely in a world I've been forced to dwell,
A thirst for life the Gods did unforgivingly dispel.

The lights dropped, the screen went black, and the music stopped until only the faint thrum could be felt through the floor.

Tattooed Memories

CHAPTER 1

JERK - NEUROTIC OUTSIDERS

Gabe

PRESENT

Have you ever been to a rock concert? Felt the adrenaline pumping through your veins while you wait for the band to come on? The high you feel when they're there right in front of you? If you're near the stage, you might even get to touch your favourite rock star. There's a heat, a frenzy, it's as close to public sex as most people will ever get.

Now imagine being the one on the stage, being the one to cause all those lust-fuelled emotions. Imagine knowing how one smile, a wink, a stroke of a cheek from you has the power to make someone's day go from mildly okay to fucking outstanding.

That's the power we wield, and often, the power we abuse. It's the power we use when we point at a girl, a guy, a couple. When we take them back to our hotel rooms, a dark alley, the bathroom in the back of a seedy club and make them do all the dirty filthy things they only dream about in their cold lonely beds.

They do it to be close to the power and fame. They do it to get a taste of how we live for a short time.

We do it because it's there for the taking. It's offered to us on silver platters. Who's going to say no to that?

Didn't think I'd admit that, did you?

But here's the thing. We aren't the only ones who abuse it, so do the fans. When you're a member of a band as big as we are, there's no such thing as privacy. Someone who wouldn't dream of touching another person inappropriately in their workplace or on the street will think nothing of asking us to sign their tits, shoving their tongues down our throats, or grabbing our dicks.

We're public property.

All the groupies, the hangers-on, the media who watch for the next screw-up, the next public break-up, the next *story*—in their minds, they made us. As far as they're concerned, without them, we would be nothing. They own us—body and soul. We're theirs for the taking.

The power musicians hold is different from that of movie stars, as far as I can see. I mean, those kinds of celebrities have their own fucked-up fans who do weird shit to get their attention. And we have ours.

Which is why when I came off the stage, dripping in sweat, the sound of the crowd still roaring in my ears, I pointed at one of the many groupies hanging around.

The girl tried to introduce herself, but I wasn't interested in her name, just in what her mouth could do for me. It wasn't like I'd remember who she was anyway, so why waste time with introductions? I cut off her stammering words by flashing the smile I was famous for, told her I wasn't interested in talking and that I couldn't wait to get her sweet, sweet mouth on my body.

While she was still gaping at me, I grabbed her hand and pulled her away from the edge of the stage, telling her I'd make her come so hard she wouldn't be able to walk for a week. Why that line worked, I just didn't question anymore. But it did, and I shamelessly used it. I used it so often it had become an automatic response whenever a woman fluttered her eyelashes at me.

I leaned against the wall in the hallway leading backstage where reporters, roadies and random people milled around. They were completely unconcerned or interested when she immediately dropped to her knees and wrapped her lips around my dick, while I took a joint from a roadie who walked by and inhaled.

I tipped my head back and stared up at the ceiling.

Fucking Christ on a stick, I was *so* bored. When did fucking become so tedious? She'd go down on me. I'd go down on her. She'd come all over my tongue, begging for me to fuck her. I'd oblige by wrapping her legs around my waist, donning a condom (because always practice safe sex!) and fucking her until she couldn't see straight. A charming smile, a vague promise to call her in a day or so, and she'd be gone. I would have forgotten her name and her face by the time I rolled out of bed the next morning.

Another nameless fuck. Another way to pass the time. Another step along the road down into hell.

This had been my life for the past eight years. Gigs, sex, drugs and alcohol—rinse and repeat. And for what? Hopefully to finally get the one thing in my life that I actually really wanted. I'd sell my soul, whore myself out if necessary, and give up my fortune, to get what I wanted.

"Gabe? Baby?" Her soft, breathy voice snagged my attention and I angled my head down to look at her. Pouting lips smeared with blood-red lipstick, big baby-blue eyes and cleavage that wouldn't quit—a blow-up doll with blood in her veins. Even if I squinted, her brassy bottle-red hair wouldn't become lavender, and her eyes wouldn't change to a unique blue so deep they looked purple.

And just like that, I'm fucking over it. I pull myself out of her mouth with a growl, shove away from the wall, and tuck my dick back into my pants.

"I'm not feeling it, babe. It's not you. You're gorgeous, it's me." Inwardly I roll my eyes at my own words. I don't even *sound* convincing. "Let me get one of the guys to organise a ride home for you." I moved to the end of the corridor before she could answer, and searched up and down for one of my security detail. They were never far away at public events like this.

"Miles?" I didn't need to raise my voice. I knew from

experience he'd be within hearing distance and, sure enough, the giant of a man appeared from around the corner, his head cocked in query. "Get rid of her for me." I jerked a thumb back to where the girl stood, wide-eyed and disappointed, and stalked away without saying goodbye or looking back.

Where was Seth?

I strode along the corridors of the backstage area until I found the room where the rest of the band and the usual hangers-on congregated, waiting for me. It was always the same after a gig. We all came down from the high in different ways.

Luca—our drummer—spent half an hour in the shower doing who the fuck knows what. There was probably a girl or two involved somewhere in his water play.

Dex—bass guitarist—would have found a high point, where he could watch the crowds leaving the stadium and smoke a joint in peace. He always needed some quiet time to come down from the onstage energies.

Seth—lead guitarist and my closest friend—would be in front of a games console killing shit.

I swept my eyes over the room until I found Seth who, as predicted, was ignoring the woman gyrating on his lap and thrusting her tits into his face. He was completely focused on the game he was playing on the large TV screen in front of him.

"I'm getting out of here," I announced.

The best part of ending an eighteen-month long tour in the city you had grown up in, and still lived, was that you knew all the places to get drunk and get laid without having to ask the locals. Seth and I had gone one better. We owned a nightclub in downtown L.A.

The added bonus of ending a tour in your home city was being able to go home to your own bed afterwards instead of a hotel.

Another upside? It was also home to a person I was determined to reel back into my life. My fingers found the lighter in my pocket and I fished it out, flicking it open and closed. If things had gone the way I'd planned, *that* should be tonight.

Seth's head slowly swung around to face me, his dark eyes bouncing over the pants still hanging low and unbuttoned on my hips, and the way my lighter was being opened and closed in a silent rhythm.

"You're done already?" he said eventually. "She looked like she'd go all night."

"She probably could." I entered the room fully and flopped down beside Seth on the lumpy couch.

He slapped the ass of the girl on his lap. "Time to go, babe."

"Seth," she whined.

We both ignored her.

"She didn't cut it. I need something more tonight. Something she didn't have." Something I'd been craving for eight years.

"Do I know what this *'something'* you're looking for is?" Seth twisted sideways, reached out and took my lighter away, then trapped my twitching fingers beneath his.

"Maybe," I said noncommittally. If he knew what I had

planned, he'd put a stop to it. I raked my free hand through my hair and cocked an eyebrow at him. "You in?"

"A night of possible unmitigated chaos while you figure out how you want to get your kicks ... or back to a hotel room with another faceless whore?" Seth pretended to weigh up the options. "It's a fucking no-brainer. How can I say no to such an offer?" He tossed the games controller to one side and rose to his feet, tumbling the girl to the floor.

"It's time for things to change, Seth. I have to do something ... something unexpected." I sucked in a deep breath and licked my lips, anticipating the night to come. "Something I should have done years ago."

"Something unexpected." Seth nodded. "Got it." He grabbed his jacket from the back of the couch. "Let's go and see what's happening at Damnation because, God knows, Gabe Mercer must get laid tonight. Otherwise, the world might end."

I laughed, feeling my mood lighten, and slung an arm across Seth's shoulders. "Wouldn't happen. If nothing else came up, there's always you."

"Great, I'm the consolation prize," my oldest friend groused, elbowed me in the ribs and shook his head. "Let's go and see if Damnation has anything for you to play with." He didn't ask, but I could see the question in his eyes. "I've *seen* your dick and there's no fucking way you're sticking that thing up my ass."

I batted my eyelashes at him and pouted. "What about your mouth? I've heard you give great head."

Seth snorted. "Unless you have a pussy hiding in your pants, you'll never have the good fortune of finding out."

<hr />

We arrived at Damnation and slipped through the back door we'd installed back when we first bought the club. The door blended into the wall, and only Seth and I had the keys. It opened onto a flight of stairs which led up to a private entrance to the VIP floor, where you had to be God, or as close as it got, to be able to enter. It had a second entrance from the main floor, which was guarded by two hulking doormen, paid so highly that *nothing* got past them unless we'd given permission. Even then, they were likely to triple-question before allowing anyone up to our private sanctuary.

Our home away from home.

The place we spent our nights when we weren't touring or recording. We even had rooms here where we could crash and fuck ... mostly fuck. Neither of us wanted to take our one-night lay back to our homes, especially me. There was only one person who would *ever* be invited to my private space and, as yet, she wasn't in my life. We might live large in the public eye, with our every escapade splattered across the news, but what little privacy we did have, we guarded jealously. That included no shitting where we lived.

I left Seth to make sure the door was locked and headed upstairs. I needed a drink, to score and to fuck—not necessarily in that order. It was the same after every gig we played, but when a tour ended and I walked off stage for that final time. When I knew the craziness of travelling the world was coming to an end and I'd be returning home, something always snapped. I needed to end the tour with a bang, a *big* one. I needed to release that final bit of energy I'd saved, kept back in reserve. Coming home made me antsy, restless and, the rest of the band would tell you, liable to fuck something or someone up.

Entering the VIP area, I went directly to the bar in the far corner. We didn't use the bar from the main floor of the club to keep us supplied in drinks, we had our own private one in the room. If we wanted something we didn't know how to mix ourselves, we'd bring a bartender up to do it, or there was always Google. I grabbed a bottle of whiskey, filled a glass with ice and took both over to the long couch which looked out over the floor below.

Before we bought Damnation, it had been a seedy backstreet club with a sticky floor, wallpaper peeling off the walls and a permanent stench of piss and sex in the air. It had appealed to the darkness inside of me.

It had also been called *Trudy's* … *fucking* Trudy's. Fucking stupid ass name.

It had been the place where local drug deals, pimps, and whores all hung out. I smoked my first joint there when I was twelve. Fucked my first girl at thirteen. I took my first sip of whiskey at fourteen and snorted my first line of coke at fifteen.

These walls could tell you a lot of the secrets I kept hidden.

Forgotten Legacy played its first gig on the shitty wooden

stage, and we'd all held our breaths every time Luca hit the drums, terrified that night would be the night we'd fall through the rotten floor.

When the owner, who *wasn't* called Trudy and didn't know anyone with the name either, said he could no longer afford to keep the place open anymore, both Seth and I had jumped straight at it.

It was a no-brainer.

The place was part of our make-up, of who we are, helped shape who we became. We did it anonymously. One of those tiny bits of privacy we hoarded so jealously. Trudy's closed down and reopened six months later, completely redesigned. Eventually, people found out who owned it, but it didn't matter by that point. Damnation had already achieved the reputation of being *the* place to be seen.

Now, instead of a reject from a Western movie set with sawdust floors, it looked more like the reception room to hell— all dark walls, plush thick carpets and low lighting. The name, *Damnation* hinted to what you might find inside.

And people loved it. Queues circled the block an hour before we opened, full of people hoping they would pass the requirements of entry, not that anyone knew what those requirements were. *Spoiler*—there weren't really any other than whatever the doormen felt like instigating. The only rule Seth and I enforced was that anyone who received a ticket *always* got in, no questions asked. The only people who could issue those tickets were the band members and our manager. Like any club, there was also a list of names—friends, certain reporters—who always had access, no matter what. As well as a list of those who were never allowed to set foot inside. What can I say? We're a vindictive bunch, especially me.

I poured my whiskey and leaned on the bar surrounding the tinted glass wall, which kept the noise of the club below to a minimum while allowing us to watch every section of the floor without being seen ourselves. Seth and I *may* have voyeuristic tendencies. We like to people-watch.

"Anything catch your eye?" Seth asked as he entered the room. He stole my whiskey and took a healthy swallow.

"Fucker," I grumbled. "Get your own." But I returned to the bar and snatched up a second glass, filled it to the brim and returned to his side.

Seth cocked an eyebrow with a half-smirk and raised his ... *my* ... glass in a salute. "Luca paid someone to hand out twenty tickets to random people before the show tonight."

"People who were at the gig?" I asked, my eyes roving over the heaving mass of bodies on the dance floor below.

"No," Seth snorted. "I think he sent the guy out to beat the streets and see what caught his fancy. Who the fuck knows what will turn up."

I felt my lip curl up into a smile. Twenty tickets out in the wild, which meant forty newcomers to the club and, if Luca had followed my instructions, one of which would have landed in the hands of someone who would fulfil the craving I'd had for forever. When I'd told Seth I was in the mood for something more than what the groupie at the gig had offered, what I really meant was that it was time to set the final stage of a plan I'd been preparing for since one night eight years ago.

In the meantime, I needed something to take the edge off. My eyes swept over the club again and fell on two blondes gyrating together on the edge of the dance floor. I pointed toward them with my glass.

"Get Ken to send them up."

"I thought you had plans for something more tonight?" Seth opened the door, which led down into the club itself, and murmured to the man standing outside it.

"I'm working up to it. Besides, what I want hasn't arrived yet." She hadn't actually turned up in the entire five years we'd owned the club, no matter how many tickets I sent to her. But tonight ... tonight something told me there was a really good chance she'd be here, and I was salivating at the thought.

❄

You'd think after performing for two hours at a sold-out live concert in front of seventy thousand plus people, then heading to a club until the early hours of the morning, I'd be tired and ready to sleep.

Sadly, I wasn't.

Oh, mentally I was exhausted. I was physically drained but ready to sleep? No, not anywhere near ready to close my eyes. I couldn't do that until I'd reached the point where exhaustion would make me blackout—no dreams, no thoughts, just unconsciousness.

That could take a day or two.

The two blondes I'd brought up from the dance floor had crashed and burned less than thirty minutes after arriving. One was asleep across the couch, the other was still half-sprawled across my lap, a line of coke neatly balanced on her thigh. I wasn't a big user of coke, or any other drug really and our manager was really hot on ensuring none of us became addicts, but on days like today when my adrenaline levels were too high for me to manage and my mind wouldn't quit, I needed something to take the edge off.

I admired the clean line it made against her California tan, then plucked a hundred-dollar bill from my money clip—just as a nod toward my decadent rock star lifestyle—rolled it, and inhaled the pure white powder in one long sniff.

I let the drug do its thing, and dropped my head back against the couch's headrest, idly patting the girl's thigh before pushing her off me. I rose to my feet and moved to the glass wall to press my head against it and looked down over my domain.

And there she was.

There ... She ... Was.

Looking completely out of place in the hedonistic setting of my club with her lavender hair and a summer dress which reached her knees. I licked my lips, already tasting her skin on my tongue. I didn't even need to see her face to know who it was, to know she'd *finally* taken the bait, to know my years of patience had paid off.

I patted my pockets, searching for my cell, fished it out and called down to the bartender. Lazy, I know, but I owned the fucking place. I can do things exactly how I want them. Bren answered almost immediately, his face lifting to look in my direction.

"What's Lavender Hair drinking?" I asked, and watched as he glanced down the bar to where my primary obsession stood.

Was she barefoot?

I pressed closer to the glass, squinting down at her. She fucking *was*, her shoes placed neatly beside her.

"Lemonade."

"With what?" I saw Bren shrug.

"With nothing."

"Fucking lemonade?" She'd been a vodka and tequila girl when I knew her ... not that she'd been legally allowed to drink the last time I'd seen her, but that didn't stop her.

"Well," Bren drawled down the line. "She's not fucking it that I can see, more taking the odd sip and muttering about her friend being dead to her."

I laughed. "Still feisty, then. Give her a vodka for me."

"She's drinking lemonade, Gabe," he repeated like I was a fucking idiot. Newsflash—I'm not, although I can behave like one sometimes.

"So? Vodka is just as clear as lemonade. It just has less fizz."

I heard Bren sigh down the line. He knew how this game played out. "Fine. Is there a message to go with the vodka?"

"No message." I wanted to see how she responded to the drink.

She refused it, shaking her head and pushing it away from her. That made me grin. It meant she wasn't easy and I was going to have to work for it. That, or she no longer drank vodka. Wait ... what if she didn't drink at all? I dismissed that as idiotic—who didn't drink alcohol? I sent Bren a text.

```
Give her gin.
```

I could see his eye-roll from where I stood, but he knew better than to argue and a few seconds later he placed a second glass in front of her. Her hair rippled with her headshake.

```
Tequila.
```

A third glass was placed in front of her, and a third refusal was given. She didn't even look around to search out who was sending the drinks. I found that the most interesting thing of all.

CHAPTER 2

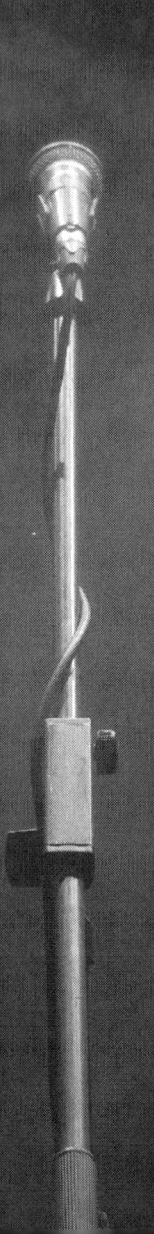

MISS JACKSON - PANIC! AT THE DISCO

Harper

PRESENT

There seemed to be two types of people who hired companies to clean their homes.

The ones who didn't view the cleaners they hired as people, just machines there to clean up their messes and so the messes they left were, at times, eye-opening to say the least.

Then there was the second type—the ones who felt that because they were paying someone to clean their homes, it meant they were paying for anything they wanted, including touching the person doing the cleaning. There were a few who thought hiring a cleaner was the same as hiring someone to fulfil their dirty French maid fantasies and we spent half our time fending off the employer.

Thankfully today wasn't one of those days. Most of the places I'd cleaned had been empty, their owners at work, so I hadn't needed to avoid the more 'hands-on' types. But still, it had been a long hard day, especially as toward the end of my shift a final job had been assigned to me. To clean a ground floor apartment of the building I was working in already because the owner had been away for the past seven months and was set to return that evening.

I'd finished and returned to the small apartment I shared with Siobhan at just gone nine PM. Siobhan had been standing in front of the mirror, with her bedroom door open, twisting and turning as she attempted to see the outfit she was wearing. When I pushed through the door and kicked it shut behind me, she greeted me with a huge smile—the type of which I *knew* meant she was after something.

And I was right. She was.

Siobhan wanted to go to Damnation—a club with a tightly controlled list of what got you inside. You could queue and take a chance, but if you managed to get an invitation—which was like gold dust, so I didn't want to even ask how Siobhan had managed it—it meant you were whisked past the queues of people waiting in the vain hope the doormen would like what they saw and let them in. It was a free pass and she wanted me to go with her.

Damnation was the last place I wanted to go to. But I couldn't tell Siobhan that without telling her the reason why—and those reasons would then require explanations. And that was a trip into the past that I had no intention of visiting any time soon.

Which was why I was propped against the bar, music thudding so loud I could feel it crashing around inside my head, and a tension headache starting.

I didn't want to be in this club. I didn't want to be out in any club, but *this* club, in particular, was one I avoided because I knew who owned Damnation and I was terrified he might be there.

I wanted to leave, but the problem was my car keys were in the pocket of my so-called friend—the girl I shared an apartment with, my best friend since I was nineteen and trying to adjust to a life I hadn't planned for, the bitch I was going to kill for deserting me. Yeah, my best friend had disappeared.

In her defence, she had stayed beside me for the first couple of hours, standing at the bar and watching, wide-eyed as numerous famous faces came to the bar—ordering drinks, dancing, having fun. She pointed out celebrity after celebrity, her excitement at being so close to many of her idols written all over her face. Which, I have to admit, looking back was weird and out of character for her. Siobhan never got star-struck.

But then she spotted a group of girls she recognised, and I'd waved her away, knowing I wasn't the best company. She promised to have a quick drink with them and come back. That had been an hour ago. It was almost two AM, I'd officially been awake for twenty hours and I wanted to go home and crawl into my bed.

I kicked off my shoes, the shoes my soon-to-be-dead roommate had talked me into wearing, and my toes curled into the thick carpet which ran the length of the bar. I took a sip of lemonade, hardcore drinker that's me, and looked up when a shadow fell across my glass. The bartender—long dirty-blond hair flopping into his eyes, tattooed from his wrists to his neck—slid a glass in front of me.

"I didn't order anything," I told him.

He grinned, showing a gold-capped front tooth, and nodded behind me. "Someone thought you looked thirsty."

"I *have* a drink." I pointed to my glass.

"Yeah, but this one has alcohol in it."

"So what you mean is someone wants to get me drunk?"

He shrugged. "I just deliver the drinks, honey. I don't ask for the reasons behind them."

I cursed Siobhan beneath my breath for leaving me alone to deal with unwanted attention. I had no idea what was in that glass, but it looked like water and that gave me a few clues—tequila, vodka, gin, for starters. None of which I drank anymore. And, even if I did, I wasn't stupid enough to down a glass of alcohol sent to me by a stranger—especially in *this* club.

The throbbing in my head grew stronger, tiredness competing with the music, and resulting in a headache that made me nauseous. I took another sip of lemonade, resisting the urge to place the chilled glass against my forehead.

Where was Siobhan?

I should have just left her a note with the bartender and grabbed an Uber. Gone home to where my bed was waiting for me.

I should have …

But I didn't.

Whoever was sending me drinks was persistent, I'd give them that. When the bartender placed the third glass in front of me, the salt frosting the rim and a slice of lime telling me exactly what it was. I shook my head.

"Could you please tell them thank you but I'm not drinking."

"I have," he told me. "A word to the wise." He leaned forward across the bar-top. "If you want his attention to move on, drink the drinks. He enjoys the chase. You're only making it worse for yourself by refusing them."

"That doesn't make it sound like he's a guy I want any attention from." I sipped my lemonade and pulled a face. It had lost its fizz, there's only so long you can cradle the same drink. "We all know accepting a drink in a bar is the first sign of showing interest," I continued.

"But *not* accepting it throws down a challenge." A new voice sounded close to my ear, low and raspy. "And *you* should know, I never back down from a challenge." Two arms appeared either side of me, inked from his fingers up—bold, black tribal patterns that covered both forearms and caused my heart to stop beating. The hands rested against the edge of the bar, boxing me in, and I could feel the heat from his body behind me.

I shifted closer to the bar and attempted to catch the bartender's eye. The blond behemoth suddenly seemed to be very interested in cleaning the already sparkling glasses and refused to look in my direction.

"Do you mind moving back, please?" I asked, hoping I wouldn't have to turn around and face him.

"I do, as a matter of fact," was the response. "I bought you three drinks. Three of your favourite drinks, I might add. The way I see it, the least you can do is say thank you."

I heard the bartender snort and shake his head, still refusing to look in my direction.

"I didn't ask you to buy them. I didn't drink them," I retorted, torn between wanting to turn around and knowing it would be a big mistake to do so.

Right then he was close enough for me to feel the heat his body generated, but he wasn't touching me ... not yet.

"Still doesn't mean you can't show some manners."

"You mean like the manners *you're* displaying?" I snapped. "Haven't you heard of personal space?"

His laugh, close to my ear, vibrated through my body. And there was something about it, a darkness, an edge that never used to be there, a wicked promise, which sent a jolt of electricity through my veins. Something touched my neck—*his lips?*—and goosebumps broke out over my skin.

"Your body likes my personal space invasion," he murmured and *yes,* those were his lips I could feel against my throat. "It always did."

"My body also likes chocolate chip cookies. Doesn't mean I jump on every single one I see." I should have ducked under his arm and moved away. The club was packed, and I didn't think he would try to stop me, not now, not with so many people around. That wasn't the way he liked to torment me.

"Do you know what my body likes?" His breath was warm against my cheek.

"Tattoos," I replied, pleased my voice didn't break when his tongue licked the shell of my ear.

He laughed again. "You're right. Why don't you turn around and see the rest I've had done since you last saw me."

"Why don't you move along and find someone who's actually interested in you?"

"Lavender hair," I watched as his right hand lifted and gently tugged a lock of my hair, "and a frosty attitude. You haven't changed at all. I think I might be in love. Will you marry me?"

I bit my lip, remembering a time when I had wanted nothing more than to hear those words. "You're not my type."

"No?" His knuckles brushed my cheek. "I used to be. How do you know you've changed your mind unless you try me?" His lips pressed against my ear. "I could become your favourite all-you-can-eat buffet." His voice dropped to a whisper. "I know *you* could definitely be mine."

I snorted, not very ladylike, I know, but I couldn't believe he was using these lines on me. I twisted to face him before I considered my action.

"Do those lines *ever* work on …" my voice trailed off as my gaze was captured by the expanse of tattooed male chest in front of me.

I lifted my eyes slowly, noting the black tribal patterns I'd seen on his arms also flowed over his shoulders until they licked like black flames along his throat.

I tipped my head back and finally met his eyes—eyes I hadn't seen in almost eight years—grey and turbulent.

Tattooed Memories

CHAPTER 3

SEX AND CANDY - MARCY PLAYGROUND

Gabe

PRESENT

Fuck.

I thought I'd been prepared to face her. But the second she spun, eyes so deep a blue they bordered on purple sparking and spitting up at me, I knew I was in trouble. Whether it was the coke finally hitting its high or just the woman in front of me, I didn't know or care. All I *did* know was that when she lifted her eyes and speared me with the same look she'd had on her face the last time we stood face to face, my dick was so hard you could have hammered nails into a fucking wall with it.

Standing behind her, feeling her heat, and smelling that subtle cotton candy scent which clung to her had been torture enough. Now, with a front seat view of curves that wouldn't quit and a mouth I knew held so much sass I wanted to swallow her whole, my plans for this woman had gone to a whole new level.

This was the *'something'* I'd mentioned to Seth. That thing the other woman hadn't had. And like any favourite toy, I was going to play with her until we were both exhausted or one of us broke.

"Bold fashion choice," she said, and my dick twitched at the way her lips pursed. "Why aren't you wearing a shirt?"

"Why aren't you wearing your shoes?" I countered.

She glanced down, breaking eye contact, which allowed me to suck in a much-needed breath. My gaze followed hers. Over her curves, the cleavage I had a bird's eye view down because I was *still* at least a foot taller than her, over her hips and down the bare tanned legs until I reached her toes. Toes that were curled into the carpet. Toes that were topped with a lavender polish. Toes I wanted to see curling because of the mind-blowing orgasm I was giving her.

By the time I stopped obsessing over her toes—*when did I get a fucking toe fetish?*—and dragged my eyes back up to her face, she was scowling at me.

"Well, as much as I appreciate you wanting to buy me a drink, you're not my type."

"*Three* drinks, Frosty," I corrected her and leaned forward to grab one of the glasses still sitting on the bar. She swayed back, attempting to avoid the collision course of my chest against hers, and I smirked. "Why are you hanging out in my club, alone, anyway? I thought you would never set foot in the place." I raised the glass and knocked the shot back. The vodka was refreshing after all the whiskey I'd been drowning in for the past few hours.

"I'm not alone."

I widened my eyes, and made a big deal of looking around, then lowered my voice conspiratorially. "Aren't you a bit old to have an imaginary friend?"

Her scowl deepened, lips twisting into an unconscious pout. And, *fuck me*, I wanted them wrapped around my dick so bad it hurt. I eyed the bar behind her, half-considering lifting her and placing her on top of it. It would put her at the perfect height for me to spread her thighs and sink my tongue, or my dick—I wasn't fussy which—inside her.

Most people would think there's no way I'd do that in a place full of people, but I would. I'd throw her down onto that bar, no matter how many fucking people were there, and I'd fuck her to the beat of the songs playing out over the speakers.

It wouldn't be the first time I'd performed for an audience, clothed and unclothed. People would gasp and look embarrassed, but they'd watch. Do you know why? Because they'd want to see if I lived up to the rumours and reputation. Spoiler alert—I *do* … and then some.

"Leave a note for your friend behind the bar and come upstairs with me."

"Why would I do that? It's not like we parted on the best of terms." That was the first time she'd acknowledged there was a history between us. Progress!

I dipped my head until my lips were against her ear. "Because

I want to take you upstairs and do dirty things to you." I let the fingers of my left hand trace a path up her thigh, drawing the hem of her dress up. "I want to slip my fingers inside the no-nonsense panties I'm sure you still wear and prove you're lying when you claim I'm not your type." When her breath hitched, I took a chance and stepped closer, curved my palm over her ass and hauled her against me.

Part of me noted, with some amusement, that I'd called it about her panties—no uncovered asscheeks for this girl. One day I'd rectify that, but for now, I was far more interested in how she fit perfectly against me. How had I forgotten that? All soft curves where I was hard. And, by fuck, was I hard.

Her hand wedged between us and pushed at my chest. "Let me go."

"We both know you don't want me to do that," I replied, tracing the shape of her ear with my tongue and letting my fingers stroke along the edge of her panties.

"I'll scream."

"That's the intention. I *do* love a screamer." My teeth caught her lobe and nipped. Her breathing stopped, started again, stopped once more.

"We're not doing this. I'm not agreeing to you touching me," she tried again and I chuckled, confident I could change her mind.

"You need to brush up on your acting skills, Frosty. Playing hard to get isn't the role for you." As I spoke, my fingers eased beneath the cotton of her panties—I wondered briefly if they were white—and discovered the wetness she'd tried to hide from me.

A soft moan escaped her lips, and her head tipped back exposing her throat. I accepted her unspoken offer and ran my tongue up the soft, fragrant skin from collarbone to jawline, my other hand delved down to unbutton my jeans and pull out my painfully hard dick. With practised moves, I hooked her leg up around my hip and pressed the tip against her through the thin material of her panties. I could feel her heat, her wetness, and I was all set to pull them aside and sink into her when she froze.

"No ... *no!*" her voice rose as she repeated herself and she shoved at my shoulders, pushing me away from her.

Colour darkened her cheeks, arousal and embarrassment merging together. Her eyes dipped down, widened at the way my hand was wrapped around my dick, stroking it idly while I stared at her, and the colour in her face deepened.

"Who do you think you are?" she hissed. "*What* do you think *I* am?" She stooped, snatched her shoes up and smoothed down the front of her dress. "Get out of my way, *Gabriel*."

CHAPTER 4

SHE HATES ME - PUDDLE OF MUDD

Harper

PRESENT

Had I really just stood there and let Gabriel Mercer, a man I hadn't seen in eight years, touch me intimately in the middle of a crowded club? Cheeks burning, I pushed past him only to find his hand gripping my arm and holding me in place.

"Don't pretend you didn't enjoy it."

My jaw dropped, and before I even thought about what I was doing I let my shoes fall to the floor and slapped his face. "How *dare* you!"

The slap didn't make him let me go. If anything, his fingers dug deeper, and the next I knew I was, once again, flattened against him, from chest to toes. His arm wrapped around my waist holding me in place and he bent his head until we were nose to nose.

That close I could see the imprint of my palm on his cheek—an angry red mark which matched the angry burn in his eyes. Eyes that had huge dilated pupils, swallowing the colour of his irises. *Was he high?*

"Just let me go, Gabe," I whispered tiredly, the fight leaving me. I didn't want to do this, not now, not *ever*.

His nose stroked against mine. "Why would I do that when I have you exactly where I want you?" He was still turned on. I could feel his erection pressing against my stomach.

"Because you don't really want me, Gabriel, and you don't want the attention you're drawing with your behaviour."

He pulled back slightly and a slow, arrogant smile spread across his face. "I could strip you naked, throw you on a table face down and fuck you while you screamed my name. And do you know what's the worst thing that would happen? The video would be released on the internet." The smile turned into a smirk. "It wouldn't be my first sex tape to go public, Frosty." He palmed my ass again. "Come upstairs with me … for old times sake."

Something snapped inside of me and I rapped his forehead with my knuckles. "Is there something *wrong* with you? Do you remember the last time we saw each other?"

"The past is the past. If spending time with me isn't incentive enough … how much?"

*"*What!*"* Was he being serious?

With his free hand, he pulled a money clip from his pocket and I was momentarily distracted by the difference between the man in front of me and the boy I'd known growing up.

"How much?" He glanced down at the bills in his hand. "There's probably around three grand there. Come with me and it's yours." He fingered the cheap material of my dress. "I don't imagine you're rolling in cash."

"Let me get this straight," I said slowly. "You are offering to *pay* me to have sex with you?"

He shrugged, and his grip on my arm eased. "It's the least I can do ... you enjoyed it last time. Don't you remember?"

I yanked my arm free. "I remember *everything*, Gabriel. Including the part where you called me a whore and walked away." I twisted out of his grip and spun away, no longer caring that I was leaving my friend in the club alone. I just needed to get away before the tears burning the back of my eyes spilled over.

He didn't stop me when I walked away from the bar, from *him*, and moved toward the exit. But then, he didn't really need to. The words he called after me were enough to tell me he wasn't done ... *we* weren't done.

"For the record, Frosty, I *am* your type. I'll be seeing you soon."

CHAPTER 5

SOMEBODY THAT I USED TO KNOW - MAYDAY PARADE

Harper

AGE 8

When I was seven, my dad died. Within six months my mom had lost the house and her job, and we had to move to an apartment block within the Fashion District in L.A. To say it was a bit of a culture shock would be an understatement. Our house had been open, airy, with large gardens front and back, and I'd had my own bedroom. The apartment we moved to had an open-plan living room/kitchen and one bedroom, which my mom and I shared.

I'd been confused, not understanding why we had to leave our beautiful home, my school and my friends. I was too young to understand that my dad had taken his own life, which meant the life insurance my parents had paid into for years wouldn't pay out. It was only years later, after Mom died, that I found all the paperwork she'd kept in a box which detailed how dad had taken out a second mortgage on our home without telling her. The monthly payments were more than she earned and it wasn't long before the house went into foreclosure and we had to leave.

In some ways, that move was the best thing that ever happened to me. In others, it was the worst.

We'd been in the apartment for two months before I met the people who lived opposite us. We'd heard them a lot—shouting, banging, fighting at all hours of the day and night—and I'd caught glimpses of a thin, gangly, dark-haired boy slinking in and out. To my eight-year-old eyes, he seemed really tall, yet he walked with his shoulders hunched inwards and his head bowed, almost like he was trying to make himself smaller than he was.

I was sitting just outside our apartment the first time I saw him properly. My mom had bought me an ice-cream, and I was sitting cross-legged on the floor in the narrow hallway between apartments. My mom was bleaching the floors inside and told me she didn't want me breathing in the fumes, so I'd be better sitting outside. She told me to stay where I could see her, but stay out of the way. So I sat with an ice-cream and a colouring book and crayons, while she got to work.

I was halfway through turning the bunny rabbit on the page purple when I saw a shadow fall over the book and a deep voice rumbled, "Whatcha doin' there, girl?"

I looked up, eyes widening at the giant towering over me—tall, broad, bearded, with straggly blond hair and flinty grey eyes. The boy I'd caught sight of a few times stood just behind him, face lowered and angled to the side. From my position on the floor, I could see his eyes were locked on the giant, and his throat moved repetitively, as he swallowed.

Carefully I placed my book and crayons to one side and rose to my feet.

"Hello," I said. "My name is Harper Jackson." I held out my hand like my daddy had taught me.

The giant's eyes dropped to my outstretched fingers, then up to my face, and he threw back his head and laughed. The sound reverberated down the hallway and the boy beside him flinched.

"Well, aren't you a proper little lady." He chuckled and reached out a hand to muss my hair. "You could learn from her, boy."

His hand moved from my head and swung out, clipping the boy around the ear. He staggered sideways but said nothing. The giant's eyes shifted from me to look beyond into the apartment where Mom was humming as she cleaned.

"Where's your da, Harper?" he asked.

"Gone," I replied softly, my eyes dropping to look at my feet. If I didn't say he was dead, maybe he'd come back.

"And left two beautiful ladies all alone?" He shook his head, and the look in his eyes made me uncomfortable. "I should introduce myself to your mom. It's the gentlemanly thing to do … isn't it, boy?" The boy nodded silently. "You stay here and keep little Harper company." He stepped around me and moved into my apartment, pushing the door closed behind him.

"Wait!" I yelped, too late as the door swung shut. "My mom said I was to keep the door open," I finished and spun to stare at the boy, who shrugged one bony shoulder.

I wasn't of an age where I could pick up on body language very well, but even at almost eight I knew this boy was sad. I could see it in the downturn of his lips, the way his eyes stayed lowered onto the floor, so I did the same thing my mom did when I felt sad.

Two small steps put me directly in front of him and, without any other thought in my head other than how happy it made me when my mom hugged me, I wrapped my short arms as far around his waist as I could reach. My head rested against his chest, and I squeezed as hard as I could.

His entire body stiffened, his heart racing beneath my ear, and I felt his hands land on my shoulders.

"Wh-what are you d-doing?" His voice was little more than a whisper, hesitant and unsure, almost like he didn't speak aloud very often.

"Squeezing the sadness out of you," I told him.

I heard the door open behind me and the boy jumped back, jerking away and putting space between us.

"The boy will babysit, and I'll pick you up at eight," the giant was telling my mom as he walked out of our apartment. I heard my mom murmur something in reply and the giant laughed. "He'll do it."

There was an edge to his voice that I didn't like. My eyes

sought out the boy, but he'd already turned away and was walking toward their own apartment door.

"Harper?" My mom's voice pulled my attention away from him and back toward her. "Time to come in and eat, honey."

※

After dinner and a shower, Mom settled me into my bed and perched on the mattress.

"Honey, Mommy is going out for a few hours with Thomas, the man who called earlier. You remember him?" She waited for my hesitant nod. "His son, Gabriel, will be coming over. He'll be in the living room if you need anything."

Gabriel—the boy with the sad eyes.

Mom was waiting for me to reply, so I gave her a smile and snuggled down into the sheets, clutching the snowman soft toy close to my face and took a deep breath. The snowman had been one of the last things my dad had given me before he died and, if I sniffed really hard, I could still smell his cologne on it.

A knock sounded at the main door and Mom rose to her feet, bending to press a kiss to my forehead.

"All right, sweetheart. I won't be late." Her hand brushed over my hair, and she smiled down at me for a second before leaving the room and closing the door quietly behind me. "If you need me, Gabriel knows how to reach me."

I must have fallen asleep shortly after because when I woke with my heart beating rapidly and a scream bursting from my throat, the room was dark.

The bad dreams had been constant since Dad had died. I woke most nights, crying and pleading for him to come home, to not leave Mom, leave me, leave *us*. Usually, I'd crawl out of my bed and find my mom, curl into her side and eventually drift back off. But when I looked, her bed was empty.

Rubbing my eyes, I climbed out of bed and padded to the door, snowman clutched in my hand. Easing it open, I peeped through the gap.

"H-hey." The soft voice of the boy—Gabriel—sounded from the opposite side of the door. "I … heard you. A-are you okay?" He paused and I saw movement—his hand lifting to rest against the door. "Do y-y-you want to come o-out here?"

I pushed the door open, watching him cautiously, and then slipped through the gap. He waited until I stood in the living room, snowman clutched to my chest, then crouched down until he was eye-level with me.

"Was it a b-bad dream?"

I nodded and he held out a hand. My eyes dropped to look at it. The knuckles looked bruised, a couple had split and scabbed over. I could see dirt beneath his nails and, when he turned his hand palm up, faint scars marred the centre of his hand and wrist. My eyes bounced back up to his.

"I-it's okay," he said. His fingers curled around mine, warm and gentle, and he led me over to the lumpy couch that had come with the apartment, before letting go of my hand. Easing onto it carefully, favouring his right side, he patted the cushion to the left of him.

I climbed up beside him and he placed a blanket over my legs, tucking it in around me and my snowman.

"W-what's his n-name?" He flicked the snowman with one finger.

"It's Frosty the Snowman. My daddy gave it to me."

He gave a slow nod. "My mom d-died when I was f-four," he told me, his voice solemn. "Before that, w-when I couldn't sleep, she'd s-s-sing to me."

I lifted my face up to look at him curiously. "What did she sing?"

His lips curled into a small smile. "Lullabies, m-mostly. Do you kn-know any?"

I shuffled closer to him, leaned against his side, into his warmth, and he carefully lifted an arm and curved it around my shoulders.

"I like "Hush Little Baby," I whispered.

"I know th-that one." I could hear the smile in his voice.

That was my first memory of hearing Gabe sing.

CHAPTER 6

SEVEN NATION ARMY - THE WHITE STRIPES

Gabe

PRESENT

Harper Jackson! I watched her stalk away from me, weaving past all the drunks as she aimed for the exit. I could have stopped her. One wave of my hand would have had security materialising to block her exit. But I let her run … for now.

We all have that 'one that got away' and she was mine. Although, if you want to get real about it, she didn't actually get away because *I* left *her*. It was the one moment in my life where I thought about somebody else. I took what she offered to me because I had to have just one taste, and then I made her hate me afterwards. Judging by the venom in her eyes, she *still* hated me, but at least she didn't hate herself as well, and that was actually important to me at the time.

Now though? Not so much. I'd bided my time, waited for

the right moment, I'd given her every opportunity to come back to me, hoped she would reach out. I told myself I'd wait until she came to me ... and now she had—whether she admitted it or not. Now I would take what I'd been so patiently waiting for, and she *would* give it to me.

She disappeared out of sight without looking back and I made my way back upstairs. The two girls from earlier were still there, and I was still turned on from my interaction with Harper.

Win/Win. But first, there was something I had to do, so I pulled out my cell and called Karl.

"I want you to arrange an interview with someone," I told him when he answered.

There was a long pause before he spoke. "What did you do?"

"Nothing ... yet. That's what the interview is for."

"Gabe—"

"Karl," I spoke over him. "It's just an interview."

"You *never* give interviews. What's going on?"

I sighed. "Just arrange the interview." I paused, thinking. "And a photographer. They'll want photos."

"You're worrying me now."

"You're not paid to worry." That was a low blow. Karl had been my friend and my manager for a long time, and I've done a *lot* of things that caused him to worry.

"Shouldn't you be sleeping?"

"I'll sleep soon, *dad*. Find me a reporter. One that'll have the largest reach. Arrange an appointment for tomorrow morning.

I'll even go to them!"

"Should I also call the lawyer?" Karl's voice was dry.

"No. It's too soon for a lawyer." I laughed at his sigh. "Trust me, Karl. This is a personal thing. Not a band thing."

"Fine. I'll text you the details when it's set up."

"Oh, and get Miles to pick me up from Damnation in the morning."

"Anything else?"

My eyes slid to the two girls. "There is, but I think I have that covered."

※

Was this what it had really come down to?

I was standing in the shower jerking myself off, while the two girls I'd chosen off the Damnation dance floor slept the sleep of the sexually satisfied in bed. And why? Because all I could think about was the day ahead and the things I'd planned to do now the ice queen from my past had finally arrived in my present.

I groaned and rested my forehead against the tiles, my dick hardening more at the thought of her and I stroked faster, building up the image of her in my mind. I could see her clearly. Those plump lips pressed together, unique eyes so blue they were almost purple, and as cold as the sky in winter, narrowed and raking over my body in a look of utter annoyance. What I wouldn't give to turn that look into one of lust. To see those lips wrapped around my dick. And I would. Very soon.

Fuck.

My fingers tightened their grip and I pumped faster, feeling the pressure build until it was almost unbearable. My eyes closed, and her face floated behind my lids—how she'd look as I fucked her, how it would feel to be buried to the hilt inside her body, how her moans and cries would sound when I made her come—and she *would* come, multiple times, I'd make sure of that.

Was this what I'd become? Gabe *fucking* Mercer, frontman of Forgotten Legacy, a man who could walk into a room and have any woman in it—jerking off over the fantasy of a girl who fucking hated the sight of me. A girl whose skin visibly crawled if I was anywhere near her.

Fuck.

Lights flared behind my eyes as I came, spilling all over my hand, and my breath left me in an explosion of expletives.

Apparently, *yes*. That's exactly who I'd become.

I washed away the evidence of my fantasy, turned off the water and stepped out of the shower. Grabbing the towel from its hook, I wrapped it around my waist and walked back into the bedroom.

The two girls were still sleeping, the bottle blonde—Jane, Jan? I don't *fucking* remember—with her hand resting on the natural blonde's breast. I glanced down, waiting for the usual twitch. Any other day and I'd be back in that bed, using my famous smile and charm to get them to fool around together while I watched and got myself off. But today? Nothing, zilch, nada. Absolutely fuck all. Not even a slight stirring at the idea.

In fact, I even regretted letting them stay. The coke-high I'd been on had dropped mid-fuck and I'd looked down at the girl beneath me and realised I didn't even want her. I didn't want either of them. I was simply going through the motions. The sad part is neither of them even noticed when I mentally switched off. I made them both scream and retreated to the bathroom to dispose of the condom before they realised I hadn't even come myself.

The even worse part of that? I didn't care that I hadn't got off. I shook my head, unable to contain a grin at the thought of *why* I hadn't come, towelled myself dry and dragged on a clean pair of jeans and a t-shirt. My cell was ringing by the time I was done, and I grabbed it from the floor beside the bed and padded out into the main VIP area.

The club below was silent and empty—the partying crowds had left hours ago, and it was still too early for the cleaning staff. I connected the call.

"I'm waiting for you outside," Miles told me and I grunted as I popped a cigarette between my lips.

"Did you bring coffee?" I asked him.

"Of course I did."

I shoved my feet into boots, pocketed my wallet and headed downstairs. When I exited the club, it was to find Karl, the band's manager, leaning against the car beside Miles. He straightened when I appeared and scowled at me. And I knew … *fucking knew* … what was going to come out of his mouth.

"What the *fuck* is wrong with you?"

Yup, there it was.

I put on my best swagger and walked toward the car. "There's probably a woman's magazine out there somewhere detailing every flaw I have. Get one of your minions to find it for you."

He threw open the car door. "Is this interview something to do with seeing Harper Jackson last night?"

Half inside the car, I stopped and twisted around. "Miles, there are two girls upstairs. Can you get rid of them for me?" I ignored Karl's question.

"For fuck's sake, Gabriel!" my manager roared.

I threw a smile at him over my shoulder. "You're gonna give yourself a heart attack, Karl." I dropped onto the leather seat and waited.

Predictably, Karl slid his ass onto the seat opposite me seconds later. "So what's this interview about?"

I smirked and linked my hands behind my head. "Well, about that ..."

Tattooed Memories

CHAPTER 7

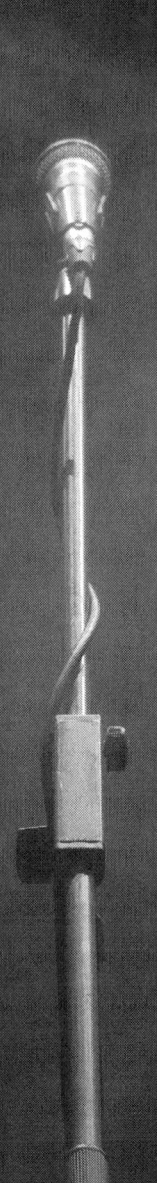

MEMORIES - MAROON FIVE

Harper

PRESENT

"And if that mockingbird don't sing, mama's gonna buy you a diamond ring."

My eyes snapped open, hearing the smoky voice singing the lines of a lullaby I hadn't heard in almost a decade. I shot upright in my bed, half-expecting to find Gabe Mercer sitting beside me, but my room was empty. Definitely nobody there—no haunted boy from my past or arrogant rock star from my present.

Throwing back the sheet, I slid out of bed and walked through the apartment to the kitchen, thinking about two nights ago when I'd sent a text to Siobhan telling her I'd taken an Uber home, found our spare key hidden beneath a small plant pot by the elevator and gone straight to bed.

Memories masked as dreams had haunted me both nights, taking me back to a past I'd worked hard to forget. In one meeting, everything had come crashing back, leaving me more exhausted than when I'd crawled beneath the sheets that first night.

Coffee. I needed coffee. I found myself in the kitchen, turning on the coffee maker on autopilot, and flopped onto the nearest chair to wait for it to brew and flicked through one of the magazines Siobhan had left on the table.

Over the noise of the machine percolating, I could hear voices, growing louder and closer, outside the window. I lived on the ground floor of a small apartment block and the area was full of people who were more likely to be out at night rather than at this hour on a Sunday morning.

Frowning, I rose to my feet, crossed to the window and peered out from between the curtains. A group of people were clustered outside the entrance to my building. Blinking, I rubbed my eyes and looked again, sure I was seeing things.

They had microphones, cameras and ... *was that a news van?* I stepped back, my frown deepening. Had there been a burglary? A murder? I shook my head. Neither would bring this kind of attention to the neighbourhood I lived in. So, *why* were there reporters outside?

I was still contemplating the mystery when the front door opened and Siobhan dashed in—hair wild, eyes wide, and her face flushed. In the middle of pouring coffee, I frowned at her.

"You're up early. Where have you been?"

"Late, Harper. I'm up *late*," she corrected me as she threw her bag down onto the floor and eyed me. "Why are you so calm? I was sure you'd be freaking out. That's why I came home."

"About what?" I paused. "Wait! Was someone murdered in our building? Is that why all those reporters are out there? Where are the police? Oh my God, it wasn't Mrs Lowry, was it? She didn't finally snap and kill her husband?"

Mrs Lowry had been threatening to off her husband for as long as I'd lived here. I'd been sure it was just an idle threat, but who knew. There was a man I'd happily do time for murdering, so why wouldn't she feel a similar urge?

"Harper..." Siobhan took the mug of coffee from me and set it on the table, then caught my shoulders and turned me toward the window. "Those reporters out there are here for you."

"Me? I'm not dead! Why do they think I've been murdered?"

"They don't think you're dead! Stop looking for murders. Jesus, what's wrong with you? Why is murder you go-to reason for everything?"

"Well, why else would there be reporters outside?"

Siobhan bent and pulled out a newspaper from her bag. "Maybe because of this?" She opened it, folded the pages over and held it out to me.

ROCK STAR'S HEART BROKEN BY HIS CHILDHOOD SWEETHEART

Beneath the headline was a photograph of Gabe Mercer, and I felt something in my chest twist and tighten. The photographer had taken an image of him gazing out over the city, his expression distant and sad. One hand rested against the pane of glass, the other captured as he rubbed the back of his neck. For some reason, it felt natural and unposed for.

Below the photograph was an article.

"Do I want to read this?" I questioned. Inwardly, I was screaming.

What have you done, Gabe?

"It'll explain why they're here," Siobhan replied. "And then *you* can explain to me why I wasn't aware you knew Gabe Mercer."

I took the newspaper from her and scanned the opening paragraphs.

```
Gabe Mercer, the lead singer of Forgotten
Legacy, chose to bare his heart with
us in an intimate one-on-one interview
yesterday in the hopes of reaching out
to the childhood sweetheart who broke his
heart.
"Harper Jackson was eight when we met,
and I knew from the first time I laid eyes
on her that she would change my life."
Gabe paused at this point to give, what
looked to me, a sad smile. "She quickly
became the most stable thing in my life,
an anchor in the storm."
I ask him why he's waited until now to
mention her and he shrugs. I wouldn't be
female if I didn't mention how the material
```

of his t-shirt stretches and tightens with the movement.

"I saw her at my club last night, and she couldn't get away from me fast enough." He laughs quickly, his grey eyes glinting with unusual humour. "I treated her badly the last time we spoke, but I want the chance to fix things. When I saw her in my club, I thought she'd finally come around to the idea and was willing to meet with me. I found out later that she wasn't there because she knew I was, but because her friend wanted to go."

I ask if that's why he wanted to do this interview and he nods. "Yeah. I figure if I lay it out there, she will get in touch or someone will know how I can reach her. I miss her. I want her in my life. I *need* her in my life. I didn't realise how much until I saw her again."

So there you have it, folks. Before you read the rest of our interview, can you help? The notorious lead singer of Forgotten Legacy is looking for the one that got away. Do you know Harper Jackson? If you have any information on her whereabouts,

```
contact me at the L.A. Inquisitor and I'll
pass the information on.
```

I threw the newspaper down in disgust. "What the hell is he playing at?"

"It's true, then? You *do* know him?"

I ignored my friend. "I'm going to kill him." I fumed. "I'm not going to rest until he's dead at my feet."

"You're not going to kill him, Harper. You're too pretty to go into the prison system over a man."

I snorted a laugh. "Do *not* be reasonable with me right now!" I reached for my cell.

"What are you doing?"

"Calling the newspaper. I want his number."

"Isn't that what he wants you to do?"

I stared helplessly at my friend. "Look out there, Von!" I jabbed a finger toward the window. "They've already found me. It's only a matter of time before Gabe shows up, and *that* out there will become even more of a circus!" While I spoke, I watched a dark car with tinted windows crawling slowly down the street. The closer it got, the more the sinking feeling in the pit of my stomach grew.

"Von … are you expecting someone?" I asked when the car parked a few feet beyond the reporters.

"No, why?" She moved closer and peered over my shoulder. We both watched in silence when a smart-dressed large man exited the driver's side and leaned against the side of the car, his arms folded across an extremely broad chest. Sunglasses masked part of his face, but his close-cropped hair and burly physique suggested he was someone at ease with being intimidating.

I wondered why he was here … and whether I should worry.

"Maybe he works for one of the TV crews?" Siobhan offered.

"*Look* at him. He looks more like a killer for hire than an executive." *Someone Gabe would know*, I thought. "I *knew* I shouldn't have gone to the club with you!"

"What? Why not? Was that why you left? Did you see Gabe Mercer there?"

I couldn't stop a pensive sigh as I turned to face my friend.

"Gabe *owns* Damnation," I told her.

"You obviously made quite the impression on him." Her tone was questioning.

I glanced at the newspaper on the table. "That?" I shook my head. "That's just him manipulating a situation to get what he wants."

"Well, clearly what he wants is you."

"No, he wants to cause trouble for me. I didn't break his heart. We didn't have some crazy love affair." My lips pressed into a thin line. "If anything, *he* broke *my* heart, but it wasn't unexpected. Gabe was a big part of my life after my dad died. I thought I was in love with him, believed if I showed him how I felt, he'd tell me he felt the same." I gave a bitter laugh. "He didn't … and made it very clear. That was the last time I saw him, until the other night."

"So why that, then?" She waved a hand toward the article.

I shrugged. "I don't know." I *did* know. It was to draw me out, to give him the attention he wanted. I turned back to the window and frowned. The car was still there but the man had disappeared.

"Where did—" A rap on the door cut me off, and I traded looks with Siobhan.

Neither of us moved.

"Will you—"

"Shall I—"

We both spoke at the same time.

"Stay out of sight," she warned me and moved toward the door to peer through the peephole. "It's the guy from the car," she hissed. "What do you want me to do?"

"Ask what he wants!"

"You know I can hear both of you, don't you?" His voice was dryly amused, and we looked at each other in horror.

"What do you want?" Siobhan demanded.

"I've been sent to collect Ms Jackson."

"Collect?" Siobhan mouthed at me.

"Ms Jackson, I know you're listening. I'm sure you've seen the article in the Inquisitor, and the press waiting for you outside. Without my help, you're going to be stuck inside your apartment unless you want to face the reporters alone. I can get you out of here and somewhere … *safer* … until it all blows over. Which it won't if you ignore the message."

"What message?" I couldn't remain quiet any longer.

The man's laugh was as dry as his words. "You know exactly what I'm talking about."

"Humour me."

"He said you'd be like this. All right, Ms Jackson, I'll *humour* you. I'm employed by Forgotten Legacy as part of their security detail. As of today, I've been reassigned to *you*. At least until I deliver you to my employer, anyway."

"You mean Gabe Mercer?" I said flatly.

"I assumed that went without saying."

"What if I say no?"

"I'm sure you already know the answer to that, Ms Jackson." He paused. "I assure you, you're in no danger. He simply wants to talk to you."

"Where?"

"He's waiting at his apartment in Carson Heights." He named a prestigious apartment block a few miles from where Damnation was located, and a place I'd actually cleaned apartments inside. "Before you refuse, he instructed me to tell you he isn't there alone. His staff are with him."

"Staff?"

"His manager, his assistant, and someone from his PR team."

"He has a PR team?" I couldn't imagine Gabe being surrounded by minions.

There was a bite to his tone when he replied. "You *have* met Mr Mercer before, haven't you? I'm sure you understand the need for such a team."

"I'm bringing my friend with me." I didn't even know I'd decided to go until I said it.

"That's fine, Ms Jackson. Are you going to open the door?"

"No. We'll be out soon. Just wait there." I waved a hand at Siobhan to get her attention and walked down the short hallway to my bedroom. My friend was hot on my heels.

"Are we seriously going with the scary guy?" she asked once we were inside with the door firmly closed.

"If I don't, Gabe won't stop at an interview. But you don't have to come if you don't want to."

Her look said everything I needed to know in reply to that.

We didn't take more than half an hour to get ready, and the 'security detail' was leaning against the wall, glasses still covering his face and arms folded across his chest. I was tempted to try and sneak past him, but the reporters were still outside and the second we opened the door he straightened to his full height.

"Ready, ladies?" he asked.

"No, but let's get this over with," I replied. "How are we going to get past *them*?" I looked pointedly at the press gathered around the entrance to the building.

Security Man, or SM in my head, smiled. "We're going to walk through them. Stay in front of me. Don't look at them. Keep your head up and focused straight ahead. Don't stop, don't answer any questions, and *don't* make eye contact." He moved away from the wall. "Ready?" he asked again.

I didn't reply, staring at the mass of bodies beyond the door.

"This is crazy," I whispered.

"Don't worry about it. I don't imagine it'll last too long." His tone was unreadable. I wanted to ask what he meant, but his palm pressed against my back, urging me forward.

When we reached the door, I stopped, tensing. "Wait!"

He ignored me. "Take a deep breath, Ms Jackson," he said and yanked the door open.

The noise outside was deafening, a cacophony of voices. People shouting, cameras flashing, microphones pushed into my face as we made our slow way through the crowd. Through it all, I could feel SM's hand firm on my back, guiding me. I didn't dare look around for Siobhan and hoped she was safely beside us.

We were almost at the car when a question stopped me in my tracks.

"Are you the girl he almost killed his father over?"

CHAPTER 8

MIGRAINE - TWENTY ONE PILOTS

Harper

AGE 13

"Gabe? *Gabe?*" I dashed out of the elevator already yelling for the boy who lived in the apartment opposite me.

"Keep it down, Frosty." His voice, wavering between that of boy and man, and without the nervous stutter he always developed when his father was nearby, came from behind me.

I spun and was running toward him, intent on throwing myself into his body, when I spotted the two boys flanking him. I skidded to a stop, eyeing them nervously.

"It's okay, Harpy." He grinned at my scowl. He knew out of the two nicknames he'd given me, *that* was the one I hated. "These are my friends. Shaun," he looked at the green eyed boy, "and Deacon." His head turned toward the other, who was brown-eyed. Both of them stared at me with the same curious expression. "This is Harper," he explained. "She lives there." He pointed toward my apartment. "What's got you so excited?" he asked me then, and I suddenly remembered why I'd been shouting for him.

I gave him a triumphant smile. "I did it! I got an A!" I pulled my bag from my shoulder and dragged out the math test to show him.

Gabe smiled. "I told you. Well done!"

"I thought we could get some ice-cream ... you know, to celebrate?"

Gabe hesitated, looking at his friends. "I'm sorry, Frosty. We're heading out of town for a couple of days."

"Oh." I scuffed the floor with the toe of my shoe, my excitement fading.

The silence stretched between us, and I shoved the paper back into my school bag and began to trudge toward my door.

"Wait." My eyes jerked up at the unfamiliar voice and met the green-eyed gaze of Shaun. "We have time." He nudged Gabe. "Let's take the pipsqueak out to celebrate her grade, then we'll get out of here."

"You're sure?" Gabe asked his friend, who smiled down at me.

"Can't let that A go by without celebrating it, right?"

I returned his smile with a shy one of my own.

❄

I was stuffed. I couldn't remember a time when I'd ever eaten so much! The three boys had taken me to Molly's, a local diner known for having the best ice-cream in the district, and a place I rarely went to because my mom couldn't afford it.

We had piled into the small booth, Gabe sitting beside me and his two friends on the opposite bench seat. Shaun had plucked one of the menus from the holder and slid it across the table in front of me.

"An A in math is a huge deal, pipsqueak," he told me. "Let's make it a proper celebration. Dinner and dessert on me."

"Shaun," Gabe began, and I knew he was going to refuse his friend's offer. He didn't like feeling as though he couldn't pay his way, I knew that.

"I'm starving, so for God's sake don't talk him out of buying dinner," Deacon piped up, forestalling Gabe's objection. His golden-brown gaze met mine and he winked. I hid a smile.

Gabe sighed beside me but didn't protest further, and Shaun ordered burgers and fries all round, followed by the biggest milkshakes I'd ever seen, and then topped it off with huge servings of multiple flavours of ice-cream, because Deacon couldn't make up his mind which flavour he wanted. I was sure he did it because he could see me wavering over three different ones, but he never said anything so neither did I.

The entire time, Shaun kept the conversation flowing. I learned that he and his brother were twins who went to the same school as Gabe. Shaun was naturally sociable, his hands waving expansively as he talked, a permanent smile fixed to his face. His twin was quieter, his dark eyes sharp and focused as he took in everything around him, and seemed content to let his brother talk for them both.

Afterwards, Shaun paid, throwing down a wad of bills that made my eyes widen, and we all trooped out.

"I think I'm going to burst!" I exclaimed on a groan as we walked back to our apartment block.

Deacon laughed and ruffled my hair. "That's what happens when you eat too much, pipsqueak."

We stopped outside my front door, and I looked up at Gabe. "How long will you be gone?" I asked him.

"We'll be back Sunday night," he replied. "Stay out of trouble until then." His gaze darted to his own apartment door and back to me. His unspoken warning was clear. *Stay away from my da.*

The twins waited outside while Gabe walked me into the apartment. I dumped my bag by the door and turned to face him.

"Does your dad know you're going away for the weekend?"

Gabe didn't reply, his eyes shifting away from me. I knew what that meant. His dad *didn't* know.

"Gabe," I said softly.

"D-don't." He grimaced when he stumbled over the word.

"He'll be mad."

Gabe shrugged and reached out to tuck a lock of hair behind my ear. "Stay away f-from him, Harper," he told me quietly. "I m-mean it."

I clutched at his wrist, feeling the faint scar lines beneath my fingertips. "He'll hurt you."

He shook his head. "Don't worry about it, Frosty. J-just promise me you'll stay out of his way."

Gabe
AGE 15

I crept into my apartment as silently as I could, hoping that my da had stayed drunk all weekend and didn't notice I was missing or hadn't been home himself. The place was in darkness when I slipped through the door, but I knew that didn't mean anything. He could have passed out in the living room or be in his bedroom or even be lying in wait for me.

I stood, one hand on the door handle, listening intently for any sound which would warn me he was nearby, but the room remained silent. I waited for a minute or two longer before stepping deeper into the room.

The blow to the side of my head sent me crashing into the wall. My hands rose automatically to cover my face, and I slid slowly to the floor when the next blow caught my shoulder. I twisted just as he buried his foot into my side, and pulled my knees up against my chest.

I didn't make a sound, having learned a long time ago that any sign of pain or weakness would enrage him further.

"Where the fuck have you been, boy?" he snarled, reaching down to wrap one meaty hand around my throat and haul me back to my feet.

I said nothing. I knew my eyes didn't hide the fear and loathing I was feeling, but I'd lost the ability to care about him seeing how I felt years ago.

"Answer me, you little shit." The whiskey fumes on his breath burned my nose and stung my eyes.

His fingers tightened, cutting off my air supply, but I still didn't react. Instead, I held his glare and slowly counted to ten inside my head. I reached nine, and my vision had started to blur when he let go of me. I didn't get a chance to draw any oxygen into my lungs before he backhanded me and my lip exploded. The metallic taste of blood filled my mouth and I spat, narrowly missing my father's foot. He growled, stepping back.

His fingers curled into the neck of my t-shirt and I felt my feet leave the floor as he lifted me up. "Where have you been?" he said slowly.

"I w-was with f-friends." The stutter I worked hard to stop when I was with friends came back with a vengeance.

"All weekend. Did you think I wouldn't notice?"

"I h-hoped," I muttered.

"What did you say?" He shook me, making the teeth rattle in my head.

"N-nothing, sir." I released a shaky sigh. It didn't matter what I said. I knew what the outcome was going to be. Nothing I did at this point would change it.

When he drew his fist back, I didn't even bother trying to avoid it. The sooner he worked the rage out of his system, the sooner he'd stop.

❄

"Gabe?" I hissed at the gentle touch on my cheek which accompanied the whisper. "I told you he'd hurt you again."

"Harper?" My voice came out as a croak. "You sh-shouldn't be here … if he catches you …" I had to force the words out from between swollen and bloodied lips.

"He's not here," she replied, her voice hushed. "He left an hour ago. I made sure to wait before I came over." Her fingers touched my face again and I winced. "School is going to ask questions this time. You can't keep this up, Gabe."

I took a deep breath, ignoring the sharp stab of pain in my side and pushed myself upright. He'd left me on the floor in the living room, unconscious and bleeding, probably hoping I'd die while he was out. Propping my back against the wall, I touched my nose gingerly. It was sore and, when I drew my hand back, blood coated my fingers, but it wasn't broken, thankfully.

"Let me help," Harper pleaded and rose to her feet. She disappeared into the bathroom, only to return a few seconds later.

I sighed, tipped my head back against the wall and closed my eyes, while I allowed Harper to wipe the blood away from my face.

CHAPTER 9

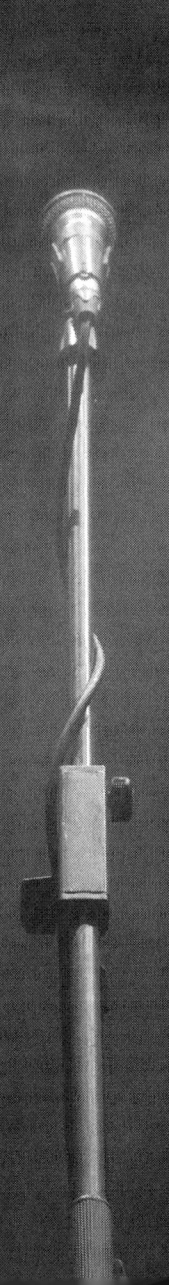

12 ROUNDS - BOHNES

Harper

PRESENT

My eyes watched the numbers rise as we stood in the elevator, and I tried to keep my breathing calm and steady.

15 … 16 … 17 …

"What floor did you say Gabe lives on?" I broke the silence and turned to face the still-nameless security guy.

"I didn't," he grunted. "But he's in the Penthouse Suite on the twenty-fifth floor."

"Twenty-fifth?" I repeated, my mouth going dry.

"It's a private building with top security, but there's always the chance of people getting to the lower floors. To access the penthouse, you need a special elevator key."

"But," I swallowed, "what if there's a fire?"

"There's a private fire escape, which reaches the ground

directly from the suite."

"Oh…" My heartbeat increased, beating rapidly in my chest, my breath became shallow, and I knew if I didn't change my focus I'd have a full-blown panic attack in the elevator.

"I'm sure the building owners have their health and safety figured out, Harp," Siobhan said lightly beside me, touching my arm and breaking through my impending panic. "She's been obsessed with things like that for as long as I've known her," she explained to the man.

He gave her a polite smile but said nothing as the elevator came to a stop and the doors slid open smoothly.

"After you." He swept out an arm, indicating we exit the elevator before him and I shook my head.

"No." My voice broke on the word. "No," I repeated more firmly. "You go first. We'll follow you."

"Are you going to press the button and return to the ground floor if I leave the elevator?"

That had absolutely been my intention and, from the slight smile on his face, he knew it. With a narrow-eyed glare at him, I stepped out of the elevator and into what appeared to be a large reception room. Two black leather couches lined the walls, with a large glass table taking centre place. On the wall directly opposite the elevator were two large oak doors.

"Follow me." The security guy strode across the room and turned the handle on one of the doors.

It swung open on silent hinges. The apartment beyond was

large and open-plan. I could see two men and a woman seated on the corner-sofa, deep in conversation. On the wall facing me, I could see numerous framed discs, awards for sales of various albums, I guessed. Mixed between them were photographs, but I couldn't see who they were from where I hovered in the doorway.

I also couldn't see Gabe in the room but, and I know it sounded weird, I could *smell* him. Sandalwood and patchouli ... and something just uniquely *him*. It permeated the air, not strong or overpowering, just ... *there*. I hadn't noticed it at Damnation, but here in his own space, I could smell him ... almost taste him in every breath I took.

"Candice." The woman seated with the two men lifted her head at the security guy's voice. "Where's Gabe?"

Candice rose to her feet, fine blonde brows dipping into a frown as her gaze bounced from him to where me and Siobhan still waited near the door.

"Is that her?" Her ice-blue eyes scanned over me and her lips puckered. "I was expecting something more ... exotic from the way he described you."

"I'm ... sorry?" I blinked at her, her comment distracting me from the fact we were on the twenty-fifth floor and I didn't know where the fire escape was. Okay so I hadn't made that much of an effort, but my black jeans weren't ripped and my Rolling Stones t-shirt, while old and faded, was clean.

She moved closer. "You're going to need a whole new wardrobe ... and *that* hair!" She tutted, reaching out to finger a lock of said lavender hair, and I jerked away.

"Leave her hair alone, Candice." I inhaled sharply at the raspy growl—a mistake when I drew in a lungful of the scent of the man who appeared through the archway on the opposite side of the room.

My senses weren't ready. *I wasn't ready.*

He looked good, *better* than I thought he should, considering the lifestyle he lived—and the fact I'd wished all sorts of illnesses on him over the years. Nothing life-threatening, I didn't really want him dead, but something to dilute the sheer ... *beauty* of him. I'd tried very hard to avoid reading about him over the years, and by that, I meant I stopped every time I saw his stupidly perfect face on whatever entertainment outlet he was on. The media loved him—his looks, his music, his behaviour—all things that made them a lot of money.

Today he was dressed in a suit—dark pants, a crisp white shirt and a black jacket hiding the tattoos which covered his chest. His usually unruly hair had been tamed, meaning he'd been too distracted to rake his hand through it. He could have easily passed as the CEO of a multi-million-dollar business, except there was three days' worth of scruff covering his face, and his sleeves were rolled up to his elbows, displaying tattooed hands and forearms. Leather bracelets wrapped around both wrists and silver rings covered his fingers. A black thong hung from his throat, whatever was on it tucked beneath the shirt. Black tattooed flames snaked up from beneath his collar and covered his neck up to his jaw.

An unlit cigarette hung between his lips, the Zippo lighter, that I knew belonged to his dad, held loosely in one hand as he idly flicked it open and closed.

To the world, he was a complete and utter bad boy rock star—inside and out. To me, he was a damaged lost soul, a misunderstood angel, who had broken my heart.

The conversation in the room ceased when he spoke and I realised the boy I'd known, the boy who'd broken my heart, had turned into a man who commanded attention with an effortless ease at odds with the person I used to know.

"*Wow*!" Siobhan's breathless whisper broke the spell he seemed to be weaving over the room and I turned my head before my eyes could meet his. His soft chuckle reached me, and I gritted my teeth against the urge to look back at him.

"Everyone out."

The command caused chaos—Candice spun around to argue with him. The two men still seated on the couch protested and the security guy who had brought us here stepped closer to Gabe, frowning.

"You heard him," he said over the cacophony of voices.

"Gladly," I snapped, thankful for the excuse, and turned on my heel, intent on heading back to the elevator and freedom.

A hand closed over my arm before I'd taken a single step, and a voice growled low in my ear.

"Oh no, Frosty, not *you*. I told you I'd be seeing you again soon." As he spoke, he drew me away from Siobhan and, like an idiot, I let him. My only defence being the misguided belief he couldn't ... *wouldn't* ... try anything in a room full of people.

When I saw where he was leading me, I stopped. "No!" I couldn't stop the word from breaking free.

A few feet ahead of us was a huge floor-to-ceiling window, with a good-sized balcony, but I could see beyond that. I could see how high we were.

"No, Gabe!" I repeated sharply and attempted to break free from his hold.

"Relax," he snapped, throwing the still unlit cigarette onto a table and pocketing his lighter. "I thought you'd prefer some privacy to catch up."

I shook my head, battling against the panic threatening to overwhelm me. *Had he forgotten?*

"Not out there!" I finally looked up into his face, meeting his eyes and the shock of the contact seared my soul.

He looked confused for a second, before he masked the emotion, leaving his eyes grey and blank. Then he blinked, his brows pulling together, and cut the direction of his gaze to the window, then back to me.

My breathing was coming in short gasps, and I knew I'd gone pale.

"Fuck," he breathed. "Fuck. I'm sorry, Harper. I forgot." He readjusted his grip, letting his hand slide down my arm until he could link his fingers with mine. His other hand reached up to brush his knuckles over my cheek. "Breathe," he whispered.

"How could you forget?" I forced through dry lips.

He shrugged. "Maybe forget is the wrong word, but it's been ten years since the fire, babe. I didn't think it would still bother you."

"Didn't think or just didn't care?"

"That's not fair, Frosty," he chided softly. "Hold me accountable for the things I did, by all means, but not for the things I *didn't* do."

"What if the things you *didn't* do hurt more?" I whispered before I could stop myself.

"Harper..."

I couldn't read the tone in his voice and he didn't finish the sentence because Candice appeared beside him.

"Gabe, you *can't* just throw us out! We're supposed to be going over your schedule for the next week."

He didn't even look at the blonde woman, his eyes locked on mine. "Tomorrow," he said.

"Gabe—"

"I *said* tomorrow. Get everyone out of here. I've got something I need to deal with."

"I'm not here to be *dealt* with," I protested. "I'm here because you gave me no choice!"

His smile didn't reach his eyes. "There's always a choice, Harper."

"You sent reporters to my home!"

He shrugged again, not even denying his part in them

finding out my address. "I wanted to talk to you."

"It's been eight years. *Eight* years, Gabe," I said shrilly. "What could possibly be important enough *now* that you need to talk to me?"

We both ignored the woman hovering beside him.

"I was waiting for the right time." He looked down at our linked fingers, frowning. "I sent you invitations to Damnation *all* the time, and you never turned up, *not once,* until the other night. I took that to mean you were *finally* ready to hear from me again."

"*You* left *me*, Gabe! You looked at me like I was less than the dirt beneath your shoe, like I was *nothing* to you! Why would I want to hear from you after that?"

He raked a hand through his hair, disrupting the work the hairstylist had done. "It wasn't supposed to be so long, Harper. I didn't expect you to run away."

"What did you *think* would happen? You threw me out!"

He sighed and dropped my hand, turning to the blonde. "Candice, get everyone the fuck out of here," he snapped. "Or you're fired."

"*What?* You can't do that!"

Gabe merely raised an eyebrow and she threw up her hands in exasperation. "Fine!" She clapped her hands loudly. "Our moody as fuck rock star wants some alone time with his childhood sweetheart. Out!"

He grabbed my hand again, ignoring my attempts to pull it

free and crossed the room.

"Miles," he called as he walked, and the security guy who'd picked us up looked over at us. "Can you take Harper's friend for coffee or something?"

"No! She stays—" Gabe turned his cool gaze to me and I faltered.

"Take her downstairs for an hour. If I don't call to say otherwise, bring her back up and pick up Harper to take them both home."

"I don't want to be alone with you," I shouted at him.

"What are you expecting me to do, Frosty?" His voice was calm and quiet compared with mine.

"At the club—"

"At the club, I was drunk, high, and horny as fuck. I'd just come off stage and needed to burn off energy."

"Is that supposed to make what you did okay?"

"I never said it was okay. It's just the facts of the situation." His shoulders moved in a shrug, which stretched the material of his jacket, and I cursed myself for even noticing. "Give me an hour, then I swear I won't stop you from leaving and returning to your life. You'll never see me again if that's what you want."

"Why should I believe you?"

"When did I ever lie to you, Harper?" he said quietly. "Even when it hurt, I never lied to you."

CHAPTER 10

BANGBANGBANG (ACOUSTIC) - DEAL CASINO

Gabe

PRESENT

I'd taken a risk doing the interview. I knew it would get her attention. I knew she'd be angry, but I *hoped* it would force her to face me. Lucky for me it worked and she was here. Okay, *fine*, she was glaring at me. I could feel her anger filling the room, but I could work with that.

I thought seeing her again would raise all the memories I'd worked hard to put behind me, and they *were* there, lurking in the dark recesses of my mind. But mostly, all I could think about was how she'd tasted, how she'd felt in my arms, the other night.

I'd wanted her when we were kids, before we knew what attraction even was. I'd wanted her when we were teens, and I still wanted her now. I hadn't realised quite how much until I finally saw her again, and realised the dissatisfaction I'd felt over the years had been because all the women I'd been with—and there had been a few—weren't her.

I just needed to convince her she wanted the same thing. Before that, though, I had to fix the mess I'd made when I was high and acting stupid.

I studied her while we waited for everyone to leave. She hadn't changed physically—she was maybe a little thinner and there was an extra level of wariness in the way she held herself, but the fire was still in her eyes.

"You know," I broke the silence and reached out to flick a finger against the material of the t-shirt she wore. "I'm pretty sure that's mine."

She scowled at me, her cheeks turning pink. "Don't be ridiculous."

"Really?" I arched a brow. "How many do you have?" Ratty old band t-shirts had been all I wore back when I was a teen and still living in the hellhole opposite her.

To her credit, she didn't deny it. "How many did you leave behind?"

Her eyes challenged me, and I bit back a smile. It *was* my shirt she'd kept, and she probably had all the others too. A good sign, right?

"Why have you brought me here, Gabe?" she asked when the silence stretched between us again.

I glanced around, noting we were finally alone and felt the tension in my shoulders ease a little. "Do you remember when we were kids? Do you ever think about those times?"

"Some of us didn't have the opportunity to remake our past and change our lives." The bitterness was clear in her voice. "You obviously know where I live. What do *you* think?"

"Why didn't you go to college? That was your plan, your dream. It was going to get you out of there."

"With *what* money?"

"You were in line for a scholarship. What happened to it?"

Her laugh was brittle. "You're seriously asking me that?"

"Obviously," I replied patiently. "I want to know." I couldn't figure out why the question made her so angry. And she was *furious*, in fact.

"You want to know what happened," she repeated, and I nodded, even though it hadn't been a question.

"*You* happened, Gabriel! After the … the …" she faltered and her eyes darted past me to the balcony. "I … I need to get out of here. Let me go." She swayed, face draining of colour. "Gabe, please," she whispered. "I can't … I …"

"Hey!" I caught her as she crumpled, her legs giving way beneath her. I swung her up into my arms and carried her over to the couch and lay her on it.

She wasn't out for long, a few minutes at most, not even long enough to find something to help wake her, and then she was surging upright. I leapt to my feet and grabbed her arm to stop her frantic dash for the door.

"Slow down. You fainted."

"We're on the twenty-fifth floor! I need to get out." Her voice was breathless, her breathing erratic.

"Harper, take a breath." I recognised what was happening. I should have considered it before bringing her here, but I'd been too wrapped up in what I wanted to think about all the little details. Something else I needed to add to my 'need to fix' list.

"Harper," I repeated her name, and cupped her chin in my palm, forcing her to look at me. "Breathe with me, Frosty," I told her, falling back into a role I'd assumed when we were kids all those years ago. "Breathe in ... that's it ... now out."

Her breathing steadied, slowed, and I found myself bending my head, my focus on her lips. I could feel her breath, warm on my cheek, see her pupils expanding to swallow those gorgeous blue-purple irises. I wanted to kiss her, *needed* to kiss her with every fibre of my being ... so I did.

The moment my mouth touched hers, I knew I was in trouble. This wasn't some desperate groupie or a random hook-up. This was *Harper*—a woman I shared a history with. She knew more about me than anyone else in my life ever had or ever would.

She could have sold me out to the highest bidder when I became famous. For a while, I'd expected to wake up one morning and find all my carefully hidden secrets printed for the whole world to see. For some reason she hadn't done it—and God knew, I would have deserved it if she had.

The smell of cotton candy surrounded me and I groaned, letting the hand cupping her chin slide over her cheek and burrow into her hair.

"Gabe." My name was a soft protest, which I swallowed and ignored, flicking my tongue out to sample the flavour of her lips.

I was so intent on the taste, the *feel*, of her mouth against mine, I missed the way she tensed—and then my head snapped sideways. I blinked in surprise and, as pain exploded outward from my cheek, I realised she'd hit me … No, not hit me—*punched* me. Clocked me with a right hook Mike Tyson would have been proud of. I shook my head and stepped back, cocking a brow at her still-raised fist.

"Jesus Christ, Harper. What the fuck did you do that for?" I resisted the urge to rub my face. The girl could hit. I should have remembered that, after all, I was the one who taught her how to defend herself.

"You can't just kiss and grope me after eight years of silence." She shoved me, her hands flat against my chest. I let her push me back a step. "Why did you bring me here?"

"You know why, Frosty. The second you decided to set foot inside Damnation, you knew what would happen."

"I didn't think you'd be there."

I laughed. *"Bullshit*! You just happened to pick the night I return from a world tour to visit my club? You expect me to believe that?"

"Yes, I do. I'm not some groupie trying to get your attention."

I raked a hand through my hair in frustration. This wasn't going the way I'd imagined.

Okay, so what if I'd imagined us falling into bed and

continuing where we'd left off at Damnation? I *knew* that wasn't going to happen, but a man could dream. But, I thought she'd at least be happy to see me.

"Okay, look. First, I don't think you're a groupie. Second—"

"Did you even know it was me?" she spoke over me.

"What?"

"At the club. When you were sending me drinks. Did you know it was me?"

"What kind of dumb question is that? Of course, I knew it was you."

"How?" she demanded. "It's been eight years."

I took a chance and reached out to tug a lock of her hair gently. "Frosty, I'd know it was you if I was blindfolded and in a dark room. I *always* know when you're nearby."

Her nose scrunched up into a look of disbelief. "That's not possible."

"Of course it's possible. Just like you knew I was standing behind you." I stepped close again. "And like you knew I'd be there … waiting for you. And how you knew where I was when you arrived here." My fingers touched her chin, lifting her head so I could see her eyes. "That awareness hasn't gone away, Harper. The amount of years that have passed hasn't changed that." My thumb brushed over her full bottom lip, and my voice lowered to a whisper. "You asked why I brought you here, but I think the better question is, why did you come?"

She jerked away from my touch. "Because you gave me

no choice."

"I told you … there's always a choice. You could have given the reporters at your door a very different version of events. You could have easily turned them against me." Her look of horror made me laugh. "You didn't even consider it, did you?"

"What type of people do you surround yourself with to even *think* that?"

She'd completely forgotten she was annoyed with me, and the fact we were twenty-five floors up, in favour of being outraged on my behalf. I hid a smile.

"It comes with the territory."

"That's sad, Gabe. You should be with people you can trust."

The concern in her voice warmed me, telling me more than she intended. She still cared about me.

"Have breakfast with me," I said.

"Breakfast?" she echoed.

"Yeah. You know … that thing when you wake up feeling hungry." I checked the time on my watch. "Although it's more brunch now. I've been at it since six, and I'm starving."

CHAPTER 11

I MISS YOU - BLINK 182

Harper

PRESENT

I heard myself agree to breakfast and internally questioned myself over what I was doing. Eight years was a long time to wait before reaching out. And did I really want anything to do with the man Gabe had become? If he thought trying to have sex with me at the club wasn't a big deal, how else had he changed? Had he even changed at all or was what I was seeing now who he had always been? When we were younger, he had always been careful to keep any girlfriends and drinking buddies away from me. I'd always thought it was to protect me, but now I wondered.

Maybe I agreed out of morbid curiosity—wanting to see if there was anything left of the boy I'd known or whether it had all been a lie. I had to admit to myself I didn't like the thought that he couldn't trust the people around him. Everyone needed someone and, if I could give him that for an hour while he ate, I could do it. He had been my closest ... my *only* ... friend once, and had saved my life before he broke my heart. I owed him that much.

As soon as he secured my agreement, he asked me to wait while he changed and disappeared back through the archway to what I assumed must be his bedroom.

Alone, I wandered around, avoiding the large windows and balcony beyond. A large black leather corner couch took up most of the room. Three guitars leaned against one wall, papers full of scribbled notes scattered on the floor in front of them.

I walked over to the wall I'd noticed when I first arrived—the one with the framed discs and photographs. Most of them were filled with people I didn't recognise. Some had Gabe in them—on stage, with his band, shaking hands or posing with other famous people. Some clearly staged for promotional use. But the one at the end made me stop and stare.

It was in the same kind of frame as all the rest. Black, with carved indents, but the photograph it held was old, burned at the edges. Before I could stop myself, I reached out to touch it, my finger stroking over the two figures frozen in time.

The girl, in tatty blue jeans, an orange tank top and bare feet, was laughing up at the boy. Her head was thrown back, hair blowing wildly around her face, as she clutched a handful of his Rolling Stones t-shirt ... the t-shirt I was currently wearing.

The boy, taller than his companion, stared down at her. Anyone would be forgiven for thinking he was angry but I knew different. He just hadn't smiled very often. I could see the gleam of amusement captured in the grey depths of his eyes.

I remembered the day the photograph had been taken. It was my fifteenth birthday, mere hours before something happened which triggered a chain of events that culminated in losing Gabe from my life completely.

"Ready to go?" I jumped away guiltily and turned.

Gabe stood beside the couch watching me. He'd changed out of the suit and now wore a pair of close-fitting black jeans and a worn Nirvana t-shirt. His dark hair was damp, but he still hadn't shaved. The fact that I was glad he hadn't shaved was something I wasn't going to question too closely. While I stared at him, he reached back and pulled a baseball cap out of his back pocket, slipped it onto his head, and pulled the bill of it down over his eyes.

"There's a place a few blocks from here if you don't mind walking?" he continued, not mentioning the fact I'd been standing in front of a photograph of us both. I *knew* he must have seen me looking at it, though, and I desperately wanted to ask him why he had kept it.

"Is it safe for you to go out?" I asked instead, and he laughed.

"I shouldn't be recognised. People are used to seeing me in my *work* clothes."

"Work clothes? Aren't you in a rock band? I'm pretty sure there's no uniform for that." I followed him to the door.

"Unbranded jeans, an old t-shirt and ratty old sneakers

don't scream rich rock star, Frosty." He stepped back to allow me out into the reception area, pulling out his cell as he walked. "Let me call Miles. He'll take your friend home, then come and pick us up afterwards ... if you want."

After calling Miles and issuing his instructions, his cell immediately rang again and he stayed on the call for the entire elevator ride to the ground floor.

I tried not to listen, but since I couldn't exactly move away, it was impossible not to overhear some of the conversation. He prowled around the small area like a caged animal, as the conversation turned into an argument.

"I don't give a fuck," he snarled down the line. "I want it taken down." He pulled a pack of cigarettes from a pocket and popped one between his lips. His Zippo appeared in the other hand and he flicked it open. I waited for him to light the cigarette, but he didn't.

"Let me make this very easy for you," he said finally. "You have until tomorrow to remove that article from your publishing schedule or I'll put you into so many court cases, you won't have time to fucking breathe." He cut the call and stared down at the cell, grey eyes flinty.

"Is everything okay?" I asked hesitantly, and his eyes jerked up to meet mine. I would swear he'd forgotten I was there.

He sighed and tugged off his cap so he could drag his hand through his hair. He shoved the cap back onto his head and pocketed his cell, then leaned against the side of the elevator and eyed me from under the bill. The Zippo flicked open and closed in his hand.

"Are you going to light that?" I nodded toward the cigarette.

"Nope."

The doors slid open and he stepped out before I could comment further.

"Are you coming?" He threw the question over his shoulder, irritably. His mood had clearly switched after the phone call he'd received.

"Maybe I should just go home instead. You obviously don't want company and I didn't want to come here anyway." My response was tart.

Gabe stopped and spun to face me, and his battle to push down the irritation he felt was evident on his face.

"No ... no." He took a deep breath. "It's been a rough morning, that's all. Let me just make one more quick call, then I'm all yours."

I held off from pointing out *he'd* been the one to bring me here, and stood quietly while he pulled out his cell again.

"Candice? I need you to call the L.A. Inquisitor ..." he stopped, and I could hear Candice's voice, not quite clear enough to make out the words, but definitely loud enough to tell she was *not* happy.

"For fuck's sake, stop yelling," he snapped. "Just do it. I know what you told me." His eyes slid to me and he turned slowly until his back was to me. "Yes, I may have fucked up, as you so delightfully put it, but that's why I pay you the big bucks, isn't it? Fix it." He listened again and scowled. "I don't want to hear it, Candice. It's none of your business unless I tell you it is. Do your job." He cut the call, rubbing the back of his neck as he scowled down at the screen.

The silence stretched and I was about to suggest, again, that I leave when he swung back to face me.

"Sorry about that. No more distractions, I promise." He made a show of turning his cell off, pocketed it and held out his hand.

I looked at it but made no move to take it in mine.

"Come on, Harper. You always hold my hand when we're going anywhere."

"And then you treated me like shit and left me," I snapped. "I'm not the same person you left behind, and I can't pretend it didn't happen."

His hand dropped. "Okay," he said, and I couldn't read the tone of his voice. "Let's go eat. You can catch me up on everything you've been doing."

He stalked off toward the entrance of his building and I trotted to catch up to him.

"Are you sure you're not going to get mobbed?" I asked and he chuckled.

"It's unlikely. People typically only see what they expect to see. Most don't know where I live or believe I'd just be wandering the streets without security, so they don't notice." He pointed to the corner. "Plus, the place I want to go is just around there. I'm a regular and they're pretty good at keeping my presence a secret."

Even with his reassuring words, I still found myself constantly watching the faces of the people around us as we walked, searching for recognition in their expressions. But no one looked twice in our direction. When we reached the little bistro and entered, I still breathed a sigh of relief.

Gabe threw me an amused look. "Relax, Frosty."

"*Gabriel!*" A tall redheaded woman strode across the room, her arms wide in greeting. "My beautiful, damaged angel!" She wrapped her arms around Gabe's shoulders and kissed both of his cheeks enthusiastically. "It's been too long, my boy."

Gabe was laughing when he untangled himself from her embrace. "Charlie, this is Harper." He reached back, found my hand, and used it to tug me up beside him.

Charlie gaped, recovered, then reached out a hand to touch my cheek.

"Ahhh, the mysterious ice maiden," she murmured, with an unreadable look at Gabe. "Come … come." She turned and led us deeper into the room until we reached a small secluded booth at the back.

"Thanks, Charlie." Gabe gave the woman a one-armed hug before sliding onto one of the bench seats.

I sat opposite, saying nothing while he placed his lighter and the still unlit cigarette onto the table between us.

"Can you bring my usual?" he asked Charlie, who still stood beside the table. "Bring Harper the same, only add cream and sugar to her coffee."

Charlie gave him a warm smile. "For you, my darling, anything."

He snorted a laugh, shaking his head. "You're laying it on a bit thick today."

Her response was to pull the cap from his head and ruffle his hair. "I'll send Melanie over with your drinks," she said and disappeared before he could reply.

I watched the exchange in surprise. The Gabe I'd grown up with had been uncomfortable with such open displays of affection. It had been years before he'd accepted my need for the security of his hand in mine—and only because I'd been terrible at crossing roads and his grip on my hand regularly stopped me from stepping out without checking for cars first. After a time, it became a habit and, by the time I *could* cross unsupervised, he'd reach for my hand automatically whenever we were out together.

"She seems to know you well…" my voice came out sharper than I had intended. I had no right to feel jealous, yet I was. I was jealous that this woman had formed a warm affection for Gabe, while I had been relegated to his past.

His eyebrow hiked and I knew I hadn't been able to hide how I felt.

"I'm just saying," I muttered and heard his quiet laugh.

"It's okay. You can ask me if you want to, Frosty."

"Ask what?"

"If I was in a relationship with her."

"It's none of my business." I sounded sulky. Five minutes

alone with him and I'd reverted to being a teenager again.

He smiled, rubbing a hand over his jaw. "You're more than welcome to make it your business."

"What? Just like that? After eight years of silence, you try and fuck me in a public place and then want to start a relationship?" My own eyebrow rose sharply, jealousy giving way to irritation.

He threw back his head and laughed, loud enough to draw glances from the other diners. "Fuck, Harper. I've missed you."

CHAPTER 12

ONE LITTLE LIE - SIMPLE CREATURES

Gabe

PRESENT

When I'd initially put my plan into action to bring Harper back into my life, a lot of things had been left to chance. I found out where she lived years ago—after I made my first million, in fact, and I knew I had the security of money behind me. I considered reaching out to her then. My life plan had *always* featured Harper in it. That was something I never questioned or deviated from.

When I started leaving access to Damnation tickets for her, I tried subtlety at first, knowing if she knew they were coming from me, she'd refuse them. I had hurt her … a *lot*. I was aware of that and, in some ways, I *was* sorry for it. But in others? Not so much. If I hadn't done what I did, I wouldn't be where I was now. In a position to give her so much more than a drug-addicted drunk, who probably knocked her about, and a home in an apartment block similar to the one we'd grown up in. I knew if I hadn't had that lucky break, I would have become my father—the odds were too high of that happening and it wasn't a risk I was willing to take. She deserved so much more than that.

That didn't mean I was a monk the entire time we were apart. I had a part to play, a role to fulfil. I had to become the rock star people wanted—unpredictable, yet charming. Sex sells—so I became a whore, musically speaking. I made sure we were front and centre of all the media outlets—for our music, for our looks, for our behaviour. It made us hot property. Everyone wanted us on their shows, and everyone wanted us in their beds.

But Harper was worth more than that—whether she agreed with me at the time or not. I knew to attain my goals, I couldn't do all the messy, dirty things I needed to do if she was by my side. It would have destroyed us both. So one of us had to make the difficult decisions, and it fell on me.

But I never lost sight of my primary goal, and I'd given myself one rule in this game I was playing. I couldn't start reeling her back in until she stepped inside Damnation without me forcing her to be there. The first move in my direction *had* to be hers. She was playing a game she didn't even know existed, and if I had my way, we'd both come out winners.

I just hadn't expected it to take this long, send me so far down the dark path of rock and roll, or be quite this difficult to bring her back to me.

She was glaring at me, her cheeks pink while she decided

whether she should yell at me or ignore me. Eight years might have passed, she might claim she wasn't the same person, but I could still read her like a book. My ice princess hadn't changed as much as she thought she had, and that gave me hope. I might have broken her heart, but I hadn't broken *her*.

"Why were you at Damnation the other night, if not to see me?" I asked, reaching across the table to take her hand.

Now she was actually here with me, I couldn't resist touching her. I needed to confirm she was real, and not a figment of my imagination. I woke up so many times at night, reaching out for her, only to find I was dreaming. It was the main reason I always slept alone. No woman wanted the man in their bed calling out someone else's name. I had a reputation for being an ass, but even I wouldn't do that to someone who shared their body with me.

No, I did something worse in some ways. I closed my eyes and imagined every single one of them was Harper while I fucked them.

"Siobhan had tickets. She was excited and didn't want to go alone." She snatched her hand back, tucking both of them beneath the table. I didn't need to check to know she'd wedged them between her knees.

"Where did she get the tickets from?" I asked idly, hooking my foot around her ankle and dragging her leg between mine. She glared at me. I smiled back innocently.

"I didn't ask her," she snapped. "Stop it!"

"Stop what?" I was holding her leg hostage between mine,

my longer ones easily pinning hers in place. "Weren't you ever tempted to visit before then?"

"No."

"Not even when you knew I was out of the country?"

She shot me a hot-eyed look. "Contrary to what you seem to think, *Gabriel*, I don't track your movements."

Gabriel. She only called me that when I struck a nerve ... and the way she said it struck a nerve of mine. I discreetly adjusted my semi and masked a smile.

"Don't lie, Frosty. You told me you only came the other night because you thought I wouldn't be there."

"Because no one *ever* sees you there! Not because I knew you were away on tour."

"I don't go in through the main entrance. I use the ... back door." The double-meaning was obvious and the pink in her cheek deepened. I threw her a wink and she tossed her head with a derisive huff.

Melanie showed up at that moment with our coffees. She flashed me a smile and placed the mugs in front of us, without even checking which was for whom. She knew what I drank.

"Thanks, honey," I smiled, caught Harper's narrowed eyes and let it turn into a smirk. "Spit it out," I instructed.

Harper shook her head and curled her fingers around the mug.

"All right then, I'll tell you what you're too stubborn to ask." I waited until Melanie was out of hearing. "I haven't slept with Charlie or Mel."

"I didn't ask."

"But you still wanted to know," I pointed out, taking a sip of my coffee. "And now you do."

She gazed at me over the rim of the mug. "Why did you lie to the newspaper? Why did you do that interview?"

"What did I lie about?"

"*Everything!*" She slammed her mug down onto the table, the coffee sloshing over the sides and spilling across the tabletop.

"I didn't lie, Harper. I broke your heart. Do you think I didn't know that? You think it was easy for me to do that to you?" I caught her hand again and tightened my grip when she tried to pull it free. "No, hear me out. I'm not asking you to forgive me, although I admit I hope you will. But I'd like you to give me a chance."

"A chance for what?"

"To remind you of what we had."

"We didn't *have* anything!" She yanked her hand free from mine. "Let me remind *you* of what the reality was. I was an eighteen-year-old girl who was in love with you. *Had* been in love with you for years ... and I saw a chance to see if you felt the same. And you *didn't*."

"Harper—"

"Don't. You hurt me. *You* hurt *me*, Gabe. But I'm glad because you made me realise that I had put you on a pedestal. I measured every other boy against you."

"Frosty—" I tried again, and she shook her head.

"You were right to leave, but I don't regret it. I don't regret a single thing about that night, except how it ended."

I loved how fierce she sounded, so I took a breath and decided to take a risk on the truth. "I knew it was you."

"What?"

"Did you really think I wouldn't recognise you? I was drunk, Harper, not blind."

"You … knew?" she whispered, looking horrified. "At which point?"

Charlie chose that moment to arrive with our food.

"Here you are, my darlings," she announced, placing the plates down. She reached out to ruffle my hair again and I ducked, which just made her try harder.

"Damn it, Charlie," I mock-growled. "You're messing with my bad boy reputation."

"We have an agreement, angel. You drop that reputation of yours before you enter my bistro, or I won't feed you."

"Yeah, yeah. You wouldn't kick me out for long. You'd miss my gorgeous face too much." I pulled the plate toward me and picked up a fork. "When are you going to take up my offer to come on tour and feed me properly?"

"Ask me again next time, my beautiful angel." She smiled at Harper's laugh. "You don't agree, little ice maiden?"

"About him being an angel? A fallen one, maybe," Harper replied.

Charlie laughed. "Aren't those the best kind, my love? Capable of the strongest kind of love, with just a hint of darkness to keep it interesting." She clapped her hands. "Enjoy your food, my darlings. I'll check back in a little while."

"Thanks, *mom*," I quipped, earning me an eye-roll before she left us alone again. "So where were we?"

"We were about to share a meal like two civilised adults," she replied, poking at the food on her plate with her fork.

"And have a long-overdue conversation." My words made her freeze for a second.

"I'm not doing this with you." She began to rise from her seat.

"If you walk out, I'll make a scene," I warned her softly. Desperate times called for desperate measures. There was no way I was letting her go. I'd blow my secrecy to keep her with me.

"No, you won't. It would draw attention to you." She stood and I don't know if she was calling my bluff or genuinely believed I was going to let her walk out.

I cocked an eyebrow at her and smirked. "Haven't you learned *anything* about me, Harper?" I slowly rose to my feet, planted my hands on the tabletop and leaned forward. "Gabe Mercer is well known for drawing attention to himself." It wasn't really what I wanted to do. This was the place where I was treated like everyone else, a sanctuary where I could watch people and relax. But if she wanted to know how serious I was, I'd step up my game. I drew my public personal around me, donning it like a disguise, turning into Gabe *fucking* Mercer, the rock star the world saw.

"Gabe ..." she began.

"Last chance," I said. "Or I'll crank up the volume to ten."

"Haven't you drawn enough attention to me with your interview?" she hissed at me.

"Baby, that was just foreplay." I lifted a leg and placed my foot onto the seat, ready to climb up. *Please back down,* I pleaded silently. I really didn't want to ruin the one haven I had, but keeping her here was more important to me than anything else.

"I thought this place was your secret? If you tell everyone you're here, you won't be able to come here again."

"That'll be on you, Frosty. Like I told you … there are always choices. You can sit down and talk to me or ruin my one sanctuary."

"This isn't fair, Gabriel!"

I shrugged. "Life isn't fair, Harper."

She glared at me helplessly, and I resisted the urge to gloat when she sank back down onto the seat. Instead, I opted for a tight smile and rounded the table to sit beside her.

"What are you doing now?" she asked with an irritable sigh.

"Do you remember when we were kids? Your mom would give you five bucks when she had spare cash, and we'd hightail it to the little cafe on the corner to share a plate of whatever the daily deal was."

There was a beat of silence and then … "I remember."

Tattooed Memories

CHAPTER 13

BETTER NOW (ACOUSTIC) - ETHAM

Harper

AGE 15

Gabe arranged a surprise for my fifteenth birthday. He picked me up after school and took me bowling with Shaun and Deacon. Afterwards, Deacon had bought dinner, Shaun had paid for dessert and Gabe had given me a snowglobe containing a snowman holding a glittering snowflake in his palms.

We'd gone back to my place afterwards and Deacon had produced a bottle of tequila. We didn't drink a lot of it, enough to make me feel warm and happy, and maybe a little bit giggly when Gabe pointed out I was falling asleep and half-carried me to my bedroom.

He pressed a kiss to my cheek, collected his friends and then left the apartment, securing the door behind him.

I was in a deep sleep when the creak of floorboards startled me awake, and I strained to listen in the dark. My mom was on a night shift and I was still home alone. Normally it wouldn't bother me but there had been a spike in burglaries over the past month in the building.

There was another creak, followed by a thud and I shot up, clutching the sheet, my heart racing. *Was someone in the apartment?*

I eased out of my bed and crept across the room. Just as I reached the door, I heard a low moan, followed by a second thud. Carefully, I opened the door and peeked through the gap. At first, I couldn't see anything, but then a figure stumbled into view, one hand outstretched to grasp the back of the couch as they staggered toward it. A gasp left my throat and I dashed through the door, all thoughts of potential invaders forgotten.

"Gabe!"

His head turned in my direction, and I got my first look at his face. One eye was swollen shut, his bottom lip was split and a dark bruise was forming over one cheek. Fear was replaced by worry and I flew across the room to him.

"What happened to you?" I demanded, fearing I already knew the answer, but hoping he'd just gotten into a fight with other boys of his age.

"You should see the other guy," he quipped, his voice slurred. I frowned at the smell of alcohol on his breath.

"You carried on drinking after you left here, didn't you? Were you at Trudy's? Did you get into a fight?"

He huffed a bitter laugh. "Nah, Frosty. I just ran onto my

da's fist a time or two."

"Oh, Gabe," I breathed and carefully took his hand. "Come into the bathroom and let me clean you up."

He didn't resist as I pulled him into the bathroom. Once inside, I switched on the light and examined him. Gabe seemed dazed, his eyes soft and unfocused, and I wasn't sure whether it was due to the beating he'd obviously taken or the alcohol he'd drunk.

I guided him to the vanity unit and pushed him down onto the toilet seat. He sprawled onto it, legs spread wide and tipped his head back. Opening the medicine cabinet, I pulled out antiseptic wipes and cotton wool, then returned to Gabe. Gently I gripped his chin and dabbed at the blood covering his lips.

"Tell me what happened?" I pleaded with him softly.

One shoulder lifted "Nothing I want to rehash."

There wasn't much I could say to that, so I simply cleaned his face as well as I could, then helped him to his feet again. With his arm draped across my shoulders, I led him back into the bedroom. He sat heavily on the bed.

"Thanks, Harpy."

"Don't call me that," I muttered.

A smile ghosted across his lips. He threaded his fingers through mine and tugged at my hand until I stepped between his legs. Even sitting, his head was still a good few inches above mine.

"I mean it," he slurred. "You're always patching me up." His head dropped to rest on my shoulder. "I don't know what I would do without you, Harper," he whispered.

Ignoring the butterflies making my stomach churn, I used my free hand to push him until he fell back onto the mattress. He sprawled there, grey eyes dark and turbulent as they stared up at me, like a broken angel who'd been thrown out of heaven, then he gave a sharp yank and I was pulled down on top of him.

My heart was hammering in my chest when his hand crept over my waist, anchoring me in place. His knuckles ran down my cheek gently, and he sighed then threw his forearm up to cover his face. I wriggled until I was lying on my side next to him.

"I'll go in a minute," he said quietly.

I shook my head. "Get some sleep. Mom will understand." I moved to swing my legs off the bed and his grip on my waist tightened.

"Stay?" he asked.

I swallowed, my heart in my throat as I froze beside him.

Gabe rolled onto his side and buried his face into the curve of my throat. "I just need you near me tonight, Harper," he whispered. "Please? You feel like home."

Tattooed Memories

CHAPTER 14

DEMONS - JACOB LEE

Gabe

AGE 17

I knew I wasn't in my own room the minute I woke up. It smelled different, *felt* different. There was also something warm and soft lying on top of me. Something that smelled of cotton candy. Something I had no business having my arms around.

My head throbbed, and I wasn't sure if it was caused by the damage my da had done or the amount of alcohol I'd downed. It didn't really matter what the cause was. All I knew was that I shouldn't be here and had to leave before Harper woke up and found me looking at her like a lovesick puppy. But having her in my arms felt right, like it was where I was meant to be. And I knew that was going to be a problem. I couldn't let her know how I felt about her. Pushing my thoughts aside, I eased out from beneath her.

It was still dark outside and I guessed the time to be around three, which meant Harper's mom wasn't due home for at least another four hours.

Harper sighed and I glanced over at where she was sprawled across the mattress. *So that's where my Nirvana t-shirt went*, I thought, spotting the band name on the shirt she wore. She changed position while I watched, drawing her knees up against her chest. The move dragged the t-shirt up over her thighs and bared her plain white panties to my gaze.

I spun away with a whispered curse and crept out of the bedroom. I shouldn't be thinking about her, about how right it felt to have her lying against me. I was no stranger to bedding women—I'd been sexually active for a long time—but she was a *kid*. I was supposed to view her like a younger sister. It didn't matter that there were only two years between us. She was *Harper*—sweet, innocent and not meant for the likes of me to put my dirty hands on her.

I moved to the window and looked down at the street five floors below us. One day I'd have a different view, I promised myself. I'd have the money to make life better for me and ... my thoughts returned to the girl sleeping in the other room ... and for Harper.

For *her*, I would make a miracle happen. I just had to survive until my eighteenth, when I could get out from under my da's control completely. Until then, I had to keep my head down, bide my time, and try to avoid the temptation which took the shape of the girl asleep behind me.

I patted my pockets until I found my cigarettes, took the packet out and popped one between my lips. The Zippo I'd stolen from my da months ago was next, the flame hovering in front of the tip ready to light, but then I stopped, frowning.

I could smell smoke and it wasn't coming from me. Leaning forward, I peered down, trying to figure out where the smell was coming from. We were too far up for it to be from the street below—although fires around here weren't unusual. But this smelled different, *stronger*. Almost as if ... my head swung around to the front door. *Almost as if it was outside the apartment*, I finished silently. Stuffing the cigarette back into my pocket, I crossed the room and laid my palm on the door.

Did it feel warm? I couldn't be sure, but I'd seen enough TV shows and movies to know I should be cautious about opening it. If there was a fire in the hallway, that was going to be a big problem. I returned to the window and cracked it open so I could lean out. The fire escape seemed intact, although it looked dodgy as fuck. But if it was our only way to escape, we'd have to risk it.

Pushing away, I went into the bedroom. Harper was still sleeping, curled up into a tight little ball. I crouched at the side of the bed and touched her shoulder.

"Harper, wake up."

She scowled and shrugged me away and, despite my growing concern, I laughed.

"Frosty, open your eyes." I shook her harder and her eyes

popped open. She pouted up at me and, I swear, the uncontrived sexiness of the look went straight to my teenage dick.

"What?" she demanded.

I cleared my throat, carefully adjusting myself so she wouldn't be aware of what she was doing to me. "Get some pants on. We need to go."

Harper sat up, pushing her hair away from her face. "What time is it? Are we late for school?" She frowned at the window. "What the hell, Gabe? It's still dark outside."

"Get moving. I think there's a fire in the hallway."

"A *fire?*" That got her moving. She shot to her feet and looked around wildly.

"Calm down," I said. "Get dressed." I rose to my feet and left the bedroom again, so she could put some clothes on.

There was definitely smoke creeping beneath the door, which meant the fire was already worse than I thought it would be.

"Gabe, is that …?" Harper's voice was small and scared behind me.

I reached back and took her hand. "It'll be fine." I eyed the smoke. "It's probably not as bad as it looks. I bet when I open the door, we'll find some idiot has set fire to one of the trash cans." I sounded far more confident than I felt.

"Should you open the door?" she asked. "In the TV shows, it always goes wrong and causes a backdraft." Her fingers tightened on mine. "Why haven't the fire alarms gone off?"

"I snorted. "Do you think the landlord keeps up on shit

like that? For the price we pay to live here, we're lucky the gas and electric works." I guided her to the far side of the room as I spoke. "Thing is, the fire escape is rusty as fuck, and I think there's more risk of that killing us than the fire. Duck down here." I pushed her shoulder until she knelt in front of the couch, on the opposite side to the door.

"Gabe, wait." She caught the hem of my shirt. "Get a towel and wet it. I'm sure I saw something about it helping with smoke inhalation."

I sent her a grin. "You're like a walking encyclopedia, you know that?"

She blushed and ducked her head. "I just like to read."

I detoured over to the kitchenette and soaked a towel in water, then wrapped it around the lower half of my face before heading back to the front door. "Stay down," I warned Harper and slowly eased the door open.

The heat was the first thing to hit me but, thankfully, there was no blowback. I quickly looked outside then just as fast retreated and closed the door. There was *no way* we were getting through the building. It was the fire escape or death. Maybe even the fire escape *and* death.

I returned to where I'd left Harper, unwinding the towel from my face. "Where are your shoes?" I asked, keeping my voice level.

"Gabe …" Her eyes darted past me to the door.

"Don't concentrate on that. Find your shoes." I tried not to let the urgency sound in my voice. I didn't want to panic her, but at the same time, I needed her to move quickly. "Come on, Frosty." I tapped the end of her nose with my forefinger. "Hop to it."

"Is it … how bad is it?"

Fucking bad enough to need to hurry, but I wasn't about to tell her that, so I gave her a lazy smile. "Nothing to be worried about. But we should leave, so get your ass moving."

I could hear the sirens of fire engines coming closer. Thank fuck someone had called them. I knew Harper didn't have a cell yet, and my da had smashed mine in the fight we'd had earlier.

She dashed back to her bedroom and reappeared seconds later with a battered pair of sneakers on her feet. I had the window open waiting for her.

"This thing is fucking old. We need to go slow and careful, okay?" I swung one leg over the windowsill and held out my hand to her. "Trust me, Harper. I won't let anything happen to you."

She took my hand and I held her steady while she climbed through the window. I kept one eye on the door, half-expecting it to burst into flames at any second. Once Harper was safely—and I use *that* word loosely—standing on the fire escape, I climbed out beside her.

"Ready?" I asked, and she shook her head, bottom lip caught between her teeth.

I squeezed her hand and lifted it to my lips, pressing a kiss to her knuckles. "We got this, Frosty. It's not our time to die today. We have too much to do."

I crouched down to examine the steps. I wasn't one hundred

percent certain they were secure, but we didn't have much in the way of choice at this point. It was go up to the roof or try and find our way down to the ground. I twisted my head to look up. The building was eleven floors in total and we were almost central. I decided it made no sense to go up ... so down it was.

"We'll take it slow. I'll be with you the whole way down. Ready?" I asked her again and straightened.

My weight on the first step caused it to creak and groan. Harper was shaking behind me, her fingers twisted into my t-shirt. I could hear her teeth chattering loudly—from fear or the cold, I wasn't sure. But I'd put money on the former.

"It's fifteen steps to the next level," I told her, my voice perfectly calm, showing none of my own terror at the situation we were in. "When we get there, we can see if anyone is in the apartment. Maybe their floor is safer than ours."

We inched down the fire escape slowly, every shift of the rusted metal beneath bringing me closer to panic. If she fell, I don't think I'd survive it. It felt like hours before we reached the next level and stepped onto it. My relieved exhale was cut short by the view into the apartment it was connected to.

The fire was clearly *not* restricted to just one floor.

That was only one of the problems I could see though. The next set of steps hadn't been visible from the other floor, but now I *could* see that midway down, the bolts connecting them to the wall had come loose. I leaned over the side, trying to figure out what we should do. The sirens were coming closer, but the fire trucks were still a few minutes away and, glancing over my shoulder at the apartment in flames behind us, I wasn't certain we could wait that long.

I gnawed on my lip, feeling the scab come away and blood fill my mouth, as I considered our options. My eyes locked onto the fire escape on the next apartment along. There was a three-foot gap between it and the one we stood on. But it looked to be in better condition. The residents had even placed plant pots on it and given it a lick of paint.

I eyed the gap and then the drop below us.

"Harper," I began slowly. "I'm gonna need you to be brave for me."

"What? Why?" her voice was shrill with panic.

I manoeuvred her to stand in front of me, facing the balcony opposite, and rested my hands on her hips, hoping the touch would calm her.

"We need to get over there."

Her eyes widened. "*How*? We'll fall." Her voice rose. "We'll die!"

"No, listen." I wrapped an arm around her waist and pulled her back against my chest. "It's not that far. If I go across first, I can hold your hands and guide you over."

"No … *No*, I can't!" Her entire body was shaking, and I knew panic was taking over.

"Harper!" I snapped her name. "If we stay here, we'll die."

I took her hands and placed them onto the railing.

"Wait here while I climb over."

She clutched at my shirt. "What if you fall?" she whispered.

I summoned a cocky grin that I was far from feeling. "Nah, that's not gonna happen. I told you, babe, it's not our time to die tonight."

Before she could reply, I climbed up and jumped. For a split second, I wondered if I was about to fall to my death, but then I hit the other side. My shoulder crashed into the ceramic pots and I rolled to my feet. Leaning back across the gap, I held my arms out.

"Take my hands, Frosty."

"I can't!"

"You have to." I could no longer hide the urgency from my voice. The flames in the window were casting an orange glow over her. "Come on. It's no worse than climbing up to the roof when it's been raining," I coaxed. "And we do that all the time."

Slowly, she stretched out and I grabbed her fingers.

"Okay, good. Now climb up and *don't* look down."

"Gabe ..." Her teeth were chattering so loud I could hear them from where I was standing.

"You're doing great. Jump toward me. I got you, Harper." I held her eyes with mine, hoping they didn't show the terror I was feeling. "I swear, I've got you. Trust me."

If she fell ... *fuck*. I didn't even want to think about that.

"Jump, Harper," I barked.

And she did...

CHAPTER 15

SCARS - BOY EPIC

Harper

PRESENT

Even though he claimed he wanted to talk to me, Gabe stayed silent while we ate or rather, *he* ate and I pushed the food around my plate with a fork. When Charlie returned a few minutes after Gabe pushed his empty plate away, she gave me a look I couldn't interpret.

"More coffee?" she asked and Gabe nodded, stretching an arm along the back of the seat.

I could see his hand dangling inches from my shoulder out of the corner of my eye, the silver thumb ring catching the light from the window. Warmth radiated from his body, wrapping around mine, yet I was shivering.

"Are you willing to meet me halfway?" He broke the silence, and I turned my head to regard him curiously.

"Halfway to what?"

His grey eyes tracked over my face and he shook his head slowly, a half-smile pulling at his lips. "You don't know, do you?" He brushed the back of his knuckles over my cheek, and I caught my breath at the familiarity of the movement, then he tucked a finger beneath my chin. "You *really* don't know." He sounded surprised. "Did you even read the interview?"

"I read enough of it." I jerked away from his touch.

"You know, Harper," he disagreed slowly. "I don't think you did." He twisted his body so he was sitting sideways facing me. "Why did you come to meet me today, if you aren't interested in being in my life?"

"You set reporters onto me, Gabe, or have you forgotten that? They were camped outside my building. Your security guy had to force a path through so we could leave. I came so I could tell you to *fix* it." I tried to ignore the way his scent weaved around me, enticing me to lean closer and breathe him in.

"All you had to do is give them the story they were after," he replied softly. "You could have stood on your steps and answered their questions, told them everything they wanted to know."

I thought about all the things I knew about him. "I could have ruined your life."

He inclined his head. "Indeed you could. I'd deserve it if that's what you want to do."

I frowned at him. "Are you serious right now? You're sitting there giving me *permission* to wreck everything you've built? Everything you've fought for!"

He sighed. "Read the full interview, Harper. It'll explain why the reporters tracked you down and are desperate to talk to you."

"I don't *want* to read it. *You* tell me what you said to them."

I held his gaze, something I'd always been uncomfortable with. His sharp grey eyes had always been able to see right through me, and I'd always been scared he'd see the way I felt about him. This time *he* was the one to look away, his lashes falling down to veil his expression.

"I want a chance to fix things between us. I know it's easy for me to say that, and I don't expect you to believe me but I *swear*, Harper, everything I did back then I did to protect you."

"Does that include letting me crawl into your bed and having sex with me?"

"Harper—"

"Or how about pretending you didn't *know* it was me until it was over and then acting shocked and horrified?"

"That wasn't—"

"Or why don't we talk about how you threw me into a cab with a warning never to contact you again?"

"*Damn it*, Harper. Shut up for a fucking second and let me speak," he roared, and the conversations in the bistro lulled as everyone turned to look.

"Gabriel Thomas Mercer!" Charlie reappeared with the coffee pot and slammed it down on the table. "Apologise to your girl this instant!"

He flinched like he always did at the reminder he was named

after his father, and I automatically reached up to grip the hand above my shoulder. I guess some habits never really died.

"It's okay, he doesn't need to apologise," I said, squeezing his fingers. I heard him sigh softly beside me. "Shouting at each other is what we've always been best at."

"No, she's right."

Charlie gave a sharp nod at his words. "Yes, I am. You *never* speak to a woman that way."

It didn't matter in that moment that eight years had passed since I last saw him, I knew *exactly* what was going through his mind at Charlie's words and my response was instinctive. I released his hand and pressed my palms to his cheeks.

"Gabe, look at me." I exerted pressure on his face to force him to turn toward me. "You're not him," I whispered. "You'll *never* be like him."

"You don't know that." His lashes dropped, shielding his expression.

"I doubt fame has corrupted you that much." That drew a begrudging laugh from him. "Are you serious about wanting me in your life?"

"As a heart attack. All this ... the fame, the money? It's just a means to an end, Harper."

"To get out from under his thumb, I know."

His smile was faint and brief. "Partially. The reasons aren't important at the moment. Are you saying you're open to seeing me again?"

"Maybe? I don't know. It's been eight years, Gabe. We're different people now." Did I want to step inside Gabe's life? The more time I spent with him, the more I was wondering what the grown man was like. I'd seen him on TV, doing interviews on chat shows, playing with his band. I'd watched, like millions of others, the *rock star*—Gabe Mercer—turning on the charm, and I was curious how much of the boy I knew remained.

"I doubt you've changed that much, Frosty."

"But you have?"

"I *had* to ... it's the only way to survive in this business."

A cleared throat had us both looking up to find Charlie still hovering. Gabe gave her an easy smile, pulled out his wallet and threw his credit card onto the table. "Take your usual tip, Charlie."

"Thank you, my darling. You'll keep us open for another week."

He laughed easily, his mood as mercurial as it had always been, and shook his head, waving her away.

"What's the story with you and her?"

His eyebrow arched. "Oh, so you're *wanting* answers now then?"

He rose to his feet and held out his hand. It hung there between us, and the familiar butterflies started waking in my stomach again. Slowly I lifted my own and slipped my palm onto his. We both looked down at where our fingers curled around each other and then I heard him take a deep breath and I felt like something important ... something *significant* ... had happened.

I stood and waited while Gabe retrieved his credit card, pocketed it, then jammed the cap back onto his head. He picked up his Zippo and cigarette and then led me out of the bistro.

"Do you want me to call Miles to take you home?" he asked.

Did I? My head said I should put some space between us, but my heart ... I'd missed him, missed his presence in my life, and I was too greedy to let it go so soon.

"Or you could come back with me?" he offered into the silence. "I'll give you a tour of the penthouse."

My mouth went dry and I swallowed. "I ... it's—"

He squeezed my fingers gently, lifted them and pressed a light kiss to each knuckle. My heartbeat increased. "I have the fire alarms checked once a week, and the fire escape every month. There are water sprinklers fitted into the ceilings of every room. They're also checked regularly. I won't let anything happen to you, Harper," he coaxed.

My heart was beating wildly when I nodded.

Tattooed Memories

CHAPTER 16

IDGAF (COVER) - PANIC! AT THE DISCO

Gabe

PRESENT

Harper was quiet during the elevator ride back up to my penthouse, and I fully expected her to change her mind and ask to be taken home before we got there. When the doors slid open, neither of us moved.

"Do you want to go back down?" I asked. I wanted this woman back in my life, I'd planned and worked toward it, but I knew this was a critical moment. If I pushed her too hard right now, it could blow up in my face.

It took her a minute to decide, but my patience was rewarded when she stepped into the reception area.

"How long have you lived here?" she asked, stopping to examine the paintings on the wall.

"I've had this place for about three years, but I was away on tour for over half of that time." I placed my hand against her back. "Through here."

The door I led her to looked the same as the rest in the penthouse. Most people assumed it was a walk-in storage cupboard for the kitchen, and I never corrected them.

"When I was looking for a new place to live, I gave my realtor specific instructions," I told her. "It needed to be the penthouse ... obviously."

"Obviously," she repeated, with a small smile.

"It had to be the only one on the floor. I don't like sharing my space. The acoustics had to be good, with a big enough room I could turn into a studio. But my biggest ask was this." I pushed the door open.

At first glance, it appeared to be an empty room, but then the lights flickered on and she saw the steps.

"Twenty-five floors is a lot more than the five we had to climb down, but this has been designed so that there is an exit on each floor. The theory being at least one of them will be safe to access."

Harper didn't say a word.

"You have no idea of the fight I had to put up to get this fitted." I forced a laugh. "The planning alone was a nightmare."

"This wasn't ... it wasn't already in place when you bought the apartment?"

I shook my head. "I don't think anywhere has something designed quite like this. I was involved in the entire process. I have a team who come in every couple of months to check the fittings."

"Why?" She turned to face me. "Why would you do that?"

She already knew the answer, I could see it in her eyes, but I didn't think either of us was ready for me to speak it aloud. Instead, I smiled and threw my arm over her shoulders.

"Let me show you around."

We walked around the penthouse, and I pointed out obvious things like the bathroom, the kitchen, the guest room (which was never used). Harper commented on the size of the shower and asked why there was a long tiled bench seat inside it, which turned into a discussion about a back injury I'd suffered a couple of years ago, that flared up occasionally and made standing painful.

"Oh, I read about that!" she exclaimed, then pressed her lips together as if admitting she'd been curious about my life was something she didn't want me to know.

"Crazy fan," I said, pretending not to have noticed. "He somehow managed to get past the security and onto the stage. He threw himself at me and Seth and took us both off the stage. They landed on top of me and *I* landed on top of the barrier. I was lucky not to break something."

"But you didn't postpone any shows."

I hid a smile because *that* hadn't been a question. She *knew* the shows hadn't been postponed. Obviously, she had followed that story a lot more closely than she was willing to admit.

"No, I didn't postpone any shows. They made me wear a back brace for a few weeks, and our stage show had to be adapted."

"What happened to the fan?"

"A signed t-shirt, some photographs with the band, and a story he can dine on for years."

"He wasn't arrested?"

"Of course not. He didn't mean to hurt anyone. He was just excited. It happens." I guided her out of the bathroom as I talked, waving a hand to another door as we passed it. "My bedroom." I didn't open the door. I knew my own limits and didn't want to tempt fate. We moved further along the hallway, up three steps and then I threw open another door. "My studio."

This was my favourite room in the entire apartment. The ceilings were high, the acoustics perfect. I spent hours … *days* … in here, perfecting the songs that swirl around my head. Harper threw a cautious glance in my direction and I nodded, telling her without words that it was okay to go inside.

I followed close behind her as she wandered around, her fingers trailing over the back of the couch, along the mixing desk until she came to a stop. I knew what had caught her eye.

"Where did you find this?" Her voice was low as she reached out to pick up the small semi-burnt snowman from his position on the upright piano.

"I went back to the apartment after the fire and found it. My intention was to give it back to you, but …" I hesitated, stroking a finger over the tattered old soft toy. "Every time anyone mentioned the fire, you'd freak out so I thought I'd just keep it safe until you were ready to take it. Then … well, shit happened, didn't it?"

"Is that why you have the photograph in your living room?"

"If you remember, that photo was taken on your birthday. I kept it in a box under my bed. My da found it and set fire to the box a couple of years later. I managed to save that and a couple of other things."

"Do you …" she licked her lips. "Do you ever see him?"

I shook my head. "He died ... about five years ago." It wasn't quite what had happened, but it'd do for now.

"Oh … I'm sorry."

"Why? You know what he was like. There was no love lost between us."

She nodded and continued examining the snowman. I watched her covertly under the pretence of fiddling with one of the guitars. My vision dimmed, went black for a moment, and I froze. My body was going to crash. I still hadn't slept since the concert and I recognised the signs of impending unconsciousness.

And, just like that, my good mood plummeted. I wanted to spend more time with her, but I didn't want to pass out with her watching, so I pulled out my cell and turned it on. It immediately started buzzing with incoming messages. "I'll call Miles to come and take you home."

"Gabe—" she began, but I swung away and stepped outside the room.

"Are you ready for me to collect your friend?" Miles answered my call with a question. "I've already dropped her roommate back home. The reporters disappeared once we left, and don't appear to have returned so far. But I doubt they'll stay away for long. I'm parked outside the building. Are you up in the penthouse?"

"Yeah," I replied. I glanced back, hearing Harper's footsteps behind me and forced a smile I wasn't feeling. "I'll bring her down now."

"I'll come up."

"No…" I didn't explain further, cutting the call and turning fully to face Harper. "The car's downstairs waiting to take you home."

"Did I say something wrong?" she asked and I shook my head. There was a buzzing in my ears, and my vision kept wavering in and out.

"No, I just remembered something I need to do." I led the way back out of the penthouse and called the elevator to take us back down.

Tattooed Memories

CHAPTER 17

EVERYTHING ABOUT YOU - UGLY KID JOE

Harper

PRESENT

I found myself hustled into the elevator and halfway down the building before I could recover from my shock at Gabe's complete about-face with his attitude. He didn't say a word the entire way down.

When the doors opened, and I was greeted by Miles' impassive stare, I scowled at him. Gabe didn't move, his back propped against the wall and his eyes closed. Not even a goodbye when I walked away from him.

"Is that how he treats everyone?" I demanded.

"If you'll follow me I'll take you home." He ignored my outburst.

"I get it. You're his employee. You can't afford to talk bad about him. But if he thinks I'm just going to let him act like that toward me—" I broke off when Miles stopped abruptly and I narrowly avoided crashing into his back.

"Are you planning on talking to the press?" he asked.

My frown deepened. "What? *No!*" He nodded and continued walking. I grabbed his sleeve. "Why would you think that?"

He shrugged. "You wouldn't be the first girl Gabe has upset. More than a few have made money from his behaviour."

"That's ... sad," I finished softly. I couldn't imagine living a life where your every move was potentially used for someone else's profit.

"That's his life. Not that he helps his situation." We reached the car and Miles opened the door for me. I climbed in and Miles bent to stick his head inside. "Listen, I know you have a history with him, but he often behaves recklessly, which means there are things we have to keep away from the media. If you stumbled onto one of those topics, he'd have shut down."

He slammed the door and strode around to the driver's side. I spent the journey thinking about the conversation I'd been having with Gabe before he threw me out. It must have been mentioning his father ... but I'd been there when he was growing up. I *knew* what his father was like. That couldn't be it, could it?

By the time we arrived at my apartment, I'd decided it didn't matter. It didn't excuse Gabe's behaviour and so I convinced myself that was the end of it. I was out of the car before Miles could get out and open the door for me.

"Thanks for dropping me off," I called back to him and almost ran into the building. I didn't even look back to see if he had driven away.

Unlocking the door, I went inside and leaned up against it,

my eyes closed.

"Well?"

My eyes snapped open at Siobhan's voice. She stood in front of me, arms folded.

"Well what?" I pushed away from the door and walked past her into the kitchen.

"When were you going to tell me you knew Gabe Mercer?"

In the middle of taking a coffee mug from the cupboard, I glanced over at her. "Never."

"Never? I thought we were friends … *best* friends. Why wouldn't you share that with me?"

Pain thudded behind my eyes, and I rubbed my temple tiredly. "There's nothing to share. He wasn't famous when I knew him. He was just another kid trying to survive."

"Have you any idea how much the papers would pay to hear your story?"

I slammed the mug down onto the countertop and spun to face her. "*No.* Promise me, Siobhan. You won't talk to the press about this."

"But—"

"I mean it." My voice was fierce.

"Harper, you could quit work on the money they would give you."

"I *said* no. If I find out you've told anyone, we're done. I mean it, Siobhan."

Siobhan huffed and tossed her head. "Fine!" But you should

at least keep it in mind."

"Why?"

She threw me an amused look. "You're so naive sometimes. He did a two-page interview with the sole intention of seeing you. He obviously wants something. He's worth *millions*, Harper, so why is he after your attention?"

I dumped instant coffee, water, and creamer into my mug and put it into the microwave. "He's probably bored."

"You think he wrote you a public love letter because he's *bored*?"

"It wasn't a love letter. It was an interview," I corrected her.

"You only read the first couple of paragraphs."

"I read enough."

The microwave beeped and I took out my drink, blew the steam away and took a sip.

"Are you going to see him again?"

I thought back to the disinterest he'd shown when the elevator closed on him.

"I doubt it."

"Something happened?"

"Only a reminder of what an asshole he is." I ignored the little voice inside my head pointing out how everything had been fine until I mentioned his father. Had his about-face been a coincidence or the reminder that I really did know all his childhood secrets?

"It doesn't matter. It was nice to see him, but it didn't end well so I guess that's just a sign to prove you can't go back."

Siobhan pursed her lips. "You don't mean that."

I didn't bother arguing. Siobhan wouldn't believe me, no matter what I said.

"What are your plans for the rest of the day?" she asked eventually.

I sat at the table. "Make the most of my day off before work tomorrow. Maybe I'll read a book."

"Or you could read that interview. I kept it."

I shook my head. "Just drop it, Siobhan."

※

The first couple of days of the following week were uncomfortable, with reporters turning up at the apartment randomly looking for a story. Once word got out that I wasn't interested in talking to them about Gabe, helped by a lack of appearance from the man himself, the attention began to ease off. By the time Friday rolled around, it almost felt like the weekend before hadn't even happened.

Late Saturday afternoon, I stopped at the local florist to pick up a bunch of my mom's favourite flowers, then walked the rest of the way to the cemetery.

"I miss you, Mom. I'm sorry I didn't visit last week." I took away the old dying flowers and replaced them with the fresh ones before sitting on the grass beside her grave. I stroked a hand over the headstone. "I ... I saw Gabe. Fame suits him. I think you'd be proud of him. He has this really high-class apartment across town. He looks good, but I think he's sad. He had this look in his eyes, like something was eating away at him like a poison." I rested my head against the cool marble. "I wish he hadn't reached out because I worry about him, Mom. And he doesn't deserve my concern." I ignored the pang of guilt those words made me feel. "He told me he wanted to spend time with me, get to know me again, Mom, and then he kicked me out and I haven't heard from him since." I sighed and pushed upright. "At least I didn't sleep with him this time, huh? I learned from that mistake, at least."

I spent a little longer clearing the area around her grave and then went back home. Siobhan was out. I hadn't seen her since Thursday—she had been working different shifts to me, so our meetings had usually been when one of us was coming home and the other going out. Friday night was her 'wind-down' night and she rarely spent it alone or in her own bed. I didn't expect to see her until Sunday, with stories of her escapades.

After a microwave meal for one and a long soak in the tub, I was curled in my bed by ten, reading a Stephen King novel. Pennywise was trying to get Georgie to go into the sewer when I saw my cell's screen brighten out of the corner of my eye. I put the book down and picked up my cell—a text from an unknown number.

Stay away from him.

Tattooed Memories

CHAPTER 18

AIN'T NO REST FOR THE WICKED - CAGE THE ELEPHANT

Gabe

PRESENT

I knew I fucked up before the elevator doors had even closed on her, but I didn't stop her leaving. I didn't ask her to stay or try to explain why I'd sent her away. I couldn't. I didn't dare. If I told her I had trouble sleeping and was about to pass out, she'd offer to stay with me. I knew Harper—she wouldn't be able to help herself. She was a bleeding heart, who couldn't ever walk away from someone if they were hurting in some way. And if she stayed, I'd have her in my bed before the day was over … and neither of us was ready for that.

I thought about the reason I walked away from her, destroying the friendship we'd cultivated as well as her budding feelings for me, and realised I was moving too fast, I needed to take a step back and reassure myself that what I was doing now wouldn't backfire.

I *needed* Harper back in my life; I'd never lost sight of that. But somewhere along the way, in pursuit of my goal, I'd forgotten why I'd let her go in the first place.

When the numbers on the elevator reached twenty-five, I straightened, waited for the doors to slide open and went back inside my apartment. My cell dinged as I walked, and I pulled it out to read a text from Miles confirming he had collected Harper.

What are you doing? I questioned myself as I made my way back into the studio. I'd planned on slowly easing myself back into her life, and instead, I started out humping her leg like a horny dog, spilled my guts in an interview she hadn't read, thrown her under the bus with reporters, and then expected her to welcome me with open arms.

I spotted the snowman sitting on top of my piano and picked it up.

"Just you and me, Frosty," I told it, positioned it so it was facing me and sat on the stool, resting my fingers on the keys.

I yawned, feeling a wave of exhaustion and stood back up. Time to hit the sack before I collapsed where I stood. But I blacked out before I reached the door, waking up face down on the carpet four hours later to the sound of my cell phone. Scrubbing a hand down my face, I hit the loudspeaker button. "Seth."

"Dude, where you at?" My lead guitarist and closest friend growled down the line.

"I'm in my apartment. Why?"

"Because you're supposed to be at the fucking studio with

the rest of us. We've been here for an hour, dude. What the fuck are you doing? Or should that be *who?*"

I grunted a laugh. "I'm not doing anyone." As I spoke, I stood, grabbed my keys and headed out of the apartment. "I'll be there in ten."

It wasn't often I drove myself anywhere, but I didn't feel like summoning Miles, so I was using the opportunity presented to me. The elevator took me down to the underground car park and I was behind the wheel of my '67 Shelby Mustang GT500 a few minutes later. I stroked my hand over the steering wheel, then gunned the engine.

※

The band and our manager all gave me the stink eye when I finally rolled up to the studio. I may have stopped on the way to grab a coffee and neglected to get them anything, but that's the way the cards fall.

"What the fuck?" Dex groused, eyeing the coffee cup.

I shrugged and smirked, dropped onto the old battered couch and propped my feet on the table, taking an exaggerated swallow while I eyed my bandmates.

Seth looked as broody as ever, his ever-present scowl directed at me. Dex was drunk. It was clear in his glassy eyes and the smell of bourbon surrounding him. Luca was twirling a drumstick around his fingers, restlessly.

I tipped my head back and yawned. "I thought we were taking a week off?"

"We were ... and then *you* decided to perform that stunt." Our manager levelled his finger at me, and Luca tossed a copy of the interview I'd done onto my lap.

"You knew I was doing it, Karl. You sat beside me during the entire thing."

"Not the entire thing, I didn't. *You* sent me out for the last fifteen minutes. I should have known ... should have *fucking* known you'd have a hidden motive. I thought it was just an end-of-tour wrap-up. But no, you have to fucking go and make some girl starry-eyed."

"That's not what happened." I caught Seth's eye and rolled my eyes. He snorted a laugh, quickly smothered by a cough when Karl's eyes speared him.

"She's the *something*, isn't she?" Seth plopped down beside me and stole my coffee. I growled at him and the asshat ignored me.

"Will you stop stealing my drinks?"

"Better your drinks than your women. So ... she?"

"It's Harper."

Seth choked on the coffee he was swallowing and I silently cheered. It served him right for taking it.

"As in *our* Harper?"

I nodded.

"Have you seen her?" Seth handed my coffee back to me.

"At Damnation the other night, and this morning."

"Harper?" Dex frowned, and I could see his alcohol-soaked brain working as he tried to place the name.

Luca smirked. "That's the bit of fluff you broke in and then chewed out, isn't it?"

I surged to my feet, dropping the coffee and burying my fist in his face in one smooth move. The rest of the guys and our manager threw themselves at us, pulling us apart before we could do too much damage.

"She's not a bit of fluff, you fucker," I snarled.

Luca just laughed harder. "You're such a fucking pussy over that girl. You always were. I never understood it back then, and I don't get it now."

"No one asked you to." I started for him again.

Seth's hand came to rest on my shoulder. "Luca's just fucking around with you. Get control of yourself. Did she ask after me?"

"Why the ever-loving fuck would she ask after *you*?" I turned on Seth.

Seth's dark eyes were dancing with amusement. "It's too easy, Gabe. Even after all these years, just the thought of her being interested in someone other than you winds you tighter than a fucking spring. Simmer down." He patted my shoulder and dropped back onto the couch. "So where is she?" He made a show of looking around. "Did you scare her off already?"

I rubbed a hand over my face. "Maybe? We'll see. I'm giving her a couple of days to get used to the idea of me being around."

"And how is that going to work? She can hardly get used to you if you're not there."

"I'm working on it," I muttered.

"Okay, enough girl-talk," Dex said and staggered over to where one of his bass guitars was standing. "Are we going to get some practice in while we're here?"

"Because we haven't just come off an eighteen-month tour playing in front of people almost every night …" Luca drawled. But he crossed to the drum kit and settled behind it.

I heaved a sigh and stood, Seth beside me.

"What do you want to warm up with?" I asked, fiddling with the mic.

"How about "Miss Jackson" by Panic! At The Disco?" Seth suggested and I threw him a dirty look. He smiled innocently back at me.

※

The rest of the week passed quickly, with me spending most of the time in the studio with the band. We'd hit onto a few riffs that needed exploring further and the days had merged together while we battled to get the words and music out.

By the time Saturday rolled around, we were cranky and sick of the sight of each other, but we had at least four new songs. We probably would have carried on, except Karl reminded us we had a premiere event to go to on Sunday night, which would require suits and, more importantly, a date.

"Gonna ask Harper?" Seth asked, following me into my apartment.

"I wasn't going to go," I replied and he groaned.

"You *have* to, otherwise Karl will have that heart attack he keeps threatening."

"Who are you taking?" I handed him a beer from the refrigerator.

"I promised Lexi she could come. It's got one of the actors she obsesses over in it."

"The lead guitarist of Forgotten Legacy is doing a red-carpet event with his baby sister?" I laughed. "Press will love that."

"Don't give a fuck."

"How's she doing?" Seth had had to fly back to L.A. mid-tour to rescue his little sister from a boyfriend who thought he could lay hands on her without consequences a few months earlier. When he'd returned, with Lexi in tow, she'd been a shadow of the vibrant full-of-fun girl I remembered.

"She says she's okay, but …" he paused to take a mouthful of his drink. "I dunno, man, she floats around my place like a ghost. This movie is the first thing she's shown any interest in. If it gets her out of the house and her mind off that bastard, I'll commit reputation suicide gladly." He tipped the bottle up and drained it. "You should ask Harper to come. You've already put her all over the news, you might as well make it official."

"Even though I haven't contacted her in a week?"

"Dude, she's waited for you for eight years. Another week isn't going to change anything."

"I doubt she's been waiting for me."

"Has she been married?"

"Not that I'm aware."

"Kids?"

I shook my head.

"Boyfriend?"

That made me growl and Seth laughed. "See." He pointed the bottle at me. "Waiting for you." His face grew serious. "She was always your one. You know that, right? I never did understand what went wrong with you two."

"It's a long story."

Tattooed Memories

CHAPTER 19

TUMBLIN' DOWN - VENUS IN FURS

Gabe

AGE 18

I leaned against the lockers watching Harper as she walked along the corridor. This was going to be the last time we were at school together. Technically, I shouldn't even be here. She was on her own now the new year had started. Not that she needed me looking out for her, she was more than capable of dealing with any trouble that came her way before it even started. But I still didn't like it. I didn't like the idea of not being around just in case she needed me.

The day after her sixteenth birthday, she had coloured her blonde hair a light purple—lavender, she informed me solemnly, when I'd commented on it. I'd been sprawled on top of her bed, an icepack pressed to yet another black eye, while she lectured me about not getting into fights.

We both knew I wasn't getting into fights, but it was a

pretence she helped me maintain and since her mom had been home, she couldn't have mentioned who had really done it.

After she was done, she had flopped down beside me, her hair still damp, and nudged me with her elbow.

"You're eighteen now," she'd pointed out.

"Yeah." My response had been a grunt.

"You can legally leave home."

"And go where, Frosty?"

"Mom would ... she said you could stay here."

I shook my head. After the fire that had half-gutted the apartment block we'd both lived in, Harper and her mom had found a new place to live. Da had insisted on staying in the dump, but I spent more time at Harper's than I did there.

"There's not enough room here, Harper."

She rolled sideways, settling her head onto my lap and looking up at me. "Most of your stuff is here."

"Only the things I don't want Da breaking." I stroked a hand through her hair. "I like this."

My attempt to change the subject failed and the discussion had turned into an argument, after which she had avoided me for three weeks. Which was why I was now leaning against her locker while her eyes—which looked just as purple as her hair—stabbed at me.

"You're in my way." Her tone was sharp.

Still angry then, I noted.

"Come on, Frosty. Don't be like that." I touched her cheek

with the knuckles of one hand. "You know I'm right."

"I know I might get a call saying you're dead if you stay there," she hissed.

"He's not going to kill me." I straightened, throwing a cocky grin at the cheerleader who stopped to stare.

Harper's eyes pinned me in place. "She your next *notch?*"

I chuckled. "My heart belongs only to you." I bent and pressed a kiss to her forehead. "But you're too good for me, so I'll settle for second best."

"You're an idiot, *Gabriel!*" Harper shook her head and shoved me back a step so she could open her locker. "Why are you here? Already wish you were back at school?"

"No, I just wanted to make sure you're going to be okay."

"I'm going to be fine." She turned, her face softening. "Pick me up after school?"

I smiled. "I can do that." She leaned against me, burying her face into my shoulder—her silent version of an apology.

"Go on, get out of here," she mumbled and spun away.

I watched her disappear into the crowd before I turned to leave.

My car, a battered old '67 Shelby Mustang that the twins' older brother Cormac had given me, was parked at an angle on the street opposite the school. One day I was determined to get it restored to its original condition, but right now its colour scheme was grey and white primer. Someone—and by *someone,* I meant Deacon—had spray-painted '*ouch*' on the left fender after I'd hit a lamppost a few months ago. I hadn't raised the funds to get it repaired yet.

Something I hoped would be resolved sooner rather than later. Whistling below my breath, I swung into the car and drove to meet my bandmates. We were supposed to be practising for a gig at Trudy's that night and I hoped to convince Harper to come and watch.

Seth was standing outside the bar, a cigarette hanging between his lips when I pulled up. He pushed away from the wall when he spotted my car and strolled over.

"You're late. You detoured to school, didn't you?"

I shrugged.

"Did you see Lexi?"

"Isn't she a cheerleader?" I licked my lips and Seth scowled.

"Stay away from my sister."

"Or what?"

"Or we'll need a new singer." He slung an arm over my shoulder. "And I don't want to go through tons of auditions to find someone to replace you."

Harper
AGE 16

I dragged myself out of school, exhaustion making each step an effort. The blare of a car horn jerked my head up and there was Gabe, dressed in ripped black jeans, and a Motorhead t-shirt, looking like a fallen angel of sin as he got out of his car.

I felt my heart skip a beat, butterflies doing somersaults in my stomach as I heard the whispers and giggles from the girls leaving the building behind me. He'd always been popular—he had that whole brooding, broken reputation that girls gravitated toward—and I knew he'd been with a lot of girls.

Not necessarily girl*friends*, he rarely stayed with one for long but it meant I was never lonely—as the girls learned quickly that the easiest way to attract Gabe's attention was to be my friend. I tried to be friendly, even when I knew the real reason they were giving me any attention at all. But sometimes it was hard and I had kind of hoped now he was no longer at school, that maybe I could make friends for *me*, instead.

But that didn't mean the relief or happiness I felt when I saw him waiting to pick me up was lessened. I bounced down the steps, my tiredness forgotten, and threw myself at him. He caught me, laughing, grabbed my bag and threw it into the back of his car.

"Hungry?" he asked and I nodded, climbing into the passenger side. "I have a gig tonight. Want to come?"

Did I want to go and watch Gabe on stage? Had I been in love with him for years? The answer to both questions was a resounding yes. There was nothing quite like Gabe up on stage with the rest of his band. He came alive. One day, I knew, he'd be discovered, become famous and I'd lose him. But, until then, I would greedily take every opportunity I was given to be with him.

"We'll have to sneak you in the back, pretend you're with the band," he said. "And you'll promise me you won't touch any alcohol. Your mom will kill me if I take you home smelling like a bar."

"I think I can control my urges." I rolled my eyes and he grinned.

"At least pretend you're listening to my big brother speech."

"I could repeat your big brother speech in my sleep, Gabe. You tell me every time you invite me to watch you play." I tugged the seatbelt over me and clipped it in place. "And you can't talk. You're not supposed to be in there either."

"I *look* twenty-one. You look like you're barely out of diapers."

"The bras I have to wear suggest otherwise." His head turned and his eyes dropped to my chest briefly, like he couldn't help himself, before his lips twisted and he returned his attention to the road.

"Is your mom working tonight?" he asked instead.

I nodded. "Yeah, night shift. She won't be home until six tomorrow."

"Okay, we'll go to the drive-thru, get dinner, then I'll take you home so you can change."

I threw him a smile and reached forward to turn on the radio. As usual, it was tuned to a classic rock station, and Deep Purple belted out through the speakers.

"What time does it start?" I asked over the music.

"We need to set up at seven, so you'll have time," he made a show of sniffing the air, "to shower first."

I punched his arm. "Ass. I don't smell."

"That's a matter of opinion." He smirked and avoided my second punch. "Don't hit the driver, Frosty."

After stopping at the drive-thru, we drove back to the apartment block I lived in and sprawled out on my bed to eat.

"How was your first day back?" he asked, shaking his head in mock disgust as I licked mayonnaise from my fingers.

"Not bad. Lexi asked if I wanted to try out for the cheer squad." He snorted and I scowled. "What's so funny?"

"I can't imagine you as a cheerleader."

"That's because the only time you think about them is when they're on their knees for you." It hurt to say it, not that he could tell from my voice. I'd walked in on him being blown by more than one cheerleader over the past year, and the image was burned into my brain.

"Jesus, Harper, when did you get such a dirty mouth?"

"Look who my best friend is. Not my fault he's a bad influence." I crammed another French fry into my mouth.

"You better not be getting on your knees for anyone," he growled.

My mouth dried up, the food suddenly tasting like cardboard. Ever since the first time I accidentally saw him with one of the cheerleaders, I'd imagined myself in that position for him. So many times, in fact, that the fantasy almost felt like a reality. I wondered what he would do if I offered, but the fear of losing our friendship stopped me from taking that step and finding out.

"So what if I was?" I said airily. "You were having sex when you were thirteen."

"That's different. If I find out any boy at school has touched you, I'll kill him."

I rolled my eyes, secretly pleased by his angry growl. "You're such a Neanderthal." I waved a French fry at him, then slid it between my lips, mimicking a blowjob. His eyes widened.

"What the fuck, Harper?"

But he couldn't mask the sudden interest in his eyes or the way he shifted uncomfortably on the bed.

Tattooed Memories

CHAPTER 20

BATH SALTS - HIGHLY SUSPECT

Harper

AGE 16

I put the finishing touches to my makeup and then stood, looking at Gabe through the mirror. His head was bent, inky black hair falling across his forehead as he scribbled in the notebook on his lap. Working on song lyrics, I guessed. Smoothing a hand down over the short skirt I wore, I took in a silent breath then turned.

"Well?" I said, and Gabe slowly raised his head.

His brows lifted as he took in the ripped Led Zeppelin tank top—*his*—with its open sides allowing my violet bra to peek through, then over the black mini skirt and down to my bare feet, before letting his eyes travel back up. I swore I could feel his touch as his gaze tracked over my skin, and my nipples puckered beneath my bra. I silently thanked the designers for adding padding enough to hide what his attention was doing to me.

"What the fuck, Harper?" His voice was low and rough.

"You said I looked like a baby." I planted my hands on my hips. "Still think that?"

"No, now you look like a jail sentence in the making," he muttered.

I bit my lip, certain he'd just insulted me, but not quite sure how. His expression darkened, brows pulling together.

"Fuck me," he whispered, scrubbing a hand over his face and throwing the notebook to one side. "Let's get out of here before—" he cut off abruptly and stalked past me to the door, shaking his head.

I pushed my feet into my sneakers and dashed after him.

❅

Despite arriving at Trudy's earlier than seven, Seth and Luca were already there. They both watched, similar curious expressions on their faces when Gabe led me over to them.

"Not like you to bring a—*Holy fuck*, is that Harper?" Luca's eyes widened and his bottom lip dropped. "Come and give me a hug, baby girl," he crooned and hauled me into his arms. I felt his palm land on my ass and squeeze.

"Luca!" Gabe barked, and he laughed, planting a wet kiss to my cheek before releasing me.

"I admire your self-restraint," he said to Gabe. "Because I would have already nailed that fine ass."

Gabe moved before anyone could stop him, and buried his fist in Luca's face.

"Back the fuck off," he snarled.

"Okay, enough you two." Seth, ever the voice of reason, slid between them. "Go and get your gear ready. Harper, grab that stool and put it beside the stage, then sit and stay."

"I'm not a dog, Seth," I grumbled and he arched a sleek black eyebrow at me.

"The men who'll be here tonight are, and *you're* prime steak." He pointed at the stool. "Sit. *Stay*."

Gabe

AGE 18

I hopped off the stage and took the bottle of water Harper held out for me. Half of it was poured over my head, cooling me down. The rest I drank. When it was empty, I handed the bottle back to her and turned to jump back up. Her hand on my shoulder stopped me, and I spun back to face her. She motioned me closer, so I bent my head and curved my hand around her waist, giving into the temptation to touch her.

Harper rose up on her toes, hooking an arm around my neck and placed her lips against my ear. "There's a guy by the bar. In the grey suit. He wants to see you all after you're done."

I lifted my gaze, scanning the dark interior of the bar until I spotted him. He was hard to miss wearing his bespoke suit in a bar full of leather and denim.

"Did he say who he was?"

Harper nodded. "Said his name is Karl and he works for NFG Records."

She pressed something into my palm and I looked down to see a glossy black business card. I brushed my knuckles over Harper's cheek, tucked the business card into my back pocket and climbed back up onto the stage to finish the set.

By the time it was over, we were all dripping in sweat. I'd peeled off my t-shirt an hour ago and was giving serious thought to stripping out of the rest of my clothes and running around outside just to cool off when I remembered the business card in my pocket. I jerked my head at Harper and she waved the stranger over.

His hand was outstretched before he reached us.

"Karl Daniels. *You* must be Gabe Mercer." I took his hand, his grip was firm, and we shook. "I've been following your gigs for the past couple of months and I like what I'm hearing." He wasted no time getting to the point. I liked that.

The rest of the band gathered around as he spoke. "The raw talent you four have can't be manufactured. I don't want to blow my own horn, but I can make you ... and *me* ... a lot of money."

"Oh?" Seth and I traded glances. "Whose souls would we have to sell to make that happen?"

Karl laughed. "No souls, not today. But I'd definitely be interested in signing you to my label. My history is in band management. I manage Black Rosary." My eyes widened. They were huge. "Over the last year, we—myself and their singer, Marley Stone—started our own label, and we're looking for fresh talent." He looked around at the raucous laughter spilling from the bar. "Can we take this outside? Somewhere we don't have to shout above the noise?"

I saw Luca glance back at his drum kit.

"Can we put away our gear first?" Seth asked and Karl nodded.

"Of course, of course. Do what you have to do."

Luca and Dex set to work dismantling the drum kit and taking it out to the van, while Seth packed away the amps and guitars. I helped where needed, keeping one eye on Harper to make sure no one bothered her. With the way she was dressed, her hair and makeup, she could easily pass for twenty-one and that bothered me ... *a lot*.

Finally, all the gear was stowed away and we collected our payment. Then, as a group, we collected Harper and went to find Karl. He was waiting outside, leaning against a black Tesla.

He straightened as we approached, his eyes flicking briefly to Harper, who was tucked into my side, my arm across her shoulders.

"She your girlfriend?" he asked and I shook my head.

"No, I'm her ride home."

He nodded. "Any of you in relationships?"

All four of us shook our heads. None of us had time for

relationships. We'd hook up with a willing partner when the urge arose, but our music always came first.

"That's good. If you want to make it in the industry, your focus can't be on girlfriends ... or boyfriends, if that's the way you lean."

He talked a little longer about the record label and then suggested the band went home to talk over everything and, if we were in agreement, to turn up at his office at ten AM sharp the following day.

I knew without even looking at the others that we'd be there.

Tattooed Memories

CHAPTER 21

MIDDLE FINGER - MISSIO

Harper

PRESENT

My phone vibrating on the bedside table woke me and I reached out to pick it up. The display told me it was almost one in the morning.

Who would be messaging me at this hour?

The first thing I noticed was that it was coming from an unknown number. Was it the same creep as earlier? Someone who'd read Gabe's piece in the paper and managed to find my number? I had blocked it without replying so I hoped not.

I swiped the message open.

UNKNOWN - Are you a creature of habit?

While I was staring at it another message came through.

UNKNOWN - Gut instinct tells me you kept the same number. Come on, Frosty, answer me.

ME - Gabriel? I mouthed the word even as I typed and

sent it.

His response was immediate.

GABE? - You DID keep the same number. That's just like you. What are you doing tomorrow night?

I frowned.

ME - You kick me out, ignore me for a week and then want to know what my Sunday plans are?

DEFINITELY GABE - I could have asked what you're wearing … or sent you a dick pic. Is that what you wanted? Am I disappointing you?

ME - GABRIEL!!!

GABE - Give me a minute. I'd hate to disappoint you.

ME - Don't you DARE send me a dick pic. How did you get my number?

GABE - It's the same number you had eight years ago. I took a chance on you not changing it. You didn't tell me what you were doing tomorrow.

ME - You didn't apologise for kicking me out last week.

GABE - I didn't kick you out. I remembered a prior engagement.

ME - That's not how I remember it.

No response came through for over five minutes. I thought he'd ghosted me and was about to try and go back to sleep when my phone vibrated again.

GABE - I'm sorry, Harper. I'm sorry for treating you like shit eight years ago. I'm sorry for going cold on you last weekend. I'm sorry I left it so long to reach out to you. I'm sorry for fucking everything up.

I read the message and then read it again. It would be so easy to let him into my life, but I wasn't sure I should. Could I take his words at face value or was it just a means of getting under my skin to get what he wanted? Whatever *that* was. I still didn't really understand why Gabe had decided he wanted me around. He'd had ample time to reach out over the past eight years and *not once* had he tried. I thought back to all the times tickets for Damnation had arrived through the post and frowned. Or had he? I'd stashed them without mentioning them to Siobhan each time because I knew she'd insist on going. She'd been *desperate* to get inside the club. *Where had she gotten the tickets from? I couldn't remember her telling me.*

I reread his message. Was he being genuine?

GABE - I should have just gone with a dick pic, huh? There's still time. Just say the word.

I laughed out loud, then clamped a hand over my mouth, casting a glance at the wall separating my room from Siobhan's.

ME - Did you know I was going to be at Damnation?

GABE - Not for certain, no.

ME - But you made sure Siobhan had those tickets, didn't you?

GABE - If I say yes, will you stop talking to me?

ME - If you send me a dick pic, I'll stop talking to you.

GABE - Shit Frosty, and I just got myself all primed and ready to send …

Even though he couldn't see me, my cheeks burned. Was it wrong that I could visualise him stroking himself in my head and the thought of it made me squirm and my nipples harden?

ME - I need you to be honest with me, Gabe.

GABE - Okay, yes, I made sure your roomie had those tickets. I was tired of waiting for you to do the right thing.

ME - The right thing? I can't believe you just said that!

GABE - I worded that badly. I meant I hoped you'd come to me. You never used to stay mad at me for long. I made sure you knew where I was and gave you a way to reach me. I thought you understood that.

ME - All I understood was that you slept with me and then threw me out. I had to do the walk of shame past your entire band, while you stood there and watched me.

There was another long pause, and then—

GABE - `Can I call you?`

Shit. He wanted to call me? I wasn't sure I was ready to hear from him again. Not after the way he abruptly sent me home or the fact I couldn't get the image of his hand fisting his dick out of my head. The phone number flashed up onto my screen a second before it burst into life. I dropped it with a startled squeak. Gabe had clearly decided for himself. Should I answer?

Swallowing, I connected the call.

"Hey, Frosty." That familiar raspy growl whispered into my ear.

"When you ask for something, you're supposed to wait for the answer," I reprimanded him.

He chuckled. "I've never been known for my patience. So about tomorrow."

"I don't remember you being this pushy." I settled back against the pillow.

"I was always pushy, Harper, just not with you." There was a beat of silence and I could hear the clink of glass and then the sound of him pouring a drink. "There's a premiere tomorrow night for a movie. The band was invited with plus ones. We may have done the soundtrack for it."

"May have?"

"Okay, we *did* do the soundtrack for it." He named the film, and the A-list actors involved. "I thought you might like to come."

"Why would you think that?"

His laugh was wicked. "Because ten years ago you waxed lyrical to me about how you would happily lose your virginity to Cole Spencer and I doubt anything has changed ... other than your virginity no longer being available for him, anyway," he ended wryly.

I felt my cheeks heat up more. We both knew I wasn't a virgin, just like we both knew who was responsible for giving me my first sexual experience.

"I think about that night a lot," he offered huskily into the silence.

"I don't." That was a lie. That night and the morning after had played a huge part in the fact that I hadn't even attempted to have a relationship since.

"You're a terrible liar. The red-carpet event starts at seven. I'll pick you up at six-thirty, okay?"

"What? No, I haven't agreed to go with you. And, anyway, I don't have anything I could wear to something like that." My excuse was lame, I knew that as soon as I said it.

"I have that covered. My assistant will send you a selection of dresses—pick the one you want and whatever accessories you need to go with it."

"Gabe—" I began to protest.

"Harper," he matched my tone. "Consider it the beginning of my apology for a long line of fucked-up decisions I've made. And now we've got that out of the way," his voice dropped to a whisper, "what are you wearing and are you sure you don't want me to send a dick pic?"

"Oh my God!" I couldn't help but laugh, then stifled the sound by burying my face in the pillow. "Stop it. I'm still mad at you."

"I'll change your mind," he said, and I could hear the confidence in his voice. "You know, I bet you still sleep in one of my old t-shirts." I heard the clink of ice and guessed he was taking a sip from whatever he was drinking.

"Why?" I was, but I wasn't about to admit that to him.

"Because, we've already proved you're a creature of habit, Frosty. You still have the same cell number. Please tell me you don't have the same phone. You do have something a little newer than the brick you were using back then?"

"It does the job I need it to." It wasn't quite the 'brick' he referred to, but it wasn't one of the newest models on the market.

"Does it take decent photographs or videos?"

"I'm not sending you nudes, Gabe."

"I'm hurt that you'd even think that's what I was going to say." I could hear the smile in his voice. "I wanted to see what t-shirt you're wearing."

"Who's the liar now?"

"Well, I can't say I'd be upset if you wanted to send me nudes, Harper. I'm happy to return the favour."

"It's your Guns N' Roses t-shirt."

"Sexy," he remarked. "What else are you wearing?"

"A frown. I'm not having phone sex with you, Gabe."

"A t-shirt *and* a frown? I like it. Kinky."

"You're crossing the line now," I warned him softly. Or was I warning myself?

"No, crossing the line would be telling you how I dream about you, or how I compare every woman I've been with to you. Or," he paused for another sip of his drink. "Or how I'm sitting here hard as a rock thinking about you sleeping in my t-shirt and nothing else."

The air left the room or was it my body? Had I forgotten how to breathe? I opened my mouth to tell him goodbye but nothing came out except a strangled squeak.

Tattooed Memories

CHAPTER 22

PORN STAR DANCING - MY DARKEST DAYS

Gabe

PRESENT

What was it about this woman that just made me want to cut myself open and offer her everything I was? Was it because we shared a history and she already knew how dark and ugly I was on the inside? Maybe I wanted to prove it to her. Show her I wasn't worthy of the friendship she'd given me all those years ago. Maybe I wanted her to prove to me I was worthy of her—I don't know.

I'm sure a psychiatrist would have a field day with the thoughts revolving on a loop inside my head. To the world, I was Gabe Mercer—the most arrogant asshole rock star they'd ever had to deal with. But at times like this, alone in my apartment, I was still that fucked-up kid being knocked around by his da, terrified that this day would be my last. And, just like then, when I was set on my own course of self-destruction, my own personal angel appeared to light my way and give me hope.

I shook my head. Listen to me being all poetic as fuck. I'd clearly had way too much to drink. Otherwise, I wouldn't have made this call, said the things I've said, and felt my cock harden at her soft intake of breath.

"Gabe."

I smiled. She'd finally found her voice again.

"Sure you don't want to have phone sex, Frosty? I could make you feel real good." I raised my whiskey to my lips, waiting for her to chew me out. When she stayed silent, I pursed my lips.

Interesting.

"You know what sticks in my mind most about that night?" I said into the silence.

She didn't reply, but I could hear her breathing quietly, so I knew she was still listening to me.

"I knew it was you from the second you slipped beneath my sheets. I knew why you were there. I knew what you wanted." I paused to take a swallow of whiskey. "I should have sent you away, but I was selfish, Harper. I didn't want some other guy to have you before me. *I* wanted that. I wanted to be your first. I wanted to be the one any other lover you took after me would be compared with. So I took what you offered. Like the greedy, selfish bastard, I am."

Harper didn't respond. I guess I'd shocked her with my blunt admission. Draining my whiskey, I stood.

"Goodnight, Harper."

"Gabe!" Her voice stopped me before I cut the call.

"Yeah?"

"Your phone sex skills need work." She hung up.

I stared at my cell, threw back my head and laughed, then realised I wasn't ready to end the conversation.

ME - My phone sex skills might need work, but I bet I can make you come without laying a finger on you.

FROSTY - Does that ever work for you?

I smirked. I didn't need to work for sex, women chased *me*. Still, *she* didn't need to know that.

ME - I don't know, Frosty. Are you turned on?

FROSTY - No, I'm really not. Is this what I'll have to deal with tomorrow?

ME - No. You'll be too busy screaming my name.

FROSTY - I thought you said Cole Spencer would be there? I'd rather scream his name.

My eyes narrowed. *Fucking Cole Spencer.* There was no way in hell I was going to put her in a position where she'd need to *say* his name, let alone scream it.

ME - You and Cole will never be a thing. The only name you're ever going to scream will be mine.

I tossed my cell onto the chair and stalked over to the kitchen and refilled my glass. By the time I returned to the living room, a new message was waiting for me. Opening it, I almost dropped my drink.

Harper had sent me a photo. She was kneeling up on her bed, the Guns N' Roses t-shirt falling off one shoulder as she posed with her middle finger raised up to the screen. If the message she was sending hadn't already been clear, the neatly written 'BITE ME' caption got her point across. I felt a grin stretch my lips.

Game on, Frosty.

Me - Gladly.

I followed that up with a close-up shot of my mouth, teeth bared and tongue licking my lips. Predictably, she didn't reply.

❄

By first light, I was ready to burst out of my skin. I recognised the signs—restless energy that needed an outlet. Usually, it would be booze and sex, the typical rock lifestyle I'd grown accustomed to, until I was ready to crash again. Instead, I lit a joint and tried to calm my racing mind, while I waited for the sun to rise so I could call Candice and get her to organise clothes for Harper.

It was seven-thirty when I hit speed dial on Candice's name.

"It's Sunday, Gabe. What the fuck?" she whined at me.

"It's that premiere tonight." I propped my feet up on the glass-topped coffee table on my balcony and took a pull on my joint.

"So? I thought you said you weren't going?"

"Changed my mind. I need you to pick out some outfits and send them to Harper. I'll send you her info."

"Harper? That's the girl from last weekend?" Her voice brightened with interest. "She doesn't seem your usual type."

I didn't engage with her curiosity. "You should probably get hold of Seth as well. He's taking Lexi tonight. She might need something to wear."

"I'm not Seth's assistant."

"But you'll do it anyway because you like Lexi."

She sighed. "One day I'm going to leave you, Gabe. You know that, right?"

"No, you won't. I pay you too well to put up with my shit." I squinted at the sun rising over the horizon. "Also, find out if Cole is going to be there tonight."

"Cole? As in Cole Spencer? Isn't he the male lead in the movie?"

"Yeah. But you know how he can be. The only time he's seen outside of his home is when he's filming."

"Did you need to speak to him?"

I laughed. "Fuck no."

"This is one of those things I don't want to know about, isn't it?" Candice said.

"Probably. Get your ass moving. I'll send you Harper's contact info." I hung up, fired off a text with Harper's address and cell number to her, then tipped my head back to enjoy the rest of the joint.

Seth showed up around midday with my clothes. He lay the bag over the back of the couch and joined me where I still lounged on the balcony. He sat in the chair opposite me, a bottle of beer in his hand.

"Not driving tonight?" I asked, with a pointed glance in the direction of the bottle.

"Nope. Lexi wants the whole red-carpet experience. Limo, a driver, showing off for the paparazzi."

"And you're not going to take a perverse delight in her ex seeing her mixing with the stars at all."

His smile was bland. "Would I do something like that?"

"No more than I would."

"Did you speak to Harper?" He sprawled back on the chair, popping his sunglasses back down over his eyes.

"Yeah. She's coming tonight." I laughed softly. "But only because she might meet Cole Spencer, apparently."

"Funny. Lexi said the same thing."

"Have you spoken to him at all?" I idly flicked my lighter open and closed.

Seth shook his head. "He won't be there long. You know he hasn't done any press events in years. Not since Sian died."

"They'll stop offering him roles soon."

"I don't think he cares. He only did this one because he was contracted for it." He lifted the bottle to his lips and took a long drink. "What about you and Harper? Is that a thing now?"

"A work in progress."

"What about—"

"As far as I'm concerned, he's dead. He can't hurt either of us now."

"Still … you need to be careful, Gabe. We don't know how much she's changed. She might not be the same girl you knew."

"She hasn't spoken to the press once since we made it. I don't think she'll start now." I squashed down the surge of anger at Seth questioning Harper's morals.

"You always did have a short fuse where she was concerned. Don't let it make you do something stupid."

CHAPTER 23

TAINTED LOVE - MARILYN MANSON

Harper

PRESENT

"What now?" I snapped down the line. My cell had been ringing continuously since eight and, thanks to Gabe, I'd barely had three hours sleep. I assumed it was him calling and was about to give him an earful when a female voice said my name.

"Harper, right? You must be. You sound exactly like me when I've been talking to Gabe."

The voice sounded vaguely familiar. "Who is this?"

"Candice. We met briefly at Gabe's place last weekend."

"And you have my number, how?"

"Well, *that* should be obvious. Our mutual asshole rock star. The why, on the other hand, knowing Gabe as I do, could be something I'm about to spring on you."

I sighed. "The premiere."

"Oh good, so you *do* know about it. That's a relief." Her voice turned brisk. "I'll be sending images of a few different things that you could wear tonight. Pick out three or four choices and let me know. I'll bring them over, along with a hairstylist and makeup artist, at two. We have a lot to do and not much time to achieve it."

"Wait, what? You're coming here?" I sat upright, all traces of sleep gone.

"You're going to the premiere of a possible blockbuster movie, headlined by Cole Spencer. There will be TV channels, news journalists, entertainment magazines all waiting to catch sight of you … thanks to Gabe and his recent interview. You're lucky they're not still knocking down your door demanding a story."

I'd thought that, but assumed Gabe had said something to stop them hanging around. "Didn't Gabe fix that?"

"Gabe?" Her laughter was loud and long. "Gabe doesn't fix things, you poor innocent child, he breaks them and leaves it to me and the rest of his entourage to repair the damage."

I bristled at her words. I was learning that the people Gabe surrounded himself with seemed to view him as a walking disaster, which didn't match the man—the *boy*—I'd known.

"I doubt he's that bad," I snapped.

There was a short silence, and then Candice replied, her voice softer. "No … no, he's not really that bad. He's actually very good to work for. I apologise." I heard her take a breath. "Let me start again. As far as I'm aware, Gabe hasn't spoken to anyone to stop the reporters surrounding your apartment, but that doesn't mean he didn't. It just means he didn't ask *me* to do it for him."

I climbed out of bed and went in search of coffee. Siobhan was sitting at the kitchen table and she frowned when she saw I was on a call.

"Who are you talking to?" she mouthed.

I shrugged and pointed at the coffee maker, silently asking if she wanted one. She shook her head.

"So, I'll send you some photos. Let me know in the next hour which ones you're interested in and your sizes, then I'll see you in a few hours," Candice was saying.

"Okay." I poured my coffee, said goodbye and cut the call.

"Who was that?" Siobhan asked the minute the call ended.

I flopped onto the chair opposite her. "Gabe is taking me to see a movie tonight."

Siobhan slowly lowered her mug to the table. "The lead singer of one of the hottest rock bands alive right now is taking you on a movie date?"

"It's not a date!" I rushed to deny. Was it? He had been flirting ... but that was just Gabe ... wasn't it?

Siobhan snorted, tossing her head. "Of course it's a date! The guy is crazy about you. He's made that perfectly clear."

"*How* did he make that clear? He practically dry-humped me in the club, plastered my name all over the news, took me for breakfast, and then ghosted me for a week!"

"And tonight he's taking you to see a movie. What if he's

recognised? That's a big risk for someone as famous as him."

"Uh … about that" I muttered, burying my face into my coffee.

"Harper!" Siobhan sat up straight and pointed a finger at me. "What aren't you telling me?"

"It's the premiere of Cole Spencer's latest," I told her, avoiding eye contact.

"What?!" Siobhan screeched. "He's taking you to a premiere? Those things are televised! Holy shit, Harper, you're going to be on television!"

"They don't talk to everyone who goes to them," I argued.

"It's Gabe *fucking* Mercer! You really think they'll let *him* walk in without wanting a soundbite?"

My heart sank. She was right. If I did this, my face was going to become linked to Gabe's. Did I want that? As if he could hear my thoughts, my phone dinged with an incoming message from him.

GABE - Has Candice been in touch yet?

"Is that him?" Siobhan asked. "That's a seriously goofy smile you're sporting."

"I am *not!*" I schooled my features while I replied to him.

ME - She woke me up.

GABE - It's 11 am. Why are you still in bed?

ME - Because SOMEONE kept me awake half the night!

GABE - Are you cheating on me already? Damn, Frosty, that's cold. Was he good? Did he make you come?

ME - Don't be an ass.

"What's he saying?" Siobhan whispered.

"He can't hear you, you know," I laughed. "He's just checking to see if his assistant contacted me."

"Is that who was on the phone?"

I nodded. "She's going to be here at two." Which reminded me—I needed to check and see if she'd sent the promised images. "She's bringing clothes for me to try."

"For tonight?"

"Yeah, and a hairstylist and someone to do my makeup."

Siobhan gaped. "Wow! He's pulling out all the stops for you."

"You don't think he's concerned I'll embarrass him?"

"What? No! I mean, he *is* known to be an asshole, but you're his chance at redemption."

"*What?*" I laughed. "Where did you get that idea from?"

"It's what he said in that interview you refused to read."

I frowned. "Why would he say something like that? You must have read it wrong."

"*Read* it for yourself. I kept a copy of it for you."

"No." I couldn't explain why I didn't want to read it. Just a gut feeling, and I'd learned to trust my instincts.

I listened to Siobhan tell me what she thought about Gabe, his band and their music as I scrolled through the messages from Candice. Most of the clothes she was suggesting weren't the kind of thing that appealed to me, but I eventually managed to pick out four and sent her a response. She replied immediately with a thumbs-up emoji.

"I'm going to take a shower and get dressed before they get here," I said and rose to my feet.

Siobhan grinned. "Look at you getting a rock star boyfriend. I'm so proud! Of course, BFF code means you need to set me up with one of his friends."

I laughed, shaking my head. "He's not my boyfriend."

"Yet!" Siobhan said with a grin.

※

"I think she's ready," Candice said, her voice rich with satisfaction.

"Does that mean I can finally see what you've done to me?" I grumbled.

She laughed at me. "I get why Gabe likes you so much now," she said and I huffed, which just made her laugh harder.

Gabe's assistant had surprised me. My first impression of her had me thinking she was abrasive and rude, but the reality was she was just very protective of the man she claimed to hate working for. She clearly adored Gabe, although she had stated within minutes of arriving that she was happily married and, while she was sure Gabe was an animal in the sack, she wasn't interested in finding out. My cheeks had been burning non-stop since then. Candice had an acerbic and wicked sense of humour, was extremely intelligent and insanely open about what she thought.

And she had put a lot of thought into what was going on between me and Gabe. Worse than that, she was more than happy to share her theories ... with me, Siobhan, the hairstylist,

Monique, and the makeup artist, Jenny. Some of those thoughts had me wanting the ground to open up and swallow me whole. I swear the woman had no filter.

"Stand up." Jenny stepped back and all four women watched as I rose to my feet. I turned to Siobhan.

"You'd tell me if I looked awful, wouldn't you?"

"You know I would," she replied. "But you don't. You look amazing." She moved toward me, placed her hands on my shoulders and turned me toward the bedroom door. "Go and look in my mirror. Put on your shoes first, though, you need the full effect." I saw her trade glances with the other women. "He's not going to be able to keep his eyes off her."

"I was going for his hands and mouth, but eyes are a start," Candice replied and I groaned.

Laughing, she handed me a pair of strappy high heels. I bent and slid my feet into them, then straightened.

"Okay?" I asked and they all followed me into Siobhan's bedroom.

It sounds cliché, but that first moment when my reflection greeted me and I finally saw what they'd done, I didn't recognise myself.

My hair fell in messy waves, shimmering with some fancy hair colour Monique had used, turning my typical lavender colour into a multitude of hues—which she called the 'mermaid' effect. The sheen also coated my skin, giving me an almost mystical look when the light hit me.

"I feel like a vampire from Twilight," I muttered to peals of laughter.

"Gabe will be your willing victim if you want to suck his blood, although I'm pretty sure he'd rather you sucked his—"

"Oh my GOD, *STOP!*" I screeched before Candice could finish and slapped my palms over my ears. "I won't be able to look at him!"

The dress, we ... *they* really ... had decided on was deep red, floor-length, with a long slit up the right side which stopped mid-thigh. The bodice was cut low—lower than I was comfortable with, especially as it was strapless—and it swooped around and down, leaving my back bare. The material felt like silk, soft and smooth, and it glimmered—like my skin—when I moved.

"Don't you think you've gone overboard on the sparkle?" I asked, and they all shook their heads in unison.

I lifted a hand to my bare neck. "I think I have a necklace that might look nice."

"No!" Candice barked. "You look perfect, and Gabe is already waiting for you. No time to be searching for cheap jewellery."

"He's here already?" I whispered, the butterflies in my stomach returning with a vengeance. *Oh god, what was I doing?* I swallowed, suddenly feeling sick. "I can't do this. Make him leave!"

"You'll be fine. Miles is waiting to escort you to the car," Candice said briskly.

"N-not Gabe?" I stuttered.

"He's *in* the car," she explained patiently. "He didn't want to risk getting seen and making the pair of you late."

CHAPTER 24

CHOKE - I DON'T KNOW HOW BUT THEY FOUND ME

Gabe

PRESENT

I'm in so much fucking trouble—that was the first thought in my head when Miles brought Harper out of her building. She was a vision, an angel poured into a red dress, a song waiting to be written. If I was a poet, I'd write a love sonnet about her, but I wasn't that pure and I wanted to dirty her up ... put my mark on her soul and make sure she belonged only to me.

I watched, my mouth dry, as she crossed the road. Miles opened the door and she bent and settled onto the seat beside me. The scent of sweet cotton candy enveloped me and my mouth watered.

"Hey." There was a slight tremor to her voice, and I saw her throat move in a nervous swallow.

"You look stunning," I told her and, at the sound of my voice, she glanced over at me.

"Thank you." Her tongue swept out over glossy red lips and I couldn't contain a groan.

"Fuck, Harper. I'd kiss you, but you'll probably punch me again. And if you didn't punch me, I wouldn't stop, which would completely fuck up your makeup and we'd fall out of the car half-naked." I raked a hand through my hair. "While they wouldn't be surprised at me doing something like that, you don't need that kind of press. But ... fuck me, Harper ... you look like temptation itself."

Her lips parted, eyes wide in surprise at my outburst, a blush staining her cheeks. I reached out to brush my knuckles down her cheek but dropped my hand before I touched her. That could be pushing my luck a step too far. I wasn't sure I could control myself if I felt her skin against mine.

I heard Miles get into the front of the car, and a second later the engine roared to life. Harper reached for her seatbelt and clipped it in place.

"Is there anything I should know about tonight?" she asked.

"Seth is bringing Lexi. Dex and Luca will be there, but I don't know who they're bringing. Probably random hook-ups it won't be worth learning the names of." She gave me a reproachful look and I shrugged. "It is what it is."

"They're still human beings, Gabe."

"Only to look at. They're mostly leeches in pretty dresses." I shifted in my seat, trying to ease the hard-on her appearance had caused without her noticing. "Other than that, the press will be there. They'll shove microphones in our faces, blind us with camera flashes and demand to know about our sex life."

"Can I tell them you need to take at least two Viagra to even get it up?" Her smile was impish, which didn't help my dick.

"You can tell them that, if you like," I replied, and allowed my eyes to linger at her cleavage, "but my retaliation will be swift and without mercy."

"What can you do in front of TV cameras and journalists?"

"Tell your story and find out," I invited with a smile.

Her eyes heated and she glared at me. "You're an asshole."

"So they tell me."

The rest of the journey was made in silence, and soon after we were in the line of limos waiting to step out onto the red carpet. Harper watched the celebrities through the tinted window, and I watched Harper.

When the car in front of us spilled out Dex, Luca and their date, I touched Harper's arm, drawing her attention to me.

"I have something for you," I said in answer to her questioning look and drew out a small black velvet box from my pants pocket. She took it gingerly, and I laughed softly. "It's not a snake, Frosty. Nothing is going to jump out and bite you. Just open it."

She lifted the lid and her surprised gasp sent a shot of lust through me. Lying inside the box on a cushion of black silk was a necklace. But I knew that wasn't the reason for her shock. That was reserved for the snowflake pendant. The design was made up of six thin bars, covered by diamonds. Eight of the diamonds were black.

If she asked me, I would tell her that each of those black diamonds stood for every year we'd been apart. If we'd reconnected a year ago, there would have been seven. If it had been another year, there would have been nine.

What I *wouldn't* tell her was that I'd had this necklace since a year after I left her—and initially, it had been embedded with seventeen normal—and by normal I mean high quality and expensive—clear diamonds. I replaced one diamond with a black one every year we were apart.

I also wouldn't tell her that it was worth almost thirty thousand dollars or that I'd originally had it designed and paid for with the first royalty check I'd received.

I'll admit, to myself at least, that I did wonder if the entire thing would be black before I saw her again.

"It's beautiful," she whispered, stroking a finger over the diamonds. I'd put money on her thinking they were fake, and I wasn't about to set her straight.

"Let me put it on you." I reached out and took the chain out of the box, and she twisted so her back was to me and lifted her hair.

I took in a steadying breath, taking in her scent, and leaned forward. My fingers brushed along the arch of her throat as I fastened the clasp.

"How does it look?" she asked, turning back to face me.

"Perfect," I replied. I wasn't talking about the necklace.

The car rolled to a stop and I looked over her shoulder through the window. "It's going to be noisy out there, and they're …" I hesitated, knowing what was coming. "They're going to expect me to behave a certain way. I have to give them what they want, Harper, or they'll never leave us alone. Do you understand?"

Her fine brows pulled together. "No. What are you going to do?"

"Nothing that should affect you, but … try not to react, okay?"

The car door was pulled open before she could reply and I fixed a wide cocky grin on my face and climbed out, reaching back to catch her hand and pull her out after me.

"Gabe … Gabe … over here … Gabe, is that Harper? … Gabe, where did you find her?"

Lights flashed, my name was called out, questions hit me from all angles and I felt Harper's hand tighten on mine. I kept my grin wide and held my head up as I moved away from the car and onto the long red carpet which led into the deluxe movie theatre.

I recognised some of the faces behind the microphones and cameras and slowed my pace.

"Charity," I acknowledged one of the journalists with a smile and she scurried forward before I changed my mind.

"Gabe, can you confirm that your plus one is the mysterious Harper?"

I dropped Harper's hand and rested my palm against the small of her back, letting my thumb brush along her spine.

"Maybe … maybe not," I said in reply and smirked.

"Gabe ... over here ... Gabe, can we get a photo of you and your girl?"

I turned toward the voice, my grin slipping before I caught it. Jefferson Thomas—the guy had been sniffing around me for years. He knew there was some kind of story to be had, but he hadn't quite figured out what it was. Miles had told me he had been one of the reporters outside Harper's after my interview was published. I should have known he'd be at the premiere.

"Jeffery," I said, and brought Harper closer to my side with a press of my palm. Thankfully, she didn't argue and I felt her arm slide around my waist.

"Jefferson," he corrected and I stared down my nose at him. Short, self-important fucker, but one who wouldn't leave me alone if he thought he could sense weakness. "But you know that."

I said nothing, waiting.

"Harper, we never did get to finish our conversation last week," he said and I stiffened. I didn't dare look at Harper, didn't want Jefferson to know he'd said something I wasn't aware of. *What conversation? What had she told him?*

I felt Harper tense beside me. "I've never seen you before," she replied.

"I spoke to you as you were leaving your apartment last weekend. I asked you a question."

"Did you?" she sounded disinterested. "I'm sorry, I don't recall. There were lots of people yelling at me that day."

"Maybe we could arrange to meet somewhere quieter?" he

offered and Harper smiled.

"I have no story to sell to you." She tilted her head to look at me. "I see Dex waving. I think he wants us to join him."

That's my girl. My grin was genuine as I nodded to Jefferson and led Harper past him.

"Well if it isn't our lucky charm!" Dex bellowed as we moved closer. He'd taken two quick strides and scooped Harper up into his arms before I could stop him. Harper shrieked, clutching the bodice of her dress with one hand and trying to not flash the entire event with the other.

"Fuck's sake, Dex, put her down," I snapped, and the idiot winked at me, planted a sloppy wet kiss onto Harper's cheek and then carefully set her on her feet.

"You grew up mighty fine," he told her.

"Holy fuck, *Harper?*" Luca's voice came from behind me and I groaned. "Let me look at that ass. Jesus Christ, baby girl. Where have you been hiding?"

Harper spun, laughing, into Luca's arms and I ground my teeth together as she received another kiss. All I needed now was for Seth to appear and stick his tongue down her throat. I looked around, just in case, but couldn't see the devil anywhere.

"Where's Seth?" I asked no one in particular.

"Already inside with Lexi," Dex said.

CHAPTER 25

TALK DIRTY TO ME - POISON

Harper

PRESENT

The noise was insanely loud. Fans screaming behind the barriers for all the different celebrities, journalists shouting questions, camera flashes blinding us as we walked toward the doors.

I felt unsettled. Uneasy, after being stopped by the reporter Gabe had called Jeffrey. When he'd insinuated that I'd already spoken to him, I had felt Gabe tense beside me. All I could do was hope he believed me when I denied it.

But the reporter's words *did* remind me of the question I'd heard when Miles had picked me up to take me to Gabe that weekend.

Are you the girl he almost killed his father over?

I needed to ask Gabe about it, find out what he meant. But it would have to wait until later—after the premiere when it was quieter and we could talk without being overheard or disturbed.

Once we met up with the rest of Forgotten Legacy, except Seth, we had to stop for more photos and interaction with the media. I hung back behind Gabe, who stared moodily across the sea of reporters at Jeffrey ... Jefferson? ... while Dex fielded questions about their recent tour and news of any upcoming new releases. Luca openly made out with his date, showing his disinterest in the proceedings around him, to the delight of his fans and irritation of the press.

Eventually, after what felt like hours under the glare of cameras, we were allowed to move on and stepped inside the venue.

"I thought you were bringing someone?" I heard Gabe say to Dex.

"I did." He waved a hand to the girl draped over Luca.

Gabe grunted. "Tag-teaming again? No wonder people think you two are hiding a relationship."

Dex shrugged. "I'm just lazy. Got better things to do than search out women. Luca enjoys the game, so I just share his pie."

"That's disgusting!" I blurted out before I could stop myself and Dex laughed, his eyes dancing.

"Is it?" Luca murmured from nearby. "Are you sure? I bet a dirty girl like you would love to be double-dicked."

"Quit it," Gabe growled.

"Why? You've done it before ... more than once, in fact." He smirked at Gabe and then turned to regard me thoughtfully. "Think about it. A dick in your mouth, another in your pussy or your ass. All attention on you, filling you up, making you scream."

He gave a slow lick of his lips. "I bet you beg real nice, baby girl."

Gabe surged forward, and then Seth was there, materialising out of nowhere and standing between them.

"Don't you give the press enough to talk about?" he asked them, his voice cool. "Do I have to babysit you all the time?"

Gabe reached for my hand and pulled me along as he stalked away without responding. I glanced back over my shoulder. Luca winked at me with a grin.

"Go get him, tiger," *he mouthed.*

I rolled my eyes and his teeth flashed as he laughed. Some things never changed. Luca had been able to push Gabe's buttons for as long as I'd known him.

An usher stood at the double doors leading into the screening room, making notes on his tablet as people passed through. I could see lots of famous faces, most of whom Gabe ignored, his flinty grey eyes staring through them until they moved away. His thumb stroked over the skin of my wrist reflexively, while his face gave off the impression of utter boredom.

I leaned closer and he must have felt me move as he turned his head to look down at me.

"Are you okay?" I whispered.

One corner of his mouth curled up, the chill in his eyes fading away. "I'll be better once we're inside and out of the goldfish bowl."

I kind of understood what he meant. It was almost surreal being here with him. I'd watched events like these on TV, and they always seemed so glamorous. I'd seen Gabe with nameless women beside him and never believed, for a second, I'd find myself becoming one of them. That *I'd* be that nameless woman walking into an event with him. Our lives had taken separate paths years ago, and I had been sure we would never meet again.

But here I was. And it was not as glamorous as it appeared on television. In some ways, it was scary—with all the noise and the screaming fans. In others, it was a fascinating display of the world's most well-known celebrities and the way they interacted with each other.

"Harper?" A soft voice behind me dragged my attention away from the chaos around us and I turned.

"Lexi? Oh my God!"

Laughing, we hugged and then broke apart to examine each other.

"Seth said you might come. You look amazing."

"So do you!" Lexi had her brother's dark good looks, but I could see a wariness in her eyes that hadn't been there before. I wondered what the past eight years had done to her.

She gave me a smile and hooked her arm through mine. "I think we're seated together. Shall we go in?"

"Do you girls want a drink?" Seth asked, nodding at the waitresses circulating the room. He already held a glass of whiskey.

I glanced at Gabe, who lifted a hand and a waitress darted over. He took two champagne flutes, handed one to me and the other to Lexi.

"Thanks, darling," he said to the waitress and sent her away. Seth gave him a pointed look.

"I'm driving," he replied.

"You came in a limo."

"And I'm leaving in the Mustang. I had Miles bring it earlier today, so we don't have to deal with all the bullshit on the way out as well."

"You still have that old thing?" I asked and he winked.

"She looks nothing like you remember, Frosty." He let go of my hand and tapped my shoulder. "Look, there's Cole. Do you want to go and meet him?"

"I thought you said I wasn't going anywhere near him?" I arched a brow.

"I'll be between the two of you the entire time," he replied and guided me across the room.

The tall, blue-eyed action star was looking down at his cell, oblivious to the people around him, when we reached him.

"Hey, assface," Gabe said and Cole looked up, his famous grin appearing.

"Dicksplash," he responded to Gabe's unconventional greeting with one of his own.

"Didn't think you'd be here."

Cole shrugged. "Part of the contract. It was this or doing the rounds of interview-hell." His gaze turned to me. "You don't usually bring your ... friends to meet me."

"This is Harper. I only brought her over to tell you she's off-limits to you."

"Gabe!" I slapped his arm, and both men laughed.

"Nice to meet you, Harper." Under Gabe's glare, Cole took my hand and raised it to his lips. "If you ever get bored of dicksplash here, you can come and visit me."

"No, she fucking won't." But there was no heat in Gabe's growl. "Shouldn't you be inside already?"

Cole sighed, the good humour fading from his features. "Yeah. You staying for the after-show party?"

Gabe shrugged. "Not sure. I have to get Cinderella home before she turns into a pumpkin. You?"

He shook his head. "No, thank fuck. My contract states I have to come to the premiere, show my face, schmooze before the film, then I can slope away afterwards and go home." He nodded his head. "Don't let him bully you into anything, Harper. Make him earn it." He bumped shoulders with Gabe and sauntered away.

"There you go. Now you can tell everyone you met Cole Spencer," Gabe said.

I sighed. "He seemed troubled. Wasn't he always in the news for his crazy behaviour until a few years ago."

"Yeah. Then he lost his daughter, and it fucked him over. Now he barely leaves his estate."

"He had a daughter? I didn't know that."

"Not many people do. Come on, let's go find our seats."

❄

The movie would be a box office smash. It had everything—a crazy good looking and charismatic lead in the form of Cole Spencer, a beautiful fiery female lead in Natalia Osmari, and a plot that took the viewer through every conceivable emotion ... at least I assumed so because I didn't pay attention to most of it.

No, from the fifteen-minute mark my entire focus was welded to the arm draped casually across the back of my seat and the thumb idly caressing my bare shoulder.

Maybe that one glass of champagne had gone to my head. Maybe I was just cold and that was causing the goosebumps on my skin. Or maybe the way I'd felt about Gabe hadn't died at all but had simply been lying dormant, waiting for its moment to return.

I was hyper-aware of the man sprawled in the seat beside me. His legs were spread across the gap, one leg pressed close against mine, the heat from his body warming my side. Every time he shifted position, my heart raced and my breath hitched.

I didn't know what I was waiting for, but anticipation had dried my mouth and turned me into a mass of nervous energy. Gabe moved again, his leg pressing firmly against mine and his hand lifted, fingers sliding up the side of my neck. I swallowed, fighting the urge to shiver. His head rolled sideways until his mouth was level with my ear.

"You okay?" he whispered, and I gave a jerky nod. "I should have kissed you in the car. It's all I can fucking think about."

I don't know if it was his low, raspy growl, the darkness of the room, or the fingers stroking my skin, but I felt every word hit me like an arrow, and I squirmed in my seat in an attempt to ease the sudden spike of lust.

"I want to mess you up, Harper," he continued. "I want to see that perfect red lipstick smeared across your face."

"Gabe!" I hissed, trying to silence him.

His tongue licked the shell of my ear. "I want to pull your dress down and play with your nipples. Are they hard, Harper? If I reached in, would I find them eager and ready for my touch? I want to slide my fingers into your panties and make you come while everyone else watches the movie. Could you stay quiet and ride my hand?"

My nipples tightened beneath my dress and I bit my lip, fighting back a moan. *What was he doing to me?*

"Would you stop me?" His other hand was on my leg, slowly pulling it closer to him, and his palm slid up over the silk of my dress. *Oh god, what was he doing?*

"What do you say, Harper?" His fingers had reached my thigh and stroked inwards, their destination clear, dipping under the material. "Want to get dirty with me?"

An explosion on the screen lit up the room briefly and I jumped, dislodging his hand. His chuckle was rich in my ear.

"I honestly don't know what's more exciting to watch. The action on the screen, or the action in your seats." Luca drawled from behind us.

Gabe lifted his hand from my shoulder to flip him a middle finger. I could feel my cheeks burning. *How many other people had heard the things he'd whispered to me?* Carefully, I checked the seats around us. No one was looking in our direction or seemed interested in what we were doing.

Gabe sighed heavily and let his head drop against the back of his seat.

"Fucking mood killer," he muttered at Luca, and his bandmate laughed.

Gabe kept his hands ... and words ... to himself for the rest of the movie. He seemed perfectly at ease next to me, but he wasn't watching the film. His head was back against the seat and his eyes were closed.

When the lights brightened to announce the end of the viewing, everyone stood up to clap. I saw Cole rise from his seat with his co-star to acknowledge the applause and they made their way to the stage.

Gabe stirred beside me, his hand finding mine and he threaded my fingers with his. The butterflies that had started to settle flew back into life. I could barely concentrate on the speech Cole was giving with Gabe touching me.

"Thank you all for coming out tonight," Cole said into the microphone. "I don't have to tell any of you how much work goes into making a film. There are hundreds of people who deserve the spotlight and your applause far more than I do, but as the primary star, it's my job to come up here and take the accolades. But I have to tell you, none of what you watched would have been possible without the amazing team who worked on it."

His blue eyes scanned the room and the smile he was famous for flashed on. "I won't keep you here any longer, I know you're all looking forward to the booze and food waiting in the other room, so go. Enjoy yourselves. And thank you again." He gave a nod and strode from the stage.

I saw Lexi lean against Seth and whisper something. He nodded and looked over at Gabe. "Lexi wants to go home, and I have no interest in spending time with the rich and shameless that'll be at the party."

"I'm not babysitting Luca and Dex." His eyes touched mine. "I have other plans."

"Karl is here. You can't be trusted alone with Luca. What are your plans?"

Gabe looked at me and I could see the heat in his eyes. I licked my lips.

"I ... uh ... whatever you want to do is fine." I managed to croak out and a smile ghosted across his face. I realised what I'd just agreed to. "Wait. I mean—"

"No, no take backs, Frosty." He tightened his grip on my hand and set off for the exit without saying goodbye to Seth.

His path was impeded by multiple people wanting to congratulate him on his part—the music—of the movie. His impatience was obvious, and he made no attempt to hide his desire to get away whenever someone called his name.

When the fourth person moved into our path, I heard him actually growl beneath his breath.

"Gabe! What did you think?" The man, who looked vaguely familiar, pumped Gabe's hand enthusiastically.

"Fucking fantastic," Gabe almost snarled and I hid a laugh behind my hand.

"Yes, yes! What was your favourite scene?"

"The one where the heroine died from an overdose of orgasms," he replied.

There was a beat of startled silence. "I don't think … There wasn't …"

"Yeah, it was great, man. Gotta go." Gabe strode around him, dragging me along behind him.

"Gabe!" I scooped up the hem of my dress to stop tripping over it and tried to slow him down.

"If we slow down, someone will try and stop us again and I have to get out of here."

"Why?" I stumbled and he stopped, turned and caught me before I crashed into him. "Why do you need to get out of here?"

"Why? You're asking me why?" He stepped closer, bending his head and lowering his voice. "Because if we don't get out of here in the next five minutes, I'm gonna pin you against the closest wall and to hell with the fucking onlookers." He took another step, his hands sliding up my arms, and I shivered. "Decide fast, Frosty. I'm good either way."

"You wouldn't!"

His eyes challenged mine. "Try me."

When I didn't reply fast enough, his hands moved the rest of their way up my arms, over my shoulders and cupped my face. Another step put his body flush against mine, and then he was kissing me.

His kiss was gentle, soft—not like I had expected. If he had kissed me harshly, demanded a response, I might have reacted differently, but this … this gentleness made me want more.

His mouth brushed against mine once, then twice, before he pulled away. I took a shaky breath, and then his lips were on me again, and this time his tongue swept over my lips, flicking, teasing until they parted for him.

The kiss changed, became more aggressive as he dropped one hand so he could wrap his arm around my waist, his fingers pressing against my bare back and driving me even closer to him. We were pressed together so firmly I could feel his erection against my stomach and just knowing he was hard for *me* sent a flood of heat between my thighs.

His tongue tangled with mine, our lips almost battling, teeth nipping at each other, and his other hand left my face to tangle in my hair. The sting as he tugged at it, changing the angle of my head so he could deepen our kiss further made me hiss against his mouth, and I heard him laugh softly, felt the vibration of it against my breasts where they were crushed against his chest.

This had to stop. There was a reason we *had* to stop! But my brain couldn't tell me why. I could focus on nothing but his touch, his mouth, his tongue. I didn't remember wrapping my arms around his neck or spearing my fingers into his hair until he lifted his head, and I found myself staring into grey eyes burning with heat and lust.

"Still want to hang around here?" he whispered and I shook my head mutely.

My face burned when I realised we were still in the theatre and people nearest to us had fallen silent to watch our display. Gabe didn't seem to care. He dipped his head to press another lingering kiss to my still-parted lips, before he reached back to unlock my arms from behind his neck, gripped my hand in his and strode toward the doors without looking back.

CHAPTER 26

CHURCH - FALL OUT BOY

Gabe

PRESENT

It took every ounce of willpower I owned to keep my hands off Harper while we waited for the valet to bring my car. Part of me was glad I'd decided to ditch the limo. The other part cursed me out. I could have dragged her into the back, put up the privacy screen and fucked her the way my body was screaming at me to do.

That would have been a huge mistake.

Maybe, subconsciously, I'd known how the evening would play out and set myself up to ensure I didn't do anything stupid … like, treat the one woman who mattered to me the way I would a common groupie. On the flip side, the more time she had to think, the higher the chance that she would decide I wasn't worth the risk.

I caught movement out of the corner of my eye and turned

my head to see Harper rubbing her arms.

"Cold?" She jumped at the sound of my voice, then gave a short nod.

I shrugged out of my jacket and draped it across her shoulders. Her fingers rose to clutch the lapels and drew it closed around her.

Fuck it.

I stepped behind her and slipped my arms around her waist. She tensed, then relaxed, leaning back against my chest. I took that as a green light and lowered my head to drag my tongue over the edge of her ear.

"My car will be here soon," I whispered. "You have a choice to make." One of my hands snaked beneath my jacket and I smoothed my palm up over her stomach to cup her breast. My lips pressed a kiss to the pulse fluttering widely at the base of her throat. "Come home with me. No pretence, no hiding. Just you and me."

Her head fell back against my shoulder, eyes closed as I nibbled at the soft skin beneath her ear, and squeezed the breast in my hand. Her lips parted on a silent gasp.

"What do you think, Frosty? Want to take a risk and play with me?"

Of course, that was the moment the valet showed up with my car. I reluctantly removed my hand from her body and guided her down the steps. The valet handed me my keys and palmed the hundred-dollar bill I held. I opened the passenger door and helped Harper inside, lingering to watch as she adjusted the dress around her legs.

Settling behind the wheel, I drove away from the theatre. Neither of us spoke. Harper hadn't said whether she wanted to go home alone or with me, and I wasn't ready to end the night. At first, I drove aimlessly, choosing random turns, and taking no notice of where we were until I started recognising landmarks.

The diner we'd go to whenever we had money to spare ... a park where we'd play ball. The green where I'd taught Harper how to defend herself ... I slammed my foot on the brake and stared up at the dilapidated apartment block we'd almost burned to death inside.

I was out of the car before I even thought about it. Rounding the front of the Mustang, I looked up at the place I'd spent the first eighteen years of my life.

"Gabe?"

I flinched at the gentle touch on my back, twisted round to lock my car, grabbed Harper's wrist and silently strode toward the entrance. She didn't protest, stumbling after me in her high heels. A part of me knew I should slow down, consider her appearance, but emotion drove me. A dark anger that required an outlet. Some of the apartments still appeared to have residents.

Why the fuck hadn't the place been pulled down?

We could hear the sound of TVs or music playing through the thin walls. Children's toys, rubbish, and furniture littered the corridors. Needles and used condoms were scattered over the stairs. I didn't let any of it stop me as I made my way up to the fifth floor.

"Gabe, we shouldn't be here," Harper ventured softly, and I glanced back at her, but kept moving.

We exited the stairwell onto the fifth floor and I felt Harper pull free from my grip. I let her go, my eyes locked onto the door hanging off the hinges of one of the apartments. This floor was empty, the walls still showing remnants of the fire which had driven Harper and her mother to leave.

I moved toward the door and stepped into the apartment beyond. It hadn't been lived in for years. Four, in fact. My steps slowed, eyeing the stain on the rotten carpet still covering the floor—dark, rust coloured.

My blood.

"Gabe?"

I swung around at my name and seeing Harper standing in the midst of all the dirt and memories—*filth* that existed only inside my mind—her flawless skin glowing under the moonlight, something snapped.

"Come here." My demand was harsh.

"We shouldn't be here." She didn't move from the doorway.

"Out of everyone who ever set foot into this building, *we* have the most fucking right to be here." I held out my hand. "Come here." I repeated my demand.

Her eyes shifted past me, taking in the mess around us, and she took a slow step forward. "Gabe, I understand why you wanted to look around, but ..."

"Stop talking." I reached out, caught her hand and pulled her toward me.

She drew breath to chew me out, so I did the only logical thing—covered her mouth with my hand, backed her against the wall, and buried my face into the curve of her throat.

"I need you, Harper," I whispered, and I sounded lost to my own ears.

I ran my thumb over her bottom lip and pressed a kiss to her shoulder. My fingers found the top of her dress and peeled the bodice down, freeing her breasts. I raised my head, my eyes meeting hers briefly before dropping down to see what I had revealed.

Slightly flushed creamy skin tipped with dusky pink nipples hard and begging for the attention of my tongue and teeth. A temptation too much to ignore, so I brushed my knuckles over one and heard her sharp intake of breath.

But she didn't stop me.

Catching it between my thumb and forefinger, I pinched, and she hissed. Her other nipple hardened more and I smiled. Lowering my head, I flicked my tongue over the tip and then sucked it into my mouth.

My hand found the slit in her dress and I ran my fingers up her thigh until I found the lacy edge of her panties.

"Gabe." My name on her lips, the touch of her fingers sinking into my hair broke the last of my control, and I thrust my fingers beneath her panties. At the same time, I nipped sharply at her nipple. Her fingers flexed, pulling my hair and I lifted my head.

"Someone could see us," she whispered.

I processed her words. It wasn't a *'please stop'*. I shrugged.

"I don't care," I told her and dropped to my knees, uncaring of the bespoke suit worth thousands I was probably spoiling. My forehead rested against her stomach while I pushed her dress away from her legs.

"Gabe …" she broke off when I kissed her through her panties, before peeling them down her legs.

"*Fuck*," I breathed. "I've missed you."

My hands curved over her hips and I buried my face into the damp curls so I could slide my tongue into her wetness.

Her gasp was like music, better than the roar of fans waiting for us to take to the stage. She was a gourmet meal and I had been starving for eight years. My tongue found her clit and I lapped at it, while I wrapped one hand around her thigh and lifted her leg to drape over my shoulder. The move opened her up to my hungry gaze.

"What would you do," I murmured, lightly tracing her clit with one finger. "If someone walked in right now and saw you like this? Wide-open for me. Your tits on display, my fingers in your pussy, my tongue fucking you." I paused to lick her again. "What would you do, Harper? Would you make me stop?"

I felt her tremble and leaned back to look up at her. Her eyes were closed, lips parted and her nipples were as hard as the fucking diamonds around her throat. I reached up with one hand to pinch one between my fingers, tugging and twisting it, taking her to the edge of pain and watched her arch her back.

"Gabe!" she hissed my name and I knew it wasn't a demand I stop.

I dove back between her legs, widening her stance with my shoulders, and lifting her up so I could suck her clit into my mouth. Her nails dug into my scalp and I welcomed the sting.

"Tell me, Harper." I pushed another finger inside her. "Would you let them watch while I eat you? What about while I fuck you?"

I'd kill anyone before they touched her. She was mine. Mine to touch, mine to taste, mine to *fuck*.

"Imagine it," I continued to whisper, feeling her tighten around my fingers. "Their hot eyes on us, their torment at knowing they can look but can't touch. Do you think they're watching us now?" She was close, I could taste it, hear it in her moans, see it in the way her body jerked. "If we get caught up here, they'll take photos. Me eating your pussy will be all over the internet." She whimpered. "Everyone will know you're mine, Harper. You've always been mine." She fell over the edge, my name on her lips as she came ... and I'd never been more satisfied without getting off myself.

Carefully, I eased back and set her leg back on the floor, then rose to my feet. Wrapping an arm around her waist, I kissed her ... hard, fast, and deep ... my tongue forcing its way between her lips. I knew she could taste herself on my tongue from the way she stiffened and jerked away.

"I don't—" she tried to say and I shook my head.

"You taste like fucking nectar," I said over her. "Better than any alcohol." I kissed her again, licked her lips until she opened them. "Taste it, Frosty. Taste how much you loved what I did to you."

She swallowed, and let me push my tongue into her mouth, slid her own along it, tasting her own arousal. I had already been hard, but that made me stiffen more. I was so fucking hard, it was painful. I wanted to pin her to the nearest surface and fuck her until she screamed but now wasn't the time. And this *definitely* wasn't the place.

I broke the kiss, and ran my knuckles over her cheek, down her throat ... and lower over her breast. I placed a kiss on each tip, then gently drew the bodice back over her, covering those beautiful nipples from my gaze. I briefly wondered if I could make her come just from playing with them and talking dirty— something I'd explore another day. Bending I tore the side of her panties, untangled them from her leg and picked them up. She watched in silence as I put them in my pants pocket.

"Ready to go?" I asked and walked toward the door.

Harper stayed where she was, her arms lifting to wrap around herself. "Those ... the things you said while you were ... were ..." she stuttered to a stop.

I swung around to face her and found her looking anywhere but at me.

"While I was eating your pussy?" I supplied helpfully, and

she blushed.

"I don't ... I wouldn't ... I'm not a freak."

My head canted. "A freak?" I repeated. Striding back to her, I tucked a finger beneath her chin and forced her to raise her head. "Harper, look at me." I waited until her eyes met mine. "Talking dirty is not freaky. If the thought of being caught excites you and turns you on ... Baby, sex is *supposed* to be exciting. Exploring boundaries *is* fun. There's nothing you can tell me that I'll think is weird." I stole another kiss and wrapped my arm around her shoulders. "Let's get out of here."

The place was just as deserted on our walk back to the car as it was when we first arrived. My car was still sitting where I'd left it—thankfully with all four wheels intact—and we were driving away less than five minutes later. Harper was silent beside me, gnawing at her bottom lip. A sign I recognised from our shared past. She was overthinking what had just happened between us.

I reached out and placed my palm on her thigh, nudging the material away with my thumb until I was touching her skin. She glanced at me from beneath her lashes.

"Are we good?"

She nodded.

"Frosty, talk to me."

"I've never done anything like that before," she blurted out. "I'm not easy, Gabe. I don't want you to think—"

"Woah, stop right there." I checked the road and pulled over to the side. "I don't think you're easy. Fuck, Harper, if this is you being easy, I'd hate to see you playing hard to get."

"It's not a joke."

"I'm not laughing." I twisted in my seat to face her. "Look, I'll take you home ... *your* home. You work tomorrow, right?" I waited for her nod. "It's been a busy night. Go home, get some sleep ... in your *own* bed ... and I'll wait for you to call me."

There was a beat of silence and then she replied with a quiet "okay".

Tattooed Memories

CHAPTER 27

PRIMAL SCREAM - MOTLEY CRUE

Gabe

AGE 19

I lay on my back, staring up at the stars, the smoke from the joint curling up from my lips. I'd finally moved out of my da's place six months ago, and moved in with Seth, Dex, and Luca. It was like living in a frat house ... or how I assumed a frat house would be, anyway. Constant noise, girls rotating in and out of bedrooms, tripping over strangers drunk on the floor.

I'd never been happier.

Yet here I was, lying on the roof, hiding from my bandmates, wishing I was on the other side of town, and wondering what Harper was doing.

We'd signed with Karl's record label soon after the gig we played at Trudy's and he'd had us playing gigs all over L.A., supporting bigger names and getting our own name out there. I hadn't seen Harper in over two months. We'd texted here and there, but she was busy with school and I was busy with ... well, life.

My phone buzzed by my hand, and I rolled my head sideways, flipping my phone up so I could see the screen.

FROSTY - `Are you going to be home next week?`

I knew what she was asking me. Would I be seeing her on her birthday? Her eighteenth. If I didn't, it would be the first one I'd missed in ten years. Could I do that to her?

I drew the smoke into my lungs and held it there until it burned, then tapped the call button. She answered immediately—like I'd known she would.

"Hey, Frosty."

"Gabe!" Her soft voice made my dick stir.

I exhaled, feeling the buzz from the weed hit. "I'm home now. Got back this morning. I was gonna call you tomorrow."

"Your dad was here yesterday."

The pleasant relaxation I'd been feeling left my body.

"What did he want?"

"He was looking for you. He didn't believe me when I told him I hadn't seen you in a few weeks."

There was a note to her voice—one I didn't like. I sat up, the buzz from the weed fading.

"You weren't alone with him?" I asked urgently. "Was your mom there?"

"No, she was working."

"Fuck, Harper. I told you not to be alone with him."

"I didn't *invite* him in, Gabriel! What was I supposed to do?"

"Did he hurt you?"

"No. Gabe, he didn't touch me, I swear."

I stood up, pinched the end of my joint and stuffed it in a pocket.

"What did he want?"

"I don't know. He forced his way into the apartment and searched my room for you. When he realised you weren't here, he left."

"Fuck." I raked a hand through my hair. "You're sure he didn't touch you?"

"I'm sure." She paused and I could see her biting her lip in my head. "I asked if he wanted me to pass on a message to you."

"But there wasn't one," I said flatly. It wasn't a question. I knew him. He didn't need to leave a message with Harper because his visit was a message in itself. He'd known I wasn't there. Known her mom was working. Known she was alone.

The message was clear. Harper was vulnerable and accessible.

Fuck ... fuck ... fuck.

"I'll deal with it," I told her and cut the call.

Swinging my legs over the side of the building, I climbed down the short distance to my window and crawled through. I could hear the guys in the other room, laughing and talking. Changing out of my dark grey sweats, I pulled on my favourite jeans and a Metallica t-shirt, shoved my feet into boots and headed out.

Dex called my name, a girl hanging on his arm.

"Dude. Charity wants to be tag-teamed. You in?"

I waved a hand, shaking my head. I didn't want to be distracted by sex or the drugs that would inevitably follow. I needed my head clear for what I was about to do. Checking I had my car keys and wallet, I grabbed my hoodie from the hook by the door, pulled it over my head and stepped outside.

Seth was leaning up against the wall, a cigarette hanging from his lip as he watched two girls kissing opposite him. His face gave nothing away—impassive, no way to know if he was enjoying their play or was bored shitless. His eyes shifted to me.

"Going somewhere?"

"My da went to Harper's."

He straightened. "She okay?"

"So she says."

"You think he—"

"No." I snapped. "He was just letting me know he could."

"Where are you going?"

My smile was tired. "To inform him he *can't*."

Seth pushed away from the wall. "Let's go."

※

The elevator was out of service at my da's apartment block, so we had to take the stairs.

"I'm surprised this shithole hasn't been pulled down," Seth remarked, kicking a used syringe down the steps.

I shrugged. "Don't think anyone gives enough of a fuck to fight about it." We walked along the hallway and stopped outside the apartment I'd shared with my da. "Wait out here."

Seth propped himself against the wall, hands shoved into his pockets. "Yell if you need help."

"I won't." I turned the handle, knowing it wouldn't be locked and walked in.

The smell of cheap beer and cigarettes assailed my nostrils. The TV played some grainy lesbian porn and my da was sprawled on the couch, his pants around his ankles as he rubbed one out.

"Fuck's sake," I muttered, rounding the table and keeping a respectable distance away.

My da was a drunk ... a *mean* drunk. He was quick on his feet, as well as being bigger and heavier than me. I'd been on the receiving end of his temper more than enough times to know I needed to be cautious in my approach.

"Da ..."

"Stop skulking over there like a pussy, boy," he snapped, his Irish accent strong and slurred. He continued to stroke his dick, eyes glued to the screen.

"You went to Harper's place."

His head swivelled and he smirked. "Now that's a fine piece of ass. You fucked her yet?"

My fists clenched and his smile widened.

"You're getting brave, boy. Ready to hit your old man? Make sure you knock me down the first time, boy, because I'll fucking kill you if you don't."

I schooled my expression. "You agreed to stay away from her."

"I *said* I wouldn't dirty her up. Not until she's legal, anyway.

It's not like she's getting what she needs from you. She's eighteen soon, and fair game. If she's anything like her old lady, she'll be really sweet too." He smacked his lips, dropping his hand from his dick and standing up.

I took a step back while he pulled up his pants, watching him warily. He caught my eye and laughed.

"Don't matter how old you get, boy, you'll always cower before me, won't you? You'll always be that little baby crying for his mama." He buckled his belt and took a step toward me. "Tell you what, *son*. I'll make you a deal."

"What kind of deal?"

"I won't touch her if you don't touch her." He turned toward the kitchen and I followed.

"You talk like it's not even her choice."

He snorted, opened the refrigerator and took out a beer. "Boy, the sooner you learn that the only way to get what you want is by taking it, the happier you'll be."

"Stay away from Harper."

He twisted off the cap and sneered at me. "Or what? You'll come and shout at me from all the way over there again?" He took a swig of beer. "Maybe I can get in on some mother/daughter action."

Something snapped inside me …

❄

"Gabe! Fuck, *Gabe!*"

I blinked, winced at the bright light, then blinked again as

Seth's face came into focus.

"Thank fuck ... I thought you were dead. Can you move?"

"What?" I tried to sit up, groaned and fell back.

"Come on, man. We need to get the fuck out of here. I'm pretty sure someone called the cops."

"The cops? Why?" I struggled to focus, the pounding in my head increasing with every word Seth said.

He pulled my arm across his shoulders and hauled me to my feet. I staggered sideways, and only Seth's grip stopped me from crashing back to the floor.

"I thought for sure you'd killed him, but he's just out cold."

"Killed? What? Who?" I shook my head—a mistake when dizziness threatened to throw me on my ass again—and fought to concentrate, to focus on what was going on around me.

"Talk later. We need to get out of here now." He half-carried, half-dragged me toward the door, and I stopped dead as everything came flooding back.

My da had talked about fucking Harper and I'd completely lost it. I twisted my head around, searching him out and finally found him sprawled out on the floor near the kitchen door.

"He's—"

"No, he's not dead. I don't think he expected you to hit him. He got a few good hits of his own in, though. I think you'll probably need stitches for the cut on your head."

I lifted a hand, touching my face and winced when my fingers came into contact with a tender part just above my right eye. My fingertips were red when I looked at them.

"I'll be fine. I need to see Harper."

"You need to go to the ER and get those cuts looked at."

I shook my head and winced again. "I'll drop you back at the apartment."

Seth glared at me, I glared back.

"Fine. Whatever. You'll do what you fucking want anyway."

Tattooed Memories

CHAPTER 28

I CAN'T GO ON WITHOUT YOU - KALEO

Harper

AGE 17

"Harper! *Harper!*"

What the hell? I grabbed my cell and checked the time. Three AM.

"*Harper!* Open the fucking door!"

"*Gabe?*" I shot out of bed and ran through the apartment, wrenching the door open. "What are you do—" My words faltered when they landed on the battered and bloodied man swaying in front of me. "*Gabriel?!*"

I grabbed his arm as he staggered forward and the smell of whiskey hit me. He wound an arm around my shoulders, gave me a hug and pressed a sloppy kiss to my cheek, then followed me inside.

"What happened? Did you go and see your dad?"

He snorted. "If he comes back here, you don't open the door,

Harper. You hear me?" He caught my arm and pulled me round to face him. "Do you understand me, Frosty?"

"Yes, I get it!!" I tried to lead him toward the bathroom. "Did you get that cut looked at?"

"I'm fine."

"Gabe, it's bleeding." I touched the side of his face. "Did he hit you? Why did you go there? You promised me you'd stay away from there once you moved out."

"Promises." He threw both arms up and stumbled. "Promises are why we're in this mess." I caught him as he keeled forwards, staggering beneath his weight.

"At least come and lie down. Don't go back home. You might have a concussion. Did you hit your head?"

"Stop fussing." He slumped onto the couch and peered up at me through cloudy grey eyes. "We're going to New York next week. Karl got us some gigs out there."

"Oh ..." I tried to hide my disappointment. "So you won't be here for my birthday?"

He tipped his head back against the headrest. "We're travelling two days after. I'm not missing your birthday." His eyes slid shut. "I'm just gonna rest for a minute."

I sank down beside him. I'd lost track of how many times we'd been in this same situation—him bloodied and bleeding, exhausted and drunk, refusing to acknowledge who had hurt him and why. It wasn't like he had to keep it a secret from me. I'd seen the things his father did, *heard* them when I still lived in the apartment opposite his. But it was as if so long as he didn't mention it, we could both pretend it hadn't happened.

Taking his hand in mine, I straightened his fingers, examining his knuckles. He wouldn't ever tell me, I knew, but I was certain he'd fought back this time. Hopefully, that meant his dad wouldn't try again. But knowing Thomas Mercer and his temper, I doubted it.

Gabe's head dropped sideways onto my shoulder and he mumbled something too low for me to hear. I threaded my fingers through his lax ones. I lived for these moments—when he dropped his guard, albeit unwillingly—and I could be close to him. I just wished that it didn't take clashes with his father to give them to me.

"Gabe, come and lie down," I whispered. I burrowed under his arm and tried to lift him to his feet.

"Can't, Frosty. You're just a kid." He grunted, his eyes opening. "Can't touch you."

"I said lie down, not strip my clothes off and screw me like you do your cheap dates," I snapped.

He lifted his head to look at me and brushed his knuckles down my cheek, a caress he'd offered to me alone for as long as I could remember. "You're not like them. I'd never treat you like that," he mumbled.

And wasn't *that* the problem, I muttered to myself. Gabe had spent so long looking at me like a little kid, he didn't see that I was becoming a woman. Okay, so I wasn't *technically* an adult yet, but I knew what I felt for Gabe was real, even if he wouldn't admit to feeling the same way. I was hoping that would change once I turned eighteen, but if he wasn't even going to be here ...

I huffed a sigh and continued hauling him off the couch.

"What are you doing, Frosty?" He gave me a lazy smile which made my toes curl into the carpet beneath my feet. I ignored it and shook my head.

"You are so drunk!" Finally, he was upright. I placed a palm against his chest, then manoeuvred his arm back over my shoulder. "Let's get you into bed, so you can sleep it off."

His hand covered mine and he canted his head to peer down at me. "Why don't you have a boyfriend? You need someone who can give you all their attention and time."

Because I gave you my heart when I was eight years old, you idiot, and no one else can compare. *I never said that, though, I just rolled my eyes at him.*

"You're drunk," I said flatly.

It took some time but I eventually got him into my room and pushed him onto my bed. He fell onto the mattress and threw a hand up over his face, while I pulled off his boots and pushed his legs over onto one side so I could sit down.

I had school in a few hours and knew I should really get some sleep. My mom wouldn't be home until after I'd left, so there was no concern about her finding Gabe in my bed. Not that I think she'd be concerned, anyway. She'd been distracted lately, and oblivious to most things around her unless I made an effort to make her notice. I made sure my alarm was set, then curled up beside Gabe. A few minutes passed and then I felt his arm settle over my waist. He shifted position, tucked me into his side and pressed a kiss to my forehead.

"Love you, Frosty," he mumbled on a yawn.

I didn't reply. I *couldn't* reply because I knew if I repeated it back to him, he'd hear the difference in the way I spoke the words.

CHAPTER 29

LOVERBOY - YOU AND ME AT SIX

Harper

PRESENT

Gabe escorted me to the door of my apartment, dropped what I can only describe as a chaste kiss on my cheek, waited until I was inside and had locked the door before he walked away. I watched him drive away from the window.

I stripped out of my dress, mortification turning my cheeks red when I remembered he'd left with my panties in his pocket, took a hurried shower and crawled into my bed ... I was just dozing off when my phone vibrated with an incoming message.

GABE - Did I mention how gorgeous you looked tonight?

I smiled.

ME - You have Candice and her friends to thank for that.

GABE - I didn't mean at the premiere, I meant

when you came all over my face.

And just like that, I was wide awake.

ME - You can't say things like that!

GABE - Why not? It's the truth.

ME - You're supposed to be waiting for me to contact you.

GABE - What can I say? I can still taste you. I have the hard-on from hell and your panties are in my pocket taunting me with your flavour. I'm tempted to jerk off with them.

My cheeks burned. Holy shit—I'd never known Gabe had such a dirty mouth.

ME - I ... I don't even know how to respond to that.

GABE - In my head you're naked on your bed, legs wide, wet and ready for me. Are you wet for me, Harper?

I hadn't been ... until he said that. His words heated my skin, made between my legs throb with need. I squeezed my thighs together, trying to ease the ache.

GABE - Are you touching yourself?

ME - NO!

GABE - You want to, though. Call me, Harper. I'll talk you through it. I'll tell you how you should touch yourself. I'll make you come with just my voice.

I swallowed.

ME - Go to bed, Gabe.

GABE - I'm not ready to sleep, Frosty. I'm lying on my back, my hand stroking my dick while I imagine you fingering yourself. If I close my eyes I can see your hard nipples, hear your moans, smell your pussy.

Oh fuck.

GABE - Do you think about that night, Harper? When you slipped into my bed and pretended you were someone else? Do you remember how it felt when I was inside you?

My nipples were so hard, they were hurting. The wetness between my legs was coating my thighs and I couldn't stop my hand from drifting down to pinch one nipple ... just to try and stop the ache.

GABE - Tell me ... when you took other men to your bed, did you imagine they were me? Did you keep your eyes closed and pretend it was me eating you out? Me filling you up? Me making you come?

He was right. I'd had two lovers since him ... both times a disaster. The first I hadn't been able to stop crying, feeling like I was cheating on Gabe—which was ridiculous because he had been plastered all over the TV after a sex-tape scandal. I'd told myself I had to stop waiting for him, he had moved on, and accepted a date with a guy who'd been asking me out for months. I let him take me home, I let him fuck me and I cried … because it wasn't Gabe.

The second time I tried not to think about. He'd reminded me of Gabe—similar build, covered in tattoos, a smoky voice that made me shiver. He'd taken me from behind and when I came, I'd screamed Gabe's name.

Needless to say, I never saw either of them again. That was when I realised I was destined to be one of those women for whom there was really only one man—anyone else would mean settling for second best.

GABE - I hope you're not answering me because you're busy playing with your pussy. I'm so fucking hard, Harper. Show me what I walked away from.

He wanted me to send him a photograph. And, I admit, I considered it. But I couldn't … the thought of having such a personal part of myself out there in cyberspace terrified me. I didn't think Gabe would share it with anyone, but I also don't think he meant for his sex tape to get published for the entire world to see, either.

When I didn't reply, my cell lit up with an incoming call.

"Put me on speaker, Frosty." His voice was a raspy growl.

"You shouldn't be calling," I whispered, but complied with his demand.

"I shouldn't do a lot of things," he replied. "I shouldn't have tongue-fucked you in the apartment I grew up in. I shouldn't be sitting here jerking myself off like some schoolboy. I shouldn't be calling you to tell you all the dirty things I'm going to do to you the next time I see you ... yet here we are."

"Gabe ..." I wanted to tell him to stop, to hang up. I wanted him to whisper every filthy word he could think up.

"Do you still sleep in my t-shirts?"

I looked down at the Motley Crue t-shirt I was wearing. "Yeah," I whispered.

"Take it off."

"Gabe—"

"Your bedroom window faces the street, right?" He spoke over me. "Switch off your light, take off your t-shirt, and lie on the bed."

"No, I'm—"

"No one is going to walk past and see you. There's no foot traffic at this hour."

I couldn't believe my own actions when I rose to my feet and crossed the room to flick the light switch, plunging the room into darkness.

"Now the shirt, Frosty."

I didn't question how he'd known I hadn't taken it off. I peeled it over my head and dropped it to the floor.

"The window's open, isn't it? Can you feel the cold air?" He remembered, after all these years, that I slept with the window open.

"Yes," I whispered.

"Turn toward the window and cup your breasts."

I turned slowly.

"Good girl," his voice was rougher, lower than it had been a moment ago. "Now pinch your nipples for me. Make it sting."

Like I was a puppet and he was pulling my strings, I pinched my nipples between my thumb and forefinger, tugging them outwards and twisting slightly until they hurt. I felt the bolt of lust right down to my pussy.

"Fuck, you look so good. Now lie on the bed and open your legs, baby. Let me see how wet you are." I backed toward the mattress and lowered myself, my legs spreading automatically.

"Keep tugging that nipple, Frosty. Slide your other hand down and spread yourself open for me."

"Gabe …" I didn't know if I was protesting his words or pleading with him.

"I'm so close, baby. I just need you to do a little more for me. Touch yourself. Let me see how you play with your clit. Come for me, Harper."

My fingers were on my clit before he stopped speaking, sliding through my wetness. I squeezed my eyes closed, imagining it was Gabe touching me. The fingers tugging my nipple clenched, and the sting of pain flooded my pussy. I groaned, panting, rubbing my clit harder until my hips jerked up off the bed and I sobbed his name.

Through my cell's speaker, I heard him groan with me and knew he was finding his own release.

"Fuck ... Harper ..." he growled softly. "Stand up and go to your window."

I rose on shaky legs and did as he asked. My lips parted in silent shock at the sight of him leaning against the side of his Mustang, his cell wedged between his ear and shoulder as he tucked himself back into his pants.

"Call me when you're ready," he whispered and swung into the driver's seat.

※

I was exhausted. There's no other way to describe it. I'd barely slept since Gabe watched me masturbate through my bedroom window. I still wasn't sure how I felt about it.

Disturbed? Check. Anyone could have walked past and seen what I was doing. Concerned about my *lack* of concern at the time? I put that down to being drunk on Gabe, post-orgasmic and drinking champagne. Clutching and in denial of the truth? Maybe, I don't care.

Mostly I was turned on every time I thought about it. I didn't think I was *that* kind of person—to get off on something like the risk of being caught, of being watched. Maybe it was something Gabe brought out in me. But I couldn't deny what he'd done ... what *we'd* done had excited me more than I would have ever thought possible.

I scrubbed the stain on the countertop furiously, glaring down at it while I contemplated the night before.

What are you worried about? *I asked myself.* List the problems.

Okay...

Problem: I wasn't sure what Gabe wanted. We'd had sex once eight years ago and he'd thrown me out, blistering my ears with words that still hurt, even now.

Counter-argument: He was here now. He claimed he wanted to fix how things ended between us.

Possible solution: Don't let him talk you into anything sexual until you're sure he's not going to disappear again.

I nodded to myself. I could do that. It wasn't like he looked and sounded like sin or made me melt into a puddle of lust when he opened that dirty mouth of his.

I bit my lip. Don't even think about that!

I moved to the bedroom, stuffing dirty washing into the linen basket.

Problem: He was part of one of the biggest rock bands around right now. Hot property—fans mobbed him in the street if they saw him. I liked my privacy.

Counter-argument: Gabe had done everything he could both times we'd been together to ensure we weren't disturbed.

Possible solution: Act like I have nothing to hide. I *did* have nothing to hide! The press would grow bored of digging for stories.

I took the linen basket into the laundry room and started separating the colours from the whites.

My cell rang as I was starting the first wash cycle. I glanced around the apartment I was in. I wasn't supposed to take personal calls during work hours, but the residents weren't home and I was alone.

I *was not* disappointed when the caller display showed it was Candice and not Gabe.

"Hi, Candice," I greeted her. "Thank you for helping me yesterday."

She made a dismissive sound. "Listen, Harper. Have you seen the papers today? Where are you?"

"At work and no, I haven't." A bad feeling was growing in the pit of my stomach.

"I doubt it's anything to worry about, but obviously you were at a very public event with Gabe last night. I just wanted to give you a heads up that there are photos of you with him, so you might find yourself getting a little more attention than you're used to." She paused. "That kiss you shared at the premiere was hot as fuck. I swear my ovaries exploded when I saw it."

I choked on my own tongue. *"What?"*

She laughed. "Oh, honey. If you're going to swap saliva with Gabe, you're going to have to get used to it being shared around."

"I didn't even think about that," I whispered, my thoughts going to what else we'd done. *God*, what if someone had seen *that*? "Is that ... That's all they took photos of ... right?"

There was a long silence. "Is there something I need to be prepared for, Harper?" Candice asked, her voice rich with curiosity. "What *else* happened between the two of you?"

"Nothing," I squeaked.

"Oh, oh, oh!" she crowed. "What did he talk you into? I smell gossip … *juicy* gossip!" She chuckled. "I have to live vicariously through you, Harper. You have to tell me what you did with that dirty, dirty boy."

My cheeks were burning and I thanked every God I could think of that she wasn't standing in front of me. "I don't know what you're talking about."

"Hmmm, well …" I heard voices in the background, one in particular.

"Are you with Gabe?" I asked before I could stop myself.

"Yes, do you want to talk to him?"

"No!" I yelled the word. "No," I repeated.

"Interesting," Candice murmured. "Gabe?" she called out and I groaned. "Do you want to talk to Harper?"

"Did she call you?" I heard him ask.

"No."

"Then, no. Tell her I'm waiting for her call." His voice rose. "Hear me, Frosty? Ball's in your court."

"I feel like I'm the third wheel in some weird kind of foreplay," Candice complained.

"You'd know if I was playing with you, Candice," was his drawled reply and I closed my eyes, praying for the strength of mind *not* to call him as soon as Candice hung up.

"I have to go," I told the woman at the other end of the line, before I started begging pathetically. "I'm not supposed to take calls at work."

"All right. Just be aware of what's happening around you.

Once people start to recognise you as the woman Gabe was with last night, you might need some security. If you start feeling concerned about *anything*, let me know."

"I doubt it'll come to that."

Candice laughed. "Oh, you have no idea." She ended the call before I could reply.

CHAPTER 30

BACK OF MY MIND - TWO FEET

Gabe

PRESENT

I twisted the cap off the bottle of water and drained half of it in one go, then poured the rest over my head. Dex had cranked up the heat in our practice studio to Gobi Desert temperatures, and I think I sweated away fifty percent of my body weight during the two hours I'd spent getting the vocals right on a track we were trying to lay down. I'd already stripped off my t-shirt and was giving serious consideration to removing my jeans as well, only I was going commando beneath them. It wouldn't be the first time any of the guys had seen my dick, I wasn't ashamed of what God had graced me with, but no one needed to see that shit during a recording session.

"Fuck's sake, man, turn the heat down," I bellowed for probably the hundredth time.

"No can do, buddy," Dex yelled back. "Karl says sweating

rock stars is a hot commodity."

I rolled my eyes. "Karl is a fucking asshole. Where is he? Why isn't he in here sweating with us?"

"He's not a rock star. He's just the man who makes them." Seth said quietly from behind me.

He was also dripping in sweat and bottled water. His fingers rested on the strings of his guitar and he idly strummed out a tune.

I quirked a brow. "If you're gonna play it, man, do it properly."

He flashed me a rare grin and started to play "Roll Over Beethoven". I wandered over to the microphone and launched into the lyrics. Dex picked up his bass and Luca settled behind his drums and before long we were having an impromptu jam session, belting out covers of our favourite classics.

Karl arrived just after I picked up one of my guitars and Seth and I were harmonising on Beatles songs. He leaned against the wall, sipping his coffee while we sang "Run For Your Life".

"Is that a warning?" he asked when we wrapped it up.

I looked around. "Don't see any women here to warn." I took the coffee cup he offered me. "Nice of you to finally show up."

"I thought you'd be safe enough here—nothing here you can get into trouble with." He sauntered over to the lounge area. "The girl you took to the premiere the other night..."

I stiffened. I hadn't heard from Harper since that night. Candice had spoken to her on Monday and assured me she had seemed fine, but now it was Thursday and I was starting to wonder if she'd ghosted me. Had I pushed it too far watching her get off for me?

"Gabe? Earth to Gabe?" Karl's fingers snapping in front of my face brought my focus back to him.

"What about her?"

"It was the chick you were dating when I first signed you ... Harper? The one you did the interview about."

"We weren't dating back then, but yeah, it was Harper."

"Why the sudden interest in her again?"

"My interest in her never left. It just took a short hiatus." I cocked a brow. "Is that a problem for you?"

Karl shook his head. "Of course not. I was surprised it took you this long to go back to her."

"You and everyone else apparently," I muttered and he laughed.

"Gabe, you've been following that girl around like a love-struck puppy since you were what ... ten? Does she even know how many of the songs you've written are about her?"

I dropped my gaze to the notebook on the coffee table. "I don't know what you're talking about," I said defensively.

"Of course you don't," he responded dryly, then raised his voice. "Seth, Dex, Luca—quit fooling around and come over here."

He waited until the rest of the band joined us and waved at us to sit down.

"Roth Fairfax called me this morning. He's opening a new venue in a couple of weeks and wants to know if you'd be available to headline." He raised a hand to silence Dex and Luca when they started to protest. "I know ... I know ... you've only just come back from a world tour and you're tired." He gave me a pointed look. "Some are less tired than others apparently. But this would be a good opportunity for you."

"We're not exactly hurting for attention," Seth said, and I nodded my agreement.

"No, I know. But having Roth owe you a favour wouldn't be a bad thing. He has his fingers in many pies—music, TV, movies. It never hurts to keep those doors wide open and available."

He rose to his feet. "Think about it. He needs an answer by the weekend. You already have a setlist. You can use the same one from the tour, as well as the show set up itself."

Seth and I traded glances. I knew we'd both agree to do it—performing was what we loved most. It kept us sane. We'd just have to convince Dex and Luca.

"We'll discuss it," I said.

"All right then. I'll get out of your hair. Gabe, can I have a word before I go?"

I frowned at the seriousness of his tone and followed him to the door.

"How serious are you about Harper?"

"Didn't we just have this conversation?"

Karl reached into his back pocket and pulled out an envelope. "This turned up mixed in with your fan mail this morning."

Frowning I took it, opened it and pulled out the contents. "What the fuck?" One piece of paper was a black and white print of me and Harper coming out of the old apartment block. The knees of my pants were clearly covered in dust and dirt, and Harper's hair was a messy tangle around her face. The second was from later that evening, of me leaning against my Mustang as I knocked one off staring into Harper's window. "Fuck."

"Someone is watching you. I don't have to remind you how out of hand this can get. If you're serious about her, reel her in and keep her close while I find out who sent these. If you're not, then cut her loose before this explodes."

"Isn't there any letter?" I opened the envelope wider, checking inside.

Karl shook his head. "No. But you know how this goes. It'll start small and escalate. I've alerted Miles and he's going to put someone on Harper. He's just waiting for your agreement."

"You have it. Anything it takes. Do *not* let her get wind of this. She's already ..." I raked a hand through my hair. I was going to say she was already having second thoughts, but I wasn't certain what she was thinking. All I knew was that she hadn't been in contact yet and I'd promised her I'd wait. "*Fuck.*"

"Do you want me to dispose of those?" he waved a hand toward the photographs I still held.

I looked down at them. "No ... no, I'll do it. These are going to be copies anyway, you know that. Whoever has the originals wouldn't be stupid enough to send the only copies they had."

He patted my shoulder. "Never a dull moment with you. I'll see you at the weekly meeting tomorrow. Talk to Dex and Luca about Roth's request."

I nodded absently, still looking down at the images. How had I missed someone watching us? Especially when I circled the block and went back to Harper's place after I dropped her off. I'd been careful to make sure I was alone. No cars, no people.

I studied the angle of the image ... unless they'd used a professional long-distance lens. Which meant they had planned to get images. The question was *who* had they been following—Harper or me.

I pulled out my cell—still no messages from her. I should call her, tell her what was going on, but I'd told her the ball was in her court. She needed to be the one to contact *me*. I needed to know this thing wasn't one-sided. That she couldn't keep away from me any more than I could keep away from her.

"Everything okay?" Seth came up behind me and I stuffed the photos in my pocket before he saw them.

"Yeah, I'm good."

"The boys want to order food and get some more songs down. You up for that?"

My Zippo was in my hand, and I flicked it open ... closed ... open ... closed. Seth tracked the movement.

"We could put it off until tomorrow if there's something you need to do." He knew my idiosyncrasies, was aware that the lighter in my hand meant I was stressed or irritated.

I squared my shoulders, forced myself to put the lighter away. "No, man. Let's do this." I pasted a smile on my face and walked back to the centre of the room.

※

Six hours later and I was ready to break Dex's bass guitar over Luca's head. Seth's was closer, but he'd gut me where I stood. Dex wasn't as attached to the bass he was using.

"I did not miss my cue," I repeated through gritted teeth.

"Yeah … you did," Luca disagreed. "It's one … two … three … sing. Not one … two … three … *four* … sing." With each count, he hit the drums, then pointed one of the drumsticks at me.

"It doesn't sound right on three."

We'd been bickering over this for the past forty minutes and I was reaching the limit of my patience. Seth, typically said nothing, watching us both out of dark eyes. Dex took the opportunity to roll and light a joint and was sitting on the floor eating the remains of the pizza we'd ordered.

"Why don't we call it a night," Seth said suddenly and I narrowed my eyes at him. He gave me a bland look. "What? I have no interest in listening to you two all night long. We've just spent eighteen months doing this every night." He placed his guitar on its stand and stretched. "I'm beat, anyway." He picked up his t-shirt from the floor and pulled it over his head.

"Who are you going to meet?"

"What makes you think I'm going to meet anyone?" His expression was sly.

"The only reason you'd leave here is if you've got a woman

waiting somewhere," I pointed out.

"Then you have your answer, don't you?" Seth bent to retrieve his jacket, then strode toward the exit. He paused before he left. "Stop waiting for a sign, Gabe," he threw over his shoulder, then disappeared through the door.

Tattooed Memories

CHAPTER 31

HEROIN - BADFLOWER

Gabe

PRESENT

Miles was leaning against my Mustang when I exited the studio, arms folded across his chest.

"It's your day off," I told him as I crossed the parking lot.

He shrugged, straightening. "There's no such thing as a day off in my job. I get a lot of free time, it's no big deal."

"So ... what? You're going to follow me around like a creeper?"

"Isn't that what Karl pays me to do?"

"I don't recall that being in your contract, no." I unlocked the car, then sighed when Miles plucked the keys from my hand.

"You've been drinking. The last thing you need is a ticket."

"I had *one* beer hours ago."

"Doesn't matter." He pointed to the passenger side. "Where are we going?"

We both climbed in before I replied. "Malibu," I said finally.

"You haven't been there since before leaving for the tour."

I shrugged, tipping my head against the headrest and closing my eyes. "I bought the place, I should probably use it occasionally."

Miles didn't answer until we were ten minutes down the road. "What's the real reason?"

I cracked open one eye. "For what?" I knew what he was asking, I just wanted to see if he'd come out and say it.

"We're going to the house in Malibu. You always complain it's too quiet."

"It *is* too quiet. Maybe that's what I need right now."

He harrumphed and I smiled.

"Like I said … what's the real reason?"

I opened the glove box and pulled out a battered packet of cigarettes. Taking one out, I stuffed it between my lips and flicked open my lighter.

"Gonna smoke that?" Miles asked with a frown.

I narrowed my eyes at him.

"Just askin'," he responded to my glare with a mild look. "No need to bite my head off."

I crumpled up the cigarette and threw it out of the window. "If I stay in the city, I'm going to go to Harper's place."

"Any reason why you shouldn't do that?"

"I'm waiting for her to call me."

"Haven't you been waiting for her to do that for a hundred years now?"

"It needs to be her choice." I bounced my head off the back of the seat and straightened. "Right?"

"You're asking my opinion?"

"No, I'm asking the fucking chicken on the back seat. Yes, I'm asking you!"

"I don't know this girl, Gabe. But from the little time I spent with her, I'd say you have to be all in or all out with her. There's no middle ground. If you want her, fight for her. If she's just something to pass the time, leave her alone. She's not that kind of girl." He paused to check traffic and took us onto the Pacific Coast Highway. "Are you waiting for her to call you, so you have an excuse when it fails or are you too scared to even try? Maybe she's waiting to see if you want to make the effort to keep her, thought about that?"

I sliced a glance at him. "You think she's waiting to see if I break first?"

"Interesting choice of words. Do you think she'll see you as weak if you contact her?"

"When did you become my therapist?"

"When Karl hired me." He pressed a button on the keys to open the gates to my house. "Look at it from her point of view. You have a reputation for not dating. A night here, an afternoon there. If you're serious about her, you need to prove it. Your past history with women isn't exactly a glowing recommendation."

"Fuck."

He pulled the Mustang to a stop outside the main doors

but didn't cut off the engine. "Are you planning on staying here tonight?"

I looked up at the house. It was in darkness ... empty, silent, cold—a little like my personal life.

Maybe one day it would light up with laughter and warmth ... but not today. I'd bought it on a whim, but hated everything it represented—the rich, shallow, asshole rock star I presented to the world.

"Let's go," I said quietly and felt the car roll forward.

※

"Do you want me to wait?" Miles asked.

I shook my head. "No."

"Very confident about your reception, I take it."

I flashed him a grin and got out of the car. "Closer to desperate and hopeful, I think. But I'm a big boy, I think I can handle calling an Uber if things go south."

"Call *me* if things go south. And don't argue," he added when I drew breath to argue. "It's what I'm paid for."

"Yes, boss," I quipped and headed inside Harper's apartment block.

I knew Miles wouldn't drive away until he was sure I was inside. He's hyper-focused like that. Inside the building, I took in the wallpaper peeling from the walls, the stained flooring, and it reminded me of where we'd grown up. Hand to mouth, her mother working all the hours she could to put food on the table for her only daughter.

There was a cluster of potted plants near her front door and I frowned. *She didn't ... did she?* I crouched and lifted each one, then swore quietly when a key dropped out from beneath one of the pots. Palming it, I rose to my feet and pushed it into the lock. The door opened with a quiet click and I slipped inside.

The apartment was quiet, and I moved stealthily through it to where I assumed Harper's bedroom was and eased the door open carefully. I could see the shape of her body beneath the covers, the spill of her hair across the light-coloured pillows and, without really thinking about how it might look, I crawled onto the mattress behind her, wrapped an arm around her waist and buried my face into the crook of her neck, breathing in her scent.

She rolled over without waking, winding her arms around my hips, her fingers burrowing beneath the back of my t-shirt and pressing against my spine. It was like old times when I'd sneak into her room and just lie with her after going a round or two with my da. Back then, her presence had soothed my battered soul, eased the physical pain caused by the man who was supposed to be my protector. Relaxation came easily—more than it had in the time we'd been apart—and I fell asleep thinking about all the times she'd allowed me to simply be ... at peace in the circle of her arms.

CHAPTER 32

SLEEPING IN - ALL TIME LOW

Harper

PRESENT

My alarm woke me, its beeping loud in the early morning. I stretched over to silence it and froze. I was sprawled out on top of a body—a body which was taking up most of my bed. More specifically, my t-shirt clad body was pressed intimately onto a naked tattoo-covered chest. I pushed up on one elbow and looked down at the real-life rock star sleeping soundly beneath me. I didn't need to uncover his face, which had a tattooed-forearm thrown across it—*and was that a snowflake on his wrist?* It looked a lot like the necklace he'd given me—to know who it was. I'd know this body blindfolded. The question was, however, why was he in my bed and when had he arrived here?

My alarm, which I'd forgotten about, sounded again, louder this time and Gabe stirred. His hand found my hip, squeezed, and he groaned.

"Fuck's sake, Frosty. Turn the screeching off." His gravelly morning voice was the stuff fantasies are made of.

His arm moved, searching out my phone and blindly stabbing at the power button until it switched off the noise *and* my cell.

"Better," he grunted and turned, wrapping his big, warm and—did I mention?—half-naked body back around mine. "Just like old times," he muttered, his lips kissing a lazy path down the back of my neck and his hand found its way under my t-shirt to palm my breast.

My traitorous body responded immediately and I fought to stop myself from arching into his touch. He was half-asleep and probably not even conscious of what he was doing.

"It's nothing like old times," I managed to reply, squirming away from the thumb brushing across my nipple. "I never woke up to you groping me."

"Big mistake." His teeth latched onto my earlobe and he nipped it gently. "All those lost opportunities."

"I have to get ready for work."

"Take a sick day." His finger joined his thumb and he rolled my nipple between them.

"So you can get a booty call?" Summoning every ounce of willpower I owned, I pushed his hand away and climbed out of bed. "I'm not here for when you're bored and horny, Gabriel."

He settled onto his back, eyes hooded as he watched me. "I

wasn't horny until I had you in my arms." I rolled my eyes and he laughed quietly. "You don't believe me."

"I see no reason to believe you." I looked pointedly at the erection straining in the jeans he still wore, sadly. No, not sadly—fortunately! A fully naked Gabe in my bed was not what I needed. What I wanted, maybe, but I wasn't even going to think about that! "How did you get in here?"

"You keep a key in your flower pots. That's a stupid risk, Harper." He lifted up onto one elbow. "Anyone could get in here. What are you thinking?"

"At the time, I thought it was handy if one of us forgot our keys and the other wasn't home. Now though, I see your point. After all, *someone* did get in here." I threw another look at him, which he ignored.

"Spend the day with me."

"I've got to work."

"Call in sick."

"Gabe," I said slowly, pretending I was talking to a five-year-old and not a twenty-eight-year-old man. "If I don't work, I don't get paid."

"What do you earn for a day's work?" He picked his wallet up from where he must have thrown it on the floor when he sneaked into my apartment. "I'll cover it."

I scowled at him. "Did you just offer to *pay* me to spend the day with you? That's sad, Gabe. You must have friends to annoy."

"It is sad. I'm pathetic and lonely." He pouted and I fought down a laugh. "Don't you feel sorry for me?"

I didn't reply, opting instead to run from temptation by getting out of my bedroom. He rolled off the mattress and followed me out into the main living area. Siobhan was already up and drinking coffee. Her eyebrow rose at the sight of Gabe, still half-naked, stalking along behind me.

"Come on, Frosty. Throw me a bone, I'm desperate here."

"You already have a bone of your own." I let my eyes drop to his groin. "And you're not desperate. You're just bored and looking for entertainment."

"That's harsh, Harper. Tell her, Roomie." His grey eyes swung to Siobhan.

"Ignore him," I told her, before she responded. "Just pretend he's an annoying ghost or something."

"Ghosts aren't usually that good looking," she replied, peering at him over the top of her mug. "Or quite so ... *present*." She smirked, her eyes dipping below his waistline.

I rolled my eyes. "Don't encourage him."

"She should absolutely encourage me. I need moral support ... and coffee."

I sighed and took a second mug out of the cupboard, pouring him a black coffee and handing it to him before busying myself making my own. The truth of it was I couldn't look at him without thinking back to the night of the premiere. Of the things he'd done to me, the things *I'd* done while he *watched* me.

That was the reason why I hadn't called him—not that he'd

asked. I didn't trust myself not to let him talk me into doing it again, doing *more*. He'd hurt me once. I wasn't sure I could survive him doing it again.

"I agree with him," Siobhan said into the charged silence. "You should take the day off. Go, have some fun. Have a long weekend. Let him spoil you." Her eyes dropped again and I knew she didn't mean he should buy me gifts.

"I'd love to spend the weekend spoiling her," Gabe replied, his grin making it clear he'd picked up on her true meaning.

He settled onto one of the kitchen chairs, the picture of relaxation and male perfection, and raised his mug.

I pursed my lips. "What are your plans for the day?" I asked him.

"I have a meeting at eleven with Karl and the rest of the band. Do you remember him?" He waited for my nod. "After that, my schedule is completely empty. We could take a drive out to Point Dume."

"Point Dume," I repeated. When Gabe had first got his car, we'd scraped a picnic together and spent the day there. Just me and him. I had photographs of that day stuffed in a box under my bed.

He shrugged, drawing my eyes to the sculpted muscles covered in dark tattoos. "I haven't been there in a while. Maybe some fresh sea air will do me good."

"And maybe some of your more *enthusiastic* fans will throw you off the cliff."

"You should wait until I put you in my will before you murder me, Frosty. But I feel all warm inside now I know you're a fan." He smirked at me over the rim of his mug.

Somehow between him and Siobhan, I found myself agreeing to take the day off work and an hour later, I was in the passenger seat of Gabe's Mustang, which had been dropped off by Miles while I was showering and getting dressed.

"I need to make a quick stop at the penthouse," Gabe said as he pulled away from my street. "Is that okay?"

I nodded, pretending to fiddle with my phone. We were alone in his car, although I could see Miles following behind us in a nondescript sedan. Gabe's hand settled on my leg, just above my knee, and squeezed.

"Frosty? No pressure, okay? We'll have a day, pretend we're eighteen again with the years ahead of us."

I bit my lip. When I was eighteen I'd made a decision that had cost me our friendship, and I'd lost him from my life.

Tattooed Memories

CHAPTER 33

IS THIS LOVE? (COVER) - BLACKTOP MOJO

Harper

AGE 18

The party was in full swing when I arrived, and everyone was either high, drunk or both. I wasn't supposed to be here, hadn't *technically* been invited, but I needed to see Gabe. I tried to call him but he hadn't picked up, and I knew he'd been back in town for a couple of weeks.

The last six months had been weird. I knew Gabe was busy with his band. They'd signed with NFG Records, which was also owned by their manager, and he had them going all over the country, boosting interest in their music. Gabe had tried to keep in touch as much as he could, dropping texts and calling me. But as time went by, and his schedule became more gruelling, our contact slowly lessened.

But now he was home and I needed to talk to him—he was my person, the one constant in my life and I *needed* him right now.

I pushed through the crowds, searching him out without success, but I spotted Luca and Dex off to one side so changed direction and fought my way to them.

"Hey, baby girl," Luca greeted me, reeling me in for a hug. With Gabe nowhere near, he made none of his usual lewd comments or tried to grope me. "Can I get you a drink?"

I shook my head. "I'm looking for Gabe."

His smile was tired. "Of course you are. Does he know you're here?"

"No." My eyes scanned the room. "I tried calling him."

"He's with Lucy."

"Oh." I bit my lip. Lucy was a girl he hooked up with. He said she *wasn't* his girlfriend, but they always seemed to end up together at parties or after gigs.

"Sorry, baby girl." Luca hooked his arm around my neck and pulled me into his body. "I think he's the only one blind to how you feel about him."

"You should confront him." Dex nudged Luca out of the way and took his place. I buried my face against his shoulder, inhaling the scent of smoke and weed.

"That's an idea," Luca agreed. "Force him to acknowledge it."

"I just need to talk to him," I mumbled against Dex's shirt.

Dex's fingers wedged beneath my chin and tipped my head up. He peered at me. "What's happened, Harper?" The shrewdness in his blue eyes belied his reputation as a stoner, and I suddenly realised what you saw with Dex was not always what was real.

I blinked and lowered my lashes, shielding my eyes from his piercing gaze. "I got some news today … I just … I need to talk to Gabe." I bit my lip to stop it trembling. My world was falling apart around my ears and I needed to cling to the only life-raft I had.

The two men exchanged a look and then Dex nodded. "He's upstairs. Go up, turn left. The fourth door. That's where you'll find him. Lucy left an hour ago."

I peeled away from Dex, and Luca caught my arm. "Harper, for what it's worth, you have nothing to lose. If you carry on the way you are, you'll lose him. If you tell him how you feel and he doesn't feel the same, you'll lose him." He shrugged broad shoulders. "Just go for it. He won't turn you away. At the very least, you'll have a fucking nice memory to keep you warm."

I found my way to the stairs and headed up, counting the doors and stopping outside the fourth. Licking dry lips, I pushed it open and went inside. The room beyond was in darkness, the blackout curtains keeping any street lights and moonlight from getting in. I let the door swing shut behind me, which muted the noise from downstairs a little, and waited for my eyes to adjust to the darkness of the room before venturing further inside.

"Gabe?" I whispered his name, suddenly unsure whether Luca would have sent me upstairs knowing Gabe was with Lucy. He had a warped sense of what was funny. "Gabe?" I hissed his name louder.

"Hey, babe." That distinctive rasp, heavy with sleep, sounded in the darkness. "Didn't think I'd see you tonight. Get over here."

I crossed the room and took his outstretched hand. He pulled me down onto the bed beside him, and snaked an arm around my waist.

"I thought about calling you, then Luca and Dex arranged this fucking party," he continued, rolling to pin me beneath him. The faint smell of whiskey reached me. "Then I came up here and crashed." His hand slipped beneath my top and covered my breast. "But I guess you're a mindreader, huh, *Luce*, because I'm fucking horny as shit."

I stiffened. He thought I was his maybe-girlfriend. I knew I should tell him he was mistaken, that it was me and I did draw breath to speak, but his lips were pressing hot, open-mouthed kisses to my throat and his fingers were plucking at my nipple and my mouth dried up.

I felt cool air on my skin as he pushed up my top and then his mouth was on my breasts, his tongue tracing over the sensitive peak of one while his fingers toyed with the other. I held still beneath him, unsure what to do. I wanted to touch him, kiss him, but was scared he'd realise it was me. I knew it was wrong staying quiet, but being with him like this was everything I'd dreamed about, everything I wanted. I didn't want my first time to be with some boy with school. I wanted it to be with Gabe.

His other hand caught my wrist and dragged it between our bodies, pressing my palm against his erection and I bit back my startled gasp at finding him naked. My fingers curled automatically around his hard length and he groaned against my breast.

"Feels good, babe," he whispered. "Feels ..." he stilled, head lifting and I could see the shadow of him looking down at me in the darkness.

I couldn't see his face ... I was sure he couldn't see mine, but something about the way his head canted made my heart beat rapidly, and I waited for him to say my name. His head lowered, hovered close to mine and then his lips were on my throat again, nibbling his way down to my breast.

"Hmm," I heard the rumble of his voice, felt the vibration against my skin. "Do you want me to stop?"

I shook my head mutely and his tongue flicked out to lick at my skin.

"Tell me if it's too much," he whispered and folded my fingers around his erection, slowly moving my hand up and down.

He felt hot under my palm—smooth, silky, and hard. Not at all how I expected and I tightened my grip. A moan escaped him and I immediately slackened my fingers.

"No ... no, that's good," he told me. "Keep going ... just like that." He used his own hand to guide mine, showing me what he liked, how fast or how slow to move. His mouth teased my nipples, biting and licking each peak before sucking it into his mouth.

My back arched on a gasp and one of his hands slipped beneath my body. He rolled, and I found myself above him, legs either side of his hips as he sat up to continue his assault on my nipples with his mouth.

"You're wearing a skirt ... almost as if you planned this." His palm ran up my thigh, pushing the material along with it.

I looked down. I hadn't changed since leaving school for the day and was still in my uniform—pleated skirt and a plain white short-sleeved blouse. I'd been in too much of a hurry to find Gabe after my mom had told me ... I faltered, my breath hitching, as I remembered why I'd come to find him. Then his fingers slid beneath my panties, slowly eased inside me and my thoughts splintered.

"Steady," he whispered, his hand holding onto my hip as I jerked against his intrusion. "Nice and slow." His thumb brushed over my clit and I cried out, throwing my head back. "Do you like that? Harder ... softer? Tell me," he coaxed.

I briefly wondered why he was asking what I liked when he so obviously thought I was Lucy, but I didn't dare speak. Instead I did what he'd done and placed my hand over his to show him how I liked to be touched. I might not have been with a man, but I had explored my own body, and in the darkness of the room I could be brave enough to show him. Our fingers tangled, grew slick with my wetness and he groaned, his head dropping to rest against my breast.

"Fuck ... you're messing with my control, baby. I need to be inside you."

The thought of taking him inside my body made me clench

around his finger.

"Tell me to fuck you." He tumbled me backwards and leaned over me, pushing my legs apart with his thigh. "Tell me you want me inside you." I felt him drag my panties down my legs, and then he came down over me. "I'm not going to fuck you until you speak, baby."

I could feel him pressing against me, ready to push inside and I clutched at him, trying to drag him forward. He didn't move, leisurely stroking himself as he waited.

I cleared my throat, attempted to sound like Lucy. "Please."

"The whole sentence," he demanded. "Say 'I want you to fuck me, Gabe.'"

"I ... I ..." I stuttered.

He bent his head, his mouth close to mine. "A bargain, then. I'll feed you an inch for every word. How does that sound? That'll be seven inches for the sentence, and then I'll give the rest as a reward."

"I ... I want ..." I felt him move, pushing the tip of his dick inside me and I tensed.

"Come on, baby, five more words to go," he whispered against my throat.

"I want you ... to ... to ..." He was further inside, I could feel him stretching me, filling me.

"Nearly there." His voice was strained, his teeth clenched. "Just a little more. You need to relax or it'll hurt. I don't want to hurt you."

"Oh god," I panted, swallowed and then blurted, "I want you to fuck me, Gabe." His name was a scream as he slammed his full length inside me and the pain … oh *god*, the pain of his intrusion.

He stayed still, almost as if he knew I needed time to adjust. One hand lifted and his knuckles brushed down my cheek.

"That's it. It's okay … just breathe." He kissed my lips, my eyes, my cheeks, murmuring nonsense while he held himself above me, *inside* me, and I breathed through the pain.

I felt strange, full, stretched wide, an unfamiliar pressure pulsing between my legs, and then he began to move, slowly at first, picking up his pace when my nails sank into his thighs. He held himself up, braced on one arm, the other hand between my legs, teasing my clit as he thrust into me.

Could he see me? Had his eyes adjusted to the darkness of the room? Was he watching me? The idea of his eyes taking in my body, splayed out beneath him, made me hot, wetter, and my hips arched up eagerly to meet his thrusts. I leaned up on my elbows, wanting to see him possessing my body and his palm wrapped around the back of my neck, holding me in place while he devoured my mouth with his.

I could feel my nerves tightening, his fingers flicking my clit, his tongue mimicking the actions of his dick, thrusting into my mouth, and I chased the feeling, my body pulsing around his. As my orgasm hit, he tore his mouth from mine and gripped my chin, forcing me to look at him.

"You're a fucking terrible actress, Harper," he ground out, and slammed into me, curses spilling from his lips as he came.

Chapter 34

CHICAGO – HIGHLY SUSPECT

Gabe

Age 20

I stood beneath the shower, one arm braced against the wall, and my eyes closed as the hot water rained down on me.

What the fuck have I done? The second I realised it was Harper, I should have sent her away. What was I thinking?

I gave an angry shake of my head. I knew *exactly* what I'd been thinking. It was *Harper* in my bed and I was greedy. I wanted her there, had wanted her there forever, but knew if we took that step … *nothing* would keep her from me. She'd drop everything, *change every plan she had*, so she could support my dreams.

And for what?

So she could be dragged around the country in a dirty old van, staying in seedy motels, watching women paw at me, so I could chase the rainbow? No, I couldn't do that to her.

She had a scholarship at UCLA and planned to become a nurse. She had an actual chance to get out of the dives we'd been raised—or, in my case, dragged up—in, and I wasn't going to take that away from her. It was bad enough that her career choice was because of *me*. If she hadn't spent so many years patching me up, she would have probably found a different career path.

I scrubbed a hand down my face. If I sat her down and explained all that to her, she wouldn't listen, and I knew I would cave because it was *Harper*. No, it had to be quick and brutal. I had to give her no chance to fight me on it.

I took my time washing and drying, then dressed. Half of me hoped she'd already left, but I knew her. She would be waiting for me, fucking stars in her eyes, heart full of hopes and dreams—all of which I'd have to destroy. My steps were heavy as I walked down the hallway back to my bedroom.

The party was still going downstairs. I couldn't have come upstairs more than a couple of hours ago, yet it felt like a lifetime had passed. Everything had changed, and it was about to get worse. I pushed open my bedroom door and stepped inside, my eyes immediately searching out Harper.

She was lying on my bed, her back to me, skirt still ruched up around her waist. My dick stirred at the sight and I squashed it down ruthlessly. I couldn't succumb to the temptation she posed. Instead I focused on the fact that she'd come to me still wearing her school uniform. And the dirty guilt I felt over that was real. I was twenty, she was still at school. It didn't matter that she was eighteen, perfectly legal. She was a fucking school girl—at least for another couple of months. And she'd crawled into my bed in her uniform. And I'd let her. I'd taken advantage of her.

Had she thought dressing like that would turn me on? Had she listened to her friends talk about male fantasies? I embraced the anger, stoked the flames, used it to drive me forward and shake her shoulder.

"Wake up." My voice cracked like a whip and she jerked under my touch, her unique eyes blinking up at me.

"Gabe …" she whispered my name, her lips curving into a welcoming smile.

I steeled myself against the desire to wrap her in my arms. "Get the fuck up, Harper, and cover your fucking ass."

Her hand reached for her skirt, tugging it down self-consciously. I crouched, found her panties on the floor and threw them at her. "Get dressed."

"Gabe, I don't … Why are you angry?"

"Why am I angry? You're fucking asking me that? Seriously?" I snapped. *"I thought you were Lucy. You crawled into my bed, let me fuck you, let me think I was fucking my girlfriend and didn't say a word."* I'd only thought it was Lucy for a few seconds when she walked in. I'd known for sure it was Harper the second I put my hands on her. One touch was all it took for me to know I couldn't do the right thing and send her away.

"But—"

"But nothing. What the fuck were you thinking?"

She scrambled to her knees, eyes wide. "I wasn't … I didn't … Gabe, I—"

"Don't. You come in here, dressed like a fucking school girl and act like a whore. Did you even know it was me? Or would any dick have done?"

She flinched, face draining of colour.

"Get out, Harper." I turned my back on her. I couldn't watch the tears in her eyes when they fell.

I heard her moving around behind me and then her hand touched my arm. I stepped away, shrugging her off. If she touched me, if I *allowed* her to touch me, I would break. I couldn't break. She deserved more than I could give her. She deserved someone less dirty than me. I closed my eyes and waited until I heard the door swing open.

"Lose my number. I don't want to hear from you again," I threw at her to drive the final nail home and heard her choked sob as she fled.

Fuck.

I waited a few minutes before following her downstairs. My hope was that she'd left immediately, but as I walked down the stairs and spotted her wrapped in Luca's arms, I realised I should have known better. My bandmates looked at her like a little sister, they were almost as protective of her as I was, and they must have known something was wrong when she appeared.

It had to be fucking *Luca* though, didn't it. He liked Harper a *little too much*. Stalking across the room, I shut off the music.

"Everyone out," I snarled.

There was a beat of silence, followed by protests. I folded my arms and stared them down. Dex moved up beside me.

"You heard the man. Time to go. Party's over."

My eyes didn't leave Luca, while Dex shoved and pushed people toward the door. Luca stared back at me over the top of Harper's head. When just the four of us remained, I crossed the room.

"I told you to get out," I said to Harper. Luca's eyes narrowed at me. "You got something to say?" I challenged him. Luca and I butted heads a *lot*, but I knew he would pick the band over a girl every single time.

His hands dropped from Harper's back and I nodded.

"We're done here. Give me your phone." I plucked it from Harper's hand before she could stop me, punched in her password and deleted my number. "Now leave."

Deleting my number didn't mean shit, I knew that. Harper knew it from memory, but it was the action, that final act, which would cut the deepest.

"G-Gabe."

I forced myself to meet her reddened eyes, kept mine devoid of emotion. "You crossed a line, Harper," I told her, turned on my heel and walked away.

I hadn't made it three steps before she was in front of me.

"Is this who you are now?" she hissed, and I could see the anger finally taking over her emotions. "Is this what you've become?"

"It's who I've always been. You were just too blind to see it."

The crack as her palm hitting my cheek was like a thunderclap in the silent room.

"I hate you," she whispered, spun and ran.

My eyes closed and my shoulders sagged. It was done. There was no coming back from what I'd just put her through.

Fuck.

Tattooed Memories

CHAPTER 35

WHY WORRY - SET IT OFF

Harper
PRESENT

I stood at the floor-to-ceiling window, which spanned one wall of the main sitting room in Gabe's penthouse apartment. He'd offered me a drink, walked over to the fire escape he'd shown me the last time I was here and unlocked the door, then left me so he could take a shower and change.

I smiled to myself. To most people, it seemed weird, foolish even, how I couldn't settle in an apartment until I knew where all the fire exits were. They assumed, wrongly, that I was scared of heights. Gabe, though, knew exactly what caused it. It was the simple things, like taking the time to show me how to get out, which reminded me of the boy I'd grown up with instead of the young man who'd broken my heart or the rock star who'd whispered dirty things down the phone line to make me come for him.

The view from the window was stunning. We were high up

enough to look out over the city, away from the noise of the streets below. I could understand why Gabe had chosen to live here.

"Ready to go?" A warm arm wrapped around my waist and pulled me back against his body.

"Are you sure it'll be okay?" I asked. "It's a band meeting, isn't it?"

"It's fine. I've already told them you're coming. We just need to confirm we're doing a gig at Roth's then we'll be out of there."

I turned to face him, and his arm dropped away. "I always knew you'd make it, you know."

"My first fan." His voice was unreadable.

"And all I got was this lousy t-shirt," I attempted to joke, to lighten the sudden heaviness in the air.

His smile was faint, and his knuckles brushed over my cheek. "I'll make it up to you."

My heart began to pound. There was a promise in his words, an acknowledgement of ... *something*. I licked my lips and took a step backwards, forcing myself to smile. His eyes dropped to my lips, then slowly rose to meet my gaze.

"We should go," he said but made no move to leave.

I nodded jerkily, the air in the room thickening with tension, a sense of anticipation, and then his cell blared into life and the spell was broken.

He cursed, pulled it from his pocket and connected the call.

"I'm on my way," he said without asking who was calling. He listened to the reply, his eyes flicking to me briefly. "Say that again?" His brows pulled together and he spun away, his hand raking through his hair. "When? *Fuck*! No, Miles is downstairs. I'll get him to drive us." He paused again. "Ten minutes." He hung up and swung back to face me.

"Is something wrong?" I asked.

"No. " He sighed. "Maybe? Karl said someone was lurking around outside his offices. She's a known face." He blew out a breath. "One of the less entertaining aspects of this job is it attracts some strange people."

"A stalker?"

"Not quite that bad. Just a slightly obsessive fan. She turns up every now and then. Makes outlandish claims." He shrugged. "She'll go away eventually."

My thoughts went back to the text message I'd received after I'd spent the day with him. *Should I mention it? Was it worth bothering him with? I hadn't heard anything else, so maybe it was just a one-time thing.* I decided against raising it for now.

"Do you want to cancel our trip out?" I asked instead and his frown deepened.

"No. Some crazy chick isn't going to spoil our plans." He turned, grabbed a jacket from the back of the couch and held out his hand. "Come on, Frosty."

I let him thread his fingers between mine and pull me out of the apartment and into the waiting elevator. He released my hand long enough to pull on his jacket and place a baseball cap onto his head, pulling down the bill.

"Does this elevator stop on any other floors?" I asked.

"Nope, it's private. My use only. There used to be a keycode, but a crazy fan discovered it and got into my place one night."

"That sounds scary."

He shrugged. "I wasn't home, thankfully. But it made me a little more focused on security. Now there are keys for the elevator. I have one, Miles, Seth, and Karl have one each. Another floats between Dex and Luca. Everyone else has to call up for me to send the elevator down to them." A slow smile spread across his face and he turned his head to look at me. "Or was there another reason you were asking?"

"No? I just noticed it hadn't stopped on any other floors each time I've used it."

"There are buttons for each floor, so, in theory, I *could* make it stop if I wanted to get out somewhere else." He paused and grinned. "There's also an emergency stop."

"Do *not* stop this elevator, Gabriel!" I moved to block the button and he laughed.

When the doors slid open, he took my hand again and we walked to the entrance of his building. I could see Miles standing on the steps outside. Gabe pulled the brim of his cap down so it shielded part of his face and we stepped outside.

"We've lost eyes on her for now," Miles greeted us. "But it's safer if I drive you to the meeting and then to wherever you want to go."

Gabe tensed beside me. "She's not ruining my plans."

"Would you rather she ruined your life?" Miles asked and I caught the glare Gabe sent toward him.

"I thought you said she wasn't anything to worry about?" I questioned him, and his hand tightened on mine.

"She's *not*. Miles is just being over-protective."

I looked over at Miles, who looked back impassively.

"Let's get you guys to the car," he said and led us to the car beside the steps.

Miles held open the door and I climbed in, Gabe close behind me. He dropped heavily onto the seat beside me and draped an arm across the backrest, his fingertips touching my shoulder.

With his other hand, he unlocked his phone and opened his email app. We drove in silence for a few minutes. I gnawed at my lip, thinking about the way he'd reacted hearing about this nameless fan and Miles' response. I *had* to tell him about the text I'd received. I was certain there was more to this person than he was telling me.

"Gabe?"

"Hmmm?" He looked up from his cell's screen.

"Does this fan threaten the people you talk to?"

"I've never heard of her doing that, no."

"Oh." Maybe it wasn't her, then.

He dropped his phone onto his lap. "Why?"

"No reason." There was no point in worrying him about it if it wasn't her.

"You're still a terrible liar. Talk to me."

I gnawed the inside of my cheek and he tutted. "Stop that. Has something happened?"

"I got a text a little while ago, the week after you took me to the bistro."

He sat forward. "What kind of text?"

"Warning me away from you."

"What the fuck, Harper? Why wouldn't you mention this? Do you still have the text?" He waited for the nod and then leaned forward and rapped on the privacy glass between us and Miles. The glass slid down. "Give me your phone," he told me.

"Gabe—"

"Give me your fucking phone." He snatched it out of my hand and passed it forward to Miles, who reached back, keeping one hand on the wheel. "There's a text from someone threatening Harper on here. Sort it out and get her a new number."

"Gabe, you can't just take my phone."

"Just did." He settled back and angled his head, so he could look at me. "Listen to me, Frosty. If you *ever* get any more messages like that, you tell me straight away, okay? I'm not fooling around about this. Promise me, you'll tell me."

"Gabe, it was just some weirdo." I tried to laugh it off.

"The last time a weirdo latched onto Gabe, he woke up with a knife to his throat while she told him how he was going to father her children." Miles said quietly from the front of the car.

My mouth opened, and I gaped at Gabe. "Seriously?"

"As a heart attack, Frosty."

"What happened."

"Lucky for me, Miles had seen her slipping into my hotel room and arrived just in time."

"And this woman who's been seen …"

"Is the one who's a little too friendly with knives, yeah."

There wasn't much I could say to that. Gabe was so matter-of-fact about the situation that I wasn't sure how to respond, so I settled for silence. I could feel him stealing glances at me the rest of the way to his manager's office.

When Miles pulled the car into the underground parking lot, Gabe caught my hand and lifted it to his lips.

"We good?"

"Until you screw it up, sure," I told him and was rewarded with a soft laugh.

"I'm not going to screw it up, Harper. I *am* going to screw *you* though … very soon." He winked at me and threw open the car door. "Maybe even tonight."

CHAPTER 36

PLAY WITH FIRE - SAM TINNESZ

Gabe

PRESENT

I loved the sound of her startled gasp at my words. When she climbed out of the car behind me, I reached for her hand again. She sent me a look from beneath her lashes, but didn't stop me and I let my thumb run over her inner wrist.

"Why did I find you in my bed this morning?" she asked.

"Why didn't you call me?" I retorted.

Her cheeks flushed and she turned her head to look around.

A thought occurred to me and I stopped. "Holy shit," I breathed. "You were embarrassed, weren't you?"

"No," she denied, but she wouldn't look at me.

"Yes, you were. By what? When we went to our old stomping ground or later?"

"Okay, yes!" she muttered. "You made me …"

"I never *made* you do anything. That was all you, I just made ... suggestions."

"But—"

I stopped and turned to face her. "But what?" My eyes drifted over her, masking a smile when I saw the outline of her nipples against her t-shirt. She was thinking about what she'd done, about the things I'd whispered to her, and she *liked* it. Her body liked it.

"Miles, we'll meet you up there," I told my security guard. "Tell Karl we'll be there in a few."

"Gabe."

"Beat it."

I heard his sigh, but knew he would do as I said. I reached out and flicked one of Harper's nipples with my forefinger.

"Feeling a little turned on there, Frosty?"

"It's cold in here."

"Is it *fuck* cold," I laughed and stepped closer, her head tipped back, eyes watching me. Keeping my movements slow, giving her time to say no, I tugged the hem of her shirt out of her jeans and slid my palm beneath it. "One day soon," I told her, running my fingers up over her stomach, "I'm going to spend an entire day just playing with these." I reached her nipple, pinched it, and saw her eyes darken. "I think you'd like that."

She didn't deny it. If anything, that little nipple between my fingers grew harder. I dragged her t-shirt up until her bra was uncovered, and slowly tugged the cups down, revealing those dusky pink tips. My mouth was watering before I even saw them.

"Gabe, shift your ass!" Seth's voice echoed across the parking lot and Harper's eyes went huge.

She lifted her hands to cover herself and I caught her wrists, holding them out to her sides. "He won't come over," I told her and leisurely bent to lick each nipple.

"Gabe, stop!" Her whisper was harsh, but her back arched in offering. An offering I accepted. My teeth closed over one stiff peak and I bit down, just hard enough to sting. A yelp tore from her throat and she pulled against my grip. "I can hear him. He's coming over." Her panicked whisper made me chuckle.

In no great rush, I straightened her clothes, covering her breasts just as Seth came around the corner. Harper's cheeks were burning with arousal and embarrassment. Seth's dark eyes flicked from her to me, and one eyebrow rose. I threw an arm across her shoulders and smirked at him.

"I don't want to know," he said before either of us could speak. "Karl sent me down for you."

"We better get moving then," I said. "We'll pick this up later."

After being greeted by the rest of the band, and a little more cautiously by Karl, Harper settled onto one of the luxury couches in the waiting room beyond Karl's office while we all went inside. I'd have taken her with me, but Karl had caught my eye and shook his head. The expression on his face told me this wasn't a time to push, so I didn't make a fuss about it.

We all took up position around his desk and waited for him

to begin.

"Did you manage to come to an agreement over the gig at Roth's?" he asked.

All eyes turned to me. "We'll do it," I said. "It's a no-brainer. We'll do a warm-up show at Damnation the night before, ramp up interest. Exclusive event. Limited tickets."

Karl nodded. "All right. I'll organise a meeting with Roth to iron out the details." His eyes swept across the four of us. "I don't have to tell you how proud I am of you, how far you've come since those early days." He stopped at me. "You gave up a lot to claw your way to where you are now."

I looked away.

"Gabe, don't shut me out."

"I'm not. I just know this speech and I'm not interested."

"You don't even know what I'm going to say," he argued.

"You're going to warn me away from Harper. Tell me no good can come of returning to a past I've buried. You're going to tell me that we're different people now, that what we had back then ... what *I* destroyed ... can't be revived."

You could have heard a pin drop in the room.

"Do you remember what I said to you after that first show Harper never showed up at?" Karl said, eventually. "You'd hung back from taking the stage, convinced she'd show up. She didn't and that night you gave everything you'd held back from her to the crowd instead. That night was the night you became the man you are now."

"That's not necessarily a good thing," I muttered.

"Are you sure about that?" he asked. "What did you have to offer her back then, Gabe?"

"Not everything is about money."

"I'm not talking about money."

I glanced around at the others, frowning. "What the fuck is this? Some kind of *intervention?*"

"No, of course not."

Seth snorted beside me. "Your crazy-ass stalker ex is back. This isn't an intervention, it's a 'you need to fucking be careful' TED talk."

"She wasn't my ex. I barely knew her," I protested.

"You fucked her after a gig," Dex pointed out. "For chicks like her, that's enough."

I groaned and tipped my head back, staring at the ceiling. "So what do you want me to do?"

"Go home. Stay home."

"You want me to hide?"

"View it as an opportunity," Seth suggested. "Ask Harper to stay with you. Reconnect. She'll love that."

I rolled my head sideways to look at him. "You've met Harper, right?"

Seth's lips twitched. "She might have changed over the years. From what I walked in on downstairs, she was more than happy to let you play your games."

I levelled a finger at him. "You wipe that memory from

your mind."

"No, I'm planning on going home tonight and taking advantage of what I saw. Spank bank material right there, buddy."

I growled and Seth laughed.

"I didn't see anything," he admitted. "Why do you think I shouted your name first? But if you keep stripping her in public, you're not going to keep her hidden from prying eyes for long."

I stiffened. *Did Seth know about the photographs?* I sent a cautious look at Karl, who shook his head.

"Do you all think I should go into hiding?" I asked.

"Don't be so dramatic." Luca rolled his eyes. "You just need to stay out of the way long enough to get rid of Meredith."

Meredith. *I sighed.* What a huge fucking mistake she was.

"Have you told Harper?" Seth asked.

"I had no reason to. Fuck, we've barely talked about anything."

"You're fucking lucky she's giving you the time of day," Luca muttered.

My head jerked around.

"I was there, remember," he continued. "I saw the mess you left her in."

"I had no choice. You sent her upstairs, you *knew* what would happen."

"I *thought* you'd see sense."

"This is an old argument," Seth spoke over us. "There's little point in rehashing it. If I'd known Harper was what you were hunting for that night at Damnation, I'd have knocked you out and locked you up."

"What is *that* supposed to mean?" I demanded.

Seth's smile was wry. "That girl makes you lose all reason. She always has."

"I've just got her back." I couldn't lose her again, not now.

"You wouldn't have fucking lost her in the first place if you hadn't behaved like such an asshole," Luca said.

"What do you want me to say?" I shouted. "I know what I did, Luc."

"Good, so fucking *fix* it," he bellowed back at me.

CHAPTER 37

SAY SOMETHING (COVER)- BOY EPIC

Harper
PRESENT

Gabe was distracted for most of the journey to Point Dume, his head buried into his cell. I wasn't sure if he was writing something or texting, but as the miles swept by, I could feel my irritation with him growing.

"You know," I snapped into the silence. "If you changed your mind, you could have just said so."

His head jerked up. "What?"

"We've been in the car for twenty minutes and you haven't said a word to me. You look furious and like you'd rather be anywhere but here. I get it, you're a badass rock star and your time is money, but—"

"What are you going on about?" he said over the top of me. "I never said I don't want to be here."

"That's my point!"

He looked confused. "*What's* your point?

"You keep blowing hot and cold. One minute you can't keep your hands off me, the next you act like I'm going to give you hives if you even look at me."

"Hives?" he repeated, his lip curling up in amusement. "I don't think you're going to give me hives."

"Then what's going on? I'm a big girl, Gabe. If you don't want to spend the day with me, just say so."

"I *do* want to spend the day with you. I just had to clear a few things." He tossed his cell onto the seat beside him. "I'm all yours now. You have my complete attention, I promise."

"Don't force yourself on my account," I muttered and turned my head to look out of the window.

It was foolish, I knew, being so annoyed. I shouldn't expect him to act the way he had when we were kids, where he always gave me his full attention whenever we were together. We were adults, we both had our own lives. His was clearly more full of drama than mine.

"Harper." His fingers touched my cheek. "Don't be angry with me. I had to arrange for extra security, that's all. It took a while to sort out."

"Extra security?" I twisted to face him. "For what? The crazy fan?"

"Yeah. She has a pattern. She'll show up, hang around outside the studio, Karl's offices, my apartment. Then she'll start sending me letters and gifts. At some point, the phone calls will start. I have no idea how she keeps finding my number. I change it so fucking often because of her. Eventually, it'll escalate into her trying to get to me, either by ambushing me when I leave somewhere or trying to get into the apartment."

"Can't the police do something?"

"They can move her along, give her warnings. But until she escalates to a point where I'm actually in fear for my life, there's not an awful lot they can do."

"That's terrible."

He shrugged. "It comes with the job."

I couldn't imagine living like that. Having to look over my shoulder constantly, worrying about someone behaving so crazy.

"Why does she think you're meant to be together?"

His eyes shifted away from mine. "We're on the road a lot … and we have a lot of fans who …" he shrugged. "I don't need to spell it out to you."

"You slept with her."

"Once."

"When? How long ago?"

"Five years ago. I had a lot on my mind and needed a distraction." He caught my hand. "I'm not gonna lie, Harper. I've had a lot of women in my bed, and I wasn't always particularly fussy about what their motives were. But I never made any of them think it was anything more than a hook-up."

"Is that what this is?" I pulled my hand free. "You've been on tour for what, eighteen months? Are you just looking for a bit of fun to ease you back into a daily routine?"

"Where the fuck is this coming from? No, that's *not* what this is."

"Then what is it, Gabe? You give my name to the papers, you take me to a premiere, you touch me like ... like ..."

"Like I can't get enough of you? Like I've missed you so fucking much that finally having you within my reach makes me desperate enough to take whatever opportunity presents itself so I can touch you, even if we could get caught?"

I stared at him. "You missed me?"

He threw me an exasperated look. "Haven't you been listening to anything I've said?"

"It's not always about what you say," I said quietly. "Sometimes what you do says more."

"So what have I done? What have my actions told you?"

He folded his arms across his chest and glowered at me.

"I *don't* know! If I knew, I wouldn't be asking, would I?" I threw myself back into the seat. I knew I was being childish, but I couldn't stop myself. "You appear in my life like you never left, crawling into my bed, acting like the boy I knew. Then you touch me, and kiss me, and all I can think about is the last time you did that and the things you said to me afterwards."

"You were fucking pretending to be someone else."

"And you knew it was me. You said so!" I yelled.

"You fucking knew I knew!" he roared back at me. "Don't pretend you were the innocent one that night, Harper. You wanted what I gave you. You knew how I felt about you. When I called you Lucy, you could have spoken up then, but you didn't. You wanted to be in my bed."

"But—"

"But *what?* You knew if you admitted it was you, I'd have put the brakes on. Just like I knew if I told you I knew it was you, you'd leave. We both wanted what happened, and we both knew it couldn't happen again. Not then."

"Why couldn't it? Why couldn't it happen again?" I demanded shrilly. "I wanted you, Gabriel. *All* of you. The good and the bad."

"And if I'd given it to you, where would we be right now? Not here, that's for sure. You'd have given up your scholarship. I wouldn't have been able to focus on the band. And we'd have resented each other for everything we couldn't do. Don't make me the bad dog in this scenario."

"It didn't matter! I lost the scholarship, anyway. I lost you. I lost my mom. I lost *everything!*" It was only when I fell silent that I realised I was screaming at him, tears streaming down my cheeks.

"Harper ..." his voice was soft in the silence of the car.

"Don't." I turned away, presenting him with my back and pressed my forehead against the cold glass of the window.

CHAPTER 38

CANCER - MY CHEMICAL ROMANCE

Harper

AGE 22

"Mom?" I called out, dumping the groceries onto the countertop. *"Mom?"*

She didn't answer me, but that wasn't unusual. How she behaved depended on her state of mind when she woke up. I crossed the living room and pushed open her bedroom door. She had the radio playing and I jolted when a familiar raspy voice sounded through the speaker.

Underneath the sadness,
Is a cold, dark rage,
Struggling to corrupt my soul
Tell me this is only a stage.

I swallowed and reached out to switch it off.

"Leave it!" my mother snapped from where she lay on the bed. "He was such a beautiful boy. I miss him."

"Well, that makes one of us," I muttered.

Never more will I wonder,
Never more will I cry.
Though I feel so empty
They will not let me die.

"I could fix that for you." I scowled at the old-style radio sitting on the dresser. "Just say the word, Gabriel. I'll happily let you die—screaming."

It had taken me a while, over a year, in fact, before I finally passed from the devastation stage Gabe had left me in and made the decision to move on with my life. Two more years had passed and now I resided firmly in anger. A feeling I didn't see myself moving beyond for a long time, since everywhere I turned I was reminded of him.

"Where did you go?" Mom asked me, and I turned around to see her sitting back against the pillows.

"Shopping. Have you been in bed all morning?" I moved over to fold back the sheets. "Why don't you come into the other room and watch some television?"

"Will Billy be back soon?" She took my hand and rose to her feet.

My mom wasn't even fifty, but she looked as frail as an eighty-year-old. She twisted her head this way and that. "Bill?" she called. "Billy?"

"Dad's not here, Mom," I told her. "You remember, don't you? It's just us."

Her fingers clutched my arm, her nails digging into my skin. "Where is he?" she demanded. "What have you done with him?"

"Mom—" My head snapped sideways with the force of her slap.

"I am *not* your mother!"

I took a steadying breath. "Why don't we go and have some lunch." I kept my voice calm and resisted the urge to rub my face. Drawing her attention to what she had done would make her cry. "Maybe Billy will be back then?"

"Yes, okay. He's probably at work."

Her outburst forgotten, she allowed me to take her into the living room and settled onto the couch to watch her favourite shows, while I prepared her some lunch. While she was distracted, I sneaked back into her room to switch off the radio. Gabe's band had been slowly gaining momentum over the past four years and had recently exploded into the stratosphere of fame. I couldn't move without seeing his face on the covers of magazines, on chat shows, on the internet.

One day I'd be proud of him. But I wasn't ready to take that step yet. I busied myself putting the groceries away, keeping one eye on my mom while she ate her lunch. I knew the time was coming when I'd have to look into finding some way of getting help for her. Her bad days were starting to outweigh her good ones, and I couldn't leave my job otherwise we'd have no money at all. But I also couldn't risk leaving her alone for long periods, not when she was starting to slip more and more.

I bit my lip. I had time. She wasn't there yet. We had time to figure this out.

"Harper?"

I looked up at her voice. She was waving a hand, wanting me to go to her. I closed the cupboard door and went over.

"Yes, Mom?"

"Look. Gabe's on television!" She pointed excitedly to the TV screen. She clapped her hands together when the camera zoomed in on his face. "Doesn't he look beautiful? Such a lovely boy. We haven't seen him for a while, have we? You should call him, Harper."

I swallowed back the laugh that bubbled up. "I'm sure he's busy, Mom."

"He'd make time for you." Her hands rose to cup my cheeks. "When I'm gone …"

"Don't say that."

"Harper, listen to me." Her tone was more serious than I'd heard in a long time. "I can feel myself drifting. I know there are times when I'm not myself. I don't want you to be alone when I'm gone. Promise me you'll call him."

"He doesn't want to see me, Mom. He's moved on from here."

She shook her head. "He's waiting for you, Harper. Look at him. He's looking around, searching." She turned my head to the TV. "You're supposed to be with him."

The cameras were still focused on Gabe who stood, with the rest of Forgotten Legacy, his gaze wandering over the crowds. He didn't even pretend to be listening to the questions the reporter was asking. A flash of silver caught my eye and I looked closer to see the old Zippo lighter he'd always carried around was in his hand, and he was flicking it open and closed.

I shook my head. "I'm sorry, but he made it clear a long time ago that he didn't want the same things as me."

"Okay, dear," she patted my cheek. "Do you know what I'd really enjoy? One of those iced teas from the diner down the road."

I quickly calculated the time involved. Ten minutes to walk there, then the wait depending on how busy they were followed by the walk back. No more than an hour.

"Okay, Mom. I'll go and get you one. Don't open the door, okay?"

I picked up my purse and, after one more look around, left the apartment, locking the door behind me.

※

I juggled the drink carton and bag with my purse while I unlocked the door and stepped back inside. The diner hadn't been too bad, and I'd made the journey there and back in just over thirty minutes.

"I got you one of those cream cakes you like," I called, kicking the door shut behind me. "Mom?"

The hairs stood up on the back of my neck.

"Mom?"

The apartment was quiet. *Too* quiet. The television was off, but I could see the shape of my mom sitting in the chair.

"Mom?" I repeated, my voice closer to a whisper.

I stepped toward her chair, my heart pounding. She must have fallen asleep, that's all. Switched off the television and took a nap while she waited for me. I touched her hand. She didn't react.

"Mom?" I knelt beside her chair and shook her gently. "Mom, wake up. Mom … Mom, please wake up."

But I knew she wasn't going to. She wasn't there. She'd gone … left me alone.

Tattooed Memories

CHAPTER 39

STAY - THIRTY SECONDS TO MARS

Gabe

PRESENT

"Miles, can you take us back home?" He glanced at me through the mirror and nodded, before pushing a button to close the privacy glass between the front and back of the car. "Harper," I repeated her name and her shoulders stiffened.

"I don't want to talk to you right now."

"Then just listen to me."

"No."

And with that snapped little word, I lost what little patience I had.

"I don't care. I'm going to fucking talk anyway."

She whirled around, her eyes blazing. "And doesn't that prove the problem? You don't give a fuck about anything other than what *you* want. You, *you, you*. It's all about you, isn't it, Gabe? The big badass rock star."

"Of course I give a fuck. Isn't that what this is all about? I give a fuck. I give *lots* of fucks. I give so many fucking fucks, I should be arrested for soliciting." I caught her shoulders and shook her. "Don't you get it, Harper? You and the band are all I give a fuck about. All this? The money, the music?" I threw a hand out, waving at the car's interior. "It's all yours, but you never fucking came to collect."

"You told me you never wanted to see me again!"

"I didn't fucking mean it!"

We were nose to nose, yelling at each other.

"How was I supposed to know that?" she demanded.

"How *didn't* you know that?" I retorted. "It's *us*, Harper. Me and you. You're the fucking air that I breathe, don't you get that?" And if my words didn't get the point across, I hoped my mouth would, so I kissed her.

She resisted. It wouldn't have been Harper if she succumbed straight away, but I didn't let the way she pressed her lips together deter me. I simply changed my focus. Releasing her shoulder, I ran my knuckles down her cheek, then slid my hand into her hair and cupped the back of her head. I pressed a kiss to the tip of her nose, across her still-damp cheeks, along her jaw.

"I was young and stupid," I whispered between kisses. "I couldn't see a way to give you what you wanted and keep you to myself, so I had to let you go. But I needed just one memory to take with me, to remind me what could be if I worked hard enough."

"You told me to leave you."

"I thought you'd come back."

"You deleted your number from my phone."

"You didn't need my number in your phone. You knew it better than I did." I nuzzled the sensitive skin behind her ear. "I kept that number for years. I left your name with security at every gig. I sent you tickets to Damnation all the fucking time. I told myself that I would be patient. I'd wait for you. Eventually, you'd reach out. You'd come and find me."

"Why didn't *you* come and find me?"

I leaned back, searching out her eyes. There was doubt in them and a world of hurt. I was the cause of both, which made me responsible for fixing it. The only way to do that was to bare everything to her, the unpolished truth and hope she forgave me. "I had it in my head that you had to make the decision. It had to be on your terms. And then you showed up at my club. I thought I was in control, that I could *make* you come back to me. But you walked away again and didn't even look back."

"So you went to the reporter."

I nodded. "An excuse to make you see me again."

"I still haven't read it," she admitted.

"You should. But I'll tell you what it said." My lips found the pulse beating at the base of her throat. "I talked about a girl I loved and lied to. How I convinced her I didn't want her, only to realise she was my anchor, my home."

"Gabe..."

"I told the reporter that eight years apart had made no

difference. I was still lost at sea without her. I am still as crazy in love with her now as I was the first day I met her. I told her that every song I sang, I sang for you."

I pulled away and sat back against the seat, letting my hand drop away from her face.

"What do you say, Frosty? Do I get a do-over?"

She didn't reply, tugging her bottom lip between her teeth as she stared at me. I waited, forced myself to be patient.

"I need some ground rules."

I almost sagged in relief. That wasn't a refusal.

"Name them." I'd sign over my entire fortune if that's what it took.

"There can't be any other women while you're with me."

"I don't *want* any other women."

"Now, you don't. But that doesn't mean you won't change your mind. You're used to a certain lifestyle. And, like you said, you go away a lot and there are always willing women."

"Harper, I don't want them. You can come with me as often as you want." I paused, unsure if that was what she wanted to hear. "Or as little as you want. It's up to you."

"If you decide you want out, you *tell* me," she pressed forward. "You don't sneak around behind my back until I find out on one of the chat shows or gossip sites."

I didn't like how she assumed that was going to happen. "I'm not going to do that."

"But you *might*."

I wouldn't, but if that's what she wanted to hear … "Fine. I swear I'll tell you. Is that it?"

I could see her trying to think up more ways to stall the inevitable. Her eyes gleamed when she found something and I swallowed a groan.

"No more groping me in public." Her voice was prim.

Oh, hell no. *"Nope."*

"What?"

"Sorry, can't agree to that one." There was no way I was going to stop touching her whenever I wanted to. Especially as she enjoyed it, too.

"Yes, you can. You shouldn't be doing things like that anyway."

"No. I *like* fooling around with you in public."

"I don't like it."

"When did you become such a fucking liar?" I smirked. I was on solid ground now. "Which, by the way, you suck at."

"How am I lying? If we got caught or reporters took photos, it'd be all over the internet! I don't want that kind of exposure." Her cheeks flamed when I arched my brow at her choice of words.

"What kind of *exposure* would you be comfortable with, I wonder."

"I'm not discussing this with you. Agree to it."

"Not gonna happen."

"Then we have nothing more to talk about." She folded her arms and scowled at me.

"Like fuck we don't." I felt the car roll to a stop and glanced out of the window. We were in the underground parking lot of my apartment building. I threw open the door, grabbed Harper's hand and rapped on the privacy screen. It slid down.

"Miles, take the rest of the day. We'll be up in the penthouse. I'll call you if I need you." I didn't wait for his response, dragging Harper out of the car and striding toward the elevator bay.

"I want to go home."

"That wasn't one of your ground rules." I found my key and shoved it in the lock, which opened the elevator doors. I pulled her in and pushed the button to take us up to the penthouse.

"Maybe not, but common decency means you should let me go." She yanked her hand free of mine and moved to the opposite side of the elevator car.

"I thought we'd already agreed I'm *not* decent?"

I followed her, step for step until she backed against the wall. My hands slapped onto the mirrored metal either side of her head.

"See, the problem I'm having with this whole no PDA thing," I continued, bending my head until our mouths were barely apart, "Is the way you react to them. If I thought for a second that leaning over to whisper how much I want to suck on your nipples or eat your pussy in the darkness of a theatre didn't get you wet, I wouldn't do it." I ran my tongue over my lips and lifted my eyes to meet hers. "But it *does* make you wet. It makes your nipples so hard, they could cut glass." Her eyes darkened, lips parting slightly as her breathing increased. "And that raises a question, doesn't it?" I lowered my voice. "If simply talking about it turns you on, what would acting on it do?"

I let one hand drop to curve over her hip, found the hem of her t-shirt and slid my fingers beneath it. "Three times now, you've let me *expose* you. I buried my face into your pussy and fucked you with my tongue. You stripped in your bedroom and spread yourself open for me, knowing anyone could walk past and see you. And today, in the parking lot, you wouldn't have stopped me if I'd carried on playing with your nipples when Seth showed up."

"I would—" she protested, but it was a weak lie.

I shook my head. "No, you wouldn't."

"I don't want Seth to touch me."

"Never said you did. But you wouldn't have stopped him watching while I fucked you. And I would do it if I thought that was your kink." My fingers crept up over her stomach, lifting her t-shirt. "But it's not. You don't actually want to be watched, you just like the idea of it. The potential danger of being caught, of being seen." I reached out with my other hand and hit the emergency stop, bringing the elevator to a halt. "There's a security camera in the top left corner behind me. It only switches on if I press the alarm on my keys." I dropped my head to press a kiss to her throat. "Do you trust me?" I peeled her t-shirt up over her bra before she replied, then pulled that up too so her breasts were free.

Her nipples were tight, puckered, the skin flushed. "Your

body doesn't lie, Harper." I took one hard tip between a finger and thumb and tugged, stretching it until she hissed. "You like a little pain. I noticed that the other day." I pinched it again. "Take the t-shirt and bra off." I brought my other hand up to her other nipple and teased them both as she obeyed my demand. Her tits bounced as she pulled the t-shirt over her head and I kept my grip on her nipples tight, forcing her to be a part of the way I tugged and pulled at them while she discarded her t-shirt and bra.

"Now your jeans," I told her and she flushed.

"Are you going to keep ..." she licked her lips, "doing that?"

I cocked my head. "No, I've got a better idea. *You* play with them and I'll remove your jeans."

Her eyes darted to the security camera and I smiled. "I haven't switched it on, but I will if you want me to."

"No!"

I pulled my keys out of my pocket. "Sure?"

"Gabe, no!"

Her nipples were so fucking hard in my grip, I wondered if it was an indication of how wet she was. Releasing one of her breasts, I reached down and popped the button on her jeans. Harper watched me, her breasts rising with each rapid breath she took.

"I don't see you playing with your tits for me, Frosty." I crouched in front of her. "If you take too long, someone will come and investigate why the elevator isn't moving." I pulled her jeans down her legs, taking her panties with them. "Do you want them to find you like this?"

Her hands went to her breasts, rolling and teasing her nipples with her fingers. I watched her for a minute. The view was incredible from where I was. Two perfect breasts between lavender tipped fingers, a flat toned stomach and a perfect pussy with just a hint of wetness slicking her inner thigh mere millimetres from my mouth.

I ran a fingertip through the damp curls in front of my face. "I'm going to enjoy fucking this."

My fingers spread her open, putting her clit on display for me, pink and glistening with her arousal. With my other hand, I took out my phone.

"What are you doing?" she asked, one hand dropping down to cover herself. I swatted it away.

"Taking a photo of the most perfect pussy in existence, so when we're apart I can look at it while I'm jerking off."

She liked that answer. Her breath hitched, her thighs tensed, hips rocking forward.

I laughed softly. "Are you posing for me? Open your legs wider then." Harper shifted, widening her stance as much as she could with her jeans still wrapped around her ankles. "Perfect." I leaned forward and swept my tongue over her clit. "Hold still for me." I snapped a couple of shots of her pussy, then licked her again. "Fucking gorgeous."

She groaned above me, so I ran my tongue over her pussy

and then thrust it inside her, taking deep long licks before dragging it back to her clit.

"Gabe!" Harper's voice was a choked whisper and her hand dropped to clutch at my hair.

I sucked on her clit, teasing it, feeling her fingers dig into my scalp as her orgasm built and just as she teetered on the edge, I pulled back and licked my lips.

"Gabe!" she protested, trying to haul me back.

I reached up to untangle her fingers from my hair and rose to my feet, hitting the emergency stop again, and the elevator jerked back into motion.

"You have about twenty seconds to get the rest of the way out of those jeans," I told her. "Once those doors open, I'm fucking you."

Tattooed Memories

CHAPTER 40

IRIS - GOO GOO DOLLS

Harper

PRESENT

They were the longest twenty seconds of my life. I just managed to get both my feet out of my jeans when the doors slid open.

Gabe smiled, his eyes gleaming. "Run, Harper," he whispered and I didn't even think.

I took off at a run across the reception area. He tackled me just as I reached the double doors, taking me to the ground. Before I hit the carpet, he rolled, cushioning my fall, and wrapped one hand around the back of my neck to pull my head down to his.

I could taste myself on his tongue when he pushed it between my lips, and the reminder of him licking at me sent a fresh surge of wetness between my legs. I groaned, trying to squeeze my thighs together, needing to ease the throbbing ache he'd left me with. His thigh pushed between mine, rubbed against my sensitive clit and I whimpered into his mouth.

"Take them off." I snatched in a greedy breath when his lips parted from mine. "Take your clothes off!"

His lips found my nipple. "You take them off." He rolled so he was above me.

I didn't need telling twice. My hands dove to his shirt, dragging it over his head, forcing him to part his mouth from my breast long enough to throw it to one side. Then I attacked his jeans. He laughed when I struggled with the button, but I finally got it open and tugged down the zip. He rolled onto his back, watching me with hooded eyes as I shoved the denim down his legs. He kicked them off, then grabbed me and tossed me onto my back. I landed on the thick carpet with a soft thud.

Gabe wasted no time. His hands were on my thighs, forcing them apart and then his mouth was on me again. Sucking, licking, flicking. My hips were jerking, my hands went to his head, pulling at his hair as he attacked my pussy. I panted, feeling my nerves tingling, and arched up, straining for the release I could almost taste.

And just as I almost fell, he stopped—*again*.

But this time he didn't give me time to protest. He crawled up my body, mouth finding mine, sucking my tongue into his mouth. And then I felt him ... sliding into me, my slick arousal making it easy for him to sheath himself inside my body. He went deep ... *deeper* ... and still kept filling me until I was stretched around him, completely possessed by the man above me.

His hand gripped my face, tilted it up, and he leaned back to look down at me, his grey eyes dark.

"This is how it should have been, Harper," he told me, his voice rough. "No pretence, no games. Just you and me." He sank his teeth into my throat, biting me, marking me. "You feel me inside you?"

I tried to speak but no words would come, so I nodded.

"This is where I belong. Inside you, on you, with you. Never doubt that."

He began to move then and this was no slow, sensitive lovemaking. It was raw and hard. His hips slammed against mine, driving himself deeper and deeper, branding me from the inside. My nails raked down his back, my teeth marked his shoulders, his chest, his throat.

We bit, we scratched, we drew blood and we *fucked*.

※

I woke up alone. The side of the bed where he'd lay was cool to the touch, meaning he'd been up awhile. I lay on my back, contemplating whether I could move. I wasn't sure I would be able to walk if I made it to my feet, but desperation drove me. I needed to pee.

I stifled a laugh. Not very romantic, but a necessary bodily function.

Carefully, wincing at the pull of over-worked muscles, I rose unsteadily to my feet, pulled one of the sheets from the bed to wrap around me and stepped out of the bedroom. I remembered where the bathroom was from the quick tour he'd given me the other day.

Once I was done, I went in search of Gabe. Walking into the main living room, I was surprised to see the sun still shining through the window. It felt like I'd been here for days, instead of a few hours, and I mustn't have slept for long. The balcony door was slightly ajar, so I guessed Gabe must be out there.

The quiet strumming of a guitar greeted me as I stepped outside. Calling it a balcony was like calling a child's paddling pool a luxury swimming pool. It was large, with high walls on two of the sides to shield it, I assumed, from being seen by the other apartments on other floors, and a high wrought-iron fence along the one which faced out over the city. I could see a barbecue set up along one side, and garden furniture scattered around.

Gabe was sprawled out on one of the loungers, an acoustic guitar resting on his thigh. His eyes were on me as I walked over to him. His fingers plucked at the strings, a half-smile on his lips. I laughed quietly when I recognised the tune as "Miss Jackson" by Panic! At The Disco. He sang the chorus to me as I settled onto the lounger beside him and I shook my head.

"So, Miss Jackson," he said, placing the guitar down beside him. "Are you?"

"Am I what?"

He rose and leaned over me. "Nasty," he whispered and dropped a kiss on my lips.

I bit his bottom lip and pulled back before he could retaliate.

"Only if the need arises."

He laughed and swung his leg over so he could straddle the recliner I'd chosen and regarded me thoughtfully as he sat down.

"Are you hungry?" he asked, and I got the distinct impression that hadn't been what he wanted to say. "We can order something if you are."

I hadn't been hungry until he mentioned it, at which point my stomach gave an unsexy rumble which made Gabe throw back his head and laugh. "I'll take that as a yes, then. Any preferences?"

I shook my head. "Whatever you want."

We finally settled on Italian, and Gabe put in the order, explaining to me that the delivery guy would buzz the elevator when he arrived with our food. It was then I remembered my clothes were still in the elevator. I shot upright, tripped over the sheet and would have tumbled if Gabe hadn't caught me.

"What's wrong?"

"My clothes!" I could feel my cheeks burning. "We left them in the elevator." I had to be thankful that it was a private one that only Gabe used.

I followed him as he walked inside, through to the reception area and called the elevator. The doors slid open almost immediately and I snatched up my clothes.

"I don't think I'll ever look at that thing in quite the same way again," he mused from behind me.

I glared at him. "I doubt it's the first time you've done that, being a rock star and all."

He gave an easy laugh. "Elevator sex, sure. Not in *this* one though, or with *you*." His eyes were warm as they tracked over me. "That makes all the difference, Frosty." He hooked his palm around my neck and pulled me into his body. "Stay tonight?"

I let myself lean against him, breathing in his scent. "I'd like that."

Tattooed Memories

Chapter 41

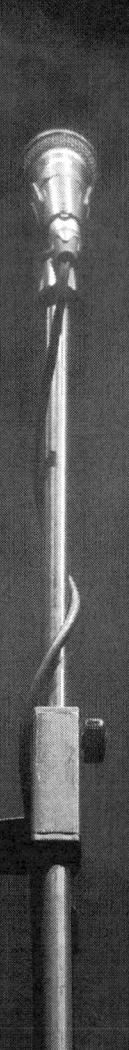

RIGHT LEFT WRONG - THREE DAYS GRACE

Gabe

PRESENT

There were food cartons scattered around the floor and a half-empty bottle of wine sat on the coffee table. We'd binged on food, squabbling like kids over who had more than their fair share of each dish. Afterwards, I opened a bottle of wine for her, and a beer for me, and we'd settled onto the couch to watch a movie, a comedy, I think. I couldn't actually tell anyone what it was. Harper was watching the movie. *I* was watching *her*.

She was tucked in front of me, one of my arms wrapped around her waist, holding her securely on the cushions, my other hand propping up my head. Her head was resting in the crook of my arm and, occasionally, she'd reach up to stroke the arm I'd draped across her stomach.

I watched the play of emotions crossing her face while she

focused on the film. The way her lips twitched in suppressed amusement at the, I'm guessing, funny parts. How her nose scrunched up when the lead actor did something she didn't think was right. And I realised I was content.

I could barely sit still for an hour, restlessness driving me to do something—*anything*—to keep my mind from dwelling on things I could do nothing about. But here I was, content to lie still so Harper could watch a movie in the comfort of my arms.

She leaned forward for her wine glass and leant up on one elbow so she could take a sip. I flattened my palm against her stomach to steady her balance. Her t-shirt—*my* t-shirt—slipped off her shoulder and I dipped my head to kiss the creamy skin it revealed. Her head tilted, baring her neck and I took the opportunity she offered, nibbling my way up to her ear. Reaching around, I took the glass from her hand and set it back down.

Twisting to face me, she wound her arms around my neck and we settled down for a serious make-out session, at least, we would have if my cell hadn't chosen that moment to ring.

"Ignore it," I muttered. "It's probably Seth." Her leg was hooked around my hip and her hands were making interesting progress down inside my sweats. There was no way I was picking a random phone call from Seth over what was happening here. My cell fell silent and I breathed a sigh of relief, only to groan when it started up again almost immediately. "Fuck's sake," I growled and stretched out a hand to grab it.

I punched the call button followed by the loudspeaker.

"What?" I snapped, and Harper buried her face against my shoulder to muffle her laughter.

"Where are you?" It was Karl at the end of the call, not Seth.

"Pent ... *fuck*." The curse left my mouth when Harper's hand curled around my dick and squeezed. "Penthouse," I said again.

"I'm on my way up."

"Wait, what? No, you—Fuck." He'd cut the call.

Harper gazed up at me, still stroking me with her soft hands and I groaned.

"Karl has an elevator key." I dropped my head against her shoulder. "We'll pick this back up later, yeah? I don't think he'll appreciate walking in to my dick in your mouth."

"Is that where it was going?" she asked, as I rolled off the couch and stood.

"It's where I planned to end up, temporarily, anyway." I held out my hand and tugged her to her feet, planted a kiss on her lips and swatted her ass. "Put some pants on before he gets up here." I bent to clear up the mess we'd left from our meal.

By the time Harper reappeared with her jeans back in place and looking presentable, the living room no longer looked like an Italian restaurant had hosted a party and the elevator door was opening to let Karl out, as well as Seth, Dex, and Luca.

Well, okay then.

"Dude, put some clothes on," Dex flicked a finger at my ribs as he walked past and into the kitchen.

"Looks like our baby girl found her claws," Luca added,

reaching out to ruffle Harper's hair, and looking at the scratches covering my shoulders.

I growled and he grinned. Seth said nothing. He disappeared down the hallway and reappeared moments later with a t-shirt, which he handed to me silently.

I pulled it over my head and followed my bandmates and manager back into the main room, where they were all making themselves at home.

I looked at them all, then over at Harper who had moved to perch on a stool near the breakfast bar.

"Did I arrange a party and forgot about it?" I queried, hiking an eyebrow.

"Someone broke into my car," Seth said into the ensuing silence.

"That sucks." I accepted the beer Dex handed to me. "Not sure why that required a group visit, though. Do you need a hug?" I opened my arms and cocked an eyebrow.

"Your elevator key was in my glovebox. It was the only thing that was taken."

My arms dropped. "Where was your car?"

"At the studio. I went to pick up one of my guitars."

"You just needed your guitar at—" I checked the time, "eleven-thirty at night?"

His expression didn't change. "So?"

"And how long did it take you to *collect* your guitar?"

I swear I saw him smile. "Two hours … give or take." His dark eyes glinted as they looked at me. "I had to … restring it."

I choked on the swallow of beer I'd taken, coughed, and wiped my mouth. "Fine. You were clearly desperate for it. Did you at least park where the CCTV could see who did the crime?"

"The camera did pick it up, but not who did it. They were careful to keep their face hidden," Karl joined the conversation. "And they were fast. As if they knew exactly where to look."

I sighed. "It has to be Meredith. That girl needs to be committed."

"She is committed," Dex snickered. "To *you*."

My eyes swung to him. "So why are you here?"

"I was at Luca's." He smirked and glanced at Harper. "We were … uhh … doubling down. Seth called for a ride. The security company called Karl because Seth didn't reset the alarm when he left the studio."

"And then you all decided it was time to party at my place?"

"No," Karl said. "Seth wanted to speak to you about the key. I wanted to speak to Seth about the alarm *and* talk to you about what happens next."

"What happens next about what?" I wandered across the room and hopped up onto the stool beside Harper. "You okay?"

She nodded. "I'd forgotten what you guys were like when you got together."

I reached out for her hand and she slipped her palm in mine.

"You two look mighty cosy," Luca said.

"We were, until you all showed up."

"Gabe, concentrate," Karl snapped. "Does Meredith know about your place in Malibu?"

"You have a place in Malibu?" Harper asked, as I snapped a reply to Karl.

"How the fuck would I know?" I sent an apologetic look toward Harper before continuing. "We fucked backstage in Montreal once. I didn't even know her name until she turned up here." I raked a hand through my hair. "I'm not going there, Karl. I'll get the keys changed out for the elevator."

"Which you won't be able to do until Monday at the earliest," he pointed out.

"Then I'll lock the fucking doors. The key only gets her to the reception hall. It doesn't get her into the apartment." I didn't think she'd be that stupid, anyway. Meredith might have been desperate enough to try it once, but no one would be crazy enough to do it twice.

"She held a knife to your throat, Gabe," Luca said.

"Someone told her I liked knife play. She didn't actually mean to hurt me." Yeah, I was defending my stalker. Life was weird like that, sometimes. "She thought it would turn me on enough to fuck her again." I threw another look at Harper. "I didn't, just for the record."

"I'm going to ask Miles to up your security detail," Karl said. "I don't want you going *anywhere* without one of them beside you." I was about to argue when his eyes moved to Harper. "*Both* of you."

"But I have to go back to work on Monday," Harper protested. "She's not going to come after me. Why would she?"

"Because you're here with Gabe … where *she* wants to be," Karl told her.

"No one knows that, though." Her eyes sought out mine. "Right?"

There was a sudden fear in the pit of my stomach that I'd lose her before we even got started, and I considered lying. But I knew, deep down, that doing that to her would bring the end around even faster, and there had been enough lies between us.

"They'll know soon enough, Frosty," I said. "Maybe not tonight, but the media will find out. And when they do, they won't keep it quiet."

"But you can stop them, can't you?" she appealed to me. "Like you did after that interview."

"It doesn't work that way." I could almost see her pulling away from me, distancing herself. "They backed off because, at the time, we weren't together."

"But—"

"The best thing you can do is stay with Gabe until it blows over," Karl said.

"I have to work," she repeated.

"We have two days before you have to think about that. Let's see how the weekend goes. You were going to stay with me tonight, anyway, and then I would have convinced you to stay tomorrow night."

"Oh you think so, do you?"

"You doubt my skills?"

"Get a room, you two," Luca groused, and I swung back to face him.

"I did ... in *my* apartment ... which *you* invaded."

"You know what," Harper slid off the stool beside me. "I'm really tired. You can continue your argument, but I'm going to bed."

Everyone watched her as she rose up on tiptoes and pressed a kiss to my cheek, before walking out of the room and heading down the hall to my bedroom.

"Well, I think that's everybody's cue to leave," Dex said, draining his beer.

"Gabe, are you going to go to Malibu?" Karl asked.

"No. I think you're making Meredith being here more of a big deal than it actually is. I'll spend the weekend here, but we need to start prepping for the gig at Roth's, so I can't stay cooped up forever. I'll agree to the extra security when we leave the penthouse, and for Harper, if she insists on going back to work, but I'm not hiding." I pointed toward the door. "Now if you all would kindly fuck off." I waved a hand in the direction Harper had gone. "I have my woman waiting for me."

Tattooed Memories

CHAPTER 42

DEVIL DEVIL - MILCK

Harper
PRESENT

I slept like a baby. Whether that was because the bed was more comfortable than my own, or because Gabe had kept me up half the night once everyone had left was questionable. At least, that's what I'd tell him if he asked. The truth was, though, he'd exhausted my mind and my body, and I hadn't so much slept as fallen into a temporary coma.

When I woke, I expected to be alone but I opened my eyes to find the lead singer of Forgotten Legacy deliciously naked and fast asleep beside me. He lay on his back, one arm thrown over his eyes, the other resting on my thigh. The sheets lay low, barely covering his hips and I could see the deep v-shaped indent which led down to a part of his anatomy that had made me *very* happy for most of the night.

I turned onto my side slowly, not wanting to wake him and

carefully eased the sheets away from his body. My eyes were greedy as I looked at him, safe in the knowledge he was asleep. I examined the tattoos which covered his torso—a multitude of images and patterns, all skilfully merging one into another and licked my lips.

"Instead of wetting your lips, you could put that tongue to a much better use." His gravelly morning voice cut through the silence. His arm dropped from his eyes and he gripped his erection, smoothing his thumb over the tip. I followed his movement, just like he knew I would, and crawled down his body to settle between his legs.

"Ahh, fuck ... Harper." His hand threaded through my hair as I took him into my mouth.

I teased him the way he'd teased me, taking him to the edge and stopping twice, making him curse and beg and finally plead for me to let him come. Having this man, this *rock star* so many fantasised over, at my mercy turned me on more than I thought it would and my fingers drifted down between my legs to satisfy myself while I satisfied him.

We both slept again afterwards and that set the tone for the weekend. From some unspoken agreement, we avoided talking about Meredith, why we were cooped up in his penthouse or what would happen when Sunday came around and I needed to go home so I could go to work on Monday. We watched movies, I listened to him sing or play guitar in his home studio, we ordered take-out, and we had sex.

Lots of sex.

Everywhere.

I don't think there was a surface in his entire penthouse that he hadn't used to do something sexual to me on and, by the time Sunday crawled around, I'd realised that if Gabe ever decided to get out of the music business, he'd make a fortune on a sex-talk hotline.

The words he'd whisper in that sex-filled rich, raspy voice of his, the scenarios he'd paint while he was fucking me or using his mouth on me had made me scream so much, my throat was sore. Gabe claimed it was sore because his dick had been down it so many times, but that just proved the point I was making.

Either way, it had been one hell of a weekend, but Sunday afternoon was creeping toward evening and I was already feeling dread at the thought of telling him I needed to go home.

"Hey, Harper?" It was the first time he'd spoken in over an hour and I could tell from the tone of his voice that he wasn't certain I was awake.

We were lying in his bed, with me sprawled out over his body, his fingers tracing patterns up and down my arm while I half-dozed. At his voice, I lifted my head to peer up at him.

"What did you mean the other day?" he continued. "In the car. You said you lost everything."

I thought back to the argument we'd had. *Oh yeah, I had said that.* I should have known he'd remember.

"I was angry. It doesn't matter." I tried to brush it off, but I knew it wouldn't work.

He moved, tumbling me onto the mattress beside him.

"Don't do that. I've been thinking about it a lot."

"When?" I couldn't help but snap. "When you're not fucking me, you're playing music, talking on the phone with Seth, or eating. *When* did you have time to think about it?"

He ignored my outburst. "You had a scholarship for UCLA, but you didn't go. Why?"

"It was eight years ago. It doesn't matter now." I tried to climb out of bed, and he hooked a hand around my arm and pulled me back down.

"You can tell me or I can figure it out for myself. Either way, I'm going to know what you meant."

"Can't you just leave it alone? It's history." I didn't want to talk about it, rehash the car crash that had been that entire time.

"No, I can't leave it alone." His grip on my wrist loosened. "You listed three things. Me, your scholarship, and your mom."

Don't ask, *I pleaded silently.* Please don't ask me.

"Where's your mom, Harper?" And with that question, reality crashed back around me.

"Gabe, I don't want to do this," I whispered. "Don't ruin things."

"Ruin them? I'm trying to fix them, Frosty. And this is gonna gnaw at me until it drives me crazy. Was it me? Did I stop you from taking the scholarship?"

"What? No!" I hadn't even considered he might think that.

"Then what was it? I feel like I'm missing this huge piece of a puzzle."

I looked at him and, for a moment, the image of the young boy I'd known overlaid the man sitting there. The self-doubt in his eyes, masked quickly, was what had always shown when he'd limped into my home bruised and battered, escaping a father who was quick to lash out for the slightest thing. Then the image cleared, and the tattooed rock star he'd become became my focus.

I reached out, running my finger over the two-days' worth of stubble on his chin, palmed his cheek and kneeled forward to kiss him. His response was immediate, kissing me back with an intensity that hadn't been there before. I ran my hands up his arms, over his shoulders and looped them around his neck, leaning into him.

He pulled his lips from mine and set me back from him. "You're not going to distract me, Harper." His voice was firm.

"Can't we just start again from here?" I pleaded softly and he shook his head.

"You had it all planned out. A scholarship at UCLA so you could become a nurse, yet here you are cleaning other people's homes for a living."

I stared at him helplessly, knowing he wasn't going to let this go. "Fine," I said eventually and climbed off the bed.

"Where are you going?"

"If you want to have this conversation, I'm not doing it naked." I opened his wardrobe and rummaged through to find a t-shirt. Pulling it over my head, I returned to the bed and perched on the edge of it.

His slight smile made me frown.

"What?"

"You're wearing a Forgotten Legacy t-shirt. I like seeing you in my merchandise."

I blushed and looked away.

"And what is *that* look for?" He leaned forward. "Ohhh, you already *have* one of my shirts, don't you? Did you buy merch, Frosty?"

"I was at one of your concerts at the start of the tour you've just finished. Siobhan had tickets and I couldn't really refuse to go without getting into an explanation … which I didn't want to do."

"Fuck," he breathed. "You came to a concert? You were in the crowd?"

"Not at the front. We were closer to the back of the venue."

"Which gig?" He leaned forward, eyes sparking with interest.

"The Hollywood Bowl."

"That was the first show of the tour. It sold out an hour after the tickets went on sale."

I shrugged. "Siobhan was determined to go. She got lucky, I guess."

"Very lucky." I waited for him to ask if I'd enjoyed it, but he didn't. Instead, he held out his hand. "Come here."

I looked at his palm, then up at his face, and placed my hand in his. He pulled me close enough to wind his arm around my waist and lifted me onto his lap, then settled back against the pillows.

"Now let's backtrack. You were about to tell me what happened to your scholarship."

I didn't want to tell him, but Gabe was stubborn and I knew he wouldn't leave it alone until he had answers.

"That night ... the one where we ..." I tried to find the words to make it sound less sordid than it was.

"The night we gave in to our urges?" Gabe offered with a wry smile.

"I called Luca to see if you were home. I needed to see you. We'd barely spoken in weeks and, every time we did talk, you were always on your way to a gig or about to go to sleep and I ... I didn't want to pile my problems onto you while something was finally going right for you."

Gabe didn't speak, his fingers stroking up and down my arm lightly, and I let my head drop against his shoulder.

"My mom had been suffering from headaches for months, and I'd started noticing her acting strangely, so she had been getting tests. When I got home from school that day, I went with her to an appointment at the hospital. We were told that she'd been diagnosed with early-onset dementia. I was warned that over time she would need more and more help and I knew there was no way I'd be able to go away to college. Even if I stayed at home, I wouldn't have the time to study.

"All I could think about was that I needed to see you. I needed to hear you tell me it would be okay. I called you, but you didn't answer, so I sent a text to Luca. He said you were home, but had crashed early and that he'd tell you I was coming over." I took a breath. "When I came into your room, I didn't mean to stay quiet. I didn't mean to lie to you."

He snorted and I lifted my head from where I'd rested it against his shoulder. "What?"

"You're lying to yourself, now. The second you realised I was in bed alone and invited you to join me, you made the decision not to tell me it was you." His tone of voice made it clear he wasn't angry about it. "Admit to that, at least."

Was he right? Had it been a conscious decision? I thought back and realised he was right. I had wanted to be something more to him, for one night at least.

"If it makes you feel better about it," he continued. "I knew it was you from the moment you walked through the door. I wasn't asleep. You called my name ... twice."

"But you called me Lucy."

"I wanted you, Harper. And you were right there in my bedroom. Exactly where I wanted you to be. If I called you Lucy and you admitted it was you, I would have known you weren't ready to go any further. But you didn't. By pretending to be her, you acknowledged what neither of us had been admitting to, and gave us both the excuse we needed. And I would take you any way I could get you. I don't regret that, but I do wish I'd handled it better after." He paused to press a kiss to my shoulder. "Carry on."

I swallowed against the lump in my throat. "After that night,

I realised I was on my own. I couldn't lean on you or anyone else. I got through the rest of the year, informed UCLA that I wouldn't be accepting the scholarship after all, and just focused on graduating. Mom wasn't too bad. She still had headaches and the occasional memory lapse, but nothing neither of us couldn't handle. But the medical bills were high. Insurance covered some of it, but not everything. I took a job to help cover the costs." I had to stop talking, my voice was quivering and the lump in my throat was growing larger.

Gabe shifted, lying down and pulling me close. His hand smoothed over my hair before his knuckles brushed over my cheek. "When did she die?"

I closed my eyes. It still hurt, even now, to think about that day.

"Four years ago," I forced out. "She'd been gradually getting worse and I was already looking at the possibility of having to find outside care so I could carry on working. The ... the day it happened." I stopped and cleared my throat. "She was watching you on television. A news report about an awards event you'd been at the night before. She said she missed you, and how handsome you'd become." I smiled at the memory. "She wanted me to call you."

"What event was it? Do you know?"

"You'd won Best Songwriter for "Regrets"." I felt him nod. "She got upset when I said we don't talk and wanted me to promise to reach out to you. Looking back, it was like she knew what was going to happen and she was trying to make sure I wasn't alone for it."

"You should have called me. I'd have come, Harper. No matter what had gone on or where I was, I'd have always come to you."

I had no response to that. Lying there in his arms, I knew he was telling me the truth, but back then I was still too angry with him, too raw over the loss. I picked up my story again. "She wanted me to go and fetch her a drink from a local diner. They did an iced tea just the way she liked it, so I went. When I got home, she was gone."

"Gone?"

I wet my lips. "I called the paramedics, but it was too late. They said it was an aneurism. It took her instantly. The doctors said she probably wouldn't have even known. But I think she did know, Gabe. When I left she was watching television. When I came home, she'd switched it off and closed the curtains. She was sitting in her chair, her eyes closed. She looked so peaceful."

"I'm sorry," he whispered. "I'm sorry you lost her, sorry I wasn't there for you."

"It still hurts, Gabe." My voice was a broken sob. "I miss her so much."

He held me while I cried, let me peel away his clothes and lose myself in his touch. He was gentle, careful, his caresses almost delicate, and it was vastly different from every other time we'd come together. The words he whispered against my skin were soft, a far cry from the dirty things he'd said before. He told me I was beautiful, sang songs against my skin, rained kisses over my body until I was a sobbing mess of ecstasy.

"I need ... I need to tell you something," I whispered as he moved above me, his lips skating over my neck.

"Tell me, then." His movements stilled and he lifted his head.

"I don't want you to look at me while I do," I muttered, and he chuckled.

"Just say it, Frosty." He gave a slow thrust of his hips, reminding me he was deep inside my body.

I closed my eyes. If he refused to look away from me, I'd hide his face from my gaze my own way.

"I love you." His pace didn't change, continuing to move in and out of me with long leisurely strokes. I cracked one eye open. "Say something!" I demanded.

He cocked an eyebrow at me, grey eyes dancing. "I'm sorry. Was I supposed to recoil in horror? Run screaming for the door at the thought of commitment?"

My other eye opened. "*Gabriel.*"

His lip curled upwards. "I fucking love it when you say my full name like that." He ground against me. "It makes me even harder."

"I just told you I loved you and *that's* your reaction?" I wasn't concerned anymore, I was irritated.

"It's not news, Harper." His hand slid down to squeeze my breast, followed by his mouth. "You've been in love with me since the day we met." His tongue tasted my nipple, flicking over the peak.

"I was *eight*!"

"And I was ten. And you were the most beautiful creature I'd seen in my entire life." He brought his mouth back up to mine. "You owned my soul from the moment we met. My heart has been yours since the first time you touched me."

"Gabe …"

"Too wordy for you?" His lips touched mine. "How about this then? I've loved you forever, Harper Jackson, and will continue to do so until the day I die." He paused and canted his head. "And beyond that, too."

Tattooed Memories

Chapter 43

NOT GONNA BREAK ME - JAMIE N COMMONS

Gabe

PRESENT

We were at an impasse. This fucking stubborn woman would not listen to reason. I wanted her to stay with me, she wanted to return to the apartment she shared with Siobhan. Okay, so maybe I also wanted her to quit her job. It made perfect sense, and she knew it. She didn't need to work her ass off. Not when I wanted that ass right where I could see it.

Only she wouldn't admit it. Instead, she glared at me from across the kitchen.

"Harper," I tried once more to reason with her. "What's the point in going back there? You're going to be spending most of your time here, anyway, right? I mean … we're not putting the brakes on just because the weekend is coming to an end."

"I still have a life. That hasn't just magically stopped

pay, my share of the rent. I can't just disappear on Siobhan and leave her with all that."

"I'm not telling you to wipe her out of existence. I'm just saying maybe you should stay here until Meredith is contained."

"*Contained?*" She laughed. "She's not an *animal*, Gabe."

I shrugged. "She should probably stop acting like one, then."

"Maybe you should as well."

"Wow." I shook my head. "Guess that moment we had earlier has left the building."

"I told you I loved you, not that I'd change my entire life for you," she snapped.

"I'm not asking you to change your *entire* life, I'm just asking you to make room for me in your existing one." I slammed down my mug of coffee, ignoring the way it sloshed over the sides and burned my hand. "For fuck's sake, Harper, how hard is it just to compromise a little?"

"You don't want a compromise. You want me to leave my job and my home and leech off you!"

"Leech? What the fuck? How is my offering to support you leeching? It's all fucking yours anyway!" I may have joked about her not being in my will, but the truth was she'd always been my sole beneficiary if anything happened to me. She wasn't ready to hear that, though. I knew she wouldn't understand.

"You've been back in my life for less than five minutes, Gabe. What else would it be?"

"It would be me wanting to make things right. We lost eight

years because of my stupidity—"

"You were right," she cut in, silencing me. "I still wouldn't have gone to UCLA and I would have still had to look after my mom, but you would have stayed with me. You wouldn't have gone off and become this world-famous rock star. It wasn't a stupid decision. You were right."

"Then let me help you *now*," I insisted. I strode across the room and looped my arms around her waist. "Once the press gets wind of us being together, they won't leave you alone. They'll follow you to work, trying to get photographs of you. They'll use the worst ones they take and they'll dig through your life, airing every decision you make publicly."

"You're not making yourself sound like much of a catch, you know." Her hands slid up my chest and curled around my neck.

I smiled down at her, sensing triumph ahead. "You'll make me look even worse than I usually do. Letting my new girlfriend scrub rich people's toilets instead of keeping her in the lap of luxury. How's that going to look? My reputation will be in tatters."

"It'll do your ego good," she countered, but her words lacked their earlier bite and she seemed more interested in touching me than arguing.

"How about this. Stay with me until the gig at Roth's. I'll cover whatever bills you have for that time." I covered her mouth with my palm when she started to argue and played my trump card. "I wasn't there for you when your mom died, let me do this now."

"Gabe, the only reason we're having this argument is because *you* can't keep your dick in your pants. It has nothing to do with my mom or you not being there."

"How do you figure that? It has *everything* to do with you." I leaned forward to kiss her because the temptation was too irresistible. "I wouldn't have spent the past eight years trying to erase you out of my mind by fucking anyone willing to look at me if you'd called me."

"Oh … so this is all *my* fault?"

I plastered a cocky grin on my face. "Not that I'd actually come right out and say that, but if the cap fits, babe …"

"Don't call me babe."

"Why not?"

"I've heard you and the other guys use it when you can't remember a girl's name. Babe, sweetheart … Luca and Dex are terrible for doing it."

"I'm not likely to ever forget your name." I brushed her cheek with my knuckles. "So, we're agreed? You'll stay with me and ditch that job?"

"I'll see if I can take a two-week vacation," she countered. "I'll stay here, but I need to go over to my apartment today for clothes and to talk to Siobhan. You gave my cell to Miles and he hasn't brought it back."

"I'll get him to bring you a new cell when I call to arrange a time for him to pick us up."

"Us?"

"You don't think I'm letting you go alone, do you? We'll go out for dinner afterwards." I picked my cell up from the countertop and dialled Miles' number. Out of the corner of my eye, I saw Harper leave the room and head toward the bathroom, presumably to take a shower.

My call to Miles was short, asking him to pick up the promised cell for Harper and to pick us up in an hour, then I called Seth.

"Harper's going to stay here. At least until Roth's gig. We'll see where we're at then," I told him. "We're heading over to her apartment in a few to grab some things, and then going to dinner. I need suggestions on where to take her."

Seth laughed quietly down the line. "You're finally taking her on a *date*? How many years in the making has that been?"

"Fuck off, Seth. Where should we go?"

"Depends what you've got planned." I heard a female voice in the background and the click of a door as he left the room.

"Where are you?"

"Damnation," he replied. "Hooked up with someone last night. Wasn't going to take them home with me." He paused and I waited. "So plans? Somewhere you can be seen ... or somewhere you can be *seen*?"

I laughed. "Somewhere quiet."

"I could give Pandora a call and get you a reservation at Joyeuse," he said after a moment's thought, mentioning a restaurant known for its high-quality food and almost rabid protection of the privacy of its guests.

Seth had had a fling with its owner, Pandora, a couple of years ago and, weirdly, they were still friends. A unique occurrence for Seth who was notorious for breaking the women he played with, leaving them devastated while he walked away without a single mark on his dark heart.

"Yeah, do that."

"I'll text you with the time." He hung up without saying goodbye and I went to hunt down Harper, hoping she was still naked, wet and slippery in the shower.

❄

Siobhan wasn't in the apartment when we arrived, and Harper took down a suitcase from above her wardrobe to pack it with all the clothes she thought she might need while she was with me. I wandered around the apartment, which was the size of a shoebox, randomly picking things up and generally just being nosy.

There was a framed photograph of her mom on one wall and quite a few of Harper and Siobhan stuck to the refrigerator. I smiled at the evidence showing me she had been happy, not that I'd ever thought she would be anything but happy. Harper wasn't one for dwelling on the bad things. She lived life with an enthusiasm that had fed my hungry soul when I was a kid. Her enthusiasm for life had kept me from topping myself more times than I could list—something I'd been very careful to keep from her.

From the first time we'd met, she'd attracted me. At ten years old, I hadn't recognised what it was, but she reeled me in with her warmth and her natural desire to heal. As the child of physical abuse, she'd given me a much-needed reprieve. She never pushed or demanded answers when I turned up at her door, bleeding and battered. As we grew closer, I sought her out more and more, while trying not to destroy her light by letting the darkness I struggled with swallow it. Even when I tore her apart and threw her away, that warmth and inner beauty remained.

I stroked a finger down the image of her face grinning up at me. Why had I thought I could barge back into her life and not have it affect me? On top of the refrigerator, mostly hidden by the boxes of cereal I caught sight of a familiar item. Reaching up, I pushed the boxes to one side and took down the snowglobe I'd bought her as a birthday present.

"Fucking idiot," I muttered to myself.

"Who is?" Her hands slid around my stomach from behind and she leaned against my back. I loved how free she was with her affection toward me.

"Doesn't matter." I carefully put the snowglobe back and turned in her arms. "Got everything?"

"I think so."

"We've got a reservation for Joyeuse at eight. Did Candice leave any of the other clothes you picked out for the premiere? You might want to bring them with you if you do. Pandora won't let me hear the last of it if we turn up in jeans." But if that's what she wanted to wear, I'd face Pandora's wrath with a smile on my face.

I waited while she went back to her bedroom to repack her suitcase, and then we went back to where Miles waited. There was a group of teenage girls on the street outside the block when we exited and I didn't pull down my cap quick enough to hide my face.

They were surrounding us less than a heartbeat later, voices high-pitched and excited. With an apologetic look at Harper, I unwound my arm from her waist and stopped. I might be an asshole, but I always made time for fans of the band. They'd made us what we were and deserved our attention when we could spare it. Harper stood to one side, while I signed their t-shirts with a pen one of them managed to dig up from a bag, and posed for photos. Then I carefully extricated myself from their clutching fingers, grabbed Harper's hand and continued our path to the car.

Miles was holding the door open before we got there.

"Thanks," Harper said to him, climbing in. I rounded the car and threw her suitcase in the back then joined her.

"Back to the penthouse," I told him. "We'll be heading to Joyeuse at seven thirty."

❋

Harper looked stunning in the silver-grey dress, which ended mid-thigh and had my mouth watering every time I looked in her direction. I knew Candice had roped in people to do her hair and makeup for the premiere, but she looked no less gorgeous without their help when she walked out of the bedroom to go to dinner.

I'd opted for black pants, black shirt, unbuttoned at the throat, and no jacket and we sized each other up across the living room. A sparkle at her throat drew my eye and I spotted she was wearing the necklace I'd given her. An almost overwhelming sense of security swept over me when I saw it. I couldn't explain it, just knowing she was wearing it calmed me.

"It's going to be difficult keeping my hands off you, Frosty," I muttered as I led her into the waiting elevator. "You look good enough to eat." I ran one finger up her thigh. "And I mean that literally."

Her nipples immediately beaded, pushing at the front of her dress, and I groaned. Tonight was going to be sheer torture. How would Pandora feel if I crawled beneath the table to slake my thirst on Harper's pussy? *I wondered idly.* She might bar me from her restaurant for life, but fuck, it would be worth it.

I shoved my hands in my pockets, out of temptation's reach, and stared at the numbers counting down above the door. When we reached the basement, I crooked my elbow for her to slide her hand through and stepped out into the building's underground parking lot.

"There is going to be press outside of Joyeuse," I told her, for probably the hundredth time. "If you want to keep our relationship a secret, now's the time to say something."

"Do *you* want to keep it secret?" she asked and I shot her what I hoped was a look of irritation, but knew was closer to pathetic adoration.

"No, I fucking don't," I growled.

She was still laughing at me when we reached the car. Miles shot me a questioning look, but said nothing as we slipped in and he drove out into the traffic. I tried to keep my hands to myself. Joyeuse was only a few minutes drive from my apartment block, but I couldn't resist letting my fingers run up the silky expanse of thigh exposed by her dress. She shifted in the seat, sending me a questioning look, her eyes darkening with a look I was beginning to recognise very well.

A sly voice at the back of my head wondered if she was like this with every lover she'd had and a sharp pang of jealousy shot through me before I squashed it down. I had no right to be jealous. I'd been the one to walk away from her, not the other way around. I'd been with more women than I could count, I couldn't exactly deny her the same right.

My cock stirred.

Although, had it been women she'd been fucking, I probably wouldn't have as big an issue with it.

"What are you scowling at?" she whispered, and the image of some unknown woman with her face buried into Harper's pussy while she sucked my dick faded. *Fuck*. Okay, so maybe it *would* be a problem. Even that made me want to hunt the faceless person down and kill them—female or not. Harper's body was mine to taste. No one else's.

"We're gonna be exclusive, right?" I demanded. I was driving myself crazy thinking about her taking other lovers, and I sounded like an idiot, I knew. A jealous idiot. "No hooking up with other people?"

She nailed me with a glare, misunderstanding my question. "If you're planning on seeing other women, I want out of this car right now."

"I'm not. But I need to know you're not going to either."

Her glare faded into a puzzled look. "Not going to what? See other women?"

"Women, men, animals, vegetables. *No one!*" I said from between clenched teeth.

"You're an idiot," she said softly, leaned across and kissed me.

Luckily, she'd used clear lip gloss so when we arrived at the restaurant, it wasn't smeared across her face from the tongue fucking I'd given her mouth.

"I'm gonna need a minute," I called out to Miles when he parked, pressing Harper's hand to the erection tenting my pants. "Want to have your starter now?"

She squeezed me through the material then drew away. "I wouldn't want to ruin my appetite." Before I could respond, she threw open the car door.

"Fucking witch," I muttered, following her out.

I spotted Jefferson Thomas lurking near the entrance and caught Harper's hand before she got too far ahead of me. He straightened when he spotted us, an oily smile lifting his lips.

"Gabe, would you like to give us a comment on what you

think about Meredith Conway being back in town?"

"Sure." I gave him an easy grin. "I don't think about it at all. I don't care."

"But you knew she was here?"

"The record label knows, and they passed it onto me, yeah."

"Has she made contact?" I was getting tired of his phone being stuck in my face, so I took a step sideways, my eyes on the doors.

"Nope, and I doubt she'll bother." I wrapped my arm around Harper's shoulders. "Now, if you don't mind, we have reservations, and everyone knows Pandora doesn't like anyone to be late."

I tipped my head at him and strode past.

"One last question," he called after me and his tone of voice had me bracing myself. Whatever he was going to say, it wasn't going to be good. "Have you seen your father lately?"

I went rigid, and slowly turned back to face him.

"My father is dead." I was surprised at how calm I sounded.

"Are you still telling everyone that?"

His smile mocked me, and I started forward, ready to knock it off his face, when a hand touched my arm.

"Gabe." Harper's voice, soft and coaxing. "Let's go inside. Ignore him." She tugged at my sleeve until my head swung around to find her. "He's just trying to get you to hit him. He'll have his story then," she said. "Come on. They've got the doors open ready for us."

I twisted once more to look at Jefferson, but he'd disappeared into the crowded street, and so I let Harper lead me inside. I was on autopilot as I greeted Pandora, and followed our assigned hostess to a secluded table inside the dim interior. Harper was a quiet presence beside me, saying nothing as I held out her chair for her to sit, before rounding the table to settle opposite her.

I caught the hostess's wrist as she placed down the menus. "Whiskey, double, neat. Keep them coming," I said.

She gave a nod and glanced at Harper, who gave me a helpless look.

"Bring a bottle of 1976 Chateau Rayas Chateauneuf-du-Pape Reserve," I said, without looking at the drinks menu.

"Coming right up, sir!" She bounced away.

My lighter was in my hand, and I flicked it open with my thumb. I stared at the flame, unseeing.

Chapter 44

HATE ME - BLUE OCTOBER

Gabe

AGE 4

Warmth enveloped me, the smell of honeysuckle and roses telling me my mom was the one wrapping her arms around me. I lay still, my eyes tightly closed, pretending to be asleep, feeling her fingers drift over my arm.

I wouldn't move.

And then she attacked, targeting the sensitive spot beneath my ribs and tickling without mercy. I gritted my teeth.

I wouldn't move!

Her hands moved—she knew all my weak spots. My ribs, the back of my neck and … uh oh … the backs of my knees. I let out a howl of laughter and squirmed away. Her own laughter was like music, washing over me.

"Come on, my beautiful boy, it's time for school." She scooped her arms around me and swung me out of bed.

I laughed again, throwing my arms around her neck and burying my face into the curve where her neck met her shoulder, breathing in her scent.

"I want to stay home with you," I told her.

"But if you do that, you won't learn all the exciting things that will take you far in this world, my love." She set me down and took my hand, leading me out of my bedroom and to the kitchen.

She set down a bowl of oatmeal, covered with a thick coating of sugar and honey, and handed me a spoon. I pulled a face.

"It's cold outside, and it'll keep you warm and make you strong. Eat up, Gabriel."

"But—"

"Do as your mama says, boy." My da appeared behind me and ruffled my hair on his way past. "The biggest lesson you'll need to remember in life is *always* keep your women happy. If they're happy, you'll be happy." He wrapped his arms around my mom's waist and kissed her cheek. "It's the rule of life."

She swatted him away with her spoon, smiling. "Get away with you now, Tommy!"

He threw me a wink, and I grinned at him around a mouthful of oatmeal.

Da had left for work by the time I was ready for school and Mom and I walked the short distance. I clung to her leg by the door, not wanting to go inside. I enjoyed school, my friends were there, but I loved spending time with my mom, and I *knew* she was going to be home all day today, but she stood firm and handed me over to the teacher. One last kiss to my forehead and she was gone.

The day passed like every other school day—full of lessons and games with my friends—until just after lunchtime. We were doing simple math questions, our heads bent to our desks as we worked through the problems and the class was silent, the air thick with concentration.

The sound of the door creaking open distracted me, and I looked up to see a man in a dark suit walk inside and bend to whisper to my teacher. Her hand rose to her mouth and she looked directly at me.

"Gabriel?" There was a note to her voice, a quiver that I didn't understand. "Come here, please."

I rose to my feet and, with the rest of my class watching, approached her, my eyes on the stranger.

"Gabriel, this is Mr Matthews, our school counsellor. Your father is waiting with the principal. He's come to take you to him."

I looked from her to the man and back again. "Did I do something wrong?" I whispered.

"No, *no*." She crouched in front of me and took my hands. "Honey, you need to be strong, okay? Go with Mr Matthews."

I didn't want to. He was big and scary and looked down at me with an expression I couldn't read.

"Hey, little man," He bent and held out his hand. "You can call me Eric. Why don't we go and find your dad?" He took my hand, but I hung back, digging my heels in.

"It's okay, Gabriel," my teacher said gently. She patted my back, sending me forward until I had no choice but to trot alongside the man ... *Eric* ... who led me away from my class.

My da was sitting in the principal's office, his head in his hands, when we entered. His head jerked up at the sound of our footsteps and he stared at me in silence. His eyes were red, wet with tears.

"Da?" I asked, my face scrunching up with confusion. My da never cried.

He lurched to his feet and grabbed me, crushing me in his arms and sobbed. Squirming, I managed to loosen his grip, looking around.

"Da?" I repeated.

"I'm so sorry for your loss, Mr Mercer," the principal said to him, his eyes on me. "Take Gabriel home and be with your son. I can get Eric to drive you, if you'd like."

Da said it was a fluke accident. Mom had been walking back from school and a car lost control, swerved and hit her. She died on the way to the hospital. The funeral was a week later. I don't remember much about that time other than my life lost its brightness and warmth and it never came back—until I met Harper.

Two months after her death, my da's drinking started to get out of control. He couldn't handle losing the love of his life, and I looked too much like her. Every time he saw me, grief struck him again, not that I understood what was happening. I was too young to really understand anything other than my mom had gone and I was slowly losing my da as well.

I tried to make him smile. I succeeded only in making him angry.

One morning, for some reason I got it into my head that if I could make oatmeal the way Mom used to before he went to work it would fix things. So I pulled out the box and tried to make him breakfast, but I misjudged the amounts and I couldn't boil the water. I was trying to clean up the mess when he staggered into the kitchen and slipped on the water.

The crash as he hit the ground had me frozen to the spot, my eyes wide.

"I-I'm sorry," I whispered. "I wanted to make breakfast for you."

He levered himself to his feet and moved toward me. I shuffled back a step.

"Don't run from me, boy," he snarled. He caught the neck of my t-shirt as I tried to dart past him and hauled me back, lifting me off my feet until I dangled in front of him.

That was the first time he hit me. A casual backhanded smack across the face which split my lip.

"Clean this mess up and then go to your room." He released his grip and stalked out.

CHAPTER 45

DIRTY LITTLE SECRET - THE ALL-AMERICAN REJECTS

Gabe

AGE 25

My phone buzzed. I ignored it, my hand on my dick and my eyes on the two girls fooling around on the bed. I was getting more enjoyment from my hand than watching the girls eating each other out, but appearances had to be maintained.

I'd carefully crafted my reputation over the years into one of a womanising temperamental rock star with a flair for dramatic outbursts and the occasional brawl with my bandmates. Okay, so maybe all of it wasn't fake, but I'd added enough embellishments to ensure we got noticed and fast-tracked through the ranks of amateurs to achieve the glory of stardom. I'd realised quickly that fame wasn't always about talent, but about being noticed, so I made sure we were front and centre whenever the opportunity arose for media coverage. Not that we weren't talented, we were—top of our game, writing our own lyrics and music. It just helped that we had that whole bad boy vibe the girls loved so much.

My phone buzzed again, vibrating against my thigh and I tapped the screen without checking the caller ID.

"Mr Mercer?" An unfamiliar voice greeted me.

"How did you get this number?"

"This is Los Angeles Sacred Saints Hospital. You were listed in Thomas Mercer's phone as his emergency contact." I managed not to flinch at my da's name.

Wait ... what? Hospital?

"What can I do for you?" I still didn't acknowledge whether I was the person they were looking for.

There was a pause before the voice continued to speak. "Well, as I explained, I'm calling from Sacred Saints. Mr Mercer was brought into the ER this morning. He was found unconscious outside his apartment and a neighbour called the paramedics. He suffered a stroke and has yet to regain consciousness."

"And you want me to do what, exactly?" I knew I sounded callous from the sharp intake of breath down the line.

"I assume you are his closest relation. With Mr Mercer unable to make decisions, we're going to need someone to come to the hospital." Their meaning was clear. They were asking me to go and take control of his medical care, and probably assuring themselves there was insurance to cover his medical bills.

I tipped my head against the seat's backrest. This was going to be a fucking PR disaster unless I could contain it.

"Mr Mercer?"

I realised I'd been silent for too long. "Fine. I'll be there in an hour. Think he'll still be alive?" Another gasp. I rolled my eyes. "I'm sorry, sweetheart, but you'll find there's no love lost between us."

I cut the call and rose to my feet. "Sorry ladies, play time's over. Get dressed and get out." I was already calling Miles and walking out of the room, ignoring their protests. "Send security up, would you? I have guests who need to leave. Once you've done that, can you bring the car round? I need to go to Sacred Saints Hospital."

"Hospital?" he queried. "What have you done now?"

"Nothing … yet. I had a call. Apparently my father is there and I'm listed as his emergency contact."

"Toby and Max are on their way up. I'll be there in five."

I ended the call, finished dressing and was ready to leave when the security detail Miles had sent weaved their way through the main floor of Damnation and arrived upstairs.

"Miles is waiting for you around the back," Max told me, moving past me to hurry the girls along.

I nodded my thanks and disappeared before he returned with them.

I called Karl on the journey to the hospital, explained the situation and left the details of how I'd get in there without being spotted in his capable hands. He was back on the line just as we pulled up.

"I've arranged for you to go in via a side entrance," he told me. "The administrator will be waiting for you. She will get you inside. Your father has been moved to one of the VIP suites away from the public areas. I'll be there in fifteen minutes or so, traffic dependent."

"You don't need to come."

"I'm not just your manager, Gabe, I'm your friend. I'll be there. Wait for me before you go up. I don't want you signing anything before I've checked it over."

I pinched the bridge of my nose. "I don't think he's had a stroke just to purposely try and rip me off."

"The fact you were his emergency contact raises a red flag. He might not have intended things to go quite this way, but considering the relationship, or lack of, between you, it's a strange thing to have done."

"Is it?" My head was starting to hurt. "I don't think he's really put that much thought into it. I'm the only relative he has." Regardless of how he treated me, I was still his son, his only blood, his hated reminder of the woman he'd loved and lost.

Miles managed to get me inside the hospital without being spotted, and the administrator was waiting, true to her word, to take us up to the private suite. I ignored Karl's request that I wait and followed her. I needed to just get this over with.

"Can I get you anything, Mr Mercer? Tea, coffee?" she asked once we were inside the VIP section.

I shook my head. "It's Gabe. Mr Mercer is my father."

She gave me a startled look. "*Gabe*? As in the singer of …"

"Yeah, that one," I shrugged.

She gave me a sympathetic smile. "I'm afraid I didn't make the connection when I received the call to move your father. My daughter is a huge fan of your music. But I'm sure you must get tired of all the recognition."

"It has its good days," I replied. "How old is your daughter?" I was making idle conversation, but the look on her face told me she thought I was being inappropriate.

"Far too young to be interested in bad boy rock stars," she told me primly.

I laughed quietly. "Contrary to my reputation, I don't jump on every girl who looks at me."

"I mean no offence." I think she suddenly remembered she was at work.

"None taken," I shrugged tiredly. "You hear the music, see the look, read the news, and make an assumption. You're certainly not the first, you won't be the last."

She stared at me for a second, then nodded. "Let me take you to see your father's specialist and he can explain the situation."

"Is he dying?" I asked.

"He's stable right now." A tall, dark-skinned man dressed in scrubs and a white lab coat, strode forward, his hand outstretched. "Dr. Franklin Jacobi."

I took his hand and shook it. Firm grip, I noted.

"Mr Mercer is your father, would I be right?" he said.

I nodded. Before he could say anything more, Karl burst

through the door.

"I thought I told you to wait for me?"

"Don't worry, I haven't signed over a kidney or anything." I returned my attention to Dr. Jacobi. "What's the prognosis? Imminent death?" My voice was hopeful.

"No," he replied, with a frown. "Your father had a stroke..." The rest of the words faded out as my attention wandered. As nasty as it sounded, I didn't really give a fuck what condition he was in, what had caused it or how long he was going to be that way. I knew Karl was listening for both of us and would give me the cliff notes for what I needed to know.

Instead, I thought about the last time I'd been in the same room as him. It had been a couple of days after my twenty-first birthday. Our first album had just hit the top of the rock charts and we were close to making our first million. He'd turned up outside one of our gigs, drunk and loud, demanding money.

I wrote him a cheque for ten thousand dollars without argument and he disappeared from my life. Occasionally, I'd receive a phone call telling me he'd run out of cash and I'd send him more. Other than that, we didn't communicate.

Karl had asked me many times why I bothered. I'd yet to figure out the answer for myself.

"Are you ready to go and see him?" The doctor's voice cut through my thoughts, and I refocused to find him and Karl both staring at me.

"Sure. I suppose I should since I'm here."

The nonchalance in my voice was feigned. There was no indication of the way my heartbeat increased or how my mouth dried up at the thought of being close to the man who had become my own personal monster when I was growing up.

No one knew our history. Well, except for one person. And *she* didn't count ... Because she wasn't here.

CHAPTER 46

CONTROL – PUDDLE OF MUDD

Harper

PRESENT

"Is that your dad's lighter?"

His eyes flicked up to meet mine when I spoke and he snapped the lighter closed, stuffing it back into his pocket.

"Yeah." He smiled his thanks when the hostess arrived with our drinks. She placed his whiskey beside his elbow and then poured a little wine into a glass and handed it to him. He took a sip, pulled a face, then grunted. "It tastes like shit to me." He nodded toward me. "You should have given it to her to try. I don't drink wine."

The hostess blushed. "Ignore him, he's being rude," I said and took the glass from Gabe. Tasting it, I smiled. "It's perfect, thank you."

"I should hope so at just over a grand a bottle," Gabe told me as she filled my glass.

"*How* much?" I demanded. "Stop pouring!"

He laughed at me. "Ignore *her*," he mimicked my words, smirking.

The hostess's eyes darted from him to me and back to Gabe.

"I'll give you a few minutes to decide on what you'd like to order," she said, her smile fixed firmly in place, and placed the bottle down on the centre of the table before she moved away at a quick walk.

"You embarrassed her," I told him.

He shrugged. "The bad boy rock star misbehaves in a restaurant—shocker."

"If embarrassing the hostess is what everyone describes as you misbehaving then I'm a little disappointed." I peered at him over the rim of my glass. "I expected more."

Gabe took a swallow of his whiskey, and his expression became wicked. "You want me to misbehave, Harper?" He leaned forward, dropping his voice. "Don't be asking for something you might regret. Because, if you *really* want me to, I can behave *very* badly."

I couldn't decide if he was teasing me or being serious. His tone of voice was low, but his eyes were bright with suppressed amusement.

"I thought you knew the owner? Wouldn't she be upset with you if you disrupted the evening and upset the other diners?"

"There's misbehaving and then there's *misbehaving*."

I studied him. Since the run-in with the reporter outside, there'd been an edge to him, a restlessness. Oh, to anyone not fine-tuned to recognise certain signs, he was behaving the same way he always did, but I recognised this Gabe. I'd patched him up a lot when we were kids.

This was the Gabe who arrived hours after a run-in with his dad, when frenetic energy would consume him. It triggered whenever he had been made to feel helpless … it seemed like the man hadn't successfully overcome that. I wondered how much of the bad behaviour that had been very publicly recorded had been down to an action or person doing or saying something that had woken up the frustrated little boy hidden inside who needed to prove to himself and the world around him that he *wasn't* helpless.

People came up, famous faces I'd seen on TV and movie screens, stopping to chat to Gabe. He smiled and laughed, shook hands and kissed cheeks, even posed for some photographs and signed pieces of paper thrust under his nose, in between the courses we were served.

I guess even other famous people had their idols.

He was charming and flirty, but there was something missing. I felt like I was sitting in a movie scene with an actor who was playing a role, but one that didn't fit properly.

After dessert had been served, I was finishing the last of my wine and Gabe was on another whiskey, I'd lost count of how many, when I finally spoke up.

"What do you need to do?" I asked him softly, and his head canted, eyes turning quizzical.

"About what?"

"I know you, Gabriel. That reporter out there upset you."

He shook his head, his smile amused. But I wasn't buying it. I was *sure* I still knew him well enough to read the signs.

"Don't do that," I told him. "What do you need to do?"

"You don't want to go down that path, Harper." His fingers drummed on the tabletop and I knew he wanted to reach for the lighter in his pocket.

I placed my hand on top of his, stilling his movements. "I already am. Tell me what you need."

He stared at me. "I n-need …" he stopped talking, eyes widening with surprise when he stumbled over the word. *"Fuck,"* he whispered.

Silently, he lifted a hand, summoning the hostess. She materialised almost immediately.

"The check," he told her. He handed her his card and she disappeared as silently as she'd arrived.

By the time we'd finished our drinks, she'd returned, handing his card back to him. Gabe didn't respond, slipping it into his wallet and rising to his feet.

"Let's go," he told me and held out his hand.

I glanced at him from beneath my lashes. That edge was still there, still needing to be burned off, and I wondered what he was planning. I slipped my hand in his and he strode toward the exit. The car glided up as soon as we stepped outside. Gabe opened the door and helped me in, and dropped onto the leather seat beside me.

"Take a slow drive back," he instructed Miles, then shut the privacy screen, sealing us inside the back of the car.

"Take the dress off."

I thought I misheard him. He was staring straight ahead, hands resting on his lap.

"Excuse me?"

"Take the dress off." His head turned. "You asked me what I needed. I need you to take the fucking dress off." His eyes were hard, his voice flat.

"Here?" I glanced toward the privacy screen.

"Yes, here. Right now." He challenged me, daring me to play his game.

I steeled my spine. "You think I won't?"

"I don't think you have the guts. You like me telling you how people might see you, but you're too scared to risk it."

"You want people to see me?" I questioned.

"No, I want to fuck you. If people see me doing that …" he shrugged, sounding bored.

He was shutting down. I could see it. Whatever the reporter had meant by his question about Gabe's dad, it had triggered something inside him. Something that forced him to lash out. As a child, he'd cut himself. I knew beneath the tattoos covering his arms, there were fine lines of scars where he'd sliced his skin. Now, it seemed, he had found other ways to fight his demons.

"If I hadn't been here, would you have picked someone up?"

"I want to fuck, Harper, not be analysed." He tipped his head back and closed his eyes. This was the rock star the world saw—arrogant, rude, demanding—to me it was unacceptable.

"So you just want to use my body?" I pushed for an answer. "Answer the question, Gabriel. Do you just want to fuck or do you want to fuck *me*?"

He didn't reply but I saw his fingers curl into fists and his jaw clenched. So it wasn't simply a case of needing a body, *any* body. He wanted *me* ... he was just too angry, too sore over the reporter's words, to say so.

I had a decision to make and no time to think it over. I could demand he take me home or I could be what he needed and trust him not to take it too far. *What was too far? What would I not be willing to do for this man?* The answer was simple. It was the same answer I would have always given—back then, and right now. I would do *anything* to stop him hurting. To make him understand that he *was* enough.

Silently, I reached back and pulled the zipper of my dress down, slid it down my legs until it fell to the floor then climbed onto Gabe's lap, straddling his thighs. His eyes shot open in surprise. I curved my fingers over his cheeks.

"You can use my body, Gabe, however you need to. I'll let you do whatever you want to me, but I want a promise from you."

His eyes were heating up, the coolness melting away, and I could feel his dick pressing against my thigh. He reached up to touch my breast and I leaned away from his touch.

"Did you hear me?" I needed him to focus on who he was with. I *would not* be treated like another nameless fuck in the back of the car.

"I heard you," his voice was raspy, low, guttural. "What kind of promise?"

"Tomorrow, you talk to me. I want to know what the reporter meant. I want to know what happened to your dad. Promise me that, and I'll be your groupie tonight." While I spoke, I rotated my hips, grinding my pussy onto his erection. "I'll be whatever you need me to be."

"Fuck." His eyes slid closed again and he licked his lips. "You don't know what you're offering or what you're demanding."

"What I know is that I love you, and you say you love me. I'll be whatever you need, Gabe, but you have to give me what I want as well."

"And what do you want, Frosty?"

"Just you. *All* of you."

In response, he hooked a hand around the back of my neck and pulled my mouth down on his. I let his tongue part my lips and thrust inside, while one of his hands curved over my hip. The other hand moved up over my breast, thumb brushing across my already hard nipple.

"I'm not going to fuck you in the car," he murmured against my mouth. "I just want you naked so I can look at you and touch you, and imagine the things I'm going to do to you." He plucked at my nipple, sending a delicious shot of arousal down between my legs.

My hand dropped down between our bodies and I rubbed him through his pants. Gabe caught my wrist, pulling me away.

"Tell me what you're going to do to me," I invited.

"Put both your hands behind your back," he instructed. "And, before you argue, don't forget you promised you'd do *whatever* I want tonight."

I did as he said, the position forcing my shoulders back and thrusting my breasts forward. He lifted his head and settled back against the seat to look at me.

"Look how hard these are." He flicked a nipple. "I wonder how they'd look with decoration."

"Decoration?" My voice was little more than a whisper.

"A chain linking them together, a clamp on each nipple," he gave each tip a pinch, "so when I tugged the centre, it will pull both of them." His finger circled one nipple, traced a line across my breasts and then circled the other. "Maybe we could add a third one down here." His hand lowered and he tapped my clit.

I hissed.

"What do you think? Should I chain you up and keep you as my submissive little slave girl?" His head cocked to the side, eyes glinting.

"No." I couldn't deny the thought that being at his mercy excited me but submissive I wasn't.

"No?" he repeated, then smiled, bending forward to run his tongue over my breast. "No, you're probably right. Submissives bore me, I prefer someone who'll match me." The finger on my clit moved, pushed inside me and I moaned, unable to stop myself clenching around the invasion.

He added a second finger, his eyes holding mine as he thrust them in and out. "What are your limits? What can't I do?"

"I don't know. What do you *want* to do?" My hips jerked when his fingers curled hitting that spot *just right*.

"*Everything,* Harper. I want to make you as dirty as I am," he whispered. "I want to fuck your pussy." He pulled his fingers out of me and ran them backwards. "I want to fuck your ass." One finger probed and I tensed. "I want to take photos of you while you come for me. I want to video us fucking. I want to watch the video *while* I fuck you." He pushed a finger slowly into my ass and claimed my lips, his tongue in my mouth matching the movements of his finger. "I wanted to crawl under the table at the restaurant and eat your pussy while you ate your meal. I wanted everyone to see you fall apart for me and wonder what was making you scream." His other hand wrapped around my hair and pulled my head back, arching my throat, his voice getting rougher as he shared his list. "I want to mark you, so everyone knows you're mine. I want to fuck you backstage after a gig. I want you to suck my dick in the corridors while the roadies tidy everything away. I want *everything* you have ... everything you *are*." His tongue ran up the column of my throat and he bit my earlobe. "Is any of that a deal-breaker, Harper? Will you let me do all that to you?"

My mind was a puddle of emotion, of arousal and need. I

could think of nothing but the feel of his hands on my body, *in* my body, his mouth on mine. On a distant level of awareness, I felt the car stop, the engine cut off, and then Gabe was lifting me off him.

"We're home," he told me, and his eyes hooded. "How brave are you feeling? Will you walk to the elevator with me the way you are?"

I blinked at him. "N-naked?" I clarified and he nodded.

"It's a short walk. The only other person here is Miles and he won't get out of the car. He'll drive away. He might take a look back through the mirror. But we'll be alone."

I swallowed. I could see Gabe wanted me to do it, could feel it in the hard length of his erection against my thigh, the excitement in his eyes. Before I could overthink it, I reached for the handle, opened the door and climbed out. The cool air hit my body, tightening my nipples, and then Gabe was there. His warm palms sliding over me, guiding me across the floor. He touched me as we walked, my breasts, my ass, and when we reached the elevator, he stepped back.

"You're so fucking beautiful," he said. I bit my lip, waiting for him to open the elevator. The car behind us hadn't moved, the engine silent. Miles was still there, and I knew he was watching us. "Get on your knees for me, Harper." He unzipped his pants and pulled out his erection, fisting it and looking at me.

I sank to my knees in front of him, placed my palms on his thighs and leaned forward to kiss the tip of his dick, licking away the precum that coated it. He jerked and groaned, and I smiled then sucked him into my mouth.

He cursed, the sound harsh in the silence of the parking lot. His length was hard and hot against my tongue. His fingers slid through my hair, tightened their grip and forced me to take him deeper. I loosened my jaw, let him fuck my mouth how he wanted, snatching a breath every time he eased back. He hit the back of my throat and I gagged, tears streaming from my eyes, but he didn't stop and I didn't pull away, adjusting my position, tipping my head, taking everything he fed me. And then he was dragging me to my feet, his tongue replacing his dick and his fingers burying themselves into my pussy.

"You're fucking perfect," he muttered. With the fingers of one hand still moving inside me, he found the key and opened the elevator, then walked me backwards inside. The door slid closed as he dropped to his knees and buried his face between my legs.

I'd come on his tongue twice before we reached the penthouse.

CHAPTER 47

STRAWBERRY LIPSTICK - YUNGBLUD

Gabe

PRESENT

She was fucking perfect.

I had her bent over the couch, head down, ass up, buried balls-deep inside her pussy and a finger in her ass. Her nails were digging into my thighs, her screams muffled by the cushions, as I coaxed another orgasm from her exhausted body. I couldn't get enough of her. The way her body felt around me. The way she begged and screamed. The sounds she made for me when she came.

Her body spasmed around me again and I eased out of her, caught her when her legs gave way and helped her onto the floor. Dropping a kiss to her shoulder, I straightened.

"Take a breath, we're not done yet," I said and walked across to the kitchen. That angry energy was still burning me up, I *still* hadn't done enough to release it. I needed more. Once I would have made myself bleed. I'd embrace the pain to distract me from feelings I couldn't control. Now I just wanted to hear Harper scream my name.

I washed my hands and opened the freezer to take out the ice-cube tray, then opened the refrigerator and studied the contents. My eyes fell on the bowl of strawberries, plump and juicy. They reminded me of Harper's pussy—wet and sweet—and I grinned.

I carefully placed the strawberries and ice cubes onto the coffee table and nudged Harper.

"Roll onto your back."

"I can't," she mumbled. "I'm already dead."

"You promised, Harper." I kissed my way down her spine. "Come on, baby. I'll make you feel good, I swear." I pressed an ice cube against her fevered skin and she jumped at the coldness. "Pussy or ass?"

"W-what?"

"It's going in one of them. If you stay on your stomach, your ass. If you roll over, your pussy."

She didn't move. Decision made, then. I pressed it against the tight puckered hole and pushed.

"Gabe!" My name was a shocked gasp.

Harper tried to scramble out of reach, but her limbs were too shaky and she didn't move fast enough. I rolled on top of her, pinning her beneath me, so I could rub my dick against the one hole I hadn't fucked yet.

"I offered you a choice, Frosty." A second ice cube followed the first and she wriggled, her ass lifting. "Gonna roll over?"

I plucked a strawberry from the bowl and slid it along her pussy. "I want some Harper-flavoured snacks to keep my strength up. Roll over."

Her body twitched, and then she slowly rolled onto her back. The melted ice cubes wet the carpet.

I brought the strawberry up to her lips. "Bite." She opened her mouth obediently and took the strawberry coated in her own juices between her teeth. "Good girl." I repeated the process with a second one, dipping it inside her to coat it in her arousal. "Fucking perfect," I whispered again, and ate it. The flavour of Harper and strawberry exploded on my tongue and I almost came from that alone.

I ran an ice-cube over her nipples, watching them stiffen and reached for the clamps I'd bought online and kept close to hand. Her gasp as I clipped them in place was like music and the way she writhed when I tugged at them was almost my undoing.

Gathering up a handful of strawberries, I took the largest and fucked her with it, pushing it in and out until she was begging to come. With a mischievous smile, I told her to spread her legs wide and filled her with the plump red fruit, then leaned back to take a photo before I buried my face between her thighs to eat them out of her.

I shared the remainder of the strawberries with her, each one slick with added Harper as seasoning, then I pushed an ice cube into her pussy, followed it with my dick and fucked us both into exhaustion.

※

I woke up, gritty-eyed, a few hours later covered in a sticky mess of strawberries and my own cum. We'd both crashed almost as soon as I came and Harper was still fast asleep, using my body as a pillow, her pussy pressed against my thigh, and her legs tangled around mine, and I half-considered waking her up for another round. The darkness that had enveloped me had receded, and I felt drained, mentally exhausted, physically sated, and perfectly content.

Carefully, not wanting to wake her, I worked my way out from under Harper and stood. She murmured a sleepy protest but didn't open her eyes. I surveyed the room and laughed quietly. The entire place reeked of sex. I was pretty sure the carpet was ruined—stained by squashed strawberries … amongst other things.

Harper was so exhausted, that she didn't even stir when I scooped her up and took her to the bedroom. Placing her onto the bed, she mumbled something I didn't catch, buried her face into the pillow and huddled beneath the sheets. I bent to press a kiss to her cheek, grabbed some clean clothes and headed into the shower.

She was still sleeping when I was done, so I made sure the room was in darkness, closed the door and crept back out to the main room. My cell rang while I was sipping my coffee and idly wondering whether the carpet could be saved, and I moved out onto the balcony to take the call.

"I'm going into Damnation today to see what we can do with the stage area." Seth didn't even say hello before stating his reason for calling. "I want to see if we can replicate the tour version of the show."

I sank onto one of the loungers and stretched out. "If we put a screen up behind it, and maybe extend the stage area out a couple of feet each side, it should work."

"I don't think we should announce it," Seth said.

"You mean a secret gig? No announcement, just surprise whoever turns up?" The idea appealed to me.

"Yeah. Open the club as normal, and then hit the stage around eleven."

"I like it."

"I thought you might." Seth's reply was dry. "So, with that said, how about you meet me at Damnation later today so we can figure out a plan?"

"Sure. What time were you thinking?" Movement to the side caught my eye, and I looked up to see Harper hovering in the doorway, wrapped in one of the sheets from the bed. I patted the front of the lounger and swung my legs either side to make room for her.

She seemed a little hesitant when she sat down, and wouldn't meet my gaze. Only half paying attention to Seth, I tucked a finger beneath her chin and turned her face toward me.

"Okay?" I mouthed at her.

She gave a partial nod, her cheeks bright red and bowed

her head again. I frowned, then sputtered a laugh. She'd walked through the mess we'd left in the living room and was probably dying with embarrassment over what she'd let me do to her. My Harper was a dirty girl when she was horny, but fucking mortified when it was over. I found it cute.

"Sorry, Seth. What was that?" I caught the tail end of his query. "I got distracted."

"I *said* get there at two. The weekend clean up should be finished by then, and we'll have the place to ourselves for a few hours," he repeated.

"Two. Got it. See you then." I hung up.

Silence hung between us. Harper sat stiffly in front of me and I studied her for a second before reaching out and brushing my knuckles down her cheek.

"You kept your end of the bargain. Are you ready for me to keep mine?" The pink in her cheeks deepened further. "Harper, why are you so embarrassed?" I swung my legs around so that they were either side of her and I was behind her, and slid my arms around her waist. My lips sought out the pulse at the base of her throat and I pressed a kiss to it. It fluttered wildly against my mouth. "We didn't do anything wrong last night and you enjoyed yourself, right? I know *I* did."

"I've never … what we did … what I let *you* do …" she was clearly struggling to find the words to tell me how she felt.

"So long as you enjoy it, you shouldn't be ashamed of anything we do. I know I'm not." I nuzzled her throat. "It's us,

Harper. Me and you. You get me? Nothing that happens between us is wrong."

I don't know whether she really agreed with what I was saying, but she relaxed against me, the tension leaving her body.

"Okay?" I asked her and she nodded, more firmly this time. "I made coffee. You want some?"

"I'd like that." I stood and took her hand, and we walked back inside.

Harper settled on one of the stools at the breakfast bar while I made her coffee. I didn't need to ask how she liked it, it was something imprinted on my brain from when we were kids ... well, teenagers, really, since her mom hadn't allowed her near coffee until she was fifteen. She liked it sweet and creamy, the complete opposite to me who was a plain black with no sweetener or cream of any kind sorta guy.

"Who was on the phone?" she asked as I moved around the kitchen.

"Seth. I need to go to Damnation this afternoon." I placed her mug in front of her. "Want to tag along?"

"Will he mind?"

"He won't care, either way. You know how he is. He hasn't changed all that much in the past eight years. Maybe got a little more ornery and standoffish with people." I opened the refrigerator and sent a silent thank you up to the woman who stocked my kitchen once a week. I took out eggs, cheese, tomatoes, ham, onions, and milk and laid it all out.

Harper watched me, her chin cupped on her hand, while I chopped, sliced, diced, and whisked the ingredients, heated oil in a pan and poured the mixture in. A few minutes later, I placed a fluffy omelette in front of her.

"I think I missed your omelettes more than I missed you," she said around a mouthful and I laughed.

"Glad to know I was handy for something."

We ate together wrapped in a comfortable silence I didn't feel the need to fill. It had always been that way with her, and I realised I'd missed that a lot. There were times when I needed quiet, to let my mind settle and rest, and it was difficult in the industry I was in to find moments to do that. Silence was examined, dissected, and questioned and, as the frontman of one of the biggest rock bands on the planet, I had to be larger than life all the fucking time.

This simple moment of just *existing* without needing to draw attention to myself was something I needed, almost *craved* at times, and she gave it to me instinctively.

When we'd finished, she helped to clear up the mess in the kitchen *and* the living room, then disappeared to take a shower.

I called Karl to let him know I was going to be at Damnation with Seth in the afternoon and asked if he knew any carpet cleaners. My manager didn't even question my need for such a service—such was our relationship—but told me he'd get something arranged and let me know the details.

"I've got a meeting in about an hour. Do you need anything

else?" he asked me.

I hesitated. There was, and he wasn't going to like it.

"Gabe?" he queried when I didn't reply.

"I need you to arrange something for me. It's short notice."

"*How* short notice?"

"Like ... this morning."

I heard the creak of his chair, and I visualised him leaning back in his big leather office chair, a frown wrinkling his brow as he ran through various scenarios I might need fast help fixing.

I didn't leave him suffering ... for too long, anyway.

"I need to visit Sacred Saints. Obviously, I don't want the press getting wind of me being there."

"*Why?*" He almost barked the word.

I told him about the run-in with Jefferson Thomas outside Joyeuse and he cursed furiously.

"It's fine. He's just trying to find a story. But Harper wants to know."

"Can't you just *tell* her?"

"No. It won't be enough. I need to show her. Can you arrange it for me?"

"Probably. I'll get back to you. *Don't* go there until I've spoken to you to confirm it."

"I won't."

"I mean it, Gabe. Don't fuck around on this. We've kept it out of the news for years. Don't slip up because Harper turned up."

"I said I *won't*."

※

"Gabe, it's so lovely to see you again." The administrator of Sacred Saints, Shirley Temple—yeah, her parents hated her that much they named her after a child star—greeted me warmly.

Over the years, I'd visited here and there and we'd built a cautious friendship. I always brought her daughter signed merchandise whenever I turned up and I hadn't forgotten this time, even though it had been twelve months or so since I'd last been there.

I handed her the bag—tour t-shirt, signed photos of the guys, limited edition vinyl and a demo CD. "Tell Riley to stop bitching about me on her blog and I'll send her tickets for a private gig soon."

Shirley laughed. "What's she been saying about you now?"

"Claims I was a beat off in Louisiana. Has she graduated yet?" I knew she hadn't, just like I had her date of graduation listed in my diary. And by diary, I meant a reminder on my phone. That reminder came in the form of Candice, who called me most days to list any appointments I had.

"Three months."

"She still want to be involved in the industry?" I followed Shirley into her office, Harper close behind me.

"It's all she talks about. I wish you'd talk her out of it," Shirley was saying as she rounded her desk.

Riley had been in the hospital one of the times I'd visited and once she'd gotten over her '*oh my God, it's Gabe Mercer in the flesh*' and realised I was an asshole, she soon got over her adoration and now behaved like the baby sister I didn't want.

She had an immensely popular blog where she reviewed gigs and new music releases. It helped that I sent her backstage passes to a lot of them, which gave her up-close and personal access to a lot of stars. Thing is, she was bloody good at it and most of the bands trusted her not to fuck them over. To get backstage, she needed to lie about her age, otherwise she would have needed to have an adult with her at all times and that was a problem because she was gorgeous and an outrageous flirt. I knew Shirley would kill me if any of the guys I knew even tried to get into her pants, so I had to double-down on the crazy whenever I let her near them.

I caught Shirley looking curiously at Harper and reached back to take her hand.

"Harper, Shirley is the administrator of Sacred Saints. Shirley, Harper is …" I paused. Girlfriend sounded childish, lover probably wasn't the wisest description to use. I opted for what was, to me, the best choice. "Harper and I grew up together. One day I'll marry her."

"Only if I let you," Harper replied without missing a beat. Christ, I fucking loved this woman. She took my shit and threw it back at me.

"You'll let me." I started down my nose at her, arrogance dripping from every word, just to see how she'd react.

"Not if you don't explain why we're here." She tossed her

hair and sniffed.

"I'm working up to it." I looked at Shirley. "Has there been any change?"

"You know I'd call you if there was."

"Change about what, *Gabriel*?" Inappropriately, my dick hardened. There was something about the way she said my full name that did something to me *every ... single ... time*. Especially now it was imprinted in my head how she screamed it when I made her come.

"Can we go up?" I ignored her question, and *tried* to ignore my erection. I failed at both when she repeated my name. Licking my lips, I met her curious gaze. "My da is here," I told her.

Tattooed Memories

CHAPTER 48

SATELLITE KID - DOGS D'AMOUR

Harper

PRESENT

Gabe's father was alive?

"But ... you said he was dead," I heard myself say.

"It wasn't really a lie. He's dead to me." His face was impassive, but his eyes ... his eyes burned with an emotion I couldn't describe.

"Thomas Mercer has been here for three years now," Shirley said into the silence as we stared at each other.

"What's wrong with him?"

"I've been asking myself that for years," Gabe muttered. He shoved his hands into his jeans pockets and turned away. "Can we go up?"

I looked at the hospital administrator.

"Could you give us a minute?" I asked her and, after a moment's hesitation while she waited in vain for Gabe to respond, she nodded. The click as the door closed on her back was loud in the silence of the room.

"Why did you tell me he was dead?"

Gabe swung back to face me, sighed and scrubbed a hand down his face. "Because he might as well be." He held out his hand. "Come with me?"

We left the office and found Shirley waiting outside. She glanced down at our clasped hands, but said nothing about his white-knuckled grip on my fingers. "Tasha is overseeing his care today. I've made sure the rest of the staff will be off the floor for the next hour, so you can take your time."

"I doubt we'll be there long," Gabe replied and led me down the corridor. "This is the VIP wing," he explained as we walked. "There's rarely more than a couple of people here. You have to have a certain level of income to afford care on this floor."

He opened a door and waved me in. I stepped through, then stopped, my eyes going to the bed. My first thought was how small and frail he looked. In my memory, Gabe's dad was a huge, loud, often terrifying man, not this shrivelled person lying in the bed.

I inched forward, taking in the tube coming from his mouth, the soft beeping of machines, the sterile smell of the room. I heard Gabe move behind me, felt his warmth as he hooked an arm around my waist and let his chin drop to rest on the top of my head. I leaned back against his chest.

"He had a stroke a few years ago. I was the emergency contact in his phone. Fuck knows why. He was unconscious when I came in. The doctors said the coma would probably only last a few weeks but here we are ... three years later."

"Do you think he knows you're here?"

"I fucking hope not."

I turned in his arms and looped my hands around his neck. "You're a good man, Gabe Mercer. A far better man than your father was. I hope you know that."

"I'm not, but I like that you think so."

"Is this what that reporter was talking about?" I felt his body tense against me.

"No. Jefferson Thomas," he spat the name out, "seemed to think I killed my da. He spent a couple of years writing articles about how it was a big mystery that no one knew who he was or where he was. I know he knows more than he's written about. I'm pretty sure he knows about the things my da did when I was a kid, and he definitely has photos of me beating the shit out of him."

I glanced back at the still form in the bed. "You beat him up?"

"It's not related to the condition he's in now. It happened years before. But that was when Karl finally forced him into an agreement to stay away from me. In return, he was given an ... allowance, but it would have ended if he fed any information to the press. I guess Jefferson took two and two and made five."

"He seemed to think your dad was still alive last night."

"Yeah," Gabe's reply was soft. "I got the same impression. And that means he's digging again."

"What will he find other than a man who still managed to make something of himself, no matter where he came from? You have nothing to be ashamed of," I told him.

"I'm not ashamed, Harper. I just don't want him to get any more attention than he deserves. He's not responsible for what I've done, *I* am."

I turned back to look at the man in the bed once again. "Do you think he'll wake up?"

"I doubt it. Shirley has been telling me it's time to consider switching off the life support." He glanced toward the machine and the emotionless mask faltered briefly, showing the raw pain he was hiding.

I palmed his cheek and brought his head back to face me. "It's not wrong to be upset, Gabe."

"I hate him, Harper, with every part of my soul. I *hate* him, but I just can't do it," he whispered, resting his forehead against mine. "I can't sign the order to end his miserable fucking life, and while I pay the bills the hospital won't force me to do it."

We stood there, together, with only the beeping of the machines breaking the silence. I mourned the little boy I'd known, the things he'd suffered, and I celebrated the man he was. How he'd clawed his way from the depths of abuse and poverty and held the world in the palm of his hand.

He pulled away from me and walked toward the door. "Come on. We have another stop to make before going to Damnation."

"What is this place?"

We'd driven for about forty minutes before Miles pulled the car off the main road and through a set of electronic gates. The building at the end of the drive was large and forbidding. Gabe smiled at my question.

"I promised to tell you everything. You already know my past, you now know about my da. You know everything about the band. This is the final piece." He threw open the car door. "You'll like this, I promise."

As we reached the top of the steps, the front door was thrown open and two little boys, no more than five years old, launched themselves at Gabe's legs. Both chattered loudly, their voices battling for dominance. Gabe squatted down and wrapped an arm around each of their thin shoulders.

"Boys, I can't listen to you both at once," he laughed. "Harper, this is Marley," he squeezed the dark-skinned boy's shoulder. "He's a crazy good artist. If you ask him nicely, he might draw you a snowman. And this is Parker." The other kid, pale-skinned with a shock of bright red hair covering his head, got a similar squeeze. "They live here, along with six or seven others and," he paused and smiled warmly at the woman exiting the building. "They live here with Bea." Smoothly he rose to his feet, untangled himself from the two boys and opened his arms.

The woman, who I assumed was Bea, walked into his embrace with a low, warm laugh. "I wondered when you'd show up." She reached up to place a kiss on his cheek and I had to stop myself from clearing my throat, jealousy at their obvious affection burning like acid in my stomach.

"Bea," he turned the woman to face me. "*This* is Harper." His tone of voice was odd ... heavy with meaning.

I found myself wrapped in her arms, as she peppered kisses over my cheeks. "Finally! I'm so so incredibly pleased to meet you at last!" I returned her embrace awkwardly. "Come inside, both of you. Boys! Leave Gabe alone. Go and wash up ready for lunch."

She caught both our hands and marched us inside. Gabe ignored my questioning glances, his eyes focused directly ahead of him, his free hand stuffed into his pocket as he walked alongside Bea.

What *was* this place?

Inside it looked like a mix between a school and childminders. There were toys scattered all over, the walls were painted brightly with murals of fairy tales, dinosaurs, cars, and giants. Through the windows opposite, I could see a large garden area. Swings, slides, rope nets, and a treehouse were visible through the glass.

"You're just in time for lunch," Bea told Gabe as we walked through the house. "The kids will all be in the dining hall, so you can get all the excitement out of the way at once."

"Do you need anything? Money? How's the budget coping?" he asked, and I frowned, trying to figure out what I was missing. What was going on here?

"One of the showers has broken, but we've got someone

coming to look at that tomorrow. We're well within budget this year, I think. Unless one of the kids sets fire to something again."

Gabe chuckled. "Let's hope not. Any birthdays coming up? Isn't Parker's soon?"

"Next month."

"I'll get something delivered to him. He still into fire trucks?"

Bea nodded. "Very much so."

"Maybe I can get one of the local firehouses to drop by and take him for a ride-along. I'll see what I can do."

"You're a good boy, Gabe." She released his hand to pat his arm. "Here we go. Brace yourself." She threw open a door.

Noise flooded out. Children's voices, talking, laughing, shouting. The smell of food made my stomach grumble and Gabe shot me a look, his eyes dancing with laughter.

"I think Harper's hungry," he said, draping an arm over my shoulders. "She'll hurt me if I starve her." I dug him in the ribs with my elbow and he smirked. "See?"

Bea's smile could only be described as indulgent as she looked at us. "I'm sure we can feed the pair of you."

She stepped through the door and clapped her hands together sharply. Silence fell over the room and then, collectively, the six children in the room shrieked Gabe's name. I stood beside Bea as he was swamped by small bodies.

"Is this a children's home?" I asked Bea.

"You don't know?" She hooked a hand through my arm and drew me further into the room. "Let's go through to the kitchen.

Gabe will be a while." She threw an affectionate look in his direction.

I smiled at the view of Gabe being dragged across the room by the kids. He sat on one of the chairs and they climbed all over him, vying for his attention. He looked up, caught my eye and winked.

"We run a home for abused children," Bea said quietly when we reached the kitchen. "I don't know how Gabe found out about us, but he showed up about five years ago, wrote a cheque for an obscene amount of money and left again. Six months later, he showed up again. After that, he became a regular visitor. He'd bring toys and clothes for the kids. Then, one night he called me sounding distressed. He'd found a boy half-dead on the streets. With being such a famous face, he didn't want to cause any kind of media circus, so he asked if I would take the boy into the hospital and find out what had happened. I met him at the hospital and took over the care of the child. From the pieces we've managed to patch together, the boy had run away after being beaten badly by his father." She gave me a long look. "I'm sure you know how that resonated with Gabe. When child services came to take him, I offered to take him in here. With Gabe's contributions, we've become a haven for children, giving another option over standard foster care."

I looked at the man in the other room. He was so much more than what people saw. I knew why he hid it, why he didn't want people to see just how deeply he did care about things. He tried to bury that side of himself beneath bad behaviour and outrageous words.

He looked up and caught me watching him and something jumped between us, a spark … an energy. His smile was slow and warm and then the moment was broken when one of the kids touched his arm and Gabe looked down at him.

※

"Why do you keep it a secret?" I asked him as we drove to Damnation. I was curled into his side in the back of the car, while he held a text conversation with Luca.

"Because I don't want reporters hanging around outside the place in the hopes of catching me there. Those kids have been through enough shit without my presence adding to it," he said after a moment. "They need to feel safe. Bea and her staff give them that."

"And it getting out would completely destroy your bad boy rock star persona," I teased lightly.

He laughed. "That too. I'm not doing it for publicity. There's no reason anyone needs to know I'm the anonymous donor."

"I'm seeing a whole new side of you. The kids in there obviously adore you, and Shirley's daughter obviously has a good relationship with you as well."

"If you tell anyone, I'll have to kill you," he deadpanned. "Are you okay with coming to Damnation? You're probably going to be bored while we figure out the logistics."

I shrugged. "I downloaded the Kindle app, so I'll just find a quiet spot and read until you're done."

Seth was already inside when we arrived, a pencil tucked

behind his ear and a tape measure in his hand.

"All you need is a tool belt and you can pass for a construction worker," Gabe quipped, bumping shoulders with him. "I'm just gonna take Harper upstairs and then I'll be back."

Seth nodded, sending me a smile and a wave, and Gabe led me to the staircase set back against the far corner of the club. Upstairs, he gave me a quick tour of their 'VIP lounge', dropped a quick kiss on my lips and disappeared back downstairs. I settled onto one of the plush couches, curled my feet up beneath me and buried my nose in my book.

Tattooed Memories

CHAPTER 49

LEVEL OF CONCERN - TWENTY ONE PILOTS

Gabe

PRESENT

I was sick of seeing the inside of the car. It wasn't even my Mustang, but the sedan Miles drove me around in. I *missed* driving myself places. I missed waking up and getting behind the wheel and just driving somewhere to clear my head.

My days currently consisted of dragging my ass out of the bed, where Harper was wrapped around me, at six in the morning, going to the studio to meet the guys where we'd work on the set for the upcoming gigs until three in the afternoon.

Harper turned up around that time with take-out. The guys had welcomed her back into the fold easily, although Luca still flirted way too fucking much for my comfort level. Which was why he did it. Wasn't the point, it pissed me off. We'd eat, then practice for a few hours longer, and then we'd head back home.

Rinse and repeat day after fucking day.

I banged my head against the soft leather of the back seat and let out a frustrated breath. It wasn't in my nature not to confront the issues head-on and all this avoidance was starting to grate on my nerves

I hadn't seen or heard from Meredith since Karl had told me she was lurking around. *Nothing*—no attempts to contact me, no lying in wait outside my building or the studio, but Karl insisted she was still around. He didn't seem to understand that I wasn't bothered by her, I didn't *care* about what she was doing. The girl had issues. She needed help. Pretending she didn't exist wasn't going to make her go away, it would just make her more determined.

"We're here," Miles' quiet voice cut through the silence of the car and I realised we were parked outside the studio. "I'll pick up Harper and drop her here at the usual time?"

"Yeah," I grunted, almost sullenly, and threw myself out of the car.

The one bright light was that my relationship with Harper was going from strength to strength. She'd practically moved in. She *claimed* she was only staying with me because of the whole stalker issue. But I didn't think she'd be moving out any time soon. And I was more than fine with that.

I was halfway across the parking lot when I realised no other cars were there, which meant I was the first to arrive.

Cursing beneath my breath, I dug out my keys and stood in front of the door trying to remember which one would unlock it.

"It's the gold one, gorgeous."

Fuck. Spoke too soon!

I turned slowly, scanning the parking lot for Miles, but the car had gone.

Double fuck.

He wasn't supposed to leave until I was inside. But it was my fault because I'd bitched the entire way here about not needing a babysitter.

"Hello, Gabe."

Meredith Parker. A one-night stand that almost turned into a live-action version of *Misery*. In fact, it hadn't even been a true one-night stand. It had been a couple of hours backstage after a gig. But, for some reason, she'd decided it was the start of something more and began following me around.

Last time I'd seen her, she'd had a knife, so I was understandably wary when I eyed her. I couldn't see anything in her hands, but I wasn't going to risk it.

"What are you doing here?" I asked.

"I know what you're thinking, but you're wrong."

"That right? I'm thinking you're not supposed to be within five hundred feet of me, and I've heard reports that you've been hanging around the studio and the record label's offices a lot."

"I have, but not because I wanted to …" she waved a hand. "Look, Gabe, what happened between us—"

"There isn't and never was an *us*," I cut in.

"I know that now," she replied quietly. "That's what I'm trying to tell you. I've been seeing a therapist and they've really helped me to understand what I was doing and why. I just ... I wanted to apologise. I know it doesn't make up for the things I've done, but ..." she shrugged. "I knew if I wrote a letter, it wouldn't get to you. This was something I had to do in person. I don't expect you to believe me, but I *am* sorry."

She was right, I didn't believe her. I thought what she was saying was just an excuse for her to have contact with me, but I'd play along.

"If that's the case, why did you threaten Harper?"

She looked confused. "Harper? I don't know who that is."

"You sent her a text, threatening her to stay away from me."

Meredith shook her head. "No, I didn't. I haven't spoken to anyone. Well, except for the receptionist at NFG to try and get an appointment to see you. I wanted to do this properly, not have to sneak around to catch up with you. But, for obvious reasons, she wouldn't give me an appointment."

She reached out a hand and I stepped back, evading her touch. Her arm dropped.

"I'm sorry, Gabe. I was sick, I know that now. I'm going back to Montreal tonight, so this is the last you'll see of me." She turned away.

"Wait." I set off after her across the parking lot. "Are you sure you didn't send that text?"

"You can check my phone records if you like. I'll send you a copy of them. I haven't texted anyone connected to you."

I shook my head. "No, I'll take your word for it."

She gave me a sad smile. "I *really* am sorry for everything I did."

I said nothing as she continued walking away, my mind already picking at the puzzle she'd left me with. I unlocked the studio door and went in, turned off the alarm, and switched on the lights. A glance at the wall told me it hadn't quite reached seven, but I pulled my cell out of my pocket and made a call anyway.

"Too early." Harper's sleepy protest when she answered the phone settled my nerves immediately.

I settled onto one of the large couches and propped my feet on the table. "Did I wake you?"

"You know you did." I heard the rustle of the sheets as she moved around. "Is everything okay?"

"You remember that stalker? The reason we've been holed up in the penthouse?" I waited for her affirmative response and then told her what Meredith had said.

"Hmmm, strange. Do you believe her?"

"I didn't at first, but I dunno, Frosty, I kinda think she did mean it." Voices reached me and I looked up to see Dex and Luca coming through the door. "Listen, the guys are here. You'll be here later, yeah?"

"Chinese today, right?"

"Yeah. I'll text you with what everyone wants."

"Do that. I'm going back to sleep for an hour."

I chuckled. "Dream of me."

She didn't reply, ending the call.

"All well in honeymoon land?" Dex asked like he did every

morning. I'm not sure whether he was expecting me to fuck it up to the point she left me, or if he was genuinely happy Harper was back in my life.

Luca didn't say anything, going over to the drum kit in the corner and fiddling with its placement. I didn't take it personally. Even though it seemed like we hated each other and bickering with each other *did* play a big part in our relationship, most of the time we got on fine. He also wasn't a morning person and, lately, something had clearly been eating at him.

I crossed to where he was bent, adjusting one of the pedals and he glanced up at me.

"What's going on with you?"

"Nothing," he grunted.

"See ... you say that, but I don't believe you."

He sighed and stood. "Nothing that will affect my performance or the band. Is that better?"

"But *something* is going on with you, isn't it?" I moved to the mic stand and shifted its position.

"We're not having a heart to heart, Gabe." He settled onto his stool. "Where's Seth?"

"He's meeting contractors at Damnation to get the stage area adapted for what we need. He'll be here later. I'll cover the guitar until then."

"Let's get on then. The setlist from the top?"

I nodded and picked up a guitar, while Dex took up his position. Luca hit his drums and our practice session began.

Tattooed Memories

CHAPTER 50

BORN FOR THIS - THE SCORE

Harper
PRESENT

Five weeks ago, I'd stepped inside Damnation and seen Gabe for the first time in eight years. It had triggered a whole series of events which I could never have predicted would have ended up with me virtually moving into his penthouse a short time later.

But here I was.

And the strange part was—I didn't regret it. It felt right, like coming home. I pondered it as I put the finishing touches on my makeup. Okay, we'd had a bit of a rocky start, but overall, I thought we were in a good place.

Tonight I was going back to Damnation, but this time Gabe and Forgotten Legacy were taking the stage in a surprise, unannounced gig, for the clubbers—and I couldn't wait to see him in action. I'd invited Siobhan, and we'd spent the day getting ready, back in the apartment I'd shared with her until two weeks ago. I hadn't said anything to Gabe, but I knew I wouldn't be moving back here. He didn't want me to leave the penthouse, he'd made that clear, but I'd refused to let him get his own way without a battle.

Gabe had left early in the morning to go to the club, dropping me off with Siobhan en route, and he'd checked in periodically throughout the day. Who knew he'd make such great boyfriend material? Especially after the way we'd left things all those years ago, but here we were making a go of it.

"Are you ready?" Siobhan appeared behind me, dressed in a slinky short red dress which should have clashed horribly with her hair but she pulled off in her usual sexy 'don't give a fuck' fashion. She'd paired it with a pair of silver strappy high heels. Her dark red hair was piled on top of her head, with curly strands falling down artfully around her pixie-shaped face.

I felt like a frump beside her. She was so effortlessly sexy it made me sick, and I told her so. In typical best-friend fashion, she laughed at me.

"This from the woman who is dating one of the sexiest men in rock?" She perched on the edge of the bed, handing me the glass of wine she'd brought in with her. "Tell me … is he as wild in the sack as the rumours suggest?"

I choked on the mouthful of Pinot Noir and spluttered. I could feel my cheeks burning as images of the things I'd done with Gabe over the past two weeks assailed me.

"Oh my gosh!" Siobhan leaned forward, green eyes sparkling. "He *is*! I want to know all about it. It's best-friend code. You *have* to share all the nasty details with me!"

I shook my head. "Not going to happen."

"At least tell me he's *good*."

I laughed into my glass. "Oh, he's *very* good."

Siobhan raised her own glass in a toast. "I'm so proud of you! Now drink up. Our ride will be here soon."

※

The club was a heaving excited mass by the time we arrived. Miles whisked us through without needing to queue and led us to the stairs which would take us up to the VIP room. The barman who'd been there the first time I'd visited caught my eye and grinned. I waved as I passed him.

"Who's *that*?" Siobhan hissed in my ear.

"Just one of the bartenders. Bran, Brax? I don't remember what Gabe said his name was."

"I might just sashay on over and say hello."

I grabbed her hand. "No, you're coming with me to meet the rest of the band!"

She stopped. "Oh no! That wasn't what I agreed to. I have no interest in meeting the men I lust over from a distance. It'll be so disappointing."

"Von!" I swung around to Miles, who stood behind us. "Tell her."

"You're to go up to the VIP suite," he said obligingly. "Come along, ladies." He rested his palm on the small of Siobhan's back and gently moved her into motion again.

At the top of the stairs, a big burly doorman stood, his arms folded over his chest. When he saw us coming, he straightened and moved to stand with the door behind him.

"It's okay. This is Gabe's girl, Harper, and her friend," Miles said from behind us and the guy relaxed.

"Nice to finally meet you," he greeted me and swung the door behind him open.

We walked through and the door closed again, muffling the noise from the bar downstairs and sealing us inside the room.

"Well, fuck …" a raspy voice drawled from my left and I turned as Gabe slid an arm around my waist and spun me to face him.

His palm slid down my spine and over the curve of my ass and he dragged me against his body. "Now that's something I've been dying to see all day long."

And then his mouth was on mine. I'd anticipated his greeting by wearing clear lip gloss because over the past two weeks I had discovered that when Gabe kissed me, he did it thoroughly. There were no quick pecks on the cheek when he was leaving for work. If he kissed me, he *kissed* me, leaving me breathless and needy, regardless of whether we were with his friends, out in public, or at home.

I pulled back. *Home?* When had his penthouse become home?

"Put her down, for fuck's sake," I heard Luca growl from the other side of the room. "And get the girl a drink."

"Charming as ever, Luc," I laughed and untangled myself from Gabe to go and give the grumpy ass a hug.

I'd missed these guys more than I realised. Hanging out with them while they practised over the last few weeks had slowly taken me back to the time when we'd always been together, and they'd reverted to treating me the way they always had—the annoying kid sister who they'd tease mercilessly ... only Gabe teased me in a very different way these days. One I wouldn't complain about at all.

"Who's the redhead?" Luca whispered before letting me go.

"Siobhan, my friend. So leave her alone," I told him.

He flashed me a grin. "Not me you need to worry about, tiger." He nodded toward Dex who was standing close to my friend, his palm resting on the wall beside her head.

"Dex," I called out and his head swung toward me. "You play nice." I pointed a finger at him. He smirked back at me.

"I always play nice, babe."

Siobhan's fingers curled over his bicep and she peered at me over the top. "I'm a big girl, Harper," she told me and winked.

Gabe's hands slid around my waist and he pressed up against my back, nuzzling my throat. "Are you watching from up here or coming down to the main floor?"

"I'm coming down. Last time we saw you on stage, we were so far away we had to watch on the screens. I'm not missing this one." I tipped my head back against his shoulder. "It looks extra busy down there tonight … or compared with when I was last here, anyway."

I felt him nod. "We had more tickets made available for tonight. There's already whispers about a live band playing, but no one knows who." He chuckled, his breath warm against my ear. "This is my favourite part about doing what we do. Getting up on stage, performing in front of screaming fans who just live for the music." He pointed down at the stage. "We're going to cut off the music at eleven, then turn off the lights. We'll come on stage from the left and the curtain will drop."

I could hear the excitement in his voice, the passion and love he had for the band and their music. The entire room was filled with a sense of anticipation, each of the men in Forgotten Legacy filled with an energy that sizzled and crackled.

We stood by the tinted glass window, looking down over the main floor of the club. Gabe stood behind me, his hands resting on the bar either side of my hips. I could feel his warmth against my back, wrapping around me, and—I laughed to myself—his erection pressing against my thigh.

"Do you always go on stage with a hard-on?" I asked him.

"No, I usually come *off stage* with one. Being out there makes me horny as fuck." His lips found the pulse in my throat. "Knowing *you* will be watching me is what's giving me the hard-on right now."

"You always say all the right things." I tilted my head, giving him better access to nip and suck at my neck.

One of his hands lifted to squeeze my breast. "If I hiked up your dress a little, and pulled down my zipper, we could have a quickie right here, right now."

"And there you go spoiling it." But my nipples were hard and my panties were wet just from his words—and he knew it.

"They wouldn't even notice … until you started screaming." He pinched my nipple and laughed when I shivered.

"That's our cue," Seth said from the other side of the room as "No Rest For The Wicked" by Cage The Elephant started playing downstairs. "Let's go."

"Saved by the song," he quipped and nipped my earlobe. "But I love the fact you're going to be wet and hot for me while I'm out there." He turned me around to face him. "Kiss for luck?"

"You don't need luck," I told him but kissed him anyway.

CHAPTER 51

ROCK BOTTOM – GRANDSON

Gabe

PRESENT

We stood beside the stage, out of sight of the club's visitors. When the music stopped and the lights went out, we crept onto the stage and took our positions. We let the club stay silent … or as silent as it could be with people milling around asking why the lights had gone out, and then Dex and Luca sang the opening to "Miss Jackson" by Panic! At The Disco—because of course, we were going to open with the song I sang to Harper all the time.

As the bassline started up and people realised there was a live band, the atmosphere changed. When I sang the first line and the lights switched on, the crowd went wild. I stalked around the stage, reaching out to touch hands with the fans straining up, while I sang. Dex and Seth prowled around behind me, guitar and bass blending perfectly with the beat of Luca's drums.

When the song ended, I hopped up onto one of the speakers and looked out over the sea of faces.

"Welcome to Damnation!" I called out and everyone roared. "We thought we'd surprise you all and get up on stage to play a few songs. Are you up for that?"

Cheers erupted.

"I love you, Gabe!" someone shrieked from the back.

I flashed a grin in the direction of the voice. "Thanks, babe. So I'm not going to waste time up here talking, let's make some noise!"

We treated the gig like every other we played, no matter that it was a much smaller stage, with fewer people than we'd played to in years. We gave it our all and by the time two hours had passed, all four of us had stripped down to our pants and we were coated in sweat.

The lights went down and I dashed off the stage to grab a bottle of water from Harper. I drained half the bottle, grabbed her for a kiss then jumped back up for our encore.

The club vibrated with the thrum of what sounded like a heartbeat, slow and steady, building up, coursing through bodies. Making them restless, turned on, hot and ready.

A light flickered, my cue to take up position in the centre of the stage. Dex's bass added a deep dark rumble, Luca's drums joined the heartbeat, the light flashed on ... off ... on ... off. Seth's guitar rang out, wailing its pain and then the lights moulded into one and shone down on where I stood, centre stage, arms outstretched with big black wings on the screen behind me. The screams of excitement washed over me, thrilling me, and I sang the final song—*"Regret"*—with my dick so hard it was painful.

When it was over and the lights dimmed again, I stalked off the stage, grabbed Harper's hand and dragged her upstairs. We were through the door and I'd locked it behind us before the rest of the guys finished up on the stage and I pushed her toward the glass wall.

I dropped a hand between us to drag down my zipper and pull out my dick. With the other hand, I pressed down on Harper's shoulder until she dropped to her knees. The minute her mouth slid over me, my legs almost buckled.

"Fuck."

I could still hear the crowd screaming downstairs, muted through the partial soundproofing of the room and my mind flashed back to the last gig we'd played. I'd been in a similar position afterwards with a girl on her knees, sucking my dick, while I could hear the crowd still roaring. Ironically, it was also the night Harper came back in my life. The difference was this time, *tonight*, I was far from bored and, when I looked down at the woman's head bobbing back and forth in front of me, I didn't have to pretend she had lavender hair or smelled like cotton candy.

My fingers slid into that silky hair, while I fought not to take control of her movements. Her tongue was licking at me, swirling around my erection, and I knew if I didn't pull her off, I was going to blow like a virgin getting his first blowjob.

I started to ease her head away, and her hand came up to

grip my thigh, stopping me.

"Harper." It was the only word I could say, could *think*. The only word I *knew*. My ability to converse in sentences went along with my control as my hips jerked and I came, spilling into her mouth. I felt her throat move as she took everything I had, and that just made me come harder. I threw my head back, snarled out a string of curses, and dragged her to her feet.

My mouth took hers, my tongue parting her lips and invading inside. I didn't care that I could taste myself, that she'd just fucked my dick with her mouth. None of that mattered to me. All I cared about was this woman was here, with *me*, in my arms and I'd finally come home.

I eased back, curving my palms over her cheeks, and kissed the tip of her nose. "Let's go home."

I unlocked the door to find the rest of the band, and Siobhan, standing outside. Seth flicked cool eyes over me, then nodded to Harper.

"We're heading out," I said.

None of them argued. They all had their own ways of coming down after a gig, and none of it included recapping or sharing our feelings. Each one clapped my shoulder as I passed them, Harper's hand in mine, and took her down the private staircase at the back of the VIP area, to where my Mustang waited.

I helped Harper into the passenger seat then strode around to the driver's side and slid in. Her hand landed on my thigh and squeezed. With a smile, I gunned the engine and headed home.

The penthouse was only a twenty-minute drive from the club and it's one I have done a million times, but every other time I wasn't distracted by a woman beside me, her fingers creeping slowly up my thigh, working down my zipper and sliding her fingers inside to grip my dick.

Maybe that was what caused the distraction, maybe the car that collided with us did it deliberately—it's hard to say. But either way, my grip on the steering wheel wasn't as secure as it could have been and when the car came out of nowhere and sideswiped us, it spun and sent us on a collision course.

Harper cried out beside me as I fought to regain control, but the car was going too fast, and we were sent headlong across the road and straight into one of the trees which lined the sidewalk.

※

There was a ringing in my ears, lights flashing above me, voices shouting and sirens. I tried to move, and pain ricocheted through my head.

"Steady. Stay still," a voice cautioned.

"What?" I tried to focus and the pain intensified, making me groan. "Fuck ... w-what ... h-happened?" I forced the words out from between gritted teeth. Agony sliced through me with every word.

"Hold still. We need to cut you out."

I think I passed out at that point because when I next opened my eyes, there was a white ceiling above me and an engine rumbling in the distance. A stranger peered down at me and shone a light into my eyes, making me wince.

"Can you hear me?"

"Yes," I ground out.

"Do you know your name?"

"What the fuck kind of stupid question is that?" I attempted to sit up and found myself pressed firmly back down.

"Name?"

"Gabriel Mercer."

"And the year?"

I told him, my tone making it clear I was done with stupid questions. "What happened?"

"You were in a car crash. We're in the ambulance."

"Harper?"

"Who?" The paramedic looked blank.

"The girl in the car. *My* girl. Is she okay?"

"I'm sorry, there was no girl in the car."

"What? No. Harper was in the car with me." I struggled to rise again. "We have to go back. Harper is there."

"Mr Mercer ... Gabriel ... calm down."

"Get the fuck off me." I shoved at him, trying to unstrap myself from the stretcher and the distraction cost me my consciousness when he pricked my neck and sedated me.

※

The next time I woke, I was in a hospital bed.

"Fuck. What time is it?" I surged upright and was stopped by rough hands grabbing my arms and hauling me back down.

"Lie the fuck still." Seth's voice, clipped and tired.

I searched him out and found him on the left side of the bed, Dex and Luca on either side of him. Karl stood on the opposite side. All of them looked exhausted, still in the clothes we'd worn to the gig.

"Where's Harper?" I demanded and watched as all four faces blanked. *"Where ... the fuck ... is Harper?"*

CHAPTER 52

BAD DAY - DANIEL POWTER

Harper

Present

C old.

Bone-jarring, teeth-chattering, breath-freezing *cold*.

I was lying on my side, knees curled up to my chest and my fingers tucked under my arms. Obviously, even while I was unconscious I'd been aware it was cold and did my best to stay warm. Tried, but failed.

My entire body was shivering. I wasn't dressed for cold weather. The dress I wore was short, the sleeves almost non-existent. I was dressed for a night in a club followed by sex with my ridiculously hot rock star boyfriend.

"Gabe!" His name left my lips in a gasp and I tried to sit up.

The minute my hands touched the floor, I snatched them back up and looked down. There was a thick layer of ice beneath me, which explained the cold. Further investigation showed that

I had been lying on a blanket. As my eyes adjusted to the dim lighting, I tried to see where I was but didn't recognise anything. I was definitely indoors ... but *where*? Ice suggested somewhere cold, and part of me questioned whether I was still in L.A. But if not there ... where *was* I? Someone *must* have brought me here.

The last thing I remembered was being in the car with Gabe. I'd been teasing him while he drove us back to the penthouse and then ... I frowned. Then what?

Oh my God!

A car's headlights had come at us from a side road and hit the Mustang. Gabe had lost control and we'd hit something. I didn't remember anything after that until I woke up here.

I drew my knees beneath me and knelt up, tugging the skirt of my dress down to cover as much of my legs as I could—which wasn't much. Now my eyes had adjusted, I could see my breath forming in the air in front of me. If I didn't get warm soon, I was going to have serious problems ... namely *death*.

"Hello?" I called out and heard my voice echo back at me. "Is anyone there?" Movement in the darkness caught my eye and I stumbled to my feet. *"Hello!?* Can you help me?" My heart was hammering in my chest, the beat of it loud in my ears as uneasiness rose.

Whoever was there didn't come closer or speak, and fear was heavy in the pit of my stomach. I'd been avoiding thinking about how I had arrived here, but I knew—*knew*—nothing good was going to come of it.

Footsteps echoed through the room and I spun around trying to figure out what direction they were coming from. Cold hands closed over my shoulders from behind and held me still.

"Sorry about this," a voice muttered and then pain exploded out from the back of my head.

CHAPTER 53

AIN'T NO SUNSHINE - SHAWN JAMES

Gabe

PRESENT

I held it together until the detective left my penthouse, but once the doors slid closed on the elevator I spun and buried my fist in the wall.

"Gabe ..." Karl spoke behind me seconds before a hand landed on my shoulder.

"Two days, Karl. It's been *two fucking days* and they've got nothing. *Found* nothing!"

"But there's been no ransom demand." He hesitated. "You have to consider the possibility she's simply decided this wasn't what she wanted and left."

"Ghosted me? No way. Harper wouldn't do that."

"You don't know that. Not really. It's been eight years, Gabe, and you've been together for less than a month."

"If you can't be fucking helpful, then get out." Maybe I was being unreasonable, but I didn't care. Harper was missing and no one could give me any answers that made sense.

When I'd finally found someone at the hospital to talk to me, I discovered she hadn't even been in the car when the paramedics had shown up. There's no way she would have just got up and walked away.

The LAPD had reluctantly opened a missing person case, mostly because I'd threatened to give so many interviews to as many media outlets as I could find if they didn't, but they had no leads at all to follow.

"Look," I said finally. "I'm not crazy. Someone took her."

"Then you have to let the police do their job."

And at his words, something clicked and settled into place. I looked around for my cell, spotted it on the kitchen counter and grabbed it. Swiping the lock screen, I punched in a number.

It connected on the second ring.

"Hey, fucktard. How's life with the filthy rich and shameless?" A lazy drawl greeted me.

"I need your help." I didn't even try to hide my panic.

"Where are you?" The amusement dropped from his voice, leaving it all business.

"L.A."

"We'll be there tonight." The line went silent. No request for information, no demands, no accusations. And the simple reassurance those words gave me eased some of the pressure building up behind my eyes.

❄

The ding of the elevator arriving dragged me from the restless sleep I'd fallen into on the couch. In my groggy state, I thought it was Harper and lurched to my feet, only to be greeted by two men, one of whom caught my arm when I staggered and lost my balance.

"Steady, brother." The low rumble of one of my oldest friends was like a catalyst opening the floodgates and I dragged both of them into a rough hug, fighting back my urge to cry like a baby.

Two sets of hands patted my back and I clung to them.

"Dude, if you're going to grope me, at least buy me a drink first," Deacon grouched and ducked under my arm to stride past me and flop onto the couch.

Shaun was a little kinder. "We heard the news. It's all over the internet and papers. We have Asher running a search." He draped an arm over my shoulder and led me over to his brother. "We'll find her."

"She's just fucking disappeared. It makes no sense."

"Actually, what makes no sense is the pipsqueak forgiving you for that bullshit move you pulled on her back in the day," Deacon commented, propping his boot-covered feet onto the table.

"DJ," Shaun sighed. "Give the man a break."

Golden eyes shone as they assessed me. "How bad have you got it?"

"Can you find her?" I ignored his question. He knew the answer, I didn't need to explain it to him.

"Unless aliens took her, I'll find her," he answered, the arrogance unhidden in his voice. "Why did you wait before calling us?"

I ran a hand through my hair tiredly. "I haven't been thinking straight. I got out of the hospital yesterday, and I've been with the cops and to the crash site, and there's just no fucking trace of her."

"And there's been no ransom demand?" Shaun asked.

I shook my head. "I don't think it's a ransom situation. I don't know what it is, but they don't want my money."

"Two days is a long time with no contact." Shaun didn't say it outright but I knew exactly what he meant. There was a high chance Harper was dead.

"I'd know."

"Would you?" Shaun questioned. "You're not like us, Gabe. It doesn't work that way for you."

"I'd *know*."

He inclined his head. "All right."

"We left Asher at the hotel. He's checking all the CCTV footage from the area where you crashed. How the fuck did that happen anyway?" Deacon joined the conversation again. "I thought we could head over there and sniff around."

"The police have already checked the CCTV, there's nothing on it."

Deacon snorted. "We won't be looking for the same things as them."

"As for how it happened. I'm not sure. A car hit us from the driver's side and sent me into a spin."

The brothers nodded as one. "You think it was a targeted hit?" Deacon asked.

"I don't know."

"Anything strange happened lately? Dropped calls, threatening messages?"

"No ... wait ... maybe. Meredith showed back up, but she said she was here to apologise for her behaviour. Harper got a text just after we first met up telling her to stay away from me. But only the one. I assumed it was from Meredith, but she denied it."

"If someone took Harper from the car, I doubt it was her. If Harper was awake, she'd have fought. If she was unconscious, carrying a deadweight isn't for people built like Meredith." Deacon stood, stretched, then glanced over at me. "You coming?"

"Of course I'm fucking coming," I snapped. I grabbed my wallet, keys, and cell and followed them to the elevator. "Wait. How did you get up here?"

Deacon rolled his eyes. "When has anywhere ever kept me out?"

CHAPTER 54

WAY DOWN WE GO - KALEO

Harper

PRESENT

I lost track of how long he had me. I hadn't seen or heard him, but I knew it was a male. His hands were large, I felt them when they gripped me to hold me still so he could inject me with whatever he was using to sedate me. He didn't talk to me, or show his face or touch me beyond that, though.

I had no idea why he had taken me or what he wanted. I asked … over and over … until my throat was hoarse, but all he did was send me to sleep, and then I woke up with duct tape sealing my mouth shut. A message telling me he didn't want to hear me talk.

Each time I woke, we were in a different location—all of them cold. I think they were warehouse refrigerators. He allowed me a sip or two of water, but no food and my stomach was cramping, which told me it had been at least twenty-four hours, but probably longer. I think he kept knocking me out to confuse me, so I couldn't track the length of time. He wasn't giving me anywhere near enough water, my lips were dry and cracking, and I felt lightheaded and disoriented, but that could also have been down to the drugs he was using.

This time when I woke up, the first thing I felt was the warmth—something I had been convinced I would never feel again. But there was a heat against my arms and my back, and my bare feet were resting on top of a stone floor which felt warm beneath my soles. I assumed it had underfloor heating.

I started to sit up, and something dug into my wrists, sending pain down my arms. I couldn't move my hands. My eyes snapped open to find I was already in a seated position and my arms were lifted with my wrists cuffed to an expensive-looking radiator at shoulder level. My hands felt funny, numb.

"What the hell?" Even whispering the words made my throat hurt and my head ache. This was the first time I'd been restricted. Every other time, my hands had been free, I'd just been too disoriented to move. *That* hadn't changed.

"You're awake." The male voice came from *close* behind me, and I couldn't stop myself from jumping in surprise at the sound. I tried to twist around to see who it was, the voice sounded so familiar, but all I could make out was one dark brown sleeve.

"I thought I might have dosed you with too much this time. I didn't *want* to kill you, but I needed you to come with me," the voice continued, and his conversational tone scared me more than it would have if he had sounded aggressive.

"Who are you? What do you want with me?" I demanded, and even while I said it, I wasn't really sure I wanted to hear the answers to either question. I was confident that no one sane would knock someone out, take them from place to place and then handcuff them to a radiator, so whatever he wanted, it could be nothing good.

"This is *his* house," my unseen captor ignored my questions. "But he hasn't told you this little secret, has he?"

"Him? Whose—"

"How often do you think he sneaks away to be with his other little whores? Meredith, Candice, Bea, Riley, Shirley ... the list is endless. You don't believe he's faithful to you, do you?"

I shook my head—big mistake!—dizziness caused my vision to blur. "I don't know what you mean." I tried to twist my wrists, hoping they would slip free of the cuffs. "Why have you brought me here? Who are you?"

"You're not fooling me with your innocent act." My captor strode around and crouched in front of me. "I thought you might have been different. Especially when you turned him down. But no, eventually you spread your legs for him. Let him use you the way he uses all the others. Just another pussy to be filled."

I closed my eyes, swallowing. Somewhere I'd read or heard that seeing the face of the person who'd kidnapped you was a clear statement you're not going to survive whatever they've taken you for. But I couldn't keep them closed, couldn't stand the fear of not knowing what was happening in front of me, so I opened them again, and recognition and fear chilled me.

Close-cut sandy blond hair, blue eyes, a face that was neither ugly nor overly handsome—*normal* looking, I realised. But he had a presence—one that said he could control a situation. Someone you would trust with your safety. His was a face you automatically trusted, one you expected to protect you. I knew he had a warm smile, rarely used. I almost laughed at the way I was describing him in my head. Like it mattered what he looked like, and more importantly, I doubted there was a way I could convince him to let me go, but I had to try.

"If you let me go, I won't tell anyone you brought me here," I said, trying desperately to not let him hear the fear in my voice.

"I can't do that. He needs to understand that he can't just do whatever he wants and still be rewarded for it. I've watched him for the past seven years squandering everything he had on drugs, women, and alcohol. Always expecting me to pick him up when he crashed. And every single time … he bounced back without a scratch. He needs to learn, Harper, don't you see that? He needs to understand there are consequences to his actions."

"He never hurt anyone," I whispered. "He never forced anyone to do anything with him."

He laughed, the sound bitter. "Tell that to my sister. She *loved* him … just like you do. And he cast her aside, leaving her broken-hearted. She gave him everything. Gave *up* everything to be with him. And what did he do? He *laughed* at her. Told her she didn't mean anything to him and to stop pestering him."

"Your sister?"

"That's why I took the job. To get close to him. To help my sister get close to him. And it was working. Then *you* showed up. His one failure. The one thing he hadn't been able to fix. I thought you'd teach him the lesson he needed, but no. Even *you* gave in to his whims, let him charm his way back into your bed." He dragged a hand through his short hair. "I tried to warn you off."

"The text message?"

He nodded. "That's right. And what did you do with it?" he demanded angrily. "You ignored it and spread your legs for him anyway."

"I love him. He loves me."

"That's what he says to make you do what he wants. You girls are all the same." His lip curled derisively. "My sister thought he loved her. So I helped her get close to him."

I tried to wet my lips, my brain sluggishly attempting to piece together what he was telling me. "Meredith ... your sister is Meredith."

"She begged me to help, to make him see how she was the one for him. I had a friend who owed me a favour and he got me a position where I could be close to him." He stopped, his head turning to the door and his brows pulled together. "I think we've run out of time." I watched as he reached behind him and lifted a gun.

"Please ... please don't kill me," I couldn't help but whisper, shrinking back against the radiator and trying to make myself as small a target as possible.

"I have to. You were supposed to stay away from him. That's all you had to do." He paused in the middle of sliding the bullets into the barrel. "He'll turn to Meredith in his grief, and she will have what she always wanted."

"I ... I ... please."

He placed his hand over my mouth, almost affectionately. "It'll be okay, you'll see," he told me, snapped the barrel of the gun closed and pointed it at me. "In life, and in death—a message will be well served."

"No, no!" I cried out, and tried to reach toward him, forgetting my wrists were cuffed and feeling the metal dig deep into my flesh.

Miles smiled and pulled the trigger.

I screamed.

Tattooed Memories

CHAPTER 55

MOTHER MARY – BADFLOWER

Gabe

PRESENT

"Did you say you were driving?" Deacon asked me from where he crouched near where I'd crashed the car.

"Yeah. We were going back to the penthouse."

"Huh."

"Have you found anything?"

"Maybe yes, maybe no." He vaulted to his feet. "There's a scent here. One that was also in your apartment."

"Karl was here to get my car towed."

Deacon shook his head. "No, not Karl. I *know* Karl. No, this one is someone I've never met." He waved Shaun over to him. "Do you recognise it?"

Shaun angled his head and took in a breath. "No ... wait ... yes!" He stooped, glanced around to see if anyone was around and then lowered his nose to the ground. "Fuck. That guy ... the one who drives you around?"

"Miles?"

"Yeah, that's the one. He's been here."

"He might have brought Karl."

Shaun was shaking his head before I finished the sentence. "No. Harper's scent is mixed in with his." Both brothers strode to where the car would have been.

Deacon mimicked opening a door. "He opened the door, made sure she wasn't conscious, then lifted her out." He turned and pointed down the street. "His scent goes a few feet that way, then ends. I'm guessing he put Harper into a car and then took off."

"Miles?" No way. The guy had been my constant shadow for years. We were friends … right?

"Doesn't matter how many times you say it, the answer isn't going to change." Deacon shrugged. "Question is, where would he have taken her?"

"*Why* would he take her? Harper has never done anything to him." I said.

"You really think this is about Harper?" Deacon asked.

"You think it's not?"

"Dude, seriously? Why would he get a hate-on for a girl he met a few weeks ago? I'll bet she's been nothing but sweet to the guy. You're the asshat, not her."

"We didn't have an employer and employee relationship. He was more like a friend," I protested. I didn't want to believe Miles would do something like this. What reason would he have?

"Was he? Are you absolutely certain about that?" Shaun asked. "Was there ever a time where you clashed or he was angry over something you did or a decision you made? Sometimes all it takes is one thing to trigger the avalanche."

"I don't think so," I replied slowly. "He wasn't a fan of the lifestyle I led … *all* of us, really. He didn't like the endless cycle of girls or the occasional time he had to extract us from sticky situations."

"Didn't like or hid how much he hated it?" Deacon moved to stand in front of me. "Think, Gabe. He has access to every part of your life. Planning and doing something like this would be easy for him. Are you *sure* we can cross him off the list?"

"I …" I hesitated. *Could I*? More to the point, *should* I? "I don't know," I admitted. Something caught my eye as I spoke and I frowned, crossed the road and crouched to pick up the snowflake pendant I'd given to Harper. I pocketed it and returned to the twins.

"Where is he now?" Shaun asked the one question I'd been hoping he wouldn't … because I didn't know. I hadn't seen him since waking up in the hospital.

Before I could tell them that, Deacon's cell rang. He held a muted conversation with whoever was on the other end, then turned to me.

"Well, we have our answer," he said grimly. "Asher cleaned up the CCTV. He spotted a car parked just on the edge of its visibility. The number plate is registered to one Miles Hargreaves. Where would he take her?"

"I *don't* know!" Frustration was driving me crazy. I didn't fucking know anything and *that* was the problem.

"Did Asher find any more footage of the car?" Shaun rested a hand on my shoulder.

"Thankfully, yes." Deacon pursed his lips. "Do you have a place in Malibu?"

"Yeah. Bought it a few years ago. Don't live there, though. Tried to do it a few times, but …" I trailed off and shrugged.

"Take us there."

❄

I directed Shaun, who was driving, to my home in Malibu, although calling it my home was a stretch since I'd bought it five years ago and stayed there for a single night once just after I took the keys. It was too big, too quiet, too ... lonely. And one thing I couldn't stand was being alone with my thoughts, so I'd gone and bought another penthouse in downtown L.A. and rarely given the place another thought—other than keeping it clean and having a housekeeper stock the kitchen ... just in case!

Shaun and Deacon were whispering in the front of the car when we reached the electronic gates, and Shaun twisted in the seat to look at me.

"Miles' scent is really strong around here. Harper's too. It's no more than a few hours old."

"He brought her here? Why would he do that?"

Shaun shrugged. "I can't answer that. You know the guy better than we do."

"I *thought* I knew him. I clearly didn't ... not as well as I thought, anyway," I muttered in return.

"Let me and DJ go in first. We don't know what we're walking into and we can get in there without being seen a lot easier than you will. Is the place alarmed?"

"Yeah, but Miles knows the code, so I guess he switched it off."

I felt sick at the thought that this man had been a part of my life for so long and I'd *never* even had a hint that he would do something like this. I didn't even want to consider what might have happened to Harper while he'd had her. If she'd been harmed ...

I cut off that train of thought. Thinking the worst wasn't going to help Harper *or* me.

"Gabe? Are you listening?" Deacon's voice prodded me for a response.

"Yeah. You go in, I'll wait for you to shout out."

The brothers swung out of the car and prowled toward the doors. If ever there was a time I noticed how different, how *unusual* they were from me—from humans in general—this was it. There was a stealthiness to their gait that "normal" people would never be able to achieve, no matter how well trained they were.

It was times like this that I was extremely glad to be able to call them friends.

I watched Shaun reach out and the door swung open silently beneath his hand. Deacon's eyes gleamed in the moonlight as he glanced back at me and then they both disappeared inside.

I don't think I breathed the entire time they were gone, and then a gunshot sounded in the silence and I shot out of the car and ran across the driveway, skidding to a stop when Deacon appeared in the doorway. He wouldn't meet my gaze, his expression troubled as he caught my arm and guided me through the silent hallway.

"I heard a gun." My voice was shaking, *I* was fucking shaking. "Where is she, Deacon? Where the *fuck* is she?"

"Through here," he said, then caught my arm as I made to run past him. "Wait. We found her *and* Miles."

Bile rose up in my throat. "Is she—" I couldn't finish the sentence, but Deacon knew what I wanted to ask.

"No. No, she's alive, but it's not a pretty sight in there. I think, for your sake, you should call the police and bring them in. I mean ... *we* can deal with it for you, but you've already got an investigation going and if Harper suddenly shows up it's going to look weird—even I know that."

"What do I say?" My eyes were on the doorway behind him. I could see light seeping under the door and the shadow of someone moving around.

"Tell them we've found Harper at your home here. That you were coming here to get away, clear your head, and you heard gunfire. Shaun's taking pictures so we have something to show them. We also need paramedics."

"I want to see her first."

"Make the call. Gabe. *Then* you can go in there. She's alive, another minute isn't going to change that."

I glared at him, something that never worked on Deacon. He stared back impassively, blocking the doorway with his arms folded.

"Fuck!" I snarled the curse, pulled my cell out and the card with the Detective's number on it. I don't recall what I said, only that they promised to be there as soon as they could and were sending a paramedic team as well. "Can I see her now?" I demanded, and Deacon stepped aside to let me past.

I pushed open the door and the smell inside rocked me back on my heels. "What the fuck?" I whispered, my eyes taking in the scene in front of me without really understanding it.

Shaun's hand touched my arm. "Down here." He redirected my gaze, and there she was.

My heart stuttered, stopped for a second, then raced when I realised she was breathing. Her eyes were closed, her head slumped forwards, but she was fucking breathing. I whispered thanks to any Gods that were listening and dropped to my knees beside her.

"Harper?" I touched her face gently, wincing at the purple bruise mottling her temple and the black eye. She didn't respond. "Fuck. Harper ... come on, baby, open your eyes."

"I don't know if he gave her something, or whether it's dehydration and lack of food." Shaun's finger drifted over her dry lips. "Maybe all three? We need to get her to a hospital. I would search the body for a key to unlock the cuffs, but we shouldn't leave our DNA all over the crime scene."

"Crime scene?" I repeated faintly, and then what I'd walked in on finally clicked in place like a jigsaw piece in my head. "That mess is Miles?"

Shaun nodded. "I got in here just as he aimed the gun at Harper. I wasn't fast enough to get the gun from him, and he turned it on himself when he saw me."

"What the fuck?"

"Gabe?" Harper's pained whisper brought my head back around to her.

Her eyes were wide, unfocused, and I wasn't sure how aware she was of her surroundings, but I carefully slid an arm around her waist, uncaring of the blood spattered across her, and buried my face into the crook of her neck.

"It's okay. We're here. We found you. You're safe now." I don't think I was saying the words to her, but assuring *myself*.

"Gabe." She breathed my name again, and I felt her body go limp against me. For a second of paralysing fear I thought she'd died, that I'd lost her, then I heard her faint breathing and sagged in relief.

She'd passed out, but she was alive. We just had to get her out of here and into the hospital where I could be certain she'd get the care she needed.

Tattooed Memories

CHAPTER 56

I'M SORRY - HOTHOUSE FLOWERS

Harper

PRESENT

The world came back into focus slowly. First I heard voices talking quietly, then noises—the beeping of machines, people moving around—and then light formed behind my closed eyes. I swallowed, trying to moisten my lips, but my mouth and tongue were too dry, so I forced my eyes to open so I could find something to drink.

There was a white ceiling above my head and I focused on that for a second, staring up at it blankly, while I collected my thoughts. And then the memories returned. The last thing I saw was Miles pulling the trigger and I cried out, struggling to sit upright.

Hands caught my shoulders, gently pushing me back down.

"Easy, tiger." A voice, one I recognised, cut through the panic making my vision swim and blur, and I clung to it while I tried to calm my breathing.

"D-Dex?" His face came into focus above me.

His smile was tired, but oh so welcome in my state of near-panic, and I clutched at his sleeve. "Gabe?"

"Sleeping." His fingers touched my cheek and gently turned my head slightly until I could see Gabe, sprawled out in a hospital chair, his eyes closed.

"H-how long?" I tried to wet my lips again and Dex accurately guessed what I needed.

He reached for the jug of water beside the bed, poured some into a plastic cup and popped a straw in it before placing it to my lips. I drank greedily.

"Not too much. It'll make you sick," he cautioned. "Luca went to tell the doctor you're awake," he continued.

I nodded, my eyes straying back to Gabe.

"He fell asleep about an hour ago," Dex explained. "He's been running on coffee and cigarettes for almost a week, so it had to happen."

"I-I thought he'd quit s-smoking?" I winced, talking hurt my throat.

"He did, but the crash, your disappearance and then …" he shrugged. "He needed the stress relief."

"So … how long?" My voice sounded strange, hoarse and rough—like I'd been screaming and shouting for hours.

"How long since the crash or since you've been in the hospital?"

"Both."

Dex scratched his ear, clearly uncertain how to answer me. He was saved from the decision by the doctor arriving.

"Shirley!" I gasped out the name of the hospital administrator, who hurried over and took my hand.

"You look a lot better than when you arrived," she told me. "This is Dr Medici," she introduced the woman who had come into the room with her. "She's just going to do a quick check of your vitals and then we'll talk, okay?" She glanced at Dex. "The rest of you outside."

"The rest?"

"Hey, baby girl," Luca appeared beside Shirley and bent to press a careful kiss to my cheek. "You gave us all a scare. Let's not do that again, right?"

He disappeared before I could respond and Seth replaced him. He looked down at me, his eyes dark and unreadable. "Harper Jackson," he pursed his lips and shook his head. "I told Gabe you were gonna be trouble." His words were cool, but he winked at me and squeezed my fingers.

Once we were alone, apart from Gabe who still slept in the chair by the window, Dr Medici did her tests. I don't know what they were but they involved a lot of poking and prodding, and grumbling on my part, before she announced she was satisfied with my results.

I asked why my throat hurt when I talked and she explained that there had been some damage to my vocal cords, which made me think of the screaming I'd done, but that it should heal given some time, then handed me some painkillers for the aches and pains she said I would soon start feeling, and departed with a warning not to talk too much.

Silence descended upon the room.

I shifted in the bed, my eyes drifting over to Gabe.

"He hasn't left your side since he found you," Shirley told me softly.

"Gabe found me?"

"He had the police searching for you but, from what I understand, he brought in two friends who specialise in tracking missing people and objects. They discovered who had taken you and where you were."

"But how?"

"I don't know the details. Karl called me when they were on their way here in the ambulance and had me secure a private room for you."

"How long?" I was trying to keep my questions short. Every word I uttered sent pain flaring down my throat.

"Nine days since the crash. Seven since they found you. It was touch and go for a couple of days. You were severely dehydrated, and your body had started to shut down." She paused, her expression grim. "If they had taken any longer to find you, we wouldn't be having this conversation."

My lips parted on a silent gasp of horror. She was saying I would have died. It was clear in her tone, even if she didn't utter the words.

"But we *did* find her in time." Another voice joined the conversation. One I hadn't heard in a long time.

"Deacon?"

"Hey, pipsqueak. We just wanted to drop in and say goodbye before we left. We have to head back home." He moved into my line of sight, his twin brother beside him.

"Shaun!"

"Hey, Harper." Shaun's smile was warm. "Been a while, huh?" He bent to give me a careful hug, then stepped back and Deacon took his place.

"Go easy on our boy, yeah?" he whispered to me before he stepped back. "He's killing himself over what happened to you."

"It wasn't his fault."

"*We* know that," Shaun looked over at the sleeping rock star. "Him ... not so much." His green eyes gleamed as he turned back to me. "He'll be waking up soon."

"How do you know?"

"We may have slipped a little something in his coffee to knock him out for a while. He was on the verge of collapsing," Deacon said, with a conspiratorial wink.

I shook my head, unwilling amusement lifting my mood. I hoped Deacon would never change.

"Tell him to call us," Shaun said. "We have a flight to catch." With another hug and kisses all around, the brothers left.

"It's time you got some rest," Shirley told me once we were alone again. "You're going to get tired easily for a while. It's normal and will get better." She fussed with the pillow behind me and pulled the covers up, tucking them around my shoulders. "Get some sleep, Harper."

"I'm not—" I broke off to yawn. Now she'd mentioned it, I *was* tired. "Fine, okay," I grumbled and closed my eyes.

※

"No! *No!*"

"Harper, hush. It's okay."

My eyes snapped open and met grey ones, dark with worry, close above my head.

"*Gabe?*" I moved without thinking and threw myself at him and felt his arms wrap around me.

"Hey … hey, it's okay," he whispered, but he held me tight and I could feel his body shaking against mine. "Fuck. I thought I'd lost you again."

I didn't think I was meant to hear him because he tensed and began to pull away. I clung tighter, shaking my head.

"Don't go. Don't leave me," I pleaded and he stilled, one hand smoothing up and down my spine.

"I'm sorry, Harper. I'm so fucking sorry." His lips sought out mine and he placed a soft kiss at each corner.

My heart was hammering in my chest, and I wanted to cry. There was something about his words, the way he touched me that told me I was losing him.

"Please, Gabe," I whispered. And I didn't know what I was pleading for.

"I love you, Frosty," he murmured. "Don't ever forget that." I felt him take my hand, place something in my palm and curl my fingers around it, and he stepped back.

"Gabe?"

He shook his head. "I'm sorry."

And then he was gone.

CHAPTER 57

LOST THE GAME - TWO FEET

Gabe

PRESENT

I strode through the hospital, uncaring that I was being recognised by everyone who looked in my direction. I looked a mess. I hadn't showered or shaved in a week, I'd barely slept, I was wearing the same bloodied clothes I turned up at the hospital in. I probably stank. I didn't fucking care.

I'd just made a decision that ranked up there with the one I'd made eight years ago … and for the same reason. Only this time I knew there wouldn't be another chance.

It was done. It was over.

I wasn't meant to keep Harper—the signs were clear. She'd nearly died. All my money and fame hadn't been enough to protect her. They had only made everything worse. All the things I'd given up, the things I'd done, the depths I'd sunk to, to claw my way up to what I thought were the heights—the money, the fame, the power—meant nothing because Harper had almost died.

Because of me.

If I'd stayed out of her life, she would have been okay, happy even. Her life hadn't been bad—she thrived on hard work. She'd been *content*. But my ego wouldn't let her. I didn't want her to be happy without me. Because I sure as fuck wasn't happy without her.

I deserved to be unhappy. I was just as much a monster as my father, just in different ways. At least he hadn't almost killed me.

"Gabe?" My eyes narrowed at the recognisable voice and I swung around to find Jefferson Thomas standing by the hospital entrance, a smile on his lips.

"What the fuck do you want?"

I was done playing nice with reporters. Fuck it. Let them do their worst. Tear me down, take it all. It was worth fuck all, anyway.

"You come to this hospital a lot," he said.

"It's a free country. So fucking what?"

"I discovered something interesting about it. There's a Thomas Mercer here. Isn't that your father's name?"

"And? I thought you believed I'd murdered him."

"He disappeared just after your band had their first hit. It was a logical assumption." He shrugged. "No matter how much I dug, I couldn't find anything on him. The last sighting was near to where your girlfriend lived. The connection seemed obvious. He was bothering her, you either took care of him yourself or had it done."

"What do you think I am? A fucking mob boss? I play music

in a rock band. I'm not some kind of fucking mafia prince, taking out hits on people." My lips curled up into a sneer. "Some kind of reporter you are."

"How about this for a story, then?" His smile broadened. "Rock star reignites his relationship with his childhood sweetheart, only for her to be taken by the bodyguard he trusted with his life. The bodyguard had plotted and planned for years to teach the rock star a lesson he'd never forget because he had fucked the bodyguard's sister and broken her heart. He was disgusted with the *bad boy's* attitude to life and women. When the new girl appeared in the rock star's life, the bodyguard thought she'd never allow him back. But no, that wasn't the case. She did, and she let the rock star do all manner of dirty things to her. So the bodyguard's sister begged her brother to take care of it, get rid of the girl, leaving the path open for her to take the girl's place. It would be a lesson the badly behaved rock star would never forget and probably live to regret for the rest of his life."

"Get to the fucking point." I managed not to flinch at his dissection of recent events.

"There are two points. One is there's a story there that all the news outlets would kill to own. I could make a small fortune selling it."

"And the other?" I asked through gritted teeth.

"The bodyguard may be dead, but his plan was a partial success."

"How'd you figure that?"

"You're leaving the hospital," he shrugged. "You wouldn't

do that unless you've left that poor girl. And you've left her because you've realised you're not good enough for her. You ruin everything you touch. You're everything your father said you were when you were growing up. Every time he told you how worthless you were is now finally echoing around your head as the truth."

I snapped.

I don't remember hitting him or being dragged off him by Seth and Luca ten minutes later. But I could relive it via the videos uploaded to Social Media as often as I wanted—I *didn't* want to, the police kept showing me—while sitting in the cells waiting for bail to be posted.

※

Footsteps scraping along the tiled floor had me raising my head and meeting Karl's gaze through the bars. I'd been sitting in this cell for twenty-four hours.

"Don't say a fucking word," he levelled a finger at me. "Officer, if you wouldn't mind letting the idiot out now."

The officer on duty snorted a laugh and unlocked the cell. "Sorry, man," he said.

I shrugged. "Just doing your job."

"The good news is Jefferson isn't pressing charges," Karl told me while I waited for my personal items to be returned.

"And the bad news?"

"You're all over the internet smashing someone's face into the wall, hitting him with a chair and then punching him into unconsciousness."

I plastered a smirk I wasn't feeling onto my face. "Not seeing the bad news in any of that."

"Of course you're not," his response was dry.

We stopped a couple of times to pose for photos and sign autographs with officers who happened to be fans of the band and then we were beside his car.

"Get in," he told me.

I knew better than to argue. Contrary to popular opinion, I did have *some* moments of clarity. We were silent as he drove to my apartment block, and rode the elevator up to my penthouse.

I faltered when we walked in, seeing Harper's jacket on the couch, a pair of her shoes discarded by the door.

"Go take a shower, shave and get some clean clothes on," Karl instructed.

"Yes, dad," I muttered, and forced myself to walk through to the bathroom without looking for any more evidence of Harper's presence.

I dragged my ass to the bathroom, stripping off my clothes as I went, and stepped into the shower. Behind the steamed-up glass and under the heated spray of water, I lost my shit.

The terror of the last two weeks, the constant tension, the necessary acting in front of media hounds waiting for a sign of weakness so they could pounce, exhaustion, and pure, unmitigated despair—all of it crashed down on me in one heavy weight, driving me to my knees. And right there, underneath the water, I begged for forgiveness for every damnable thing I'd ever done.

Nothing of my breakdown showed when I returned to the living room. My hair was still damp, my face freshly tidied and back to my usual stubble. I definitely *smelled* better than I had in days and I was clothed in a clean pair of black jeans and a dark grey t-shirt. The only sign of my mood was the lighter in my hand, flicking open and closed as I paced restlessly.

"Are you going to sit down and eat something?" Karl asked me.

"Not hungry."

"How about a drink then?"

"I'm good, thanks."

"Maybe you should smoke a joint?"

I turned at that. Karl lectured long and hard about drug usage. It was an ongoing battle he had with Dex.

He shrugged at my questioning look. "I'm just saying you need to relax a little."

"You've just picked me up from a jail cell after I made a series of fucked-up decisions ... and your answer to that is *smoke a joint?*"

"So you agree you've made some bad choices in the last couple of days? That's a good start. I thought we'd still be in the denial phase."

My eyes narrowed at him and I turned back to look out of the floor-to-ceiling window. The ding and swish of the elevator doors opening caused me to tense. *Who the fuck was it now?*

I saw the reflection of Karl in the window as he rose to his feet. "Okay, my shift is over. My replacement is here. We need to talk about the rescheduling of the gig at Roth's. You have a week to get yourself straightened out." He patted my shoulder and walked away.

I grunted and didn't bother acknowledging whoever my new keeper was.

CHAPTER 58

I SEE YOU - MISSIO

Harper

PRESENT

When Gabe walked out of the hospital room, my initial reaction was to cry. He was walking away, leaving me—another heartless decision like the one he'd made eight years ago. But then I paused and thought about his words, his actions and, most importantly, the expression on his face.

I looked down at my hand, still curled into a fist. Whatever Gabe had placed there, it was pressing against my palm, so I slowly opened my fingers. The snowflake necklace he'd given to me in the car before we went into the movie premiere was laying there. I stroked a finger over the diamonds, feeling their sharp edges against my skin. Lifting the chain, I held the pendant up, watching as it caught the light from the sun.

A snowflake.

I'd seen the pattern before somewhere, but *where?* And then I realised. It was tattooed on Gabe's body. On both his shoulders in fact, and there was a smaller version on his inner left wrist. Why hadn't I noticed it before? But I knew the answer to that. Whenever he was naked, my concentration hadn't been focused on his tattoos!

Damn it, Gabe!

He thought he was doing the right thing, protecting me from the dangers that might happen because of who he was. Putting what he thought *I* needed above what *he* wanted. And I realised that was also what he had chosen to do eight years ago. He hadn't been rejecting *me* all that time ago. He had been rejecting his own happiness. And he *was* happy when he was with me, I knew that. I'd witnessed it.

The more I thought about it, the angrier I became. At him, at his father for making him believe he shouldn't be happy, at Miles for taking that happiness away, at myself for not realising it sooner. Inside, Gabe Mercer was still that little boy who believed every bad thing his father said about him. He believed he deserved the things the man had done to him, the beatings and the insults, and the claim he didn't deserve to be loved, that he had no right to be happy because his mother had died.

Stuck in that hospital bed, I thought about nothing else and I planned.

And then Dex told me he'd been arrested for assaulting someone … a reporter and I knew what I needed to do.

※

Jefferson Thomas' face was a mess of purple and yellow bruises, one black eye, and a split lip when he was escorted into my hospital room. My first thought was that he'd been lucky to be in the hospital when Gabe had hit him, followed by concern at the state of mind my running-scared rock star was in.

He gingerly took a seat beside my bed.

"Why did you ask to see me?" he said.

I waved a hand at his face. "Gabe did quite a number on you. Are you pressing charges?"

"I could. He assaulted me. There are witnesses and video evidence to prove it was unprovoked."

"Was it, though?" My question was soft. "You didn't hit him first but you *did* speak to him, didn't you? Something you said triggered his physical response." His eyes shifted away from me and I knew I was right. "What was it? Something about his father?"

"I said a number of things."

"None of them pleasant, I'm guessing."

"I'm a reporter, Ms Jackson. My job is to find the truth."

"Is it? Your job isn't to harass people and dig for information that is no one's business but theirs?"

"People deserve to know the truth about their heroes."

I let a smile cross my face. "I'm so glad you said that. Because I want you to know *my* truth about Gabriel Mercer."

We sat in that hospital room and talked for hours and, as I told my story, I could see Jefferson's demeanour changing. It wasn't quick or obvious but a subtle loosening of his shoulders and in the way he leaned forward, intent on my words. He interrupted to ask a question here and there, but mostly he stayed silent and recorded everything I said.

And I told him a lot. I told him *everything*. Well, not quite everything. I kept all mention of the things we did behind closed doors very much to myself. This wasn't a dirt-sharing moment. This was me showing the world the Gabe Mercer *I* knew, the one they *deserved* to meet.

As I was winding down, Siobhan arrived. I'd asked her to go to the apartment I shared with her and find the box I kept at the back of my wardrobe. She'd been in and out of the hospital the entire time I was there and had been outside when Gabe walked away.

She hovered in the doorway, seeing I had company and I waved her in, thanked her for the box and opened it under both their curious gazes. I spread the contents out over the bed. Photographs of me with Gabe as we grew up. Some were burnt at the edges, salvaged from the fire that destroyed the apartment I'd lived in with my mom, some were sneaky ones I'd taken with my cell and then had printed off. I showed them the birthday cards, the random gifts, the scribbled poems and the hundreds of Damnation tickets he'd sent over the years. The ones he thought I'd thrown away.

"This is *my* Gabe," I said to Jefferson.

"What do you want me to do with all this?" he asked finally.

I held his gaze. "I want you to do what's right."

※

I watched the numbers above the elevator doors, and as they

increased so did the beat of my heart. I gripped the newspaper in my hand, my knuckles white, my palms sweaty. Jefferson had written a masterpiece, using photographs I'd supplied. He'd sought out and spoken to Bea, and while he hadn't mentioned her by name, I recognised her words of praise for everything Gabe had done. He had dropped me a copy of the finished article along with a large bouquet of flowers earlier that morning, just as I was getting ready to leave the hospital.

Now I was here… riding the elevator up to Gabe's penthouse, using the key Dex had given to me, with my heart in my throat and terror coursing through my veins.

The doors slid open and I froze.

What was I doing? What if he threw me out? What if he was angry over what I'd done?

Then I heard Karl's voice telling him his replacement had arrived and I was out of time. I stepped out of the elevator and met Karl's gaze as he moved toward me. He didn't speak but reached out to squeeze my fingers as he passed. The elevator doors closed on him and I was alone.

Alone with Gabe.

With no means of escape.

I almost turned and fled.

Summoning up the tattered remains of my courage, I walked inside, placed the newspaper and small parcel I'd picked up on my way onto the kitchen countertop, and then turned to look at the man standing at the window. I thought he'd turn, but he didn't.

I went into the kitchen and turned on the coffee machine, took out two mugs, not bothering to be quiet about it, keeping one eye on him. I could see him fiddling with his lighter, the flame flickering on and off—a clear indication of his mood.

"I figured it out, you know." I kept my voice purposely casual and watched as his entire body locked up. The hand holding the lighter froze, the flame burning orange briefly before he snapped it closed. "You asked yourself why you don't switch off your dad's life support," I continued, while I poured coffee. "And I know the answer."

Opening the refrigerator, I took out cream, added it to my coffee along with sweetener and then crossed the room to place both mugs down on the coffee table. He still hadn't turned to face me.

"Do you want to know?" I asked, knowing he wouldn't reply. I sank down onto the plush cushions and crossed my legs, lifted my coffee mug and took a sip. "It's because you're better than him."

That got a reaction. He flinched and slowly, *very* slowly, turned to face me.

"What are you doing here?" His voice was distant, cool and I knew he was trying hard to make me believe he didn't care.

He was failing. His mistake was looking at me. I could see his eyes ... and his eyes had never lied to me—even when I didn't realise it. They were full of pain, sorrow, and a hunger he couldn't hide when they swept over me.

"I wrote you a letter," I told him and waved a hand toward

the folded newspaper behind me.

His eyes glanced over at it and then back at me. "What does it say?"

"You should read it." I put down my mug and stood, skirted the coffee table and stopped in front of him. "But I'll tell you." I saw his realisation when it dawned on him I was repeating what *he*'d said to me about the interview he'd done. "It talks about a boy who arrived in my life. One that lived under a dark shadow yet was always kind and thoughtful. One who helped me with school work, cheered everything I did, turned up at every school event. A boy who had nothing yet gave everything." I reached up to touch his cheek and he jerked away from my touch, so I stepped closer until he couldn't evade me. "It's about a boy who held my heart in his hands, and shattered it because he thought he wasn't worthy of love."

"Harper." He closed his eyes, masking the pain burning in them. "Don't do this."

"Everyone is going to see you how I see you, Gabriel. Only you refuse to open your eyes."

He raked a hand through his hair, pocketing his lighter. "I can't do this with you."

"So that's it? You're just going to walk away, give up?" I folded my arms and glared at him.

"What do you want me to do? You nearly died. And why? Because of me!"

"I *lived* because of you. Because you didn't give up, you

found me."

"*Deacon* found you."

"Only because *you* called him." I reached out again and placed my hand against his chest. This time he didn't avoid me. "Stop running, Gabe. Stop hiding."

"What if I end up like him?" He sounded broken and tired.

"You won't."

"You don't know that," he insisted. But I *did* know. Everything he did, his actions all proved he would *never* become his father.

"If you were like him, you would have switched off his life support. You wouldn't have come back to me. You wouldn't have saved that little boy or supported the home Bea provides for them." I risked rejection and wound my arms around his neck. "You're not your father, Gabe. You never have been."

I could feel his tension, his body was almost vibrating with it. Dropping one hand, I found the hem of his shirt and slid my palm beneath it, over the taut abs and up. My fingertips touched the stainless steel of the bar piercing his nipple.

"Take your shirt off."

"Harper, stop. It's done. *We're* done." He started to step away.

"No, we're not," I argued. I moved my hand up his body further, and paused where I knew one of his snowflake tattoos were. "This proves it."

He stilled.

"I didn't make the connection until yesterday … after you'd left. But you couldn't walk away without leaving a part of you with me, could you?" I unwound my arm from his neck and moved my hand to where the pendant hung from my throat. "You left *this* with me. Which came first, Gabe? The pendant or the tattoos?"

He stayed silent, his lids lowering to hide his eyes, and then in a burst of movement he pulled off his t-shirt and threw it to one side. "Fine," he snapped. "Look your fill."

I did. Not only did I look, I touched. I traced the snowflakes on his shoulders, the string of lavender-coloured hearts along his left pectoral muscle. I turned his left arm to display the smaller snowflake on his wrist and then I reached for the leather bracelets covering the scars on his right wrist. He tensed, but he didn't stop me from pushing them further up his arm to see my name hidden there. Everywhere I looked, I found references to our history—flames for the fire we'd barely survived, musical notes for the music he loved so much. Everything was bold, black and stark, apart from the hints of lavender breaking it up.

My eyes darted up to his, but his expression was blank—a look he'd perfected over years of abuse from his father. His eyes, though, he couldn't hide the truth in his eyes. I bit my lip.

"These are all memories of us," I whispered. "Tattooed onto your skin. *Why?* Why would you do that?"

"To keep you close." He still wouldn't meet my gaze. "To remind me of what I'd lost when I drove you away."

"I'm here now." I curved my palms over his jaw.

His hands settled onto my hips and he bent his head.

"What am I going to do with you, Harper?" he whispered.

I rose up on tiptoes and rested my lips against his. "I brought strawberries ..."

Tattooed Memories

EPILOGUE

RED BALLOON - DEAL CASINO

Harper

THREE MONTHS LATER

"Are you ready to do this?" I asked him and saw Gabe's chest move as he took a deep breath.

"No?" he said.

I leaned against him and his arm settled over my shoulders. "But you know it's the right thing to do, don't you?"

"Logically, sure. Yeah, I know." He shrugged. "But there's this voice, Harper, whispering that I'm doing it out of revenge."

I pressed my palm to his cheek and turned his head toward me. "Look at me. You've seen the reports. He's not in there. Only the machine is keeping him alive. Turning it off now would be mercy, not revenge."

"I know."

"If you would rather wait, everyone will understand."

"No." He stiffened his spine and dropped his arm to take my hand. "Let's do this."

We walked together into the hospital room where his father lay. Shirley was waiting inside. She rose to her feet when we entered and moved around the bed to lay her hand on Gabe's arm.

"Ready?"

He gave a jerky nod, and Shirley issued instructions to the doctors and nurses in the room. Gabe's grip on my hand was bone-crushing, but I didn't say a word.

"Once the machine is turned off, it might take a little while," Dr Jacobi explained quietly. "It may look like he's breathing but it's just an automatic response and will slowly stop." He hesitated, then touched Gabe's shoulder. "I'm sorry for your loss."

We stood as the doctors did their job and the machines fell silent. With solemn nods and whispers of condolences, they all left the room until we were alone. Gabe's eyes were fixed on the figure of the man in the bed.

"He was a good dad at one time," he said, breaking the silence. "Before Mom died. When she ... when we lost her, something broke inside him and he couldn't come back from it."

I wrapped my arms around his waist, feeling his body shaking beside me.

"I tried to be what he needed, but I just couldn't do it. I couldn't replace her."

"Don't do that, Gabe. You lost someone, too." I pulled his head down and he buried his face against my shoulder, his arms sliding around me.

He sucked in a shuddering breath and I let the lead singer of Forgotten Legacy, the larger than life bad boy rock star, the love of my life, mourn the loss of his parents in my arms.

We left the hospital an hour later. Gabe was quiet but I knew the time we had spent in his father's room had been cathartic. We had talked about his mom, his better memories of his dad, and he seemed much lighter when we finally headed back out to the car.

His driver, a recommendation from Deacon Jacobs, straightened from his position against the car and opened the door. There was something about him that raised the hairs on the back of my neck. Deacon assured me he could be trusted implicitly and I caught a look which passed between him and Gabe, which caused Gabe to nod and hire him on the spot.

"Thanks, Remy," Gabe said as he followed me into the dark interior of the car.

"Where to?" Remy asked as he settled into the driver's seat.

"We have a graduation to attend. I promised Riley I'd bring the guys to boost her street cred, so can we pick them up on the way to her school?"

"You got it." He slid the privacy glass shut and started the engine.

Seth

Why the fuck had I agreed to go to some kid's graduation? I must have been drunk when Gabe had raised it because no one in their right mind sat through shit like that. Fuck, I didn't even go to my *own*.

I shrugged into my dark jacket and straightened my tie. All of which I was wearing because the asshole singer of our band had insisted we all wear suits and since he was still feeling a bit fragile we were all fucking pandering to his whims—which were getting more questionable by the day. I was quite sure he was just making shit up now to see how far he could push us.

My cell rang as I was slipping my feet into boots and I connected the call.

"We're outside," Gabe said and I grunted a response. "Love you too, man." He hung up.

Pocketing my keys, I strode out of my house and, sure enough, the sleek black limo was waiting on the circular drive. A fucking limo. Whoever this kid was, Gabe was giving her the full-on rock star treatment.

My bandmates and Harper all greeted me when I climbed inside. Dex and Luca were bickering over a game they were both playing on their phones, Gabe had his head back and his eyes closed, and Harper was curled up against the side of his body, like a sexy little kitten.

"Who's this girl again?" I asked.

One grey eye cracked open. "Daughter of someone I know. Riley Temple."

I frowned. Why did that name sound familiar? Wait ... *Fuck* ... no way.

"Is that the blogger? She does the interviews?" I asked slowly, dread creeping up my spine. *Please say it's not.*

"Yeah, that's her." Gabe yawned. "She's graduating high school today. I told her we'd show up and make her look good." He squinted at me. "You okay, man? You look like you're about to throw up?"

No, I fucking wasn't okay. I was breaking out in a cold sweat.

"She hasn't finished school? Was she kept back a couple of years?"

"What?" Gabe laughed. "Why would you think that?"

"I thought she was twenty or something."

"Nah, man, she was eighteen last week."

Oh, for fuck's sake. I was in so much trouble.

Luca

My cell kept vibrating in my pocket. Message after message, increasingly urgent. Stealthily, I slid it out, onto my thigh and tapped the screen.

Fifteen messages, all from the same number. I checked to make sure no one was watching and opened them.

```
Where is she?
I know you've been with her. WHERE IS SHE?
You think your fame will protect you?
Answer me.
I'm coming for her.
She's MINE.
```

I deleted the rest—they were all the same thing. He wasn't creative enough to come up with anything new. I pocketed my phone and leaned forward to look down the row of chairs. Dex was beside me, oblivious to his surroundings, Seth beyond him. Lexi was next, her eyes on the ground and her lip caught between her teeth. Whatever was on her mind, it was bothering her. Harper sat next to her and Gabe at the end. My eyes returned to Lexi and, almost as if she could feel my gaze, she turned her head.

The moment our eyes locked, I knew. He'd contacted her already, told her he was coming, and she was ready to give up. It was all there in that one troubled look.

No fucking way. That wasn't the way our story was going to end.

Dex

Okay, so dropping acid before going to a high school graduation hadn't been the smartest decision of my life. But, gotta be honest, it wasn't even close to being the worst either.

It made the tedium of the graduation bearable, even entertaining. The speeches turned into colours as the words spilled from the students' mouths. Their gowns and graduation caps became beautiful giant butterflies in the gentle breeze and flew away. The only downer was Seth, who was doing a great impersonation of a bear with the hangover from hell beside me.

Everyone, other than Seth, was happy, laughing, celebrating with … Someone. I actually had no clue why we were even there, but I rolled with it. Gabe had told me to come, and so I did. It made him happy. And a happy Gabe meant a peaceful life for the rest of us. I'd actually never seen him so happy. He stood with his arm wrapped around Harper, signing autographs and posing for pictures.

I thought the girl they were standing with was someone I'd met before, not a relation of Gabe's though—as far as I was aware he was an only child—but she and the older woman, who I assumed was her mother appeared to be really pleased we'd showed up.

To anyone who didn't know me, I probably looked a little spaced out. The happy little space cadet. The bass guitarist, the stoner, the approachable one in the band. The *nice* one. I let out a snort. *Pie* was nice.

A flash of red on my right caught my eye and I turned my head slowly, the air feeling thick and heavy, making the movement a struggle.

"Are you okay?"

I should have recognised the voice but it sounded distorted, like the speaker it was playing through was broken, and I frowned.

"Dex?" Another voice, this one deeper, but just as warped. I turned toward it, stumbled, and slowly—at least that's how it felt to me, anyway—crashed to the floor and rolled onto my back laughing.

Voices, frantically calling my name, floated above my head—each one a pretty colour—and I smiled, reaching up to grasp them with my fingers. Each time I got close, they dissolved, which was frustrating. The more I grasped, the darker the colours turned and the angrier the voices sounded until I was no longer laughing, but screaming and begging and crying.

At least I was doing all those things until I started vomiting and frothing at the mouth.

Tattooed Memories

FORGOTTEN LEGACY

AUTHOR NOTE

Did you make it this far? Now you've read the book, you need to go and examine the cover. There are so many Easter eggs waiting to be discovered there. Find them, email me at lann.author@gmail.com and tell me what you discovered! If you find them all, I might send you some goodies!

Thank you for taking a chance on my broken rock star and the girl whose heart he broke. This story has been years in the making. I got a little sidetracked by wolf shifters and bogeymen. I hope you'll carry on the journey of Forgotten Legacy with me when the next book is released. Who will it be? Seth? Dex? Luca? Only time will tell!

If you're not already a member, you can join me in my
Facebook Group
https://facebook.com/groups/lannsliterati

Or you can come into the **spoiler group** to discuss what you've just read
https://facebook.com/groups/LAnnsSpoilerGroup/

If you're not a Facebook user, then I have a private **VIP Reader group**, which you can find here
https://clubdamnation.com

I also have a **newsletter** where you not only get a free novella for signing up, but you're the first to see cover reveals and get free chapters of upcoming releases before anyone else!
https://lannauthor.com/keep-in-touch

OTHER BOOKS BY L. ANN

Midnight Pack Series

Midnight Touch - Book 1
Midnight Temptation - Book 2
Midnight Torment - Book 3
Midnight Hunt Book 3.5
Midnight Fury - Book 4

Printed in Great Britain
by Amazon